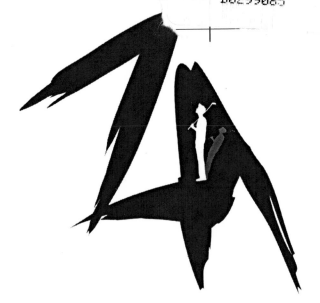

MOLLY LOOBY

MOLTEN PUBLISHING

ZA

First published in 2016 in Great Britain by Molten Publishing Ltd

Molten Publishing Ltd, 14 Clachar Close, Chelmsford, Essex, CM2 6RX

ISBN 978 0 993 59290 4

www.moltenpublishing.co.uk
www.mollylooby.com

For Nick and James Looby,
the forever ZA ready.

ONE

I was so ready. My heart was pulsing through my body, fierce and alive. I could feel it in my ears, behind my eyes. Every muscle was coiled to spring. Ready.

"Go!"

I leapt into action, launching down the track. The wind fired in my ears. Ignoring the rush of joy, I pumped my arms and drove my legs faster. My name was catching on the wind as all mouths opened to cheer me on. I was aware of the eyes on me, ogling my performance. It had to be faster than last time. Had to be.

Crossing the finish line had a chorus of whoops drifting in and out of my awareness. I jogged to a stop, at last feeling my legs and my stomach and my lungs. High fives surrounded me, and I received them without a word, staring at Mr Henderson.

He smirked at me. "It's fast, but you're not qualifying for the Olympics yet, Zane."

I rubbed the back of my neck as I made my way over to him. "Did I beat my personal best at least?"

"Not quite. 10.37."

I dropped my hand, chewing on my lip to hide disappointment. "Monday," I said. "Monday I'll set a new best."

Mr Henderson didn't say anything more as I took off in the direction of the field, catching up with the long-distance runners. I always pushed myself to run the same distance as them, regardless of how many sprints I'd done. Anything to make my legs stronger, to shave milliseconds off my time.

When everything was packed away, we trudged to the showers. I shut my eyes before enduring the water, scalding hot from whoever had been in last and then freezing cold with no warning as the temperature balanced out. With my skin tingling from the icy water, I showered as fast as I could, not stopping to ponder my efforts. I could save that for the bus ride home.

In my favourite jogging bottoms and hoodie, I waved a quick goodbye before power-walking to the bus stop, my legs screaming, and my heavy rucksack bouncing along. As usual, I arrived before the bus and waited with a woman chatting on her phone as though she wanted the world to know her business. Almost every week I panicked and rushed to the bus stop, heart galloping in my chest. Not because I had a fear of being late, but because I knew if I took the earlier bus I'd be with her sooner.

By the time the bus arrived, my hair had blown dry in the wind and was sticking up at all angles. Attempting to flatten it as I stepped onto the sweaty bus, I muttered to myself about Mum's car and its lack of being in the college car park. It'd been the most exciting thing in the world when I'd passed my driving test, and Mum had insured me on her car. Now it seemed like a waste of time the amount I used the thing. It was never in the place I needed it to be.

As I untangled my headphones, the man sitting in front of me turned the page of his newspaper to reveal another headline. My eyes darted over the words almost without my permission. What was it about reading over a stranger's shoulder that was so appealing?

MENINGITIS VACCINE FAILURE

The man decided this page was entertaining enough and read on, allowing me to skim the subheading. *Clinical trial shows all patients declining as a result of the new vaccine.*

I pulled my hood up and leant my head against the window, shutting my eyes. Only thirty minutes to go.

The George and Dragon was a happy sight, and a smile crept onto my cheeks as I hopped off the bus and pushed my hood off. I made my way down George Street, where all the lawns were tidy and all the flowers in line. There was even someone sweeping leaves off their front path. Gnomes and ornaments eyed me as I passed.

Ashford House was the red brick beauty at the top of the street. Two proud trees sat on either side of their front path, and unlike the rest of their neighbours, the Ashfords hadn't felt the need to erase any evidence of leaves from their lawn.

As I raised my hand to press the bell, the door flung open, and Callie launched herself into my arms. I toppled back a step before squeezing her tight, inhaling her sweet perfume. Something uncoiled inside me, and I relaxed into her embrace, feeling as though I could breathe again.

"I missed you," she whispered into my ear.

"I missed you too."

She pulled back to kiss me, and I lost myself in a moment of perfection, heart swelling at her touch. Her lips drew into a smile, and I couldn't help but laugh, breaking the kiss and meeting her sea-green eyes. They roamed over my face, taking in every line and surface. She didn't unravel her arms from around my neck as we parted, only held us there in the moment, noses almost touching. My face grew hot, and I set her down, skin and heart and soul on fire.

"Good day?" She took my hand and led me inside, where I wiped my feet and took off my newish Nike trainers.

"Of course." I followed her into the dining room. A selection of papers and books were laid out on the table along with her laptop. "How was yours?"

"Busy." She exhaled as she sat down, pushing her light-golden hair behind her ears. "Still is."

There was a thundering on the stairs, and Jay appeared

in the doorway wearing a strange combination of clothes. His grey combat trousers were ripped and bloodstained, as was his T-shirt and the baggy shirt he wore over the top. The whole thing was topped off with an oversized blazer and two bandanas, one round his neck and the other round his head.

"I'll have face paint on, obviously," was how he chose to announce himself. "What do you think?"

Callie chewed on the top of her pen. "It's interesting."

Jay looked down at himself. "It's awesome. Zane?"

"Yeah." I nodded. "Awesome."

Jay rolled his eyes. "Like either of your costumes are any better. Imagine it with more blood. On my face and stuff."

"I'm not sure I get it." Callie went back to her screen.

"I'm a survivor, duh."

I furrowed my eyebrows. "I thought we were supposed to be going as zombies?"

"I am a zombie. I'm a survivor that's clearly been infected."

"Right. I didn't realise we had to put that much thought into it."

"Why? What does your costume look like?"

"It's just some ripped, old clothes."

"So inventive." He put his hands in his pockets. "You reminded Gemma, right?" He was looking at Callie. "She has a costume?"

"Yes, yes. She's coming."

Jay shot me a look before opening his mouth again. "Show me what you've got then, Zane."

I followed him upstairs with my rucksack and plonked it down on the bed in the spare room, rooting through it for my costume. Jay sat on the bed and picked up my watch, which I'd forgotten on Sunday.

"Do you live here now?" He held it up.

"Don't say that." I took it off him and fastened it to my wrist. "Your mum might hear."

"I've heard her refer to this as 'Zane's room' more than once. Chill out."

"Even so." I threw him my old combat trousers and plain T-shirt.

He raised his eyebrows as he held them up. "Really?"

"What?"

"There's not even any blood on here."

"Not everyone's thought about the apocalypse as much as you have."

"ZA, Zane. Zed-ay."

"Huh?"

"Zombie Armageddon."

"Right, sorry." I took the shirt back. "What's wrong with apocalypse?"

"Doesn't have such a ring to it."

"Because I'm sure that's what we'd all be saying."

"We will if it catches on." He jumped up. "Come on. I'll get you some blood for those clothes."

His bedroom was covered in discarded garments that obviously weren't *awesome* enough for him. The TV had a loading screen of some description displaying on it, and he swore when he caught sight of it. I watched him root through piles of who knew what, pushing his golden skater-boy hair back with the bandana.

"I had it. It was in my hand."

I crossed my arms and leant against his doorframe. "How much use would you be in the apocalypse? You can't even find something you used five minutes ago."

"Don't underestimate me. I'm ZA ready."

I pressed my lips together to stop from laughing. "What?"

"Isn't it self-explanatory?" He stood up, tube of fake blood in his hand. "ZA ready. Ready for the Zombie Armageddon."

I just looked at him.

"Useless." He shook his head. "Utterly useless."

"Well, I don't know about that. I think I'd be all right."

"Yeah," he scoffed. "Like you're ZA ready."

TWO

After dinner, I curled up on the sofa with Callie, eyes drooping from the warm or the food or the pure bliss of being next to her. She was already asleep, making tiny snoring noises. Did she snore in the night? Was it loud? I wondered when I'd be able to sleep next to her.

I gave an awkward grin to Michael as he entered the room and grabbed the TV remote, like he could read my mind or something. "All right?" I said, unable to think of anything else.

"Great." His smile was wide and true, and I relaxed as he sat himself on the other sofa. He flicked through the channels and tutted, stopping on the news. "Terrible, isn't it?"

"—*health of the clinical trial participants is declining at an alarming rate.*" The news anchor went to speak to the correspondent.

"Is this that meningitis thing?" I asked.

"Yeah."

"—*appears to be attacking the immune system in a way researchers hadn't anticipated.*"

He changed the channel again to some old comedy. "Never any good news stories any more."

Michael and I watched TV until the lights from a car appeared on the driveway. I tried to move Callie off me to answer the door, but Lisa beat me to it.

"Gem! Come in, come in."

"Why do you sound so surprised to see me? Didn't Callie say I was coming?"

Callie stirred and rubbed her eyes.

"Cal? Did you not—" Gemma stopped as she entered the living room. She was taller than Callie and stronger-looking.

Her dark-coffee hair was tied up in a ponytail. "Is that why your mum seems so surprised? You've been asleep all evening?"

Callie sat up. "How long have I been asleep?"

"Ages," Michael answered, throwing a smirk my way. "Right, Zane?"

"Hours. Dribbling and everything."

Callie narrowed her eyes at me and tried not to smile. If Michael wasn't part of the conversation, I would have kissed her then.

Gemma dropped her huge bag to the floor and threw herself on the sofa next to Callie, giving her a pressed lip look before turning to Lisa again. "Is it all right if I stay tonight? I'm guessing she didn't ask you that either?"

"It's all fine. You've got that zombie thing tomorrow, haven't you?"

"Yeah." Gemma looked at Callie. "What is even going on with that?"

She shrugged. "Ask Jay. It's his thing. You did bring a costume, right? He'll kill me if you didn't."

"Of course I did."

Callie yawned and stood up. "I'll go ask him what we're even doing tomorrow."

There was silence in the living room for what must have been two whole minutes after Callie left.

Michael spoke first. "How's it going, Gem?"

"Pretty good."

"Are you falling asleep over your work every night?"

"Nope." She looked at her hands for a moment as though she had something under her nail. "Of course not. Why? Is Little Miss Perfect?"

He chuckled. "Do you expect anything less?"

Gemma shook her head. "Grades come at a terrible price."

Lisa called Michael from the kitchen, and he threw the

remote our way before leaving the room. Neither of us went for it.

"So?" Gemma clicked her tongue. "Broken any world records yet?"

"Not yet."

She let her hair down from its ponytail only to put it back up again in the exact same spot.

"Looking forward to this thing tomorrow?" I asked after another minute.

"I think so." She dropped her hand from her hair. "I mean, I'm not totally sure what we're doing. It starts at the pier, right?"

"Think so."

"There are worse ways to spend a Saturday. Though this'll be my first one surrounded by the undead."

"Hope it doesn't rain."

Her eyes met mine. I had never noticed the colour before. They were a stormy-grey. "Really, Zane? We're talking about the weather now?"

I only looked at her, unsure how she wanted me to respond.

She played with her ponytail. "You're in love with my best friend. Have been for a year. And look at us. Why is it so hard?"

I wasn't going to admit that Callie's love for her best friend intimidated me. Or was it Gemma in general? I had never met anyone like her before and was yet to work her out.

"I do want to be friends with you, Zane."

I rubbed my hand on the back of my neck and looked away from her.

"Talk to me. Do you have a problem with me? Have I done something wrong? What?"

"No, no. You've never done anything wrong."

"Then what's the problem?"

"I dunno."

"Callie keeps asking me if I even like you. It's hard for her. Us not talking."

I nodded. "I wanna be your friend too, Gemma. But we're so..."

"Different." She wet her lips before shooting me a grin. "We can sort this out, right? For Callie."

"Of course."

"Right. Let's start off easy. Call me Gem." She winked.

My eyes widened, and I didn't know what to do with my hands. Gemma was cackling when Callie joined us.

The smile that lit up Callie's face almost made her mouth open with joy. "What's this?" She sat between us, taking my hand.

"Nothing. Just chatting with my buddy Zane."

"Oh yeah?" Callie glanced my way, and I was lost in her beautiful eyes, feeling at home again.

"Yeah. Right, Zane?" Gemma winked again, but this time I managed to regain control of myself and wink back.

"Apparently I'm funny," I said.

"Shocked us both."

Callie shut her eyes as she leant back on the sofa cushions. "Jay's being an arse."

"What else is new? Did he say what the plan was for tomorrow?"

"He doesn't have a plan, obviously. He told me to look it up. So I guess that's another thing I have to do. I'm not even bothered. He's the one who wants to go."

"Don't worry your pretty little head. I'll sort it." Gemma whipped out her phone.

"I don't even really want to go."

"It's fine. We'll sort it out. It'll be fun. Surreal, but fun," Gemma said.

"A crowd full of Jays." I shook my head. "It's gonna be weird, isn't it?"

"It will be okay though, right?" Callie bit her lip. "People won't be too scary, will they?"

"I don't think it's scary," Gemma said. "Oh wait. Says something here about scaring the locals."

Callie's eyes crinkled, and I squeezed her hand.

"We won't let them scare you. I'll protect you. I promise."

"And if Zane can't manage it, I'll be there, Cal." Gemma pulled out her ponytail again, but this time she left her hair down so she could rest her head against the back of the sofa. It tumbled in thick waves down her back, unlike Callie's fine, straight hair. "Looks like a lot of fun actually."

"It's so crazy," Callie said. "Who thinks of these things? It's not my idea of a good time."

"You don't know. It'll be fun."

"Yeah, a load of weirdos like Jay all congregating in one place. Sounds fantastic."

"Come on." Gemma put her phone down and nudged Callie. "We'll make it fun. Won't we, Zane?"

I nodded. "And anyway, what's the worst that could happen?"

THREE

We were the only zombies when we first stepped onto the bus, but with every stop, more members of the undead joined us.

"You're taking that hoodie off when we get there, right?" Jay turned to me. Gemma and Callie were chatting and giggling behind us.

"What? No. It's freezing." The sharp October air was growing colder and colder by the day.

"But it's not even ripped." He crossed his arms. "You didn't commit."

"Nobody committed like you did."

Hair ruffled and smeared with fake blood, eyes covered in dark makeup, and blood dribbling from his lips, Jay was by far the scariest person I'd sat next to on a bus. And that was saying something. He'd wanted to create a wound on his whitened face but had run out of time. Callie had gone pale when he'd descended the stairs with moments to spare.

"You wait. You'll have the lamest costume."

When the bus stopped, the undead shuffled to the front and out onto the street. I did a double take when I took in the number of zombies. The pavement was crammed with them, chatting, drinking coffee, and eating chips. Some of their costumes looked expensive, like they'd had a makeup artist working on them. A few people looked like zombies down to the finest detail. Well, how I imagined zombies to look. I hid a shudder by rubbing my arms. Zombies didn't exist.

Callie grabbed my hand tight, and Gemma whistled as she took in the sight surrounding us.

"Wow. That's a lot of dead people."

Jay turned to us, blue eyes brighter than I'd ever seen them, even behind the dark makeup. "This is awesome."

We followed behind him, nudging our way through the crowd of people who didn't seem to notice us. The closer we grew to the pier, the more toes I almost stepped on. The undead might not care about their toes being crushed, but I did. A broken toe was not an option.

"Jay!" I had to yell over the hum of voices. I pointed to a fish and chip shop on the other side of the street. Jay nodded, leading us away from the horde.

"This is incredible," Jay said as he wiped the rain water off his rusty seat and sat down. "Crazy."

Callie zipped her fleece up over her mouth. "Can't we go in?"

"Erm, Cal." Gemma sat next to Jay. "We don't wanna disturb the living." She went to put her hand in her hair and stopped as she felt its hugeness. Gemma's hair had been backcombed and left to its wild devices. Massive was the only way I could describe it. I was glad Callie had sat next to her on the bus.

As the least scary of the group, Callie and I went in to order. She twisted a strand of hair around in her fingers. Callie had backcombed her hair this morning too. She'd also slept with it in a plait to create some kind of volume. It hadn't gone to plan though as it just looked wavier than normal. She wasn't scary-looking even when she was trying to be.

Even so, people were gawping at us like they hadn't seen the horde outside. I listened to the radio and pretended to be interested in the menu on the wall to hide from their stares.

"*—taken a turn for the worse with almost all participants, most of which are children, showing fatal decline. The worst cases are becoming unresponsive, and the death rate is rising by the hour. Professionals*

13

worked through the night to do whatever they could to slow the effect of the vaccine that some are now calling Juvenile Virus."

"Cool costumes," the guy behind the counter said, breaking my concentration from the radio. "Looks huge this year. I've never seen anything like it."

"Neither have we."

Gemma and Jay were staring at the crowd of people when we returned. The table wobbled as I put everything down and leant on it, the metal legs squeaking.

"Am I even going to be able to see anything?" Callie asked as she sat down.

"Good point," Jay said, wrenching his eyes from the zombies. "I didn't think of that. You guys'll be fine." He looked to me and Gemma. "It sucks being short."

"I dunno what you're worried about, Jay." Gemma had only just finished her chip and another was making its way to her mouth. "There's nothing to look at."

We all fell silent as someone dressed as a zombie bride raced to her group of friends, almost toppling over she was going so fast. They caught and steadied her. It was almost as though the entire group froze. One of them leant in closer, and the zombie bride nodded. Their faces dropped, their eyes widened, and they were running down the street like it was their last chance to beat their personal bests.

"What's going on?" Callie narrowed her eyes as the horde watched them sprint out of sight.

"That was weird." Gemma wiped her hands on her combat trousers and didn't go for another chip.

Somebody who'd been behind the group was shaking his head and pulling his friend's arm, saying something. Nobody took any notice of him for another minute or so until he started talking to the lady next to him. She, like the zombie bride before her, rushed to her pack of friends. They all seemed to laugh at her, grins on their faces, except a girl with red hair who took her hand, yelling something to those around her.

At once, feet were moving, and the crowd scattered in every direction. People were running. Sprinting. A wave of something was happening. The moment it hit us, I stood up.

"I don't like this."

Callie's hand was in mine.

"Hey!" Gemma jumped up and tried to catch the attention of a cheerleader zombie. People whizzed by, crossing the street without paying much attention. They flew past Gemma as though she wasn't there.

My breath seemed too loud as I watched hundreds of people all decide to move at once. I squashed Callie's hand in mine, like she could ground me. My heart was thumping hard, and my stomach was writhing.

"Hey!" Gemma grabbed a guy by the shoulders this time, stopping him. "What is going on?"

"Get off me!" He flung her towards the fish and chip shop. She landed on the table, breaking it, the old legs giving way.

"Hey!" I stepped in his path as he went to take off again, Callie letting go of me to help Gemma. "What's your problem?"

He darted round me and kept running. All I could do was turn and watch him go.

"You all right, Gem?" I dragged my eyes from all the commotion as Callie and Jay pulled her up.

"Fine." She looked at her hands as she stood up, groaning. "What a jerk."

People inside the fish and chip shop piled up at the window, looking to where the table had stood.

Jay stepped closer to the road and beckoned us over. "Come on."

Gemma shouted an apology about the table as we crossed the road again to a spot where hundreds of people had been five minutes ago. The chaos seemed to be spreading in both directions, more people freaking out and running for their lives every second.

"There." Jay pointed to a man sitting on a bench, watching the disarray unfold. He had made a similar effort to us, wearing bloodstained, old clothes, nothing too wild. "He might answer us."

Callie had her phone pressed against her ear as we approached the man. "Dad! Dad, please come and pick us up." Her eyes were big as they darted from one person to another. "I don't know, but please come fast."

"Hey." Jay gave half a wave to the man. "Do you know what's going on here?"

The man shook his head.

"Hello?"

He put his head in his hands. "Oh god."

"Jay." Gemma pulled Jay back. "Come on." She led us down the street, closer and closer to all the drama. "This doesn't make any sense. They're acting like a bomb has gone off or something."

My muscles wound tight as we grew nearer to the crazy scatter of people, stepping over belongings that had been dropped and forgotten. Callie's voice was growing more high-pitched as she begged Michael to collect us.

I was wishing for Mum's car even more than yesterday.

We found ourselves in a line as we reached a crowd of people again, Gemma at the front, ketchup down the back of her hoodie. I positioned myself at the back where I could see Callie.

Everyone was talking so fast I couldn't understand them. Only a few words broke through to me.

Alive. No. Dead. Awake. Run.

"I don't like this, Jay," I called to him over Callie's head. He shot me a look, pressing his lips together.

We couldn't move faster than the panic. The casual group of zombies sipping coffee bolted before we could get close enough to ask a question. Worried faces wobbled in and out of sight. Gemma picked up the pace.

"Hey!" She jumped up, waving an arm in the air before leading us to a group of twenty-somethings who were smirking at the whole situation. "Do you guys know what's going on?"

"People are crazy, that's what's going on." The man wiped fake blood from his mouth.

"It's hysterical," one of his friends said. "They're lunatics."

"But do you know exactly what's going on?" Gemma pulled up her huge hair with a hairband on her wrist. "Seems pretty serious."

Callie yelped as a woman bumped into her, spilling tea all down her fleece. The woman didn't even apologise, dropping the paper cup and continuing.

Callie buried her face in my hoodie. "I don't like this."

I stroked her hair and wrapped my arms around her. "It'll be all right."

"They're saying something about zombies," a girl said, rolling her eyes. "They're freaks."

"They said what?" Jay stepped forward.

"Something about the vaccine. They think the people dying from it are getting back up."

"Wait. Someone came back to life?"

The girl chuckled, but it didn't sound right in the air. "Of course not. Just a misunderstanding."

Jay took a step back, biting down on his lip. "Let's get out of here."

"What?" Gemma spun him to face her. "You can't seriously

believe that's what's happening?"

"Mob mentality," one of the guys said. "It's a powerful thing."

"I don't care. We're going."

We all looked up the road as a bone-shaking scream cut through us. It was followed by yells and shrieks.

And everything was noise.

FOUR

My heart was in my throat, and I forgot to breathe for an immeasurable count of seconds. There were no words surrounding us, only cries of fear.

"What's happening?" Callie's voice pulled me out of my trance, and there were tears on her cheeks, leaving pink marks in her white makeup.

"Callie." Jay was in front of her. "Dad's coming, right? Where's he meeting us?"

"In the car park he always waits in. What's going on, Jay?"

"We need to get out of here." He grabbed Callie's hand and yanked her up the street.

The group of twenty-somethings were arguing amongst themselves, the fear biting through everything.

We didn't speak as we hurried—just short of jogging—up the street towards whichever of the many car parks Michael would arrive in. Sooner rather than later, I hoped. My eyes tried to take in everything, surveying the mess, trying to work out how much danger we were in.

I noticed it the same moment Jay skidded to a halt and let out a noise between a scream and a cry.

We were running in the opposite direction to everyone else.

A man was barrelling towards us, shrieking like I'd never heard, arms and legs flying as though he wanted to take off. His hand was covering his neck. It was red with blood.

"That was makeup, right?" Gemma's voice was shaking.

In the distance, everyone was running this way. People dressed as zombies and ordinary people and people in work uniforms. There seemed to be something on the floor up there. Heaps.

Before I could think too much about it, Jay had pulled Callie across the road and through an alleyway.

"This isn't happening," Gemma said. "This isn't happening."

"Shut up," Jay hissed. "We need to get out of here."

Screams punched through us as we ran, coming from the street. And other noises too. Something that sounded like snarling. I concentrated on the thud of my feet on the pavement and the firing of my breath instead.

As we tore round a bend, Callie stopped, heaving Jay back, staring ahead of her.

"What?" he growled.

"Look." She pointed to the end of the alley to our right. There was a shadow of a small girl standing there. Watching us. Wearing a hospital gown.

"Cal." Jay tugged on her hand again. "We need to leave, right now."

"But she's on her own."

The girl's head snapped up. My stomach jumped. I went to push Callie out the way but her feet were grounded.

"Run! Now!"

The girl charged towards us like someone had pulled the trigger of a starting pistol. The sound that escaped her lips was not human. The blood around her mouth was not fake.

Callie screamed as Jay pulled and Gemma and I pushed her up the thin side street. The girl was gaining on us. Fast.

"Run!"

Gemma grabbed Callie's hand and jerked her forwards, forcing her to run faster. Jay was right behind them, and I was almost stepping on his heels.

I couldn't look back. That would slow me down. But the

sound was getting louder. I could almost feel her on me. My skin crawled. Don't look back. A guttural roar deafened me, and I felt it on the back of my neck. I tripped, crashing to the ground.

I scuttled towards the wall on my hands. The girl leapt. A door opened in her face as she jumped, a terrific clanging sound bouncing in my head.

A man stepped out of the doorway. "What's goi—" He never finished that thought because the girl tackled him and dug her teeth into his neck, the two of them tumbling back through the door.

I cried out, scurrying to stand, limbs shaking.

"Come on!" Jay grabbed my arm, and we pelted up the street. Gemma and Callie were a few metres ahead.

"Zane!" Callie looked round to me, but Gemma hauled her forward.

"Just run! He's fine."

My legs tried to find their rhythm through the fear and the rain water my old combat trousers had soaked up. I ran through the trembling, picturing people cheering me on to a finish line up ahead.

Gemma jumped back and ducked down, Callie almost falling on top of her. Jay stopped so fast I crashed right into him.

Gemma put a finger to her lips and pointed to the other side of the wall. "Zombie," she mouthed.

I let the word wash over me, not believing it, but altogether accepting that to be the truth.

After a shriek and a rumbling growl and footsteps growing quieter, Gemma held her breath and stuck her head round. When she faced us again, she let all her air out in one big gust. I was so close I could smell the chips on her breath.

"Clear," she said, struggling to pull herself to standing again.

"How far are we from the car park?" I whispered the words, terrified they would hear me.

"Not far," Jay whispered back. "But Dad won't be here yet. It takes half an hour. When did you call him?"

Callie's hands were shaking so much she struggled to fish her phone out of her pocket. It almost went spinning to the ground. "Fifteen minutes ago. What do we do? Where do we go?"

"We go to the car park," Jay said. "We wait there."

"But what if...?" Callie didn't need to finish her sentence. We all knew what she'd been going to say.

"I don't know. We'll deal with it when we get there."

I took Callie's hand as we tiptoed down the street, trying to hurry but not make any noise. I wanted to dash down the street, everything blurring behind me. But what if we had to wait for Michael?

Callie's eyes kept meeting my face as we rushed through the streets, tears dripping off her nose and chin. I wanted to reassure her, but I didn't dare make a sound.

Jay stooped behind a four-by-four as we darted into the car park. We fell in beside him, breaths too loud. Jay peeked through the windows for a moment before dropping down again.

"He's not here yet."

Gemma wet her mouth. "Are there any of them out there?"

"Not that I could see."

"It can't be true, right?" Gemma said. "It doesn't make any sense."

"I don't know about you, but I know what I saw."

"It's crazy." I put my hand to the back of my neck. "This can't be happening. Can it?"

Heavy footsteps shot by on the other side of the car. We all shut up. My blood was so loud in my ears I almost didn't hear his words.

"Oh no. This isn't real. This isn't real."

Gemma opened her mouth, but Jay covered it with his hand and shook his head.

The man cried out in pain. A dull thud sounded. "Please no."

With my back pressed against the car, I slid up to peek through the windows. He was on his knees, clutching one of his hands to a huge gash on his forearm. Blood was dripping onto the pavement. He was covered in it. His jeans and shirt were dark with it. He bent over, heaving, vomiting on the pool of blood. In the streetlight, his skin looked yellow. When had twilight crept up on us? I crinkled my nose up as the wind blew the stink of vomit our way.

"Help me." The man collapsed into the filth. Blood spouted out of the wound now he wasn't holding on to it. If all that blood was his then...

Before I could finish that thought, his body convulsed, and there was silence.

Someone pulled on the bottom of my hoodie. I couldn't look down to see who it was.

"Zane," Gemma hissed. "What's going on?"

I put my finger to my lips without looking at her.

I didn't breathe.

The man's arms twitched and—

—he pulled himself up.

I almost cried out, but I clamped my hand over my mouth before any sound could escape. The man looked around, as though he was listening. His arms hung dead at his sides. His face looked limp. He threw his head back and roared. I squeezed my hand tighter to my face, trying to keep my heart inside my body.

His head snapped round at the sound of a car engine. He raced in the direction of the sound. This direction. I pulled the three of them up and edged round the car, hoping to remain out of sight. Someone stepped on the back of my trainer, and I staggered forward a step, slamming my hand on the car as I caught myself.

A snarl.

Four intakes of breath.

Brakes squealing.

A crash.

I opened my eyes, realising I'd shut them as the world remained quiet. The four of us stood motionless until a car door opened.

"Oh god. No."

"Dad!" Callie burst out.

"No! Don't come round here!" His voice was shaking.

Jay shot to his side. My limbs were so stiff I felt like I was moving at half speed.

"What have I done?" Michael put his hand over his mouth.

"Get in the car." Jay was shoving him back into the car.

"Jay, no! We have to call somebody."

The man's head cracked as he turned to face us, snarl rising to his lips.

"Now!" Jay gave one final shove, and Michael fell into the car.

I bundled Callie in first as Jay climbed over his dad to reach the passenger seat. I almost landed on top of Gemma as I threw myself in.

"Go," Jay said. "Drive!"

Michael stomped his foot to the floor. The car jolted forwards, skidding out of the car park and away from the dead man dying to reach us.

FIVE

"What the *hell* is going on?" Gemma screeched, eyes alight. "What was that thing?" She pointed her finger at Jay. "And don't you say what I think you're gonna say."

Jay stared ahead. "You're the one who said it."

"I didn't. It's ridiculous."

Michael's breath caught in his throat. "I hit someone."

"Something," Gemma corrected. "Not someone. That thing was coming for us."

"But I could've killed him."

"No." I had to clear my throat before speaking again. "No, you couldn't. I watched him die. He was dead. He..."

Callie wrapped herself around my arm and sobbed big and loud, tears choking her.

"It's okay, Cal." Gemma's voice softened. "We're all right now. We're safe."

"No, we're not." Jay's voice was dark. "It's happening."

"What is?" Michael asked.

"The ZA."

Gemma exchanged a look with me. I had to press my lips together to stop from screaming obscenities into the world. This couldn't be happening. It didn't make any sense.

"No." Michael shook his head. "There's got to be another explanation."

"That guy got back up." Jay spun round to face us. "That girl nearly took a chunk out of Zane. How can you deny this?"

"I'm—I'm s-sorry." Callie clung to me tighter. "I didn't realise what was happening. I—I'm sorry. So sorry. You could've—could've..."

Shushing her and stroking her hair, I leant my cheek on the top of her head. She pressed her lips against mine, hard and desperate, before disappearing into my chest and howling.

I sat there blinking for a moment before I could answer. "I'm okay now. I'm fine. She didn't touch me."

Gemma bit her lip. "It was close though. Too close."

A hush fell on the car as we listened to Callie weep. I had no words to console her. I wanted to make it better, but I couldn't. My brain wasn't working right. I couldn't figure out what had happened.

"I love you." She said it over and over again. "I love you. I love you. I love you."

I couldn't do anything more than say it back.

Jay switched on the radio, the volume of the voice shouting through the speaker making us all jump.

"Breaking news. The number dead from Juvenile Virus increases by the minute, and an astonishing phenomenon has the dead seemingly returning to life."

"What? What is—what is?" Michael tripped over his words.

"Shush, we need to listen to this." Jay turned the radio up even more.

"With almost all of the meningitis vaccine clinical trial participants now dead, panic has spread throughout the country to the new spectacle that is causing the bodies of those affected to rise. The virus is violent, and scientists have yet to explain this bizarre turn of events. Members of the public are calling it the zombie apocalypse."

"Armageddon," I muttered.

My heart dropped when Jay's lips didn't even twitch.

"Thousands of people are flooding hospitals with wounds caused by those infected with Juvenile Virus. The virus seems to be spreading through bodily fluids, and those bitten by the infected population have started to show the initial symptoms of Juvenile Virus. The more extensive the wound, the faster the virus acts. Symptoms include high *fever, vomiting, and fatigue. Medical professionals are asking people to remain in their homes and not attempt a trip to any hospital or medical centre. Do not attempt contact with the infected until more information is known. We have been told a cure is in development and will be released as soon as possible. Until then, please remain in your homes."*

"It might be okay," Michael said. "They're working on a cure."

"How fast can they do that?" I turned to Jay.

"Not fast enough. How many people are infected? How many more people will they infect? There's no way." Jay wrung his hands. "We've got to go to a supermarket. You heard what the radio said. We won't be able to go out again. It's not safe."

"Shouldn't we go back?" I asked. "They said not to leave our homes."

"We won't be able to stay at home unless we get some supplies. Who knows how long we'll be stuck there?"

Michael nodded, and we were silent again.

The closer we grew to the supermarket, the busier it became. Cars were revving their engines and blaring their horns. People were everywhere in every direction, moving for the sake of moving.

"We're not gonna get close enough." Gemma pressed her face against the window.

"Park here," Jay said, unbuckling his seat belt.

"I can't park here. It's illegal."

Jay pointed out the window. "You think this is legal? You think anyone cares? We've got to get supplies. Now!"

He opened the car door and jumped out without another word, snaking his way through the traffic. Michael threw the car up onto the pavement and put the hazard lights on before hurling the door open and jogging to catch up with Jay, calling after him as he went.

"Come on." Gemma grabbed Michael's keys.

I took one of Callie's hands and Gemma took the other.

We exchanged glances, took a collective breath, and slipped into the chaos.

People were yelling and dashing back and forth. Crying and shrieking pierced my ears as well as the rumbling of car engines and the thumping of feet.

Cars were parked every which way, white lines and lanes disregarded. Doors had been left open. Lights were left on. Engines left running, keys still in the ignition. Profanities filled the air as people couldn't escape, their cars trapped. As some sped to flee, pedestrians had to dive out the way.

The closer we grew to the doors, the more food was scattered across the floor, bags overflowing and splitting and no one stopping to pick anything up. No time for that now.

We squashed tight together and entered the crush, not letting go of each other. Eyes found mine over and over again. Mouths opened to scream as they took in my bloodstained clothes and pale face. I repeated words over and over again to keep from being tackled to the ground.

"It's okay. I'm not dead. Just dressing up. We went out. Stupid now. Really stupid. Should've stayed at home. I'm still talking. It's all fine."

Gemma led us further into the crowd, pushing her way through, elbowing and shoving and swearing. The ketchup on her hoodie had dribbled its way down to her trousers. Callie's breath puffed through the pandemonium, and I clasped her hand tighter. Hands were everywhere grabbing for everything. Food and drink were spilt all over the floor. Trolleys jammed into my legs as people tried to run us down.

An empty basket was lying on its side next to one of the shelves, and I snatched it before the hungry hands could reach it. Gemma pulled us into the canned aisle where there was no space to breathe. Up on my tiptoes, I spotted Jay's red-streaked golden hair.

"Excellent," Jay said as we jostled up next to him. He pulled the basket towards the shelf and pushed as many cans as he could into it, my arm shuddering as the weight piled on and on. The trolley was already like a mountain. "We need another basket. We've got to get water and other stuff."

"I've got it." Gemma was gone before I could open my mouth.

Jay and Michael shuffled towards the drinks without another word. Callie let go of my hand to pick up bottles of whatever was left—squash and fizzy in all colours and flavours. There wasn't any water anywhere. The bottles were piled on top of the trolley until it was about ready to topple.

"Sorry," Callie said as she piled my basket ever higher.

I looked up to see an empty basket held high. Gemma's voice cut through the drone of panic. "Get the hell outta my way!"

The second she was in reaching distance, Jay had filled her basket up and was beckoning for us to follow him once more. Sweat was beading on my forehead, and I had to puff my breaths in and out in order to make carrying this load bearable.

When we reached our next destination, I needed to put the basket down, squeezing it between my feet so as not to have it taken by the greedy hands. I rested my hands on my knees and breathed for a minute as Jay threw small boxes at me. Painkillers. Callie and Gemma stuffed as many boxes as they could in the gaps in the baskets and trolley, crushing them in order to make them fit.

Then we were off again, Jay piling matches into Michael's arms and the many pockets of his blazer. Callie and Gemma's pockets were already full of painkillers.

"We're running out of room, Jay!" Gemma had to yell to be heard.

"One last stop."

My muscles were shaking and screaming by the time we reached the candles, and Gemma was hunched over to catch her breath.

Callie pressed her lips together. "I'm sorry, Gem."

Gemma held her hand up. "No bother."

Jay crammed bags of tea lights and thick candles into our hoods. Callie stuffed them in the pockets of my trousers before stretching her arms out, letting Gemma and Jay pile them up to her chin.

Jay's eyes were bright and big when he looked to us. "What now?"

"We need to get out of here," I forced through gritted teeth.

"What else do we need?"

"Nothing. We need to go."

"What about weapons?" He turned to Michael.

"Weapons? Are you mad?"

Gemma stood up. "There aren't any weapons here, Jay. And I don't know about anyone else, but I'm about done with what I can carry."

"But—"

"There's stuff at the house!" Callie shrieked at her brother. "We need to leave."

Legs wobbling and arms trembling, I followed the trolley out of the shop, Jay barking at anyone who came anywhere near our supplies. People soon backed off when they saw us covered in fake blood.

"Wait," Michael said as we threw the baskets in the car as they were and emptied our pockets. "We didn't pay."

"Dad." Jay put his hand on Michael's arm. "If we get through this, I'll pay for it myself."

SIX

There was quiet in the car as we listened to the radio repeat its breaking news report over and over. I let out a huge gust of air as Ashford House came into view. My heart leapt and raced as I saw Mum's red Fiesta on the drive.

After fumbling with the handle, I almost fell out the car, pelting up the path. Lisa flung the door open before I had time to knock.

"What is going on?" Her shoulders relaxed when her eyes fell on Callie and Jay.

I pushed Lisa to one side to see Mum standing in the doorway fiddling with her bracelet.

"Zane!" Her arms were around me, pressing me close to her. I didn't mind her dark-chocolate hair in my face where it'd fallen out of her plait. She put her hand in my hair, and when she pulled away, there were tears in her blue eyes. I wished my eyes were blue like hers instead of my father's russet-brown. I didn't want any trace of him on me.

Gemma collapsed onto the sofa, dropping her basket, painkillers jumping out. She bit her lip and pressed her phone to her ear. "Mum? Mum? Where are you?"

Lisa wouldn't let go of Callie and Jay as the Ashfords joined us.

Jay shook her off. "We need to get water." He disappeared into the kitchen, and the tap sounded.

I raced back to the car and helped Michael pick up armfuls and armfuls of cans as well as my basket. Mum hurried out to help us, and I piled her arms high too. We went back and forth over and over until the car was empty and the hallway was a mess.

When the front door was shut and locked, the sound of running water was still coming from the kitchen.

Jay yelled over the sound of the spurting jet. "Dad? We need to board up the house."

"Seriously?" Lisa took Michael's hand. "What is happening?"

"Mum, no!"

I turned to see Gemma's face red and her cheeks covered in tears.

"Mum, please. I'm serious. This is serious." She raked her hand through her hair. "No, Mum. It's not a joke. We got attacked on the seafront." She let out a burst of noise, somewhere between a cough and a sob. "Why would I say something like that if it wasn't true? You need to lock yourselves in the house and stay there. Don't go out for anything."

Mum came to stand next to me, putting her arm around my waist and resting her head on my arm. She didn't say a word.

"Forget work, Mum. There are dead people walking the streets. No! Listen to me. Dad? Dad, please. No, wait. No. Don't. This is real. This is happening. And—it *is* happening! I swear to you. We were chased and almost attacked. Have you not listened to the radio? They—no it isn't a load of rubbish. Dad, it's real. I—don't. I'm telling you the truth. It's not safe. No!"

Her mouth popped open. She pulled the phone away from her ear, staring at it. It took at least a whole minute for her to notice us all watching her.

She swallowed and stood up. "My parents don't believe me."

The sound of the tap spraying water everywhere filled my ears again.

"Can I stay here tonight? I don't...I won't feel safe at home."

Callie freed herself from Lisa and bundled Gemma up into a hug, whispering something into her ear. Tears were rolling down Gemma's face, but she wasn't making a sound.

"Of course you can stay," Lisa said, wrapping her arms around herself now she had no children to smother with them. "We've got plenty of room."

"What about us?" Mum was looking at me as she spoke. "Do we go home?"

"Stay," Michael said.

"Really, Mick? Only if it's no bother. We don't want to get in your way."

He shook his head. "We've got to look out for each other." He met my eye. "We're family."

Callie let out a squeak and looked at me without letting go of Gemma, lip wobbling.

Mum took a deep breath in through her nose and nodded. "Thank you."

Michael hugged both Mum and I. It was strange being in his embrace. It brought a wave of emotion I wasn't ready for.

I sniffed the feeling back inside me. "What's Jay doing?"

Everyone turned to the doorway, listening, before making their way into the dining room and kitchen. The table and worktops were covered with glasses and bowls and pots and pans, all being filled with water.

"What?" Jay said as he spotted us. "We don't know how long the water's gonna last. Is the food inside? Is the house boarded up?"

"Jay." Michael shook his head. "What do you expect me to use to board up the house?"

"Wood from the shed. We don't need it."

"You want me to take the shed apart?"

Jay looked at him for a long moment. "Yes."

Michael stared back before nodding. "Fine. That's what we'll do."

I followed Michael into the garage and then the garden, Mum and Gemma behind me, piles of odd wood and power tools in our arms. We stood and looked at the shed a moment.

"This is insane," Michael said.

"Jay's right though." Gemma's voice wasn't as clear and strong as it'd been in the car. "We've got to stay safe here. We can buy you a new shed. We can't buy our way out of here."

"It's ridiculous." He picked up a saw and let out a big puff of breath, shaking his head. "Let's do this thing."

Gemma and I both went to pick up the odd pieces of wood and tools at the same time. We retracted our hands as they almost touched.

"You take the wood," she said, pulling on her ponytail and not looking at me. "I'll take the tools."

We went round the front of the house and started working without a word, she holding the wood and me drilling it into the brick.

"Thank you," she said after a while.

I wiped the sweat off my forehead with the back of my hand. "For what?"

"For standing up for me earlier. When that guy pushed me into the table."

"Oh."

"You didn't have to do that."

"I…" I didn't know how to finish, so I shuffled my feet.

"And for letting me run off with Callie."

I rubbed my hand over the back of my neck. "I needed her to be safe."

"You could've been bitten. I'm no expert at this, but I'm guessing that's not good."

"I really needed her to be safe."

She picked up another bit of wood. "You really love her, huh?"

"More than anything."

There were no words between us as we fixed the next two pieces.

I spoke first. "Thank you."

She furrowed her eyebrows. "What are you thanking me for?"

"Not letting go of her."

She watched me for a moment. "I couldn't. She's my best friend. I love her. I guess I really needed her to be safe too."

With the wood from the shed and the odd pieces from the garage, we managed to cover the outside of the windows on the ground floor. It was pitch-black by the time we'd finished, and the drill I'd been using was almost out of battery.

Inside, all the containers had been filled with water, and the shopping was stacked under the stairs. Callie, Jay, and Lisa were sitting on the same sofa in the living room not talking. Callie had her pyjamas on and her hair up. Her face was clean of face paint and blood, as was Jay's.

Callie threw the makeup wipes my way as we entered the room. Michael went to sit with his family, and the rest of us took the other sofa. Gemma sat next to me and removed a wipe, exclaiming with joy as she put it to her face.

"This is the best. My reflection was starting to creep me out."

"Your reflection always creeps me out." Jay looked up from his phone, smirking.

"What?" Lisa burst out, making me jump. "So we're not going to talk about it? I've been here worried sick hearing about the virus and the mad people running around on the streets. Then we get a hysterical call from Callie, and then all the food and water and now this." She was heaving breaths in and out, eyes swimming with tears. "Someone needs to tell me what's going on."

I looked to Jay who looked to Gemma who looked to Callie who looked back at me.

Jay scratched his head. "Where do you want me to start?"

SEVEN

When the story had been told and enough silence had passed for it to sink in, Michael turned the TV on. Images of people fleeing, cars weaving in and out of the chaos, crowded hospitals, screaming, and all out pandemonium filled the screen. It looked like the report was going around and around like on the radio.

"With all of the meningitis vaccine clinical trial participants dead, everyone is turning to the pandemic sweeping the nation. Juvenile Virus has been confirmed in seven countries."

"How?" Jay sat forward, staring at the screen.

"It has been discovered that the virus shuts down the body's immune system and then shuts down the brain before taking control and reanimating its host. It appears to be spread through the saliva like rabies. We have Dr Hastings here to give us some more information."

The screen split to show a haggard man with bags under his eyes. His hair was sticking up at all angles and his glasses weren't straight.

My stomach was squeezing tight, making me feel sick. I dug my hands into the cushions of the sofa.

"Dr Hastings, if the virus is being spread through bites, how has it managed to travel into other countries?"

Dr Hastings cleared his throat before speaking. *"Flights should've been grounded before they were, but unfortunately we couldn't foresee the unprecedented tragedy that's developing by the minute. Victims with bites may have boarded planes or boats without knowing the danger they were becoming. The virus seems to be developing slowly in those who are healthy. However, as soon as death occurs, it leaps into action, so to speak. The virus itself takes a while to weaken the body enough to kill it."*

"What should people look out for to check for infected among them?"

"Anyone with a bite from an infected person will themselves be infected. This appears to be the case a hundred percent of the time. Symptoms include high fever, vomiting, fatigue, shivering, and a paling of the skin. If you, or anyone around you, display these symptoms, I urge you to take action."

"Action?" The news anchor's face was tense and unnatural. She was pressing her lips together as though she wanted to say so much more. *"I thought people were being advised to stay away from hospitals?"*

"They are. We cannot do anything for the infected thus far. The virus is working faster than we can, and more and more medical professionals are contracting the virus themselves. This is the last place you want to be."

"So what do you urge viewers to do?"

He pulled in a breath. *"Whatever they can to stay healthy. The only way I've discovered to stop an infected person from attacking is to dispose of them."*

The anchor's hands hit the table with force, and I jumped in my seat, swallowing down a wave of anxiety. *"You can't be suggesting to kill the infected?"*

"There's nothing else for me to suggest." Dr Hastings took off his glasses and rubbed his eyes. *"There doesn't seem to be any way to stop it. We need to keep as many people alive as possible. I'm sorry. That is what I'm suggesting. And the only way it appears we can stop them is by shutting down the brain in whatever way we can. The virus controls the infected host from there. Without that, it can't attack, though we're assuming it remains alive in the body for at least a little while, so be wary if you come across any infected corpses."*

"This is ridiculous." The news anchor was looking to someone off camera. *"Are we allowed to air this?"* There was a pause. *"He's suggesting killing people. We can't—"*

Another news anchor appeared in the same seat in the blink of an eye.

"Juvenile Virus continues to ravage the nation with every corner of the country affected. Charlotte Rochendale has the latest."

The screen changed to show a blonde woman with wide eyes staring into the camera. Behind her was the pier. The sofa rocked as Mum and Gemma leant forward.

"Good evening, Matthew." Her voice was stronger than the fear in her eyes. *"I'm here at Brighton Pier where earlier today—"*

There was a flash of colour, a scream, and blood splattered the camera. Everything went shaky as the cameraman raced over to her.

Nobody in the room dared to breathe.

"Charlotte!"

The camera dropped to the ground on its side, showing all the waiting country the dead, empty eyes of Charlotte Rochendale. Her throat was black with blood. The cameraman's jeans filled the screen as he bent down to her aid.

"Charlotte? Charlotte? Oh god."

From the corner of my eye, I saw Mum put her hand to her face. I wanted to reach for her, but I couldn't move.

"Charlotte?" the cameraman said one more time before he leapt up, screaming as though the world was ending.

It was.

Before he could run, the body of Charlotte Rochendale was on top of him. The camera captured a shot of her ripping a chunk out of his flesh as he screamed.

I wanted to vomit.

The screen changed to a new anchor and a new person in a white coat talking to them. This time it was a woman with her hair up in a messy bun. She looked as tired and defeated as Dr Hastings. Mum grabbed for my hand.

"Now, Dr Collins. What new information do you have about Juvenile Virus?"

"In the last few hours, we have identified a dormant version in people who've come into contact with the infected but were not bitten."

"What sort of contact?"

Dr Collins thought about this for a moment. *"Skin to skin contact or breathing too close to them. Any close contact. Think of how a cold spreads."*

My heart leapt up in my throat, whole body tensing.

"Does this mean thousands more people are infected than we first thought?"

"Not necessarily."

I slumped back, puffing out a gust of air, blinking the tears out of my eyes.

"The dormant virus doesn't seem to be able to attack the body unless already weakened. It doesn't have enough strength to shut down the immune system by itself like the live one that enters through the bloodstream. Many people already fighting off disease will be at risk, as will the elderly and young children."

"How do you know if you're infected with the dormant virus?"

"If you're healthy, you won't know. The dormant virus in a healthy person makes the host a sort of carrier, not affected themselves but able to pass it on. However, the dormant virus will become active in those at risk and behave as normal. The symptoms are the same. All those we've studied so far with the dormant virus appear to be healthy and acting as normal thus far. The exceptions are children, the elderly, and those fighting disease, like I already mentioned."

"So the advice remains the same?"

Dr Collins nodded, more hair falling out of her bun. *"Indeed. Stay indoors and away from the infected until further notice. We are working as fast as we can and will release any new information as and when we discover it."*

"Thank you, Dr Collins."

The TV moved on to another report with much the same content, but I couldn't focus on it. The room felt like it was moving. Like I was going to fall through the floor.

"Zane?" Mum squeezed my hand.

I yanked it away from her, jumping up.

"What's wrong? You don't look too good."

I shook my head. "What if I'm infected?"

"What?"

"No," Jay said.

Gemma pulled a cushion into her lap. "You can't be. That's stupid."

"She was this close to me." I held up my finger and thumb with a centimetre between them. "She breathed all over me. What if I'm infected?"

Callie stood up to join me, and I leapt back.

"Don't come near me!"

"Zane." The pleading in her voice cut through me. The tears were fighting their way back. "It's okay."

"What if I infect all of you?"

"You won't."

"How do you know that? You can't know that. I need to get out of here." I pulled my hair as I stumbled towards the doorframe.

A hand seized my arm and dug its nails in.

"Let go of me!"

"You listen to me, Zane Carlisle." Gemma's voice hissed through her teeth. "If you're infected, we're all infected. Didn't you hear what she said? Like a cold virus. I don't know about you, but I smelt that dead guy's vomit earlier. That means I'm infected too. And look, I'm touching you. You think I care?"

"But—"

"No. It doesn't matter. We are all strong, healthy people. The virus can't get to us."

"I don't want to—"

"Shut up. If you're infected, we're all infected. Big deal. It doesn't matter. You hugged Callie who hugged Lisa who hugged Jay and Mick. You hugged your mum. I hugged Callie. Done. We're all infected. So what?"

I turned to face her.

"I don't care. I'm still good. We're all safer in this house infected with the dormant virus than we are risking our chances out there with the live one. And I don't know about all these people behind us, but I think they'd rather have you right here than out there."

Callie crept closer. "Zane, it was my fault you almost got attacked. I'm not letting you go. I love you."

I relaxed my muscles, and Gemma released me.

"I love you too, Cal."

She scurried into my arms, and I let her, holding back the tears as her shape pressed into mine.

"Good," Gemma said. "Glad we sorted that mess out." She threw herself back on the sofa.

"Thank you," Mum said, smiling at Gemma and holding out her hand. "My name's Jennifer by the way. You can call me Jen."

Gemma grinned and shook her hand. "Gemma. You can call me Gem."

"Wait." Jay was looking at the wall, and I wondered who he was speaking to. "If we're all infected, what if one of us dies?"

"Jay!" Lisa snapped. "Don't say things like that. None of us are going to die."

"But what if they did?" He looked at her. "They'd become a zombie."

"Infected," Gemma cut in. "Can we call them an Infected instead?"

"Same difference. Whatever we call them, they'd still try and attack us. That means—"

"It means nothing," Michael said. "We'll cross that bridge if we come to it. And let's hope we never do."

EIGHT

I slept on the sofa under one of Callie's blankets, letting Mum have the spare room. I must have only slept for a handful of hours. The house was quiet when I awoke for the last time, light not yet shining through the curtains. When there was movement on the stairs, I shut my eyes, pretending to be asleep. The door creaked open, and I held my breath.

"Zane?"

I peeked out of the covers to find Callie in the doorway, wrapped in her fluffy dressing gown.

"Hey." I sat up and patted the space beside me. "Can't sleep either?"

She buried herself in my arms and shook her head. "No way. How can I sleep now? Every time I shut my eyes I see her standing there, looking at me." She shuddered.

I squeezed her tight. "I know. Me too. Is everyone else asleep?"

"I dunno. Gemma's awake, trying to get a response from her mum and dad and sister."

"They really don't believe her?"

Her sea-green eyes met mine. "Would you believe her? If you hadn't seen anything?"

"But the news and the radio are only talking about the virus. How can you pretend it's made up?"

"They're scared. Too scared to think for one moment that this is real. She's trying to get them to come here, but they're not going to."

"It doesn't feel real."

"I know." She wove her fingers through mine. "I love you, Zane. No matter what happens."

I kissed her nose. "No matter what."

"We'll get through this, won't we? Even if things get really tough? Even if things change?"

"Of course we will." My stomach started to squirm. It didn't sound like she was talking about the virus any more. "What's the matter, Cal?"

"I..." She knotted her fingers even closer to mine. "I'm..." She looked at me for a moment before hanging her head and letting out a lungful of air. "I'm scared."

"It'll be all right. I promise." I wasn't sure if my promise was realistic, but I had to make it anyway. I had to make everything all right. Even if the weight of something unsaid was hanging between us.

"I really am sorry," she said into my pyjama T-shirt after a while. "About the girl. I wanted to help."

I kissed the top of her head. "I know you did. That's why I love you."

"But she could've..."

"But she didn't."

"But what if she had?"

I pressed my lips together. "I don't know. It doesn't matter."

"I don't know what I'd do, Zane. I need you here next to me. Don't go anywhere."

"I promise I'll never go anywhere."

"Never?"

"Never." I tipped her chin up so her eyes would meet mine. "I promise."

She closed the gap first, and we were kissing like this was our last moment on earth. My hand was in her hair and hers were behind my neck, keeping us squashed together. Her body was soft against mine. She felt strong and fragile all at once as I traced my fingers up her back. She melted up against me and sighed. It was the most magnificent sound in all the world.

"Dammit!"

We jumped apart as Gemma appeared in the doorway.

"Oh." She smirked and put her hand through her hair. "Am I interrupting something?"

"No." Callie cleared her throat. "Nothing."

"Animals." Gemma tutted as she sat next to Callie.

"What did Katie say?"

"She said she wants me to come home."

"Do you want to go home?"

Gemma licked her lips and looked at her hands for a moment before meeting Callie's eye again. "Yes and no. I want to be with them. I want to make sure they're safe. I want what they're saying to be true and for this not to be happening. But the other side of me knows this is happening and knows I'm safer here. My survival instinct is keeping me right where I am." She looked to the window. "I know I don't want to be out there."

Callie hugged her close. "You've got me."

"I know. I can't seem to get rid of you." Gemma looked straight at Callie. A wave of intensity pressed down on us as she mouthed something to her I couldn't make out.

Callie pretended not to have seen, and Gemma ignored the questioning look I gave her. What was going on? What was it they weren't telling me?

Callie went back upstairs to get dressed as soon as there was any hint of daylight, and Gemma jumped up to follow her. I remained where I was, puzzling over what'd passed between them.

After the sun started peeping through the curtains, Mum appeared fresh from the shower wearing clothes I'd never seen.

I furrowed my eyebrows. "Where'd you get them?"

"They're Lisa's. I didn't bring anything with me. I didn't realise we'd be staying here."

I tried to fold the blanket without getting tangled up in it. "You don't mind, do you?"

"Of course I don't." She grabbed the other end and helped me fold it. "What would we be doing at home just the two of us? You'd be begging me to come here no doubt."

I tried to hide a smirk.

"Don't deny it. I know you'd be doing nothing but worrying about Callie."

"What gave me away?"

The corners of her mouth pulled up. "You are a sweetie, Zane."

"Thanks." I put the blanket behind the sofa and straightened the cushions, aware of Mum's eyes on me.

"Are you all right?"

"Yeah. Why?"

She shook her head. "This is all such a mess. And you seemed to have a horrendous day yesterday."

A flash of the little girl's mouth dripping blood came back to me, and I tried not to shiver. "I'm fine."

"How did you get to be so brave and grown-up? Where did those eighteen years go?"

"Seventeen and three-quarters."

She rolled her eyes. "Seventeen and three-quarters then. I feel like I'm still seventeen and three-quarters."

"When you were seventeen and three-quarters you had to look after me."

She looked at me with her ice-blue eyes, mouth dropping into a straight line. "You say 'had to' like it's a bad thing."

"Wasn't it?"

She continued to stare at me. "Of course it wasn't. You're the best thing that's ever happened to me."

"Now."

"No, always." She bundled me up in a hug all close and warm. "Don't ever think about yourself that way." She pulled away to look at me again, smiling this time, before ordering me to get dressed with an 'I love you' tagged at the end.

When I returned downstairs, everyone except Jay was in the living room drinking tea and coffee and eating toast like nothing had happened last night. Like the world hadn't started to end. Like we weren't all trapped in Ashford House for the foreseeable future.

"So," Gemma put her plate on the side table, "what do we do now?"

We all looked to one another until Jay appeared, throwing himself onto the sofa. "Someone online got scratched by an Infected and is mapping the virus as it kills them."

"What? We can be killed by a scratch now?" Gemma asked.

"If it breaks the skin. It's all about getting into the bloodstream. The worse the wound, the faster it can kill you. Also, the weaker you are, the faster it can kill you."

"Fantastic. Anything else?"

"Yeah. If you're infected with the dormant virus and die, you come back capital I Infected for sure."

Everyone stared at him for a moment before he grabbed for the remote.

"Jay, please." Lisa's voice begged. "Do we have to watch that again?"

"What if there's new information? We've got to know what's going on. The internet can only tell me so much."

I could see that Lisa wanted to argue back, but she crossed her arms instead.

The news report was showing the same clips as yesterday, round and round and round again, until the male news anchor appeared in a new shirt and tie.

"We have just discovered some new information about Juvenile Virus. Dr Collins is back with us to relay the news. Welcome back, Dr Collins."

"I wish it were under better circumstances."

"So what have you discovered about the virus this morning? Is it naive to wish for good news?"

"I believe at this point it is. We established yesterday that the dormant virus cannot kill the healthy. However, now the dormant virus is everywhere, we've learnt something rather distressing." Dr Collins paused, wetting her lips. "As well as the diseased, the elderly, and the young, pregnant women are also at risk."

There was movement from somewhere beside me. I looked to see Callie standing, unable to wrench her eyes from the screen.

"In what way?" the news anchor asked. "You said the dormant virus wasn't strong enough to affect the majority of the population."

"That remains the case. However, it appears the dormant virus spreads through the entire body looking for a weakness to take advantage of. In this case, the virus can infect an unborn baby and re-enter the mother's bloodstream in its live and violent form."

Gemma stood too and clasped Callie's hand. My heart was thudding so loud in my chest it was hard to pick out words. I couldn't look at the screen any more. Only at Callie.

"When you say its live form?"

"I mean it's the same as a bite from an infected host. It will get to work at once. It truly is a nasty virus, stopping at nothing to kill any host it enters. I advise viewers to be wary of expectant mothers along with the other parties at risk."

I didn't hear any more as Callie shot from the room, Gemma close to her heels. The world blurred together as the realisation punched me in the head.

NINE

"Zane?" I heard Mum's voice from somewhere, but everything was slow and lacking definition. "Zane?"

I shut my eyes and put my head in my hands. Thoughts swam back and forth, the torment growing louder by the second. Shouting, screaming. I pushed my hands further into my hair, but nothing could quiet the thunderous swarm.

This couldn't be happening. Among everything else that was happening, this couldn't be real. It couldn't.

Wake up! Wake up!

"What's happening, Zane?" I felt Mum's hand on mine, and I shot up, racing after Callie, barrelling up the stairs, throwing her bedroom door open with a crash.

They stopped talking. Callie's face was covered in tears. Gemma's hand was on her back.

I had to take a minute to organise my words. "What the hell is going on?"

"Zane," Callie forced through her tears. "I wanted to tell you."

"What?" Gemma jumped up. "I thought you were going to tell him this morning? You promised me you would."

"I tried." Callie's face was red, and her body was shaking.

"How hard? How difficult is it?"

Callie shook her head and clutched the tissue tight.

"What the *hell* is going on?" The raging inside me was like a storm, whipping me about all over the place. My heart felt too heavy. The room felt too small.

Gemma looked at Callie. "Well?"

Callie pressed her lips together and shook her head.

"Come on, Callie. Step up. He asked you a question."

Her breath caught in her throat. She wiped her eyes. "I know. I need to talk to you, Zane."

I was frozen in my place by the door.

"Gem, can you give us a minute?"

"Fine. What do I tell them?"

Callie looked to her bedroom window. "I don't know."

"You know this is your responsibility?"

"I know."

Gemma's shoulders relaxed at Callie's squeak. She rubbed her hand over her face. "I can tell them, Cal. But..."

Callie collapsed into a sobbing heap, and I managed to wrench my feet from the floor. Gemma met my eyes as she passed, staring straight into me.

My legs wobbled as I made my way over to Callie. I dropped onto the bed beside her and looked at the wall, listening to her cry. I couldn't bring myself to do anything else.

When she pulled herself together, she took my hand. "I'm sorry, Zane."

I didn't look at her.

"I truly am sorry. I was going to tell you but then, well, you know, yesterday."

I shut my eyes.

"I love you, Zane. I'm sorry. Please say something. Please look at me."

I couldn't look at her. I couldn't speak a word.

She sat there for a few minutes stroking my hand. I found the strength to open my eyes when the silence started eating me alive.

"I love you too, Callie."

She flung herself into my chest, wrapping her arms around my neck and her legs around my waist. Her tears soaked into my T-shirt. My own tears were caught in my chest and throat but wouldn't come out. I couldn't even breathe.

The words rebounded around my skull again and again as she whispered them into my ear. "I'm pregnant."

Everything paused. The universe stopped. It felt like I jumped out of my body, pulled my hair out in clumps, and screamed my throat raw. But all I did was sit there and let her hold me.

"I love you. I love you. I love you." She repeated the words over and over like they could make this okay. Like anything could make this okay.

She pulled back and looked into my eyes, but I gazed straight through her. This couldn't be happening. This couldn't be real.

"Zane?" She shuffled closer and put her hand to my cheek. "Please. Say something."

I shook my head from side to side and tried to breathe even. The tears were creeping closer and closer to my eyes.

"I'm so sorry."

I snapped, jumping up again. "Sorry? Why are you sorry? I should be the one who's sorry." I raked my hands through my hair. "What have I done? This isn't happening. This isn't real."

She stood up on her bed. "This is happening. I promise you."

"No. This shouldn't be happening. Not to us. Not to you."

A new wave of tears rolled down her cheeks.

This time they cut through me, and my heart leapt. "Please don't cry, Cal." I took both her hands in mine.

"I'm so sorry."

"I'm sorry too."

"You don't have to be sorry."

"Neither do you."

She chuckled and smiled. It was the saddest thing I'd ever seen. "Listen to us." She rested her forehead on mine and shut her eyes.

We listened to the commotion downstairs for a moment. The voices swelled at varying volumes and pitches. The only one I could distinguish through the floor was Michael's.

"I guess Gemma told them." Callie pulled back to look at me.

"You only told Gemma?"

She nodded. "I was going to tell you, but I couldn't. I was too scared."

"Scared of me?"

"Scared of everything." She pushed hair behind her ears that wasn't even there. "I didn't think this could happen to me. I never..."

I drew her into my shoulder and inhaled her floral scent without perfume.

"What a mess," she whispered.

The longer we stood there, the heavier I felt. I crumpled onto the bed, breathing too fast. I was going to vomit.

"Zane?"

"Stay back." Everything was dripping back to me bit by bit. It felt like acid soaking through to my brain.

"What?"

I retreated to her doorway. This was much worse than I thought. A hundred thousand times over. Why did this have to happen now?

"I don't want to infect you."

"Zane." She went to take a step closer.

"Get back there!"

Her eyes widened, but I couldn't back down.

"Don't you come anywhere near me. I can't let this happen to you. What would I do?"

"It doesn't make any difference. I've been right next to you all morning."

"Do you feel all right? Do you feel any different to normal?"

"I'm fine."

"You promise?"

"I promise."

"Don't...don't leave me." The tears, at last, escaped. I dropped to the ground and sobbed big and loud, bringing my knees up to my chest, burying my face in them. I couldn't take in enough air. I choked on my breath, on my tears, on my tongue. Trying to hold my breath didn't work. I couldn't calm down. Tears were in my hair, in my mouth, down my chest.

Callie sat beside me. I shuffled away from her, facing the opposite way. What would I do if I infected her? What could I do? She couldn't leave me. I wouldn't know what to do. I didn't know how to be without her any more.

"Zane, I'm fine. Like Gemma said yesterday, either none of us are infected or all of us are. Staying away from you now wouldn't make any difference."

"You don't know that." My voice was husky and dark. "I can't let this happen."

"So what? You're going to ignore me? You're going to leave a room when I enter it? That's ridiculous. I'm fine. But I still need you. I can't do this on my own." She took my hand. I let her, two sides of me warring.

I needed to keep her safe, but I needed to stay close to her. And she was right. I couldn't leave her alone and back off. Not now.

"I'm sorry." I ran my hand through the back of my hair. "You're right. Nothing would help now, would it?"

She tipped my chin up with her finger. "Don't look so sad. Everything's all right."

"Everything is far from all right."

"Well, you're always telling me everything's going to be okay, so now I'm telling it to you." Her smile was almost believable.

"You promise?" I had to whisper the words to make them come out.

"I promise." She stood up and dragged me with her. "I guess we have to face them now."

The nausea was back with a fury. "Can't we stay in here?"

"Forever?"

"Yeah. Just the two of us."

She cringed. The nausea did a jump in my stomach, and I had to hold it down.

I swallowed before speaking. "I guess that's impossible now, huh?"

She bit her lip. "I don't want to go down there either."

I took in a huge gust of air through my nose to clear my head. "I won't let go of your hand."

"And I won't let go of yours."

The door screeched as we opened it, crying for us to stay in Callie's bedroom where it was safe. But we had to face them sooner or later. And nowhere was safe. Not any more.

TEN

They were all standing except Lisa, who had her hands in her honey-blonde hair. She pulled her head up to meet our faces when we entered the room. She looked pale, her eyes too big. Gemma was standing to one side, chewing on her lip with her arms folded. Michael looked bigger than he ever had before, chest billowing up and down as he met my eye. I looked instead to Jay next to him. Jay was shaking his head from side to side, a look of disgust pulling up one corner of his mouth. Mum's eyes were kind and understanding. She opened her lips as though to say something before shutting them again.

Callie exchanged a look with me. The smile she'd forced on a minute ago had long disappeared. Any moment now I was going to vomit. By the quick breaths she was taking, I assumed Callie felt the same way.

There was silence for the longest thirty seconds of my life.

"Who's going to explain then?" The words burst from Michael's mouth, and my whole body tensed.

Callie's voice was quiet when it sounded. "I guess Gemma told you what was going on?"

"I'm hoping she's lying, Callie Ashford." Michael took a step closer. "And if she isn't, I need to hear it from you."

"All right." She cleared her throat. "What Gemma said is true. I'm pregnant."

I had no idea where this inner strength had come from. Had she drained some of it out of Gemma, who was quieter than I'd ever seen her? I watched Callie, afraid to catch anyone else's eye. Every pair flicked between us as another wave of hush fell on the room.

"You're only a baby yourself." Lisa was the next to speak up.

When I had enough courage to look around the room, Michael had fallen back onto the sofa. Mum opened her mouth again and snapped it shut before she could say anything. She crossed her arms tight. There were white marks where her fingers were digging in.

"How did this happen?" Lisa shook her head. "What are we going to do?"

No one said anything.

"Well, what do you have to say for yourself?" She was looking at both of us, but I wasn't sure how she wanted us to respond.

Lucky for me, Callie found her voice again. Mine had abandoned me. "Nothing. What do you want me to say, Mum? I'm sorry. I didn't want this to happen. I didn't do it on purpose."

"You don't seem that concerned."

"That's because I've been freaking out about it for weeks!"

"And you didn't say anything?"

"What was I supposed to say? I had no idea how to bring it up. I was trying to avoid a situation like this." She motioned to the whole room. "I didn't realise I'd have to reveal it for the safety of the group."

"Are you all right, Cal?" Gemma moved to her side. "You know, you don't feel sick or anything?"

"No. I'm fine."

Gemma put her hand to Callie's forehead. "You feel all right to me."

"I'm not infected!" She screamed it, and no one said a word. No one even moved. Callie wiped her eyes. "I can't be infected. This isn't going to happen to us. I feel the same as yesterday, so everyone can stop looking at me like that."

Gemma held both her hands up and stepped back. "I'm convinced."

"That's not even the matter at hand here." Michael stood back up.

"Why not?" Callie's face was growing redder. "I think whether or not I have the virus is a much more sensible thing to talk about."

"Not if you say you're fine. And I want you to promise me you're okay."

Her shoulders dropped. "I'm okay, Dad. Really."

He nodded. "Okay."

"Michael!" Lisa shot out of her seat. "It is *not* okay."

"What do you want me to say? What do you want me to do?"

"Something! Anything!"

"Like what? Force them to get married? Pretend this was always the plan? What? Because if you haven't noticed, it's the end of the world out there, and none of that stuff matters any more."

"What about when this is over? We'll still have a pregnant seventeen-year-old daughter."

Michael pinched the bridge of his nose. "I guess that's true."

"We need to know what's going to happen."

They were both looking at Callie now who'd returned to her normal colour. "What?"

"What are you going to do?" Lisa's accusing tone was slicing through me.

"I haven't discussed it with Zane."

"This is your decision. Who knows how long he's going to be around?"

"Hey!" Mum stepped forward at last. "How dare you? Don't speak about my son like that. He's standing right in front of you. Why don't you ask him what he wants? I haven't seen any sympathy directed his way."

"My daughter's pregnant because of your son."

"You think this is entirely his fault? You know that's not right. What if this was Jay? Your opinion would change then, wouldn't it?"

"Jay would never do something so stupid."

"This isn't Zane's fault. There are two people in this."

"Will there be two people at the end of this? He can run away. Callie can't."

I gritted my teeth.

"This is as much our problem as it is yours," Mum said.

"Well, you don't have a daughter. You don't know how this feels."

Mum chuckled, and it was dark and scary. "Believe me, I know exactly how this feels."

"Her life is over. What is she supposed to do now?"

"What?" Callie dropped my hand and took a step closer to Lisa. "You think my life is over?"

"Don't you?"

"No." She looked to Mum. "Jen's still standing here, isn't she? She's happy."

"What's that got to do with this?"

"Do you even know how old Jen is?"

All eyes directed to Mum as the Ashfords took in her youthful face. She looked younger than her age and had been referred to as my sister more than once.

Lisa's eyes widened. "And that's the reason you think all of this is okay? Because this is the family you've decided you want to be a part of? Well, the apple doesn't fall far from the tree, does it?" Her eyes were on me.

Something deep within me snapped, and everything cleared, anxiety draining. I clenched my hands into fists. "Take that back."

"Zane." Mum stood beside me. "She doesn't know what

she's saying. She doesn't know."

"Yes, she does. I am nothing like my father. Don't you dare compare us."

Michael put his hands on Lisa's shoulders as she went to speak again, silencing her.

"I would never do what he did. Never."

Callie's big green eyes were gazing at me.

"I am not my father."

She took my hand and went onto her tiptoes to kiss my cheek. "And I'm not my mother. I know you'll stand by me whatever happens." She looked to her family again. "I was never in any doubt about Zane. You've known him for over a year. How can you suddenly turn against him like this?"

Lisa's voice was pleading now. "Look what he's done, Callie. Look at this mess."

"He's a good person. A wonderful person. And if you can't see that, maybe I'd rather be a part of his family than a part of this one."

"Callie?" Michael came forward, extending his arms.

Without a word, Callie buried herself in her father's embrace. Tears were crawling down her cheeks again.

Mum bundled me up into her own arms, and I had to hold my breath so as not to cry myself. "It's going to be okay," she whispered to me. "I promise."

"Lisa?" Michael turned to his wife.

She shook her head. "What happens now?"

"I have no idea."

"Nothing," Callie said, clearing her throat. "There's nothing we can do. We're trapped in this house as we were before. We'll figure stuff out once this is over."

"Cal?" Gemma was twisting her hair around in her fingers. "I don't know how long this is gonna be around for. We've no idea when this is gonna be over. They're gonna have to think up a cure that works and go around giving it to pretty much everyone and killing all the Infected. That's gonna take months. I think we're gonna have to consider the fact that the baby might be born here."

My knees felt weak at the word 'baby', but Mum held me steady.

Everyone watched Gemma.

"How long does it take to clear up after the ZA?"

Callie shook her head. "It doesn't make any difference. We still can't do anything. Like I said, we're trapped here until this is over." She met my eye. "Whatever happens."

ELEVEN

I found myself staring out the window, gazing at the rain. If I turned around, I would have six pairs of eyes on me in an instant. Then the chatter would return. If another person asked me if I was all right, I was going to scream.

No, I wasn't all right. Everything was different now. And it took all my strength to hold myself together.

Jay filled the silence with talk of the Infected and the web pages he'd found on the internet of people recording the infection in family and friends. I blocked it out. I had other things to worry about.

My heart tried to escape my mouth as a figure appeared in the street. His head whipped from side to side as he looked for an escape.

"There's someone outside!"

A bundle of bodies pushed against the window as everyone crowded to look. The man was joined by the stumbling figure of an Infected, and we all took a breath.

I shook my head as we watched. "We've got to help him."

Someone grabbed my arm as I went to race off, and I was met with Michael's soft-blue eyes. "Are you mad?"

"We've got to save him."

"No. We don't."

No one else dared to speak.

"We can't risk our lives for a stranger."

My heart fell back into my chest, and I swallowed. "But—"

"No."

The lack of argument made it hard to breathe. Had we sunk this low? Already?

When I wrenched myself from Michael's stare, it was already too late. The man and the Infected trailing him were gone.

No one had much to say for the rest of the day, and everyone went to bed early. It was long after midnight that I closed my eyes and stopped staring at the ceiling. The man and the Infected plagued my mind for a while but not nearly long enough. There was another pressing matter at hand.

I couldn't be a father. I wouldn't know what to do. There'd never been a male role model in my life other than my grandfather, but he'd never tried to take the place of my non-existent father. No one had. They thought I didn't need one. I'd agreed until now.

How was I supposed to be something I didn't even understand? How was I supposed to care for Callie and a baby at seventeen? Eighteen, I guessed.

I didn't know the first thing about babies. I'd never been around them for more than an hour or so. I'd never had any brothers or sisters to look out for.

I couldn't be a father. And did I even want to be?

No. Of course I didn't. Why would I want that? The list of things I wanted stretched miles long, but this wasn't on it.

Nothing I could do about that now though. We were trapped in these few rooms for the foreseeable future. Helpless. Us against the world.

I yelled myself awake. A thudding drove me into consciousness. My head swirled for a moment as I tried to grab hold of my bearings.

Thud.

Throwing the blanket back, I hopped off the sofa and moved towards the back wall where the sound had come from. Almost like...

Thud.

Someone banging on the window.

I ducked down against the floor and held my breath, shutting my eyes, willing myself to take a quick peek. If there was something out there, it shouldn't be able to break in. The windows were all shut and locked and covered with wood.

Thud.

The wood sounded strong and like it was doing its job, so I could afford to take a quick look and see what was going on. I had to talk in my head for a few minutes before having the courage to stand though. Holding my breath, I moved the curtain an inch and caught a glimpse of a pale face with blood caking his misshapen nose.

Slapping my hand across my mouth, I crept out of the living room and up the stairs where Michael appeared, rubbing the sleep from his eyes.

"Zane!" He jumped when he saw me.

I held my finger to my lips and dragged him back into his bedroom to look out the window. "There's one out there."

His eyes widened as he saw it. "Do we leave it?"

"I dunno."

"What if there are more of them?"

I pulled my eyes away from the Infected and gazed into the distance. "I can't see any others."

"They could be hiding."

"I don't know if they're clever enough to do that."

Lisa stirred and shrieked as she saw us.

"Shush!" Michael hissed.

"What, what?" She fell out of bed and stumbled towards us.

Michael clamped his hand over her mouth as her eyes met the Infected and grew huge. "Don't make a sound. We don't want it to know we're in here."

Lisa stared straight at Michael, not blinking. She nodded.

He released her, and she started hyperventilating.

"If...if it's banging on the window," I said as the thought occurred to me, "does that mean it knows we're in here?"

Michael shook his head. "I don't know. Maybe it knows something's in here that it wants. Or maybe the house is just in its way?"

I swallowed down the unease and creep of fear. "What do we do? Do we wake them?"

He took a moment before nodding. "Yeah. I think that's a good idea."

I went into the spare room to wake Mum, and she didn't let go of my hand as we met Michael and Jay on the landing. Jay shot into his parents' room, Michael knocking on Callie's door.

Gemma gave a yelp. "Scared the bloody life out of me." She wrenched open the door, her hair huge like she'd backcombed it again. "Morning. What's with the wake-up call?"

"There's an Infected outside."

Michael didn't have to say any more. Gemma sped to the window next to Jay. I pulled Callie and Mum into the master bedroom. Michael, Gemma, and Jay were all pressed up against the window and Lisa was sitting on the edge of the bed. Mum dropped my hand to take a look. Callie did not. No one spoke for at least two entire minutes.

"What do we do?" Gemma asked. "Do we ignore it and hope it goes away or do we...you know, get it?"

"Get it?" Michael looked at her. "I don't know about you, but I don't really want to go out there while it's out there."

"I think we need to kill it," Jay said.

"What?" Michael's eyes were on him. "You can't be serious."

"What else are we supposed to do? What if it just keeps doing that until it gets in?"

"It can't get through the boards and the window."

"Why not? We need to get it before it gets us."

"We don't even know how to...kill it."

"I imagine it's fairly straightforward," Gemma said. "There's one of him and seven of us."

"No." I shook my head. "We're not all going out there."

"Agreed," Michael said.

"Right." Gemma pulled her eyes away from the window. "Then who goes out there, and who stays in here?"

There was silence.

"No volunteers?" She pulled her hair up into a ponytail. "I guess I'll go. I want to know how exactly to take these things down."

"Me too," Jay said.

"No." Michael shook his head. "You are not going out there."

"Who would you rather out there, Dad? Mum? Callie? I want to see how easy it is. You think we're going to survive this thing without taking at least a few of them out?"

Michael's eyes darted around the room before he gave in. "You're only coming out there if you remain behind me at all times."

"Fine. Anyone else?"

Jay was looking at me. I opened my mouth to speak, but no sound came out, so I nodded.

"Me too." Mum stepped beside me and took my hand.

"Mum, no. I don't want you to go out there."

She pressed her lips together. "And I don't want you to go out there. Either we both go or neither of us do."

I watched her ice-blue eyes for a moment, trying to work out which of the two options she wanted me to pick, but her face gave nothing away.

"Okay," I said. "We'll both go."

"Good." Jay stood in front of us all. "Now that's decided, what are we actually going to do?"

"Let's go kill it," Gemma said. "I'm not comfortable in here if he's trying to get in. We need to get rid of him."

"We'll need weapons. I knew I needed a machete."

"Jay," Michael said. "You do not need a machete."

"Would've come in handy right about now. It would've been awesome. Unfortunately, Dad thought it was too dangerous, so we're going to have to use what we have."

"What do we have?" Gemma crossed her arms.

Jay shrugged. "Whatever we can find."

TWELVE

We dressed quicker than we ever had before and rooted around in the garage for weapons before standing at the back door, building up the courage to go outside.

"How fast do you think it'll run?" Michael asked, holding up an axe.

"They were pretty fast the other day, but I'm hoping that decomposing will be slowing them down. Speedy over here should work to our advantage." Gemma pointed at me.

"How can I be an advantage? I'm not super strong. I can't pick you all up and run back in here."

"That would be useful, but this one doesn't look as scary as the other ones." Jay had his face pressed up against the window part of the back door.

"Not as scary?" Mum squeezed her golf club until her knuckles went white. "How scary were the other ones?"

Jay ignored her. "So what's the plan? Are we just going to go barrelling out there and kill it?"

"What, all at once?" Gemma spun the baseball bat around in her hands. "Won't we get in each other's way? And make loads of noise? I reckon we let one person kill it and just be there for support. We want to be as quiet as possible."

"Makes sense," Jay said. "Who?"

We looked around at each other, fear lighting every pair of eyes.

Michael cleared his throat. "I'll give it a go. How hard can it be?"

"Remember, remove the head or destroy the brain." Jay clapped Michael on the back. "Everyone ready?"

We took a collective breath.

"Let's go."

We scurried out in a line, weapons held tight. The wind whipped at my hair. I tensed against the cold, hoping the temperature would slow them down.

The Infected turned to look at us before shuffling this way on what looked like a broken ankle. He had to haul it along with him, trailing it across the ground as though he couldn't balance on it.

"Speed is not a problem," Gemma whispered.

For a while, no one did anything. We stood there and observed the dead man in the garden. His face was grey other than the explosion of red around the nose and mouth area. In fact, his nose was missing other than a chunk of cartilage. The deep-red blood was clotted and filled the oval hole in his face. His mouth was too wide, ripped at either side to show more teeth. He was snarling, spittle dripping onto the grass along with old blood. He looked like he used to be wearing a white shirt, but there was not one patch of white left. Just red, black, and brown, along with dirt and grass stains.

The stench didn't reach me until he was a few metres away, but the moment it did, I gagged and had to bend over and rest on my knees to refrain from vomiting. Gemma threw her hand over her mouth. Mum screwed up her face. The rancid decay bit into me, and I had to repeat the word 'no' in my head over and over as I retched and tried to remain upright.

Michael stepped forward, and the Infected hissed and reached out to him with his filthy bloodstained hands. Everyone else took a step back as Michael edged closer and closer. He lifted the axe over his shoulders, adjusting his grip, before powering the weapon downwards onto the Infected's head. The blade connected with the decaying skull, and there was a tremendous crack. The Infected dropped to the floor still growling. Still moving.

The axe was stuck. Michael yanked but it wouldn't budge. It was buried in bone. Blood was squirting from the Infected's cranium and covering the grass. But it was still coming for us.

Michael was panting, sweat beginning to show on his forehead, eyes growing distant with fear as the hands grew closer to his ankles. When the fingers were centimetres from him, he yelped and jumped back into the line.

"Now what?" He wiped his arm across his forehead.

Gemma held up her hand. "I'll go."

I went to grab her arm, but she dodged my grip and threw her baseball bat down with full fury on the Infected's face. Blood and saliva blasted from the impact. My stomach heaved. I had to use my whole arm to cover my mouth and nose. Gemma huffed with each strike, driving the undead man further and further into the ground. He stopped groaning, but Gemma didn't. Not until brains leaked onto the grass. With a final squelch, Gemma was satisfied and staggered back to the line.

"Well…" She toppled to one side, and Mum held her up.

I dragged my arm away from my mouth, but the second the smell hit me along with the visual aid of a collapsed skull, I dropped to my hands and knees and vomited.

"That…" Gemma struggled for breath. "That went well."

Jay pulled the axe out of the Infected's skull—Gemma's brutal attack having dislodged it—and handed it back to Michael. "Is everyone all right?"

They all nodded. I pulled myself back to standing, wiping my mouth with the back of my hand. My legs were shaking, and I struggled to stay up.

"That wasn't as easy as I expected." Jay was biting his lip.

"Look at us." His eyes lingered on me. "What if there had been more of them?"

Gemma swiped her hand through the air as though waving the thought away. "That was just a practice. Now we know what we're up against, it'll be easier. And maybe next time Zane won't throw up all over the bloody place."

I wanted to respond, but to open my mouth would be asking for it. My breath was shallow and rapid as I tried to force the nausea back down.

"What now?" Michael looked to Jay. "We can't just leave it there. It might attract the others."

"You're not suggesting burying it? There's no way."

"We could burn it?" Gemma suggested.

I gagged once more.

"Won't that attract any others?" Michael dropped his axe. "We don't really know what attracts them, do we? It could be light."

"Well, we need to do something. The smell's just gonna get worse." Gemma wrinkled up her nose.

"You guys figure it out." I swallowed. "I need to sit down."

Mum put her arm around me as we made our way inside, supporting me in case I fell. She shuddered as we turned away from the mess that was the garden.

Callie and Lisa were waiting for us in the kitchen.

"What happened?" Lisa's eyes were big and wide.

"They got it," Mum said as I dropped to the kitchen floor. "It's dead."

"Everyone's all right?"

"Yeah, all fine. Discussing what they're going to do next. Very calmly, I might add."

I shut my eyes and felt a hand in my hair.

"You okay?"

I nodded at Callie's voice.

She pressed a glass into my hand, and I took big gulps of water, spilling it down my front thanks to Jay filling them all to the brim. If this was going to happen every time we encountered an Infected, I was going to be a liability. I had to do something about my weak stomach.

"Jen?" Lisa was rubbing her hands up and down her arms. "I'm really sorry about what I said yesterday. I wasn't thinking straight. I feel so stupid now with all of this going on."

Mum's mouth pulled up in that gentle smile of hers. "It's okay. No hard feelings."

"Are you sure? I was truly awful. I know I would've been so rude if someone was saying those things to me. But you weren't."

Mum shook her head. "I was just being the person I'd wanted my mother to be, that's all. I know you didn't mean what you said."

"I didn't, and I regret saying all of it now. I'm truly sorry, Zane."

I opened my eyes to meet Lisa's.

"I didn't mean what I said. That wasn't fair."

I shook my head and cleared my throat, pulling myself up with the help of the counter. "It's really all right. It could've gone worse."

"That doesn't make it right of me. I feel awful about it. I just didn't know what to think."

"Me neither." I looked at Callie as she clung to my arm.

"I love you both."

Callie smiled. "Thank you, Mum. That means a lot. I didn't mean to spring it on all of you like that I…"

"I know." Lisa chewed on a nail. "Gosh, what a mess. I still can't believe this is happening."

I shook my head, trying to block out the thoughts cramming their way in. I couldn't think about babies when I should've been thinking about fighting the Infected. Survival should've been at the front of my mind, but how could it be now? Nothing could overshadow this terror. I'd rather be cleaning up brain juice than think about it.

"Well, I guess we're all family now, right?" Lisa's closed mouth smile wasn't convincing. Her eyes were too wide with fear.

Mum seemed to be the only comfortable person in the room. She chuckled. "I guess we are."

THIRTEEN

Two days later, another Infected wandered its way into the garden.

"They must know we're here." Jay was shaking his head. "Why else would they come this way and not carry on?"

"I guess you're right." I pointed to the broken fence. "She smashed right through the panels."

"It, Zane. Not she."

"Right, sorry."

"I guess it's our turn this time."

"What makes you say that?"

"We didn't exactly do anything the other day. Well, that's not true. You puked all over the grass."

"All right, all right. Enough with that already."

"I'm just joking." He smirked before gathering the troops in the living room.

Everyone sat on the sofa closer to the front of the house, like the Infected could break through the brick in a couple of minutes. We were silent, staring at Jay, waiting for his command.

"I think we go as before, but Zane and I get a turn at, you know, killing it."

"Jay—"

"Dad, it'll be fine. You'll be right there. There's just one. We can handle it. Gem? You coming?"

"Of course."

"Jen?"

Mum cringed and fiddled with her bracelet. "I'll come outside if that's what you're asking, but I'm going to stand way back." She looked at me. "Do you really need to do this?"

I nodded. "We've all got to be prepared. I want to protect you all."

"But, Zane, you know what happened last time."

Gemma bit her lip to hold back whatever it was she wanted to say.

"It won't happen again." I fought down the blush creeping up my neck. "I know what to expect this time. It won't be such a shock."

"If you're sure?"

"Positive." I wasn't going to throw up. I couldn't afford to make that mistake again. Not if I wanted to be treated like an equal.

The five of us grabbed our weapons from last time and waited by the back door.

"Zane, if you don't mind going first, I think that would be better." Michael put his hand up to stop Jay from arguing. "If it comes to it, Zane can easily outrun it. I don't think you can, Jay."

"Fine," Jay said. "But let me do something."

My heart was throwing itself against my ribcage as I stepped outside. I didn't even feel the cold. Just the adrenaline shooting through my body, making me tremble, making me dizzy.

This Infected was in much better shape, and her—its—head snapped around the second we left the house. Its straggly, limp hair flicked as it moved, spraying blood in an arc.

It charged towards us. I flung the golf club round and connected with its teeth. Bone and blood exploded from the impact, and it dropped to the ground.

Before I could catch my breath, it was up again, grabbing for me. I shoved as hard as I could with the golf club and kicked out with my leg. It caught its balance before I was ready and leapt at me again, broken teeth bared, a shriek piercing my ears.

We tumbled to the ground, the Infected on top of me, centimetres from my face. I used the golf club as my shield, but I couldn't throw it off. Its body was too heavy, and my arms were shuddering under the force. The damp decay in its breath was all over me, but this time I didn't gag.

Yelling through the strain, I gave one last shove, and it jumped up a little. Enough for Gemma's baseball bat to slam into its head.

Jay was at her side, holding the hedge clippers high before driving them through the Infected's forehead.

The noise stopped.

Gemma fell to her knees beside me, pushing hair out of her face. Jay swayed before vomiting all over the grass. I couldn't stop staring at her—its—bloody face. I couldn't throw up even if I'd wanted to. Nothing was working right.

"Are you okay?" Gemma's voice sounded too far away.

I couldn't respond. The Infected was all I could see. It'd been centimetres from ending my life. From digging its teeth into my neck. Infecting me. Or killing me on the spot. What was the difference, really?

"Zane?" Gemma put her face in front of mine. I had no choice but to look into her stormy-grey eyes. "Are you all right?"

I gave a sharp nod.

"Okay." Gemma hauled me up with her and supported my weight until I broke out of my daze. "This has *got* to get easier."

"Well, it can't get any harder," Jay groaned as Michael pulled him up.

"Look out!" The screech came from Mum.

An Infected had stumbled through the hole in the fence,

arms outstretched, teeth gnashing, spittle flung everywhere. It was only a metre away from reaching Michael.

Before we could scrabble around in the grass for our weapons, Mum had leapt in front of the Infected and smashed her golf club into its face. Michael was the first to recover, but Mum brought the weapon down again and again before dropping it and scurrying into my arms. I wasn't ready for the impact. I stumbled at her force but held tight, digging my fingers into her back, never wanting to let go.

Michael's axe sliced through its neck. We were all quiet, looking at one another.

"Well." Gemma swallowed. "I think they know where we live."

"They must be coming from the city." Jay wiped the hedge clippers in the grass once he'd pulled them from the Infected's skull. "We know there were plenty there."

"But that means…"

Jay nodded. "I think most everyone in the city will be dead."

Mum whimpered, and I rested my head on top of hers.

"So what?" Gemma asked. "They're all spreading out randomly? Looking for people to infect?"

"I guess," Jay said. "What else does the virus want to do?"

"Well, what can we do?"

"Nothing. I mean, for now. We seem safe here so far."

Gemma crossed her arms. "I'd definitely rather be behind brick walls than out in the open."

Michael disappeared into the house before returning with some tools and heading over to the pile of things that used to sit in the shed. "As long as we're safe here, I'm going to keep fixing the fence."

"And in case things get worse, I'm going to figure out a plan." Jay jogged back into the house.

I watched Gemma and Michael fuss with the panels for a minute before I pulled back from Mum. "Do you want to go inside?"

She shook her head and wiped her eyes. "Nope. Not while there's a fence to fix."

I could only watch her as she joined them. It took every ounce of strength I possessed to make my feet move in their direction. All I wanted to do was sit down and try not to think.

But that wasn't an option now. Not in the ZA.

FOURTEEN

When the four of us, shivering, returned inside, the light was starting to fade behind a wall of dark cloud. The wind was whistling through the trees behind Ashford House. My hands were numb and tingling as I rubbed them together for warmth. Jay was sitting at the dining table with paper balled up and scattered everywhere.

Gemma and I joined him, heaving colossal sighs as we sat.

"Cheers for all your help, Jay." Gemma was resting her head back and had her eyes closed. "I have no idea how we could've done it without you."

"Shut up. I've been busy."

"What are you doing?" I asked, sitting on my hands to heat them up.

"Trying to come up with a list of what would be useful to take with us if we have to leave here. We'll need to pack bags we can grab at a moment's notice."

Gemma rubbed her eyes. "Good plan. What've you got so far?"

"Food, water, painkillers, matches, candles, toilet paper, and probably some form of knife or something. We'll have to carry the baseball bat and golf clubs and stuff in our hands unless they can stick out the top."

"Seems fair enough." Gemma sat forward. "What about blankets or something? It's winter out there."

"Another reason why I hope we don't have to leave here." Jay scratched the back of his head with the pencil. "The blankets will take up loads of room."

"Whatever. I'd rather be warm."

"Would you rather die of starvation or hypothermia?"

"Tough choice." Gemma continued before Jay could argue any more. "But if we were to leave, where would we go?"

"Somewhere without people. Without Infected."

"If you hadn't noticed, you live in the middle of nowhere. Where can we go that's better than here?"

He slammed his hands down on the table. "I didn't say I wanted to leave. We need to be ready, that's all. I want to stay here until everything goes back to normal. But we have to come to terms with the fact that we might have to leave. I'm just being realistic."

"What about socks?" I asked after a moment of silence.

"Socks?" Gemma raised her eyebrows.

"Very important. Wet feet are the worst. I'll be putting socks in my bag."

Gemma rolled her eyes, but Jay scribbled down my suggestion.

"We're each going to have to carry one of these things too." Jay looked to his second list. "Binoculars, map, first aid kit, torch."

"Batteries," Gemma said, "for the torch."

Jay made a note of it.

"Toothbrush," I added. "Toothpaste."

"Really, Zane?" Gemma looked at me. "Minty freshness is a priority?"

I shrugged. "Takes up no room really."

Gemma clicked her fingers. "What about a radio?"

This time I raised my eyebrows.

"Oh, come on. This is better than your sock idea. If we had a radio, we could listen to the news. They might be organising some sort of safe house for survivors or something."

Jay nodded. "It's an idea. I don't think the radio in my room is battery operated, but Callie might have one."

I looked round to try and catch a glimpse of Callie's blonde hair in the living room, but I could only see Michael and Mum's heads sticking up from the back of the sofa.

"Where is Callie?"

Jay grabbed for my wrist as I went to stand. "In her room. And you will not be going in there."

"What?"

"I've quarantined her and Mum."

Gemma exchanged a look with me. "Come again?"

Jay shook his head. "Fair enough we might not have been infected before, but without a doubt Zane is infected now. She was millimetres from licking your face. You are banned from going anywhere near Callie."

I wanted to argue, but I bit my tongue. He was right. It may pierce me like a blade to be separated from her, but knowing she was safe and all right was more important. It was the most important.

"And because I have no idea how close you have to be for the virus to spread, it's safer to assume we're all infected with the dormant virus, and Mum and Callie aren't."

"Cheery." Gemma let down her hair. "All my stuff is in your sister's room."

"It's out on the landing now."

"Where am I supposed to go?"

"Share with Jen in the spare room, or take the other sofa."

"Great. Thanks. A little heads-up would've been nice."

"What else was I supposed to do?" He flung his arms out wide. "I needed to do something. What the hell would happen if she got infected?"

I shook my head. "Don't say that."

"See." Jay pointed at me. "We can't afford a mistake like that, so I'm sorry, Gemma, but you can sleep under the stairs for all I care."

Gemma rose from her chair and dashed round to Jay's side

of the table, bundling him up in a hug. "I'm sorry. Of course you're right."

He buried his face in his hands, and Gemma and I pretended we couldn't hear him cry.

"Jay?" Gemma cleared her throat. "Not to make matters worse or anything but what about the other day? I killed that Infected and then went and slept in the same bed as Callie. According to your theory, that means she's already infected."

My heart sank, and tears blurred my eyes. No. She couldn't be infected. I needed her. This couldn't be happening. It couldn't. My breath was ragged, and I couldn't take back what little control I had over my emotions.

Jay raked in a huge breath and sobbed. The more I tried to blink away tears, the faster they fell. I hid my face in my hands, and the next thing I knew, there were arms around me.

A kiss was planted on the side of my head. Mum gave me a small smile and squeezed me tight.

"What is going on in here?" Michael asked. "And where are Lisa and Callie?"

"Jay quarantined them," Gemma explained without letting go of Jay. "Jay thinks we're certainly infected now. Well, Zane is, and I guess maybe I am, and I probably infected Jay. Jen, you might be too, at least after that hug so…"

"So you're expecting us to carry on without them?"

"I guess. I mean, that's the case as long as…well, as long as Callie's not already infected."

"Don't!" I cried. "Don't say that."

"It's a possibility, Zane. I don't like it either. I'm just being realistic. She's my best friend in the universe. Of course I want her to be safe. So if being safe means staying away from us then she's staying the hell away from us. Okay?"

Michael took in a huge breath but nodded. "Fine. I suppose we have no choice really, do we?"

"So?" Gemma pulled herself away from Jay and sat next to him. "Hypothetically, the plan is to stay here killing the Infected in the garden until all this blows over?"

Jay nodded.

"I dunno about you guys, but I can live with that. And I guess I can live with not seeing Callie for...what? The next six months? You really think they'll be all right in there?"

"They'll be all right." Jay's voice was hoarse.

I rubbed my hand over the back of my neck, wanting to say a thousand things but stopping myself.

"We've just got to hope this all sorts itself out by then because..." Gemma looked at me.

"You really want them to stay in there?" The words burst out of me. "You're saying it's okay that Callie goes through this almost entirely alone? That I'm not allowed to be a part of it now?"

"That's beside the point." Jay's hands were clenched. "I'm not the one who complicated all of this."

I stood up. "What?"

"Hey, hey, hey." Gemma jumped up too. "Enough of this. It's ridiculous. Yes, Jay. Deal with it. Your sister's pregnant. Don't blame Zane. There's nothing we can do about it now." She turned to me. "Yes, Zane. Deal with it. You can't see her until the world is fixed or the baby's born."

"Not even then."

"What?" She faced Jay.

"Callie will have to look after it and remain uninfected to do that. We will all still be infected."

"Wait, wait." I shook my head. "Are you telling me I can't be with her until they've come up with a cure? If that's even possible?"

"That's exactly what I'm telling you."

FIFTEEN

I closed my eyes and smiled as she picked up.

"Hey. How's life downstairs?" Her voice sounded further away than it really was.

"Same as ever. Eating cans of food and drinking water out of a saucepan."

She giggled, and it warmed my heart. "Anything on the news?"

"Nothing new at all. Just the same stuff over and over again. I can probably recite some of it word for word."

"How old's the newest report?"

"The newest one is still the pregnant women one. Nothing since then. Jay's making lists of everything he knows about the Infected and the virus, but I don't think he's added anything today."

"So it's not getting better then?" There was a sigh in her voice.

"We don't know that."

"I don't really know what to hope for, Zane."

I bit my lip. "Me neither. I miss you."

"I miss you too. It feels like you're in a different country."

"I might as well be." I rubbed my hand across my face. "How are you feeling?"

"Fine." She answered too fast. There was an edge in her voice.

"What is it?" All four pairs of eyes turned to me, so I stared at the wall to block them out.

"It's nothing, really. I don't want you freaking out."

My heart crashed in my chest. "It's too late for that. I'm already freaking out."

Someone muted the TV.

"It's really nothing to be panicking about. I was just sick a couple of times. Nothing. Really."

I didn't believe her. "But do you feel all right?"

"I'm tired and sick of this room already, but yes. I'm fine."

"Is this the first time you've been sick?"

"I'm sure it's nothing."

"Callie, please."

There was silence for a long minute. "Yes."

I jumped up from the sofa and started pacing.

"It's really nothing to worry about. Honest."

"I worry about you every second of every day. You think just telling me you're all right is enough?"

"It should be. Are you calling me a liar?"

I pinched the bridge of my nose, trying to fight down the burning emotion coiling inside me. "No, of course not. I'm just saying there's nothing you can say to make this better. I'm terrified."

"You think I'm not? The throwing up might be due to the fact that I'm so unbelievably petrified I'm going to die!"

I shook my head. "Please don't say that, Cal."

"It's a reasonable thing to think about. I'm supposed to stay in here for the foreseeable future. What if this is it? There are so many things that could go wrong from here."

I heard Lisa ask for the phone.

"Callie. Please, stop it."

She was arguing with Lisa, and there were tears in her voice. "Cal? Callie?"

"Zane?" It was Lisa. "What's going on?"

"Does she look ill to you?"

"No, but it's hard to tell when she's like this. She's just fragile and upset. I'm sure it'll be okay." The sentences grew more high-pitched as they went on.

It felt like a huge boulder had been thrown at me and pinned me down. I dropped onto the sofa. It took me a few minutes to force the sentence out. "Does she look better than yesterday?"

There was a long pause. My stomach squeezed so tight I couldn't breathe. My shoulders felt tense. My heart sprinted too hard and too fast. It felt like there was something in my throat.

"No."

I sucked in a huge breath and pressed my lips together to stop from sobbing in her ear. Gemma snatched the phone off me. I couldn't make my arm work fast enough to take it back.

"Lisa, talk to me. What's going on? I've got everyone here wondering what on earth you guys are talking about. Tell me what's happening. Now."

There was quiet in the room as Gemma listened. Michael was only centimetres away from her, leaning his head close to the phone. I looked to the carpet, afraid meeting any eyes would make me lose it.

"All right. You better keep us updated. Call us even if you think it's nothing. We need to know what's going on."

"What is going on?" Jay hissed.

"It doesn't seem to be anything to worry about." Gemma pushed some hair off her face. "Nothing out of the ordinary. We're keeping an eye on it."

"Keeping an eye on what?"

"Callie's been throwing up and getting a little hysterical. It's all fine."

I wasn't sure whether Gemma was saying it to calm us, Lisa, or herself.

Before anyone could say anything more, darkness surrounded us. Everyone jumped out of their seats. There was a scream from down the phone and upstairs.

"Lisa? You all right up there?"

Everything was dead. The lights, the TV, the electric fireplace.

"Yeah. Nothing down here either."

Michael pulled his head from the phone to flick the lights on and off. Nothing happened. "I'll check the fuse." He disappeared from the room.

I collapsed onto the sofa again and rubbed my hand across the back of my head and neck, trying to calm the storm in my heart.

"We don't know," Gemma said. "Mick's checking the fuse."

Mum left the room and returned with some of the bigger candles. When she lit the match, I could see how much her hands were shaking. The light cast an eerie glow across the room, throwing dark shadows behind everything. She blew the match out and pulled a pillow close to her, catching my eye. I wanted to go to her, but I couldn't make my arms and legs coordinate.

"I don't know, but we'll figure it out," Gemma was saying. "It's all gonna be okay. It's just a couple 'a lights."

Michael reappeared, shaking his head. "The fuse is fine. Power must be out."

Jay raced to the window. "There's nothing. No lights anywhere." His face looked pale in the candlelight. "The power's gone."

"What do we do now?" Mum whispered.

"Nothing." Jay went to sit beside her. "As usual."

"The water still works." Michael joined them.

"For now. We need to refill everything as soon as we've emptied it. Who knows when that's gonna stop?"

Gemma put her hand to the radiator. "Gas seems fine," she said as she paced up and down, listening to whatever it was Lisa was saying.

Michael put his arm around Jay. "We're going to be all right."

Jay nodded and sniffed. "Yeah. We're all doing great." He pulled himself up. "Where are the rucksacks?"

"By the front door where we put them last night and where

they've remained all day. Don't worry, they're there."

Jay went to leave the room.

"Where are you going?"

"I need to check the rucksacks again. Make sure they all have candles and matches and lighters, and that I found all the torches and batteries."

"We checked them this morning."

"I have to be doing something. Where's the list?"

"Jay—"

"Where's the list?"

"Callie Ashford!" Gemma's volume made me jump. "Don't you ever scare me like that ever again. No, no. I don't care. Stop it. You listen to me. It's all gonna be fine. I've been telling you over and over, and one of these days you're gonna listen to me. Okay? Good. You need to chill out. You're scaring us half to death down here. We can't see you. We don't know if you look sick or fine or scared or whatever. You can't freak us out like this again." There was a pause. "Yes, you can. You're one of the strongest people I know. No. No arguing. No. I love you, okay? I love you. Zane?" Gemma held the phone out to me. "Callie wants to speak to you again."

I couldn't help but snatch the phone off her. "Cal?"

"Zane."

I let my breath out in one huge gust, wondering how long I'd been holding it. "Are you all right?"

"We're fine. I'm sorry."

"It's okay." I shook my head. "I just really need you to be okay."

"I know." There was a moment of quiet. "I love you, Zane Thomas Carlisle."

From somewhere deep inside, I found a smile. "I love you too, Cal. More than anything. Everything's gonna be all right."

"You promise?"

"I promise."

SIXTEEN

I was tapping my fingers on the arm of the sofa and bouncing my leg up and down when Gemma threw the book onto her lap.

"Jay? If I carry Zane's rucksack, can I kill him?"

Jay didn't look up from his list, which he hadn't put down since last night. "No. He's a good asset to the team."

"How exactly?"

I slammed my hand down.

She didn't flinch. "Just because he can run fast doesn't mean he's particularly helpful."

"He's good," was all Jay had to say.

I jumped up and walked up and down the room instead. I needed to be doing something with my restless legs.

"And now with the pacing? Really? What's wrong with you? They're fine."

"It's not just that." My voice came out harsher than I meant it to. "I...I need to do something. I need to run."

"No." Gemma pulled herself up more. "You are not starting jogging round the house. I will have to trip you up if you do that."

"No tripping. If you break him, we're screwed."

Gemma rolled her eyes. "I'm bored too, but you don't see me making annoying noises. You can read this book when I'm done with it."

"I need to be moving, not reading."

"Moving where? We're not going anywhere."

"It doesn't matter. I need to run." I raced upstairs and changed into my running gear from college. It felt like a lifetime ago my heart had dropped when I hadn't beaten my personal best. As though that mattered at all. Like that made a difference. Like that was going to save my life.

Jay was waiting for me at the bottom of the stairs. "You're not going out there."

"I'm just going in the garden. I won't leave your sight." I tried to squeeze by him.

"You can't go out by yourself. Anything could happen."

"Jay, I need to move. I need to do something. Please."

He tapped his foot for a moment. "Fine. We'll come out with you. Keep watch while you run around like a lunatic."

They all ended up trailing outside with me, Gemma appearing in her zombie costume, tying her hair up.

"Gem?" Jay pulled his hat down over his ears. "What the hell are you doing?"

"Running with psycho. Can't hurt, can it?"

I jogged back and forth at a gentle pace, looking up to Callie's window every now and then, hoping to catch sight of her. Gemma ran alongside me, breath puffing loud and hard after only a few minutes. My body fell into the rhythm of pumping my legs and arms, and a wash of calm filled me up.

When I felt warm and alive, I picked up the pace, stretching my legs. Gemma was left behind, not rising to my challenge.

"Show off," she wheezed as I lapped her.

I laughed for the first time in what felt like forever. It ached in my cheeks and my lungs and my heart. I felt lighter and more human for it, and I couldn't stop smiling.

Once my heart was pounding, I stopped at one end of the garden, wiping the sweat from my forehead before lowering myself towards the ground and leaping into a sprint. I had to skid to a stop before I went through the fence, mud caking my favourite trainers. But I didn't care.

I went back and forth until I couldn't hear anything but my own blood rushing in my ears, my heart drumming, and my breath gasping. My legs were splattered with mud which was cracking along my skin as it dried. Gemma was still jogging from one side to the other, face red.

She slowed to reach me and took a minute before she could speak. "You really are speedy, aren't you?"

I shrugged.

"Ugh, don't be modest. It's sickening." She rested her hands on her hips. "If I started in the middle of the garden, would you still beat me?"

I shook my head. "It's too short. If we had a bigger run, maybe."

"Okay. What if I was only like two metres in front of you? Could you beat me then?"

"Yeah," I said without hesitation.

She raised her eyebrows. "I would never have thought you were this cocky."

I smirked. "What did you want me to say?"

"Nothing, nothing. So how about it?"

I just looked at her.

"Come on. Let's race."

Mum, Michael, and Jay were buried by their coats and sitting on the patio furniture. They had amused looks on their faces and took it in turns to shake their heads at us.

I put my hand on the fence, and Gemma took two huge strides forward.

"That's more than two metres," I called to her.

"What? You scared?"

"Bring it."

Jay gave us a countdown, and I launched myself as fast as I could, head down, arms and legs powering. Gemma was laughing when I passed her and slid to a halt.

"Again," she forced out when she reached me.

"You sure?"

"Positive."

We raced twice more, but Gemma couldn't hope to reach the speed she had the first time. I would have been chuckling when I beat her again had I not been struggling for air.

She reached the fence and leant back on it, gulping mammoth breaths. "All right, all right, all right. You win." She shut her eyes. "Man alive."

"All right?"

"I feel like I'm eating my own heart."

Before I could respond, there was a crack, and her eyes shot open. A hand appeared above the fence. I jumped back, slipping and landing hard in the mud.

The Infected must have thrown itself into the fence panel because the thing collapsed, splinters of wood snapping every which way. Gemma yelped and dashed back a few steps as Mum, Michael, and Jay leapt into action. The Infected snarled as it hobbled towards them, bone sticking out of its raw elbow.

I shook my head as I pulled myself to standing, every nerve jittery and live. As I lurched for my golf club, another Infected pushed its way through the commotion, skin shades of grey and green. Mum whacked it, but it spun the other way and locked its eyes onto Gemma.

She was looking from the Infected, to me, her baseball bat, and the others. I could almost see her brain working as the Infected drew ever closer.

"Gem! Run!" The voice was Callie's, and Gemma came crashing back down to earth.

As Gemma threw herself in my direction, the Infected grabbed hold of her ponytail and yanked her back. She screamed as she tumbled to the ground. I didn't think as I surged towards them, flinging my golf club round with an immense strength I didn't know I had. The Infected dropped to the ground, writhing, but it let go of Gemma, who scurried away on her hands and knees in the mud.

I brought the club down until I broke through the skull, chest heaving. As I staggered back a step, my vision blurred, and someone caught me before I fell.

"We are never playing that stupid game again. What the hell were you thinking? We can't make ourselves vulnerable like that." Jay propped me back up. "Are you okay though?"

I nodded, looking for Gemma. "Gem?"

She was leaning against the house, repeating a few choice swear words over and over, eyes wide. Her combat trousers were covered in mud, but she didn't seem to notice as she brought her knees up to her chest and hugged them.

I made my way towards her and bent down to her level, fixing my eyes to hers like she'd done for me. "Gem?" I felt I had to whisper. "Are you okay?" I took her mucky hand, and she seemed to see me all at once, clutching it tight.

I pulled her up to standing on her shaking legs, and she flung herself into my arms, burying her face in my neck. She shuddered, and I felt tears on my skin, so I held her tight, stroking her thick hair.

"You're safe," I told her. "It's all okay. We're safe."

I rocked her from side to side until she stopped shaking with the force of her tears. When she pulled away, I pretended I didn't see the marks they'd left on her face or the fear they'd left in her eyes. I tried to hide the way that terrified me.

"Thank you." Her words were soft and quiet. "For saving my life."

I smiled. "I was just repaying the favour."

She shook her head and hugged me close again, taking a deep breath. "Thank you."

"Come on." I gave her a quick squeeze. "What are friends for?"

SEVENTEEN

We assured Gemma we could fix the fence without her and convinced her to go and have a bath.

"I don't know what's attracting them here," Jay said as he picked up a piece of wood. "It could be the noise or the smell or something. The bloggers are assuming noise."

I wiped my arm over my sweaty forehead. "I don't think it's the smell. They've still got human bodies. Our sense of smell isn't that good. I reckon they're right. It has to be noise."

Callie was standing at her window the next time I looked up. She was huddled in a blanket and gazing right at me. I waved, and she gave a tiny smile and waved back. I didn't much like the expression on her face. There was a sadness about her mouth as it pulled up to respond and a tiredness in her eyes I had never seen before.

I took a step closer to take a better look. It might have been the angle or the window or the sun going down, but she looked paler than usual. Her hair was all static and askew, but she didn't seem to notice. If she had noticed, she didn't care, and there was something that unsettled me about that. I wanted a second opinion but didn't want to upset Jay, so I carried on as before, waiting for my turn in the bath.

I had never been more thankful for lukewarm running water in all my life. What was I going to do now the warm water was at an end? I tried not to think about it as I stepped into the puddle of water. I hadn't dared use any more. No one wanted to be the one to finish it.

I couldn't relax as the water turned brown with mud, and my mind filled up with panic about Callie. She couldn't be infected. Couldn't be. What would I do? What could I do? There was nothing we could do. Nothing we could even try. We'd have to watch her—no. I couldn't even think it. It was too horrible. This couldn't be happening. The world could be ending, and the Infected could be crawling all over the place, and we could be forced onto the street without shelter and fight off an army of them. I didn't care. Anything but that. At least I could fight everything else that was happening. There was a plan. I had a purpose.

But not if she was infected.

And there would be no one to blame but myself.

She wasn't infected. No. She couldn't be infected. She wasn't. I said it over and over again to try and convince myself, but nothing was working. I agonised over the symptoms, wondering if there was any way to know the difference between morning sickness and vomiting due to Juvenile Virus.

Vomiting, yes. Fatigue, yes. Paling of the skin, yes. Shivering, maybe. I called her image from the window to mind. She'd been under a blanket. Was that because she was cold? Or did she have a fever? High fever, maybe.

It wasn't looking good.

I needed to know. Or did I? I wanted the misery of not knowing to stop, but only if she was okay. I would much rather be tortured with not knowing than have my worst fear realised. Wouldn't I?

Each step was heavy as I made my way down the stairs, trying to hold my tears in, not wanting to make everyone else uncomfortable. I didn't want them to try and make me feel better. I wanted to feel this way. I needed to be punished for what I'd done. I didn't want them to tell me everything was going to be okay because there was an enormous chance nothing was ever going to be okay ever again. I'd single-handedly ruined my entire life and hers. There was no redemption for that.

Gemma wiped her eyes as I entered the living room. She was wearing one of Jay's beanies, but something didn't look right about it.

We didn't say a word as the others appeared one by one.

Jay's eyebrows came together as he looked at Gemma. "Why are you wearing my hat?"

"My head's cold."

"What? You've got more hair than all of us put together. How can your head be cold?"

"Well, I don't any more." She pressed her lips together as the room stared at her.

That was what looked wrong. There was no hair sticking out the bottom of the beanie.

"Gem?" Jay's eyes were wide. "What have you done?"

"I've made sure that *never* happens again."

"Well, show us then." He sat beside her, reaching for the hat.

She pulled it down further. "Why? It's not a fashion choice, it's good sense."

Mum tucked some of her hair behind her ear. "Are you suggesting we all do that?"

Gemma shrugged. "I think it makes sense. I'm not having anything hold me back. I'm gonna survive this."

Mum nodded, and I could see her considering it.

"So what?" Jay sat back on the sofa. "You're going to wear my hat forever?"

"No. I told you. My head's cold."

"Yeah." He rolled his eyes.

"You should cut your hair too," she said.

"Excuse me?"

"Yours is longer than mine now."

"I am not cutting my hair."

Michael cleared his throat. "I think you should, Jay."

"What?" He jumped up. "What is this?"

"The ZA." Gemma pulled the hat off, and there was silence. Her hair was now the same length mine was. It was fluffy in places and tufty like it had no idea what'd happened. Some places looked choppy or wonky, and other parts were shorter than the rest. If I walked by her in the street, I wasn't sure I'd be able to recognise her.

"I'm not doing that to my hair." Jay ran his hand through his golden skater mop.

"Gem?" Mum stood up. "I'll even it out for you if you want. You can do mine."

Gemma smiled and a weight lifted inside me I didn't even know was there. "Okay."

Michael and I watched as Mum cut Jay's hair. It was still longer than mine and Michael's and Gemma's but less grabable, and he was happier with the result than I'd expected. Gemma cut Mum's to her chin. I sat on my hands the entire time, seeming to be the only one concerned as the two of them laughed the whole way through it. By the time Mum evened out Gemma's into something less chaotic, there was an air of calm across the house. Perhaps we were creating a new kind of normal.

That was, until there was a noise from upstairs.

"Zane?" It was Lisa. "Pick up your phone."

We all stiffened and looked to one another. Jay had given Lisa and Callie strict instructions to only use the phones in an emergency. Their battery life was limited and useless.

My hand was shaking as I switched my phone on and waited for the call. Though I knew it was coming, it still made my heart leap.

"I don't know what to do." For some reason, she was whispering.

"About what?" I had to swallow past the lump in my throat. "Callie."

"Why? What's happening? Why are you whispering?"

"She's asleep. She…she's got a fever. I don't know what to do."

"It might not be, you know. She could just be sick."

The faces around me dropped, and they pressed their lips together.

"I don't know. She seems really sick." She sniffed, and her breath caught in her throat. "If it's not…the virus, then it's something really bad, and I can't do anything about it. Nothing's helping at all."

"How do we…?" I had to take a moment. "How do we know if it's the virus?"

"I don't know. I think if the fever doesn't get any better or if she keeps throwing up or, or…"

I lost her in a mouthful of tears, and I couldn't blink my own away any more. The realisation was dribbling into me so slowly I thought my body would stop working. I wanted it to stop working. I didn't want to process this.

Lisa regained control of herself before I could make my mouth move. "What do we do?"

I shook my head.

"I don't know what to do. What am I supposed to do? Zane? Zane? Pass Michael over."

I held the phone out to Michael without a word and stared at the wall. If I remained in this state of shock, I wouldn't have to think about what was happening. What was going to happen next. Maybe I could live like this forever in the bliss of not understanding.

Gemma sat beside me and took my hand without looking at me. She squeezed hard, but I couldn't find it within myself to squeeze back.

Jay was pacing up and down, shaking his head. He was muttering under his breath to himself. Tears dripped off his nose and onto the carpet.

Michael shrunk smaller and smaller as he listened to Lisa. "I don't know," was all he could say when it was his turn. "I just don't know. What is there to do? What can we do?"

Gemma looked at me as she spoke. "Nothing."

EIGHTEEN

I didn't speak another word all evening. I tried not to function at all as Jay screamed, and Gemma held back her tears. Mum sat hugging me, whispering that everything was going to be okay.

Gemma watched me for most of the night from her place on the other sofa. She didn't try and start a conversation, but she wouldn't take her eyes off me. I didn't sleep all night. Every time I shut my eyes, I would see Callie's face at the window. I let the tears drip off my nose in silence as I stared up at the ceiling and waited for the world to end for real.

"Zane?" Gemma hissed a few hours before the sun came up. "How you doing?"

I didn't bother to move.

"You're scaring me. Please, Zane. Say something." She propped herself up on one hand. "You can't shut down like this. Not now."

"Why?" My voice felt croaky.

"Because we can't have you non-responsive like this. What if more of them came at once? You'd just sit there?"

Again, I didn't answer.

"Zane, you can't just sit here and wait for life to happen around you?"

"Why?"

"Because that's not being realistic. If you haven't noticed, we've kinda got a huge situation happening around here."

I faced her. "Bigger than what I've done to Callie?"

"Is that what this is all about? You're blaming yourself? Don't be so stupid."

"Who else's fault is it if it's not mine?"

"Any one of us could've infected her. Not just you. You're

not the only one she got close to. If anything, you should blame me for this."

"You know that's not what I mean."

There was quiet again for a moment.

"Please talk to me," she said. "I'm not going to tell you everything's all right, or it might not be the virus. In fact, I'm telling you everything is not going to be all right, and it probably is the virus. You feel better now?"

"How could that make me feel better?"

"I'm just trying to make you feel *something*. We need you back in the game, Carlisle."

"Maybe I don't want to play any more."

"You think we all want to be playing? I didn't sign up for this. My entire family is dead."

I rubbed my eyes and sat up. "You don't know that."

"And you know they're alive?" She sat up too. "They had no idea what was going on. We're just about managing here with loads of food and water and weapons. What do they have?"

"Gem."

"What? You wanna tell me it's gonna be okay?"

"No."

"Good. Because we both know that's not true." She ran her hand through her short hair. "You want to talk about it yet?"

"No."

"So you're gonna let yourself die next time there's an Infected?"

"No."

"I don't believe you."

"It's not for you to believe."

"Really? I think for the safety of the group we all need to believe it. Convince me." She crossed her arms.

"Convince you of what?"

"That you're still feeling something."

The storm was growing wilder inside my chest, and it was getting more difficult to ignore my heart. I wanted to turn to sludge and seep down the drain. I wanted to sleep for a thousand years, wake up the only man alive, and wander the earth alone forever. I wanted something drastic to happen so I didn't have to explain why my life was over. I wanted everyone to see it for themselves.

"I…" There were tears caught in my throat that could not fall. "I'm not feeling nothing. I'm feeling everything. I want to never feel again. And if I do, I want to feel nothing but misery for the rest of my life."

"Good. Me too."

"Really?"

"Really." She shut her eyes. "Because how can the virus be killing Callie Ashford, my best friend in the whole world? If I'm honest with myself, my only true friend. And certainly my only friend in this world. How can I be healthy and she be dying? She's the good one. The perfect one. She's got so much promise. What have I got?" Tears were falling onto her lap, but she didn't seem to notice. "How? I just don't understand how this is happening. I get that it's the freaking Zombie Armageddon. I get that we have to kill the Infected. I get that if I get bitten I'll die. I get that. I don't have a problem with that. If anything, it's fairly easy to process. But this?"

I chewed on my lip. "I know."

She sniffed. "Oh really?"

"Yeah. I know it sounds stupid, but I don't want life to carry on. Life should stop. Everything should stop. The universe should be taking notice."

"Damn right." The tears were flowing faster now. "Why isn't it stopping and taking notice? Why hasn't the earth stopped turning?"

"I don't know."

"How can everything carry on, Zane?" She wiped her eyes. "I know it will. I know the virus will kill her, and everything will carry on as normal but—what are we going to do?"

My own tears started falling. I couldn't stop them any longer. "Do we just...pretend?"

She gave a dark chuckle. "Like we could ever pretend this wasn't happening."

"Then what?"

"I don't know." She blew out a puff of air. "I never considered I'd have to think about a world without her in it. Now I'm stuck in this house with her family. Don't get me wrong, I love them all, but they're not the reason I'm here. They're not the reason I stayed."

"You don't think it's the same for me? You think I stayed here for anyone else? I brought Mum here because I couldn't leave Callie, and now I've ruined everything."

"You've got to stop blaming yourself."

I pulled on my hair. "Why should I? It's my fault."

"Everyone's thinking it's their fault, but it isn't anybody's."

"How? I'm the one who..."

She came to sit next to me, but we didn't touch. "Everything that's happened couldn't be avoided."

"But—"

"No. Don't argue. She was pregnant before this mess. You just didn't know about it. I haven't heard about anything else. I blame her a little bit because maybe things would've turned out differently if she'd told you before all this."

"It's still my fault."

"If you have to believe that, please just take half the blame."

"I want all the blame. I want... I don't know what I want."

"I know. But we're going to have to carry on. We'll have her family to look after. And I'll have someone even more important to look after."

My eyebrows came together.

"You."

I shook my head.

"Argue all you want, but that girl's universe revolves around you, and if something happened to you, I would feel guilty about it for the rest of my life. I'm going to be watching you like a hawk, Carlisle. I'm now considering myself your keeper. I owe it to Callie."

"Then I'll repay the favour." As I spoke, something warm and real took hold of my heart and let me carry on for a little while at least. "As far as I see it, you're her favourite person in the world. And if anything were to happen to you, I couldn't live with myself. So I guess we're even."

She offered her hand to me. "Deal."

I took her hand and shook it.

"I think I see what she's been banging on about for all this time. You really are a wonderful person."

I pushed her arm. "And I see how annoying you can be."

She laughed a little freer than before. "Oh please, you don't know the half of it."

The silence swallowed us up again. The wind whistled outside. I twisted my string bracelet around my wrist. Callie had made it for me a few months ago. Gemma pushed her wrist up against mine to show me hers. I managed a smile.

"It's gonna happen, Zane." She took my hand and looked into my eyes. "But I'm gonna be right here when it does."

I nodded and looked down to my wrist again. "You were wrong before. When you said you didn't have any other true friends. You've got me."

"That's true. I do. And you've got me. And if I can help it, I'm not going anywhere."

NINETEEN

Gemma managed to fall back to sleep, but I fiddled with my bracelet until the sun came up. What she'd said was ringing in my ears. I knew I would have to keep going. For the Ashfords, for Mum, for her. Of course I would. I just couldn't imagine doing any of it. I couldn't imagine a world without Callie Ashford by my side.

When there was a soft groaning coming from the front of the house, I tiptoed over, peeking through a gap in the curtain. My breath caught in my throat, and I stumbled back, forgetting how close the sofa was and falling onto Gemma.

She screamed and whacked me. "What the *hell* are you doing?"

I moaned and rubbed my now throbbing head.

"You scared the freaking life out of me! What do you thi—"

I clapped my hand over her mouth to quiet her. "Shut up!"

Her chest was heaving up and down as she regained control of herself. She pulled my hand away and whispered this time. "What's going on?"

"There are a group of Infected out there."

"A group?" She leapt up and poked her face through the curtains for a second. "Where did they come from? Do we get them?"

"I dunno."

Jay appeared in the doorway. "There are two Infected in the garden."

"There are at least four out there." Gemma pointed to the front of the house.

I rubbed the back of my neck. "Do we bother to kill them, or would that be a risk?"

"There are only five of us," Jay said. "I wouldn't be happy going against four. The two in the back garden maybe, but not out the front."

Gemma shook her head. "Are we fighting a losing battle with this? They're always gonna keep coming."

"What do you suggest we do?" Jay threw his arms out wide. "Just let them bang on the windows until they get in?"

"Would it be better to keep killing them until we can't? Would that buy us more time here?" I asked.

"We need to stay here." Gemma crossed her arms. "For as long as we possibly can. For the moment at least."

None of us spoke aloud the reason we couldn't pack up and leave.

"So what?" Jay scratched his shorter hair. "Do we go outside and kill them or do we not?"

"I guess we should vote," Gemma said.

Jay raised his eyebrows.

"What? We're a democracy aren't we? Let's have a vote."

With Mum and Michael bustled into the living room, Jay explained our situation.

"I don't much like the sound of either." Michael pulled on his ear.

"So who votes for killing the ones in the garden?" Jay asked.

We all raised our hands.

"What about the ones out the front?"

No one moved.

Gemma cleared her throat. "Maybe we should vote on that once we've sorted the two in the garden?"

They all nodded and jumped up.

"Jay," Michael said. "You're with me."

"Zane?" Mum nodded to me.

Gemma picked up her baseball bat. "I guess I go where I'm needed. Everyone ready?"

We threw open the back door and shot to an Infected. The one to the left of the garden, facing Mum and I, was huge and blue-looking. He was double the width of me and almost as tall. The smell didn't bother me so much now. Perhaps that was because I expected it and braced myself, trying to breathe through my mouth.

I swallowed and squeezed my golf club before throwing all my weight at the Infected. It was easier and easier to take them down. Not just because each day brought them closer to total decay, but because it was hard to feel bad about it once you'd seen them attack. These weren't people any more. If the person who'd once lived in that body could see the damage they were causing, they would forgive me for stopping them. I knew I would. What was worse than becoming an Infected? Killing innocent after innocent.

When the Infected stopped twitching and moaning, I looked to the others, who were standing over the other body.

Gemma's baseball bat wasn't even dirty. "I gotta say, I'm glad that seemed easy. I was getting a little worried about our chances in the wild."

"What about the ones out front?" Jay looked to each of us.

"What if there are more down the street and our presence causes commotion?" Michael asked. "It seems as though they'll come this way once they figure out we're in here, but we don't want to speed them up."

"How long will it take them to get into the house?" Mum shuffled her feet from side to side. "They have to get through the boards and the glass, and there aren't enough of them to cause a threat."

"Except attract other ones." Gemma bit her lip. "The only

way they can get in is by sheer force. The more there are and the louder they start screaming, the more will join. I think you're right. They're not causing a huge threat at the moment. Only a group large enough will actually get in. But do we go and kill those four to silence the noise? At least then more won't show up looking for the party."

"Unless we attract them by going out there," I said, rubbing the back of my neck. "I really don't know what would be best."

Gemma shrugged. "Who feels up to going out there?" Her own hand was raised.

Jay raised his hand too. "I think we should go. If we come back inside and four more start coming over here, we'll know not to do it again, but this might save us some time. If there are none out there, that means another one has to figure out where we are."

Michael and Mum were looking at each other, neither wanting to be the one to sway the decision in case something went wrong. So I saved them both the trouble and raised my hand, stomach leaping into my mouth.

"I think we can do it. If it turns out we can't, we'll just run back inside."

"And hope they don't follow us." Michael shook his head. "It's madness."

"The madness has spoken." Jay lifted his hedge clippers high. "Let's go."

We followed him through the kitchen and into the dining room where he tapped on the window.

"What're you doing?" Michael whispered.

"Trying to get them away from the door. Someone needs to do the same in the living room."

Gemma and I went to the living room and started beating on the glass with the tips of our nails.

"Is this totally insane?" Gemma asked as two Infected stumbled towards us.

"Yeah. I think maybe it is."

There was a tremble working its way along my body as we crept into the hall with the others.

"Same as before?" Jay asked.

I squeezed Mum in a quick hug, having to drag myself away from her before I lost the strength to let go. She kissed me on the cheek before we nodded, holding our weapons ready. My heart felt like it was developing a stutter. My skin was clammy with being both roasting and freezing all at once.

"No big deal. Just like before." I wasn't sure whether Jay was trying to make us feel better or trying to convince himself. "We'll go left. Jen and Zane, you go right."

I took a wave of air into my lungs and held it as Jay clicked the door open. There was no time for fear. There was no time to overthink it. We bundled outside.

Mum and I jogged to the right, coming face to face with a woman with patches of hair ripped out and blood dripping off the ends. Before I could raise my club, Mum had smacked her in the face with her own and driven it into her eye.

In lesser situations, I would have stopped to vomit, but not now.

I skirted round the Infected on the floor and came across a boy about my own age, skin ripped and blackened. His milky eyes met mine, and something told me I knew him. I slammed my golf club into his head before that could hold me back. Mum again went for the eye.

We turned around in time to see Jay checking the Infected were staying down by plunging the hedge clippers through their skulls. Mum took my hand, and we crept inside. My heart was flinging itself round in my chest. I sat on the floor as soon as Michael had locked the door behind us, limbs shaking.

"You all right?" Gemma sat next to me.

I nodded, shutting my eyes, trying to make the Infected go away. "I didn't realise how scared I was."

"Well, I'll say that was mission accomplished. We really are getting better at this." Jay's satisfied smile filled the room.

Mum gave a short laugh, covering her mouth with her hand. Something tickled in my chest, and I couldn't help but chuckle too. Gemma pushed her leg against mine and pressed her lips together, catching my eye.

"Madness." Michael was shaking his head as he entered the living room. "Utter madness."

TWENTY

"Lisa?" I tapped on the door. "If I ring, will you pick up?"

The phone jumped in my hand, and I sat myself at the top of the stairs to answer it, everyone else still in the living room trying to process the six Infected we'd taken down today.

"What's the matter?"

"How's Callie? Is she any better?"

It took Lisa too many seconds to answer. "No. No better."

"Any worse?"

She cleared her throat and took a breath. "I think so. How long do we carry on like this? At what point do we decide it's the virus? All she wants to do is be out of this room. And I can't say I want to stay in here either, but is that giving up?"

I rubbed my hand across my face. My heart felt too big and heavy. "I don't know. What else could it be?"

"I don't know. There's nothing I can do. Nothing's making her feel any better. She's started trembling nonstop apart from when she's asleep. Her fever's as bad as it was yesterday, and she's still being sick quite often. She won't seem to eat much either. I don't know what to do."

My chest felt tight. "Do you want to speak to Michael?"

"Nothing anyone can say will make this any easier. I know none of you could do anything more than I'm doing. But how's everything going down there?"

"We're fine. Don't worry about us."

"I'd like something else to worry about."

"I don't think there's anything else to worry about. We cleared the outside of the house of Infected. We're as safe as we can be."

"How's your phone's battery?"

"Not great. It won't be long until we have to use someone else's, but I'm not sure how long we can keep this up."

"I'm not sure how long we'll have to." She gave a strangled squeak.

There was a mumbling in the background and my heart leapt.

"Oh, Callie. I thought you were asleep. It's Zane. No, everything's fine…all right. Callie wants to speak to you."

"Okay." I had to force the word out through my dry throat. "Zane?"

"Callie." I breathed it out all at once. The tears had been locked away in my heart, but now they were brimming in my eyes. Her voice was so beautiful. Everything about her was. "I miss you so much. And I love you. I love you so much."

"I love you too." There was no rise or fall in her voice. I had to clutch the phone tight to stop from sobbing. "I'm sorry."

"Sorry?" I rubbed my hand over the back of my neck. "Why are you sorry? What do you have to be sorry about?"

"Everything."

"Don't be silly."

"It's my own fault I'm in this mess. I'm sorry. I'm so sorry about all of this. I didn't want this to happen. I don't…I don't want to die."

Tears were blinding me, and I tried to hide them from my voice as best I could. "You won't. You won't die. I won't let you."

"Zane, please. I've never been so sick in my entire life. I feel awful. I can hardly stand. I can barely sit up. I just wake up to be sick and fall back to sleep again until I wake up sweating and on fire and shove my duvet off, and then I start to freeze even though my skin is burning and sweat is dripping off me. I…" Her voice caught in her throat. "I want it to stop."

"What are you saying?"

"I know it's gonna get worse, but I don't think I can stand it. How many days will this go on for? How many do I have left? And how many do I have left that I can be conscious enough to talk to you?" She was sucking in huge, rasping breaths, but I couldn't think of anything to say to calm her down. "I want to see you."

"No." I shook my head. "No, you can't."

"Why? In case it's not the virus? I think we can safely assume I'm dying, and there are days left. Maximum."

"Please, Callie." I could taste the sorrow on my tongue, my heart making it hard to breathe. "Please don't talk like this."

"How do you want me to talk? Do you want me to pretend this isn't happening? I have to think of some crazy way to get over this. All I have so far is that at least I won't get eaten."

Lisa told Callie to stop it, but she either didn't hear or ignored her.

"I need to see you, Zane. I miss you so much. There's nothing in this world that can make this any better. But maybe being next to you will."

"Of course I want to see you too, but I can't just say yes and come in."

"Why not?"

I wanted to smash through the wall and bundle her up into my arms and race down the road and never return to this house ever again, but I couldn't think like that. There was no more 'I' and 'me' any more. It was all 'we' and 'us'. We were a team. That was the only way we could survive this.

I wiped the tears off my face. "For one, Jay would kill me dead. And second, we apparently vote on this sort of thing now, so I can't make this decision."

"What about me? This is my life. Can't I make the decision?"

I pressed my fingers into my eyes. "I think the others would have something to say about this."

"This is ridiculous. I should decide. This is my life—or lack of one. I should get to decide when I want to leave this damn room."

"Callie, I love you. I'm sorry."

Her voice was shrill and loud, and I had to pull my ear away from the phone. I coughed through my tears and put my head in my spare hand.

When she was quiet, I whispered into the phone. "Can I talk to your mum?"

"What?"

"Please, Cal. I just want to talk to her for a minute."

She didn't even say goodbye to me. My heart crawled out of my mouth and curled up to die.

"Zane?" Lisa's voice sounded again. "I'm so sorry."

"It doesn't matter. I know she's just upset, but what's wrong with her? How long has she been acting this way?"

"Just this morning. I think it's dawning on her that…"

"I know," I said so Lisa didn't finish her sentence. "Do you think it's the virus?"

There was a long pause. The longest of my life. "Yes."

I didn't have anything in my body left to feel. It already felt as though I'd used everything up. I was a big blob of tears and heartbreak.

"Do you think her leaving her room would be a bad idea?" I asked.

"It won't hurt, will it? Nothing can make it any worse than it already is. I need to see Michael and Jay too."

"Do you want me to ask them if it's all right? We've started voting on stuff like this."

"All right."

"I'm going to hang up now." I had to swallow to keep the next wave of tears back. "I'll call you, or I guess we'll just knock on the door."

"All right. I guess we'll just wait here."

I dropped my phone to the ground and stared down the stairs. Before my brain could try and kill me with thoughts of grief and despair, I counted my breaths on the way in and on the way out. It took a few minutes, but I managed to regain control over my own body.

Dragging myself down the stairs, I kept my composure, making sure all the tears had been wiped off my cheeks. My face must have looked awful, because as soon as I entered the doorframe, they all stopped talking.

"Callie has a request," I said before anyone could ask me a question I couldn't answer. "And I told her we vote on stuff now." I pulled in a huge breath through my nose. "She wants to leave her bedroom."

"She what?" Jay stood up. "Is she crazy?"

"She's convinced she's got the virus. She doesn't want to be trapped in there without seeing the rest of us. She's convinced she's going to die."

"But is she any worse?" Gemma asked.

I couldn't bring myself to go into detail, so I only nodded.

"What does Lisa have to say about this?" Michael spun his wedding ring around his finger. "She can't agree with her?"

I had to clear my throat. "Lisa also believes it's the virus."

A collective gasp filled the room. Jay fell back onto the sofa.

"She said it can't make it any worse than it already is. She wants to see you both." I looked at Michael and Jay.

"So you're asking us to vote on whether Callie can come out of her bedroom?" Mum pushed some hair off her face.

"No." Gemma's voice was dead. "He's asking us to vote on whether we accept the fact she's dying."

There was silence, but nobody corrected her.

Gemma shook her head. "When did it come to this? When did it get this hard?" She stood up, filling her lungs with air and meeting my eye. "I vote we let her out." A single tear dripped onto her cheek. The ache inside me pulled at my shredded heart.

Mum stood and took Gemma's hand. "Me too."

Jay put his hands in his hair. "How do we know for sure?"

"We don't," I said. "But she's getting worse every day. She's miserable. She told me she wanted it to stop."

Michael raised his hand. "We let her out."

"Dad! You can't be serious?"

"Jay." Michael took Jay in his arms. "There's nothing we can do."

Everyone but Jay was looking at me.

"So we let her out?" I asked, my hands shaking.

"Zane?" Mum took a step towards me. "What do you want?"

"It doesn't matter." I squeezed my eyes shut for a moment. "We voted to let her out. Not to mention Lisa and Callie already voted."

"Zane?" Gemma was holding tight to her bracelet.

I looked around for an answer, but one wasn't going to drop down from the sky. I didn't want this to be happening. I wanted this to stop. I wanted to wake up and have this all be a dream. I wanted the virus to disappear and Callie to be happy and healthy again. I wanted Callie to be okay. I wanted Callie.

I squeezed my hands into fists until my nails bit into flesh. "I vote we let her out."

TWENTY-ONE

When Lisa creaked open the door, what hit me most was the hot, stuffy smell of illness. But all that fell away when my eyes drank in Callie. Her face had no colour. Her hair looked damp with sweat or grease. It was pushed back with a headband and hung limp down her back. There were dark marks under her eyes. They bugged when they saw me. At least they were still the bright sea-green of my dreams.

"Zane."

I held her close to me, unable to stop the tears falling into her hair. She felt smaller somehow. All at once everyone was trying to hug Callie and speak to her and look at her. The world fizzled and blurred as everything started to feel real.

Michael carried her downstairs and we watched her sleep on the sofa, no one talking. Lisa was curled up in Michael's arms and drifting in and out of sleep herself.

"It's the virus." Jay was looking at the candle as it dripped. "Isn't it?"

"Yeah," Gemma breathed. "I think it is."

Only a handful of words were passed round for the rest of the day, and before I knew it, I was lying next to Callie, stroking through her hair as everyone dragged themselves to bed.

I awoke with a jump many hours later when Callie said my name.

"What? What?" My heart was throwing itself against my chest, body jolting in fear.

"Shush." Callie's eyes flicked to Gemma, who was snoring on the other sofa.

It took me a few moments to realise I was in the living

room, and Callie was next to me. "What? What are you still doing here?"

"I didn't want to go back upstairs." She put her hand through my hair. I shut my eyes at her touch, trying to calm my heart again.

I had dreamt of sleeping next to Callie for months on end but never like this. If I could take it back, I would never wish for something so stupid again. All I wanted now was for her to be better. She was so hot in my arms I was beginning to sweat. But I wasn't about to let her go.

"I'm sorry about before," she whispered. "I'm sorry I shouted at you."

"It doesn't matter."

"And I'm sorry all this is happening."

"It isn't your fault."

Her eyes locked with mine. "I'm still sorry." Her breath was shuddery and she squeezed me tighter. "I love you, Zane. I don't want to leave you."

"I know." Tears were brewing in my heart but were silent for now.

"But it'll be okay."

I shook my head.

"It will. It'll be okay. You're strong. You can get through this. You can get through anything anybody throws at you."

"Not without you."

"Yes, you can." Somehow, she smiled. "You have to. I'm telling you so." She ran her hand through my hair again. "You can get through this and you will. It'll be okay. They need you. You need to keep them safe."

"I can try but..."

"No. Promise me." Her voice was firm. "Promise me you'll do whatever you can to keep them safe. All of them."

I nodded. "I promise."

With her head pressed against my chest, I fell asleep watching her breathe in and out, in and out, in and out.

The next day, I watched Callie laughing with Gemma and listening to Jay. She cuddled with Michael and let Mum plait her hair. She was never sitting up unless there was something to lean on. She couldn't stay awake for more than an hour or so. Her face was sallow and sunken, like she was wasting away in front of my eyes. But there was nothing I could do about it. I watched, numb, as the love of my life grew weaker by the hour and slipped away from me.

Infected appeared out the front and back every couple of hours, and when they were noticed, they were killed. I couldn't wrench my eyes from Callie to help them.

"Zane?" Callie blinked open her eyes.

"Shush," I told her, kissing her forehead. "Go back to sleep. Everything's okay."

She tried to prop herself up on her elbows, but her arms were shaking too much to hold her steady. "Can you help me?" She sighed.

I pulled her up, and she leant her head back on the sofa, shutting her eyes for a moment before looking right at me, tears in her eyes and a tiny smile on her face. She took a big breath before she spoke.

"I always imagined that when I went to university, you would take the train or your mum's car and come and visit me every weekend. I'd tell you not to but you would anyway. You'd surprise me at my door with flowers or chocolates and a huge smile on your face. I'd rush to meet you and cry my eyes out because I'd miss you so much."

I stroked her hand.

"But it would be okay because you'd tell me so. You'd tell me that I had to follow my dreams, and you'd always be at home waiting for me to call. I imagined you meeting all my uni friends and becoming the best of friends with them too, and they'd be the kinds of people you never lose contact with as long as you live. They'd be our friends for life, and when we got a little older, and they visited us a few times a year, they'd joke about how you used to come all the way just to see me and how in love we were.

"You'd win your place in the Olympics and train your heart out all day and all night. I'd come out of uni wondering what to do with my life, and you'd be there to support me while I figured it out. We'd buy a flat or a tiny house together and talk our way through the nights and not care because at last we'd be together, just the two of us, and our life would be starting.

"After a while, people would stop referring to one of us without the other. We'd get joint cards and presents at Christmas because we'd be inseparable. People would comment on how couples getting together and staying together is so rare at such a young age, and we'd smile and give each other a look because we were never in any doubt.

"I'd be dreaming about engagement rings pretty soon after that. You'd surprise me, again with flowers and chocolates and a huge smile on your face. I'd cry, and you'd be so nervous even though not a single cell in your body would be in any doubt of my answer.

"We'd get married in the spring. I'd have flowers in my hair. My dress would be long but understated. As I walked down the aisle, people would smile and stare. But I wouldn't see any of them because you'd be right there waiting for me, lighting up my whole life.

"We'd maybe buy a bigger house somewhere quieter and start a family. One or maybe two, a boy and a girl, and you'd be the most fantastic dad there ever was. They'd squeal as you tossed them up in the air. We'd be so happy and people would be so jealous of us because our life would be like a postcard."

She wiped a tear off my face I hadn't realised was there.

"Our kids would be beautiful and clever and kind and make us so proud. We'd go to all their school plays and jump up and clap at the end, and I'd cry and embarrass them. Their friends would always want to come to our house because we were the fun parents who let them eat sweets and stay up late at sleepovers.

"When they moved out, you'd miss them more than you missed me when I was at uni. But then we'd spend our lives travelling, and people would always stop and ask if you were Zane Carlisle, fastest man alive. You'd always stop to talk to people and take pictures with them. And I'd just stand there so proud of you that words wouldn't be enough.

"And when our daughter walked down the aisle, you would hold her hand tight and not want to let her go. But you'd let her go start her own story with her new family. And you'd stand by our son too as he did the same. And when they started having children of their own, we'd be the best grandparents there ever were, and they'd always want to come to us for Christmas and for the school holidays.

"We would be the happiest couple there had ever been. Our children and grandchildren would aspire to be like us and make sure they were happy and healthy and loved and... Everything was going to be so perfect. Everything was going to be so good." She sniffed. "I couldn't wait for my life with you to start. I didn't want to break the image." She looked down at our entwined hands. "That's why I was scared to tell you. I didn't want to shatter my plans. I wanted everything to happen in the right order and now—now I guess it can't happen in any order, can it?"

I was stunned. Numb. There was nothing I could say. I wanted every tiny little thing she'd said, but we just sat there, looking at each other, knowing we couldn't have even one piece of it.

TWENTY-TWO

The next day, Callie hardly spoke a word. She looked around at all of us as we tried to cheer her up by telling her a joke or playing a board game. She couldn't stop shivering whether she was hot or cold, and she couldn't prop herself up any more. She complained of a dry mouth and headache but sweated off all the water we gave her. Then she fell asleep or into unconsciousness. What was the difference?

Michael carried her back upstairs, and we all sat round her bed in a circle, terrified this hour was going to be the one. Or maybe the next hour. Or the one after that.

"Cal?" Jay wiped his eyes and sniffed. "Remember when I bought that new game, just after school had started? I asked you to sit with me because the internet was down, and I couldn't play it with my friends. You told me you were too busy doing your homework, and I shouted at you because it was the start of term, and what could you possibly have to do? I'm sorry I shouted at you. I didn't—I still don't—understand why you felt you needed to do your work the second you got home, but for some reason, it was important to you, and I acted like I didn't care. I'm sorry. But thank you for coming in and sitting with me anyway. I knew you weren't interested in what I was doing, but you stayed, asking questions like you were actually getting into it." He took her hand. "I just need you to know that you're the greatest sister anyone could ever ask for, and I never say it, but I love you."

Tears dripped off my nose and made my entire face itch, but the second I wiped them away, more would appear.

Mum disappeared to make everyone hot drinks on the

stove. In our silence, the Infected sang their melancholy, tuneless drone, but no one seemed to notice or care. The Infected could wait. Callie could not.

The mug of hot chocolate pressed into my hands was a comforting presence, though the idea of taking a sip repulsed me. But the warmth and normality of such a thing kept me grounded, and I held on tight.

"Cal?" Michael moved closer, and Jay let go of her hand so Michael could take it. "I hope you know how very proud of you I am. You're everything I ever dreamt of when I thought of having a daughter.

"I love you so much, so much more than I can ever say. For all the times I lost my temper with you, I'm sorry. For all the times I told you I was too busy or needed to just do something quick. If I could do this all again, I would give you every spare minute." He brought her hand to his lips. "I love you."

Lisa buried herself in Michael's back, and the two of them shed silent tears. Fear was eating my stomach alive. It'd been hours since she'd last woken up. Had I told her I loved her? What was the last thing I'd said?

Another hour passed, or maybe two. The candles were lit, and the undead kept moaning. My hot chocolate went cold.

When darkness fell outside, Gemma stood up and brushed Callie's hair back, staring into her face.

"You know?" She exhaled. "I'm actually not that good at making friends. I know a lot of people at school talk to me and spend time with me and it looks like I do, but they're just acquaintances. I know a lot of people. It doesn't mean I like them. It doesn't mean I want to spend time with them. But then there's you. You're the best friend I could ever ask for. You always listen when I have something to say, and let's be honest, that's most of the time. You're always there to offer advice or just tell me it's okay. You're so sweet and kind and caring, and I could never be all of those things. I'm not your best friend because you love me the most, I'm your best friend because I love you the most. I'm your best friend because I never let anyone else get too close to you. I've always been so damn protective. I wanted to be the only friend in your life worth calling up every night, the only one you thought of when you had a plus-one. But did I deserve it? What sort of a friend have I been to you?

"I was never a good enough friend for you, but I thank you every day that you were the best one to me. I don't care how many years pass, *you* are my best friend, Callie Ashford. Best friends forever. I guess I didn't have to worry after all. No one can replace me any more.

"I love you, you silly, sensitive girl. I wish I could've been better. But…" Gemma sniffed as the tears fell. She had to wipe them away before they hit Callie's face. "I don't know how I'm going to carry on without you. I don't know if I'll even want another friend again. I just want you. I need you, Callie. I love you."

"Gem?" Mum tried to coax her back into her seat, but Gemma continued to sit there, perched by Callie's head, stroking her golden hair over and over again.

I wanted to be there too. Holding her hand. Caressing her hair. Stroking her face. But I was frozen to the spot, watching everything unfurl around me.

Lisa went to lie on the other side of Callie when full darkness had surrounded us for hours.

"Callie Elizabeth Ashford." She gave a small smile. "I was so happy with your name. It suited you and was so pretty, and I knew you were special. You were the most precious thing I'd ever laid eyes on. I never knew I could love something so fast and so completely. I would've done anything for you—I still would. If there was some way I could swap with you, I would in a heartbeat. All I wanted was for you to be happy and live an amazing life.

"Do you know how much I love you? I must've done something right to deserve you, and I wish I knew what that was. It must have been something wonderful. And for someone to be taking you away means you are far too good for us, but we knew that already.

"I don't want you to go. I don't want to live the rest of my life without you. And I love you. I love you. I love you." She kissed her forehead and held her closer.

I couldn't breathe.

When the sun came up again, Callie's breaths were getting slower and slower. Mum put her arm around me.

"Zane? Did you want to say something?"

I shook my head.

"I don't want to push you, but this might be your last chance."

I couldn't see through my tears. "What would I say? That I love her? I've told her a hundred thousand times every day that I love her. That I'll miss her? I won't be the same person I am right now because I won't know how to be. I'm nowhere near done loving her. I didn't know I could feel like this until I met her. I wasn't like this before, but I can't remember what that felt like. I don't want to remember. I don't want this to happen. I don't want her to go."

"I know." Mum stroked my hair. "But you'll regret the things you don't say now."

I took in a colossal breath through my nose, held it for what felt like forever, and let it out, standing to take Callie's hand.

"Cal? I'm sorry." I shook my head. "So sorry. I know this is all my fault. As much as anyone tries to convince me otherwise, I know it is. Without me, you wouldn't be in this mess. I wish I could take it back. But I can't.

"I'll do what you said. I'll look after them, for you. I'll keep them safe. We'll survive this. I can't believe I'm here right now saying these things. I can't believe you're going to leave me. I mean, I was always afraid you would, but not like this. I…everyone's said such lovely things, and I can't even string a sentence together. There's so much I want to say, Callie, and so little time for me to say it. But I guess the only thing I really want you to know is that I love you.

"And I wish, more than anything in this universe, that you could say it back to me. One last time.

"I love you, Callie Elizabeth Ashford. I promise."

TWENTY-THREE

We all gathered close as Callie's breaths became so infrequent I was sure each one was going to be the last one. I couldn't believe she hadn't woken up. I hadn't thought for one minute that I would never see her again. Even though I was looking at her right now, I knew it wasn't enough.

The tears cleared from my vision just enough for me to catch the last stutter of her lungs and utter silence. No one even dared to cry. We stood there, motionless, watching her. Someone grabbed and squeezed my hand.

That was it. It seemed anticlimactic somehow. I wanted lightning to strike or the world to shake or something. Something had to take notice she was gone.

I would never hear her laugh again. Never be surrounded by her fresh smell when she appeared from the shower. Never see those beautiful sea-green eyes again.

But then I did.

She opened them.

Everyone jumped back a step. Callie let out a horrendous screech that reminded me of a vicious dinosaur. Those were not the eyes of Callie Ashford, the girl I loved. They were blurry and dim. The intelligence had gone. So had the beauty. She sat up, chest heaving up and down, saliva drooling from her mouth as she made a hungry, guttural sound.

I knew this wasn't Callie. This was an Infected using her body to bring my worst nightmare to life. But even so, I couldn't move.

A hand tried to pull me back as they each slipped from the room. But I was stuck there. Her eyes devoured me, watching my every twitch.

"Zane!" Gemma hissed. "Run!"

Callie leapt and pinned me to the floor, teeth bared and ready to strike.

Gemma kicked her in the side of the head. "Sorry, Cal."

Callie drew herself up and roared as I scrambled to my feet, but she was there in my face again, faster than any other Infected I'd seen. She was weak and slow no longer. I shoved as hard as I could, but she only stumbled back a step before recovering and pouncing yet again.

I dived out of the way and smacked my head on her bedside cabinet, the world going blurry as I tried to stand.

"Zane, get out of here!" I couldn't pinpoint Gemma's voice, but something went whizzing by my head and smashed as it reached Callie.

I crawled over her bed to try and reach safety on the other side as Gemma threw everything she put her hands on. Callie was slowed but not deterred, and she went for the closer target. Gemma threw her leg out with such force and speed that she toppled over, landing on me.

"Jay, hurry!" She screamed as we pulled ourselves up, both panting for breath and me struggling to find upright. "Zane, get out of here!"

"No!" I growled. The only thing worse than an Infected that looked like Callie, was the image of that Infected feasting on Gemma.

Mum flung open the door and lobbed Jay's Xbox at Callie's head. She dropped hard to the floor.

We scuttled towards the door, where Lisa was waiting with a pile of lamps and ornaments to throw at her daughter's reanimated corpse. I turned my head too fast and my vision warped and snapped. All at once I wanted to vomit.

Gemma held her hands across me as Callie stood and locked eyes with us.

"Please, Cal." I found myself begging. "Please don't do this. We don't want to hurt you."

"Shut up, Zane. Of course we do. That thing isn't Callie any more. It needs to be destroyed. What would she say? She'd tell us to run."

Mum passed objects forward. I was handed a vase.

"Then why aren't we running?"

"There's nowhere to run." Gemma squared her shoulders and chucked her lamp with as much force as she could manage. It caught the side of Callie's head, leaving an ugly red mark on her once stunning face.

I pushed myself forward a few steps to get a decent swing on my vase, and it smashed as it connected with Callie's head. A sharp pain sliced through my finger. There was blood dribbling into Callie's light-golden hair.

She snarled, grabbing for me, and there was nothing left for me to do but punch her square in the face. She didn't even slow down, just went for me again, leaving me with throbbing knuckles and disgust in my heart.

I dived onto the bed out of her way as her eyes moved to the crowd of people in the doorway. Rolling off the bed and onto the floor, I seized her desk chair before whistling to catch her attention. She returned her interest to me once Gemma had smashed a photo frame over her head. I flung a book at her for good measure.

Holding her back, I was squished between the wall and the chair. "Where's Jay?" I barked. Callie's arms were flailing for me as she threw herself into the wheels again and again. Her face was now dripping blood, and a few of her teeth were broken.

"He's here." Gemma had her baseball bat in hand and was creeping this way. Her foot landed on a piece of glass. The crunch was louder than it had any right to be.

Before I could comprehend it, Callie had spun round and leapt on top of Gemma.

"Gem!" I shrieked her name as I hurled the chair around Callie's head. She hit the wall with a thud, and Gemma scurried away, grabbing for the bat.

As Callie stood, I whacked her with the chair again, catching the side of her face. She let out a high-pitched shriek that made me want to cover my ears. One of her eyes was red inside, making her look like something from a horror film. It shook my bones with fear. She cocked her head to the side and went for me again.

The chair connected with less force, and she kept on coming. My arms were trembling with the effort. My shoulders pulled. I hadn't slept for over twenty-four hours. My mind was close to sludge, and I was close to tears.

Gemma's baseball bat made a terrific cracking sound on impact, and Callie fell to the floor, writhing, drooling, and yelling. Jay and Michael burst through the door carrying the rest of the weapons. Jay threw a golf club in my direction. I went to snatch it out of the air but missed. It made a clatter as it hit the ground.

Everything moved as I bent down to pick it up, and I fell to my knees.

There was a thwack and a groan and a thump.

"Zane!" Gemma yelled. "You all right?"

I went to open my mouth and vomited all over Callie's bloodstained carpet. Pushing myself onto my knees, I saw Callie's twitching body, and Jay standing above her with his hedge clippers ready to strike.

"Go on, Jay." Gemma's bat was ready, waiting for more trouble. "It's all right."

Jay lifted them higher before dropping his arm and shaking his head. Tears dripped onto Callie, and he handed the hedge clippers to Michael, retreating onto the landing. Michael looked at the tool in his hands as I managed to find full height again with the help of the windowsill.

"Mick." Gemma put her hand on Michael's arm. "It's okay. Don't do this. Don't remember her like this. Go." She tucked her bat under her arm and held out her hand for the hedge clippers. "I'll do it. Go."

Callie was scrabbling against the wall, trying to work out how to stand. Her jaws were snapping shut like she expected one of us to be stupid enough to go that close.

Michael handed Gemma the weapon and took two slow steps back before disappearing with Lisa. Mum was still in the doorframe, watching over us.

"Zane?" Gemma looked to me as I picked up my golf club. "You wanna leave?"

I climbed over the bed and stood next to her. "No."

"You don't have to stay."

"Neither do you."

Her eyes met mine for the briefest of moments before falling on Callie again.

"You don't have to do this," I said.

"Yes." She sniffed. "Yes, I do."

I held out my hand. "I'll do it." I didn't know where the conclusion had come from, but it felt right. I had to do this. I had to kill the thing that'd murdered my beloved Callie.

"Zane, no. Don't."

"I did this to her."

"You didn't. Don't say that."

"Gemma. Please."

Her eyes flickered back and forth between mine before something made her give in. She handed me the hedge clippers and took a few steps back.

I stood over Callie, taking in anything that could be left of her, but there was nothing. She was gone. Sucking in a huge breath, I held the clippers high.

"I'm sorry, Callie."

Before I could think, before I could stop myself, I thrust them into her head, blood squirting out on impact. My hands were shaking as I dropped the weapon. I went to move back, away, out of this room forever, and my vision twisted again, throwing me into blackness before I reached the ground.

TWENTY-FOUR

My head was thumping and buzzing when I groaned back into consciousness.

"Oh!" Mum cried. "Zane!"

Before I could open my eyes and figure out what was going on, her arms were around me. It was all I could do to squeeze her back and not throw up all over her. As I tried to push myself up, the muscles in my arms gave way, shaking as though it was impossible to lift me.

"Zane, Zane, are you okay?" Mum pulled back and stroked my face. "I was so worried."

I blinked open my eyes and found everyone crowded around the bed in the spare room, Mum sitting next to me with a bloody flannel in her hand. Shuffling up the bed into a sitting position, my head spun and felt heavy.

"I'm okay." I had to force the words through the confusion as everything sharpened again. I could still taste sick in my mouth. "I hit my head. I'm all right." I touched where I'd whacked it on the bedside cabinet. My hair was damp, but my hand came back clean.

"We were going to get you frozen peas." Gemma was leant up against the wall with her arms crossed. "But nothing's frozen any more."

I looked around, cataloguing everyone's faces and expressions. Jay was looking to the ground, Michael and Lisa either side of him, edging closer and closer.

"Everyone's okay though? No one got hurt?" I asked.

Mum put her hand over mine. "Just you."

Jay was shaking his head. "I can't believe…"

Michael put his arm around him. "I know."

"We should've done something. We should've realised."

"It's okay, Jay." Lisa squeezed his other side. "Everyone's okay."

Jay shook them off and thudded down the stairs. I wondered why he didn't go into his room. But then I realised he'd have to walk by Callie's door.

Michael and Lisa looked to each other.

"I'd leave him alone." Gemma's face was pale and her mouth and eyes seemed droopy. "At least for a little while. I wouldn't want to be around people. Not at first."

Their faces seemed tight as they tried to communicate something without opening their mouths.

"Go," Gemma said. "Go. Be with each other. We're all fine here. Just go."

They nodded and left without a word. Gemma flopped down onto the foot of the bed and shut her eyes. She rubbed her hands over her face and through her short hair.

"Well, I'll never sleep again."

"Are you sure you're okay?" I focused all my attention on Gemma. I didn't want to think about Callie and that room. Not yet.

She rolled onto her side and held her head up with one hand. "Yeah, I'm all right. Traumatised forever, but all right. I just couldn't deal with the Ashfords right now. I can't. I don't exactly know what I'm supposed to be feeling."

"Me neither."

"How you doing?" Mum wriggled her hand on top of mine. It almost made me want to smile.

"I'm fine. Honest. I thought I'd be trying to throw myself out the window, but I'm not."

Gemma chuckled. It didn't sound real. It sounded more like noise for the sake of noise. "Gonna admit, I thought that would happen too. I was worried I was gonna have to pull you away from the window and tie you to a chair."

"I'm okay. I have no idea what's happening in my head. I guess I have no idea what on earth is going on right now. It doesn't make sense. I didn't realise that…" I went to shake my head but stopped as it brought fire to my brain. "Jay is right though. We shouldn't have been so stupid."

Gemma rolled onto her stomach. "We weren't exactly on top form. My eyes feel like they're about to fall out of my head."

"You two should get some sleep." Mum crawled up the bed and dropped her head onto the pillow. She wouldn't take her eyes off me.

"What?"

"I love you." She grabbed for my hand and gave it a quick pulse.

A shot of pain flew through my hand, and I snatched it back. There was a cut near the bottom of my index finger. Blood had dried all around it. Mum took my hand in hers without a word and wiped away the dried blood.

"I don't even remember how I got this," I whispered.

Gemma was checking her hands over. "We're lucky that's all you got. It was so close. I thought maybe you'd been really hurt or bitten."

"I thought you were going to get bitten too."

In the quiet, the roar of the Infected crashed against the walls.

"How many are out there?"

Gemma shrugged. "Loads. There were loads yesterday, and we made quite a racket so now there are a whole party down there. Both sides."

"We should leave."

"Yeah. I'm not sure there's anything else for it. We can't stay here now. It's only a matter of time before they find a way in. And the later we leave, the more of them we're going to have to barge through." Gemma pinched the bridge of her nose. "I have no idea where we'll go or what we'll do, but it'll be damn better than staying here forever. I'm sick of this place. I need to get out." She rested her head on her arms. "Tomorrow. I can't put up with anything more today. I'm done. I don't want to get up ever again. I don't think we've got a working brain among us. We'll figure it out. Tomorrow."

"Tomorrow." I nodded and watched as she drifted off to sleep in a matter of moments.

Mum was still watching me, giving me a small smile.

"What?"

She stroked her hand over my face again. "I love you. I didn't realise how lucky I was to have you. I don't want to take you for granted again. I could never do what Lisa and Michael had to do. I couldn't."

I wiped a tear off her cheek and rested my head on the pillow next to her. "You won't have to. I'm not going anywhere. I promise."

She sniffed and kissed my forehead. "I know."

"I mean it. I promised—" For some reason I couldn't say her name aloud. An ache blossomed in my chest. A wave of emotion swallowed me up. "I promised I'd look after everyone, and I will. We'll get through this. All of us."

"I hope you're right. I don't know whether it's worse not to survive this or to go back to our empty house alone."

"Neither of those things will happen. I won't let them."

She pushed her hair behind her ear where it had just enough room to hook over and stay. "How did you get to be so brave?"

I smiled. The ache went away for a moment. "I learnt from the best."

She pulled me into a hug, and with the familiar scent and warmth of Mum, I found myself asleep in a matter of minutes. For now the thoughts couldn't reach me. They were still too fresh to process. For now I was safe in my bubble of comfort and warmth.

For now.

TWENTY-FIVE

When I awoke in the morning, my shoulder muscles screamed every time I moved. I pushed through it as I sat up and checked my head and finger. My skull felt bruised but otherwise fine, and there was a fresh-looking scab on my finger. As I looked in my rucksack for a plaster to cover the cut, Gemma moaned from her place on the sofa, dragging herself up.

"Why do I feel like...?" She tailed off before throwing herself onto the pillow again. "Never mind."

The pain stung in my chest, but I ignored it. I couldn't give it much attention. I didn't want to lose myself. I couldn't.

Gemma growled into the pillow before jumping up and trying to shove her blanket into her rucksack. "I feel like a total idiot." She was shaking her head. "How can you forget a thing like that?"

The hum of the Infected outside grabbed my attention, and I had a peep through the curtains. I dropped to my knees, breath firing in my chest, heart trying to escape.

"What?" Gemma fluffed her hair though it didn't move at her touch.

I swallowed. "I shouldn't have looked."

"Is it really that bad?"

"It's worse."

There were a line of Infected surrounding the entire house, and behind them were their friends, all ready for the feast. They were varying shades of blue, grey, and white, and in varying states of decay. But their aim was unanimous.

"Yikes." Gemma's eyes were wide when she pulled away

from the curtain. "How the hell are we going to fight our way through these freaks?"

"We're not going to."

Jay's voice made me yelp, heart sprouting wings and taking off. I held my hand to my chest, trying to breathe like a normal person.

Gemma didn't seem startled. "What do you mean we're not going to?"

"Are you mad? We can't get through that lot."

Gemma put her hands on her hips. "What else are we supposed to do?"

"We need to divert them for a little while."

"But they'll follow us."

"Not if we use Dad's car."

"But won't they all hear the engine and start trekking our way?"

"What would you rather? Walking and never being able to stop because they're not far behind you? Or being in a car that would have to move every so often?" He held his hands up like scales and tipped them from side to side.

"What about petrol?"

"I don't care right now. We need to get out of here before we can't."

"All right." Gemma sat on the arm of the sofa. "So what's the plan, genius?"

"Get dressed and get ready. You've got ten minutes."

Gemma and I exchanged a look as Jay left the room.

"And I'm not kidding," he called behind him.

I jumped to work, trying to stuff my blanket into my bulging rucksack. It was the only thing that tipped it over the edge. Without it, I'd fit everything in easy, but I'd also freeze to death.

When I returned from the bathroom, dressed in as many layers as I could, Gemma was wrestling with a piece of string.

"Where'd you get that?" I pulled my Nikes as tight as they would go, my feet swollen with three pairs of socks.

"Kitchen." She didn't look at me as she continued. She was trying to tie her pillow to the outside of her rucksack.

"You really need to take that?"

"I don't want to sleep with my head on the ground. That'd be too sad."

"Zane?" Mum appeared in the doorway holding out my phone. "Did you want this?"

I took it, turning it over in my hand. "Nah. It's useless," I said, throwing it onto the sofa. Callie jumped to mind before I could suppress it. The amount of conversations we'd had on that phone. The amount of texts with a stream of kisses at the end.

A thought struck me.

I grabbed Mum's jumper sleeve and pulled her into the room. Gemma flung the pillow onto the floor, giving up, as I beckoned her over too.

After double-checking there weren't any Ashfords around, I bent my head low, drawing them into the huddle. "What happened to…?" I had to shut my eyes and swallow before finishing the sentence. "Callie?"

Mum and Gemma's eyes widened as they looked to one another.

"Nothing, I guess." Gemma was grimacing. "What do you want us to do about it? We can't exactly bury her. There are Infected everywhere."

I ran my hand through my hair. "This isn't fair. We shouldn't just—"

"We have to," Gemma said. "We can't do anything now."

"You want to just leave her there?" The tears were creeping up on me. I had to take big gulps of air to keep them at bay.

"It's not her any more. You know it isn't. Anyway, I don't wanna go back in there. Do you?"

I hung my head, shame crawling into my system. She was right. I couldn't go back in there.

Mum kissed my cheek and tried to smile. "It'll be okay. This is a different world now. Nothing's the same as it was."

"You're right." I pulled away from the huddle, yanking my coat on. "Let's just get the hell out of here."

As we stood by the front door, coats on, rucksacks by our feet, Jay barked orders to his parents as they made their way down the stairs.

"Who can carry these?" Jay motioned to the two spare bags on the ground. One was supposed to belong to Callie.

"I'll take one." Michael grabbed the emergency rucksack.

I cleared my throat. "I guess I'll have the other one."

Gemma complained about her pillow as I tried to shoulder two rucksacks at once with my aching body. Jay chucked a balled up plastic bag at her and continued.

"We leave by the front door, bundle into the car, and go. I don't care that there aren't enough seats. I don't care in which direction we drive in. We just go." He pulled his hat lower over his golden hair. "We'll bang against the back of the house and throw things out the upstairs windows to draw them all round to the back. Then we sneak out the front. Understood?"

We all nodded as he eyed us one by one.

"Make sure you have everything because there's no way I'm coming back here unless the world is fixed." He hopped down the last few steps. "Maybe not even then."

When we'd all finished faffing about—and Gemma had shoved her pillow into the plastic bag—Jay faced us again.

"Right. Are we all ready now?"

We all looked to each other before nodding.

"Good. It's now or never. I need two people upstairs with me throwing things and the rest of you down here banging on the windows."

"Got it." Gemma shot into the living room and slapped her hands on the glass.

Michael and Lisa followed Jay upstairs.

Mum looked at me for a moment. "You really think this is a good idea?"

I shrugged, heading into the downstairs bathroom. "It's the only plan we've got."

I slammed my hands so hard on the tiny window that they stung. It didn't take long before things were smashing in the garden and more Infected shuffled round to meet us. The Ashfords had a lot of stuff. The rain of belongings continued on and on.

Gemma was swearing from the living room as the garden became crammed with bodies all reaching up, trying to grab us. My stomach flipped every time the murky eyes of the Infected met mine. I wanted nothing more than to curl up in a ball and cover my head, but I kept smacking my hands on the window until Jay appeared at the bottom of the stairs.

"Are they gone?" I asked.

He didn't look at me as he spoke. "No. Just less."

"How many?"

He shook his head and ignored me.

We regrouped by the front door, all grabbing our weapons and clutching them tight.

"It's been fun," Gemma said as we all looked to one another. "Please don't die." She gave everyone a quick hug, almost tumbling me over with the force of her embrace.

Mum rubbed my arm and gave me a kiss on the cheek. "Love you."

"Love you too."

Michael and Lisa clasped hands and looked to each other before Lisa buried her face in Michael's chest, pulling Jay in with her.

"Right." Jay straightened his hat as he escaped their arms. "Good luck everyone. Let's do this."

TWENTY-SIX

Jay threw open the front door, everyone piling out, almost throwing themselves on top of Michael's car. Gemma took down an Infected in her way, as did Mum. The fear was everywhere, all around me, swallowing me up, making it hard to breathe. I was nothing in this sea. Just a dot, bobbing along, trying not to drown.

I felt the need to slam the door behind me. The second the wood left my hand, I realised my mistake and tensed for the sound.

All the Infected looked this way, arms out, mouths open.

A terrified wobble cry escaped my lips as I hurried to the car. There were groaning bodies covering the floor, knocked down but not dead, trying to pull me down with them. I swung my golf club into an Infected's skull and didn't stop to take notice.

The car's lights illuminated, the engine revving to life. I used my golf club to push the Infected back, clearing a path for myself as voices called my name. Dodging the Infected's teeth and hands, I threw myself into the car. But before I could close the door behind me, there was a body in the way.

I shrieked and tried to shut the door, but it only brought the Infected further into the car. Its skin had a green tinge, and it was missing fingers as it tried to rip me from my safety. I kicked out with my legs over and over, crying out as I did so, Gemma and Mum and Jay all trying to pull me further into the car.

Michael began to reverse, the roar of the engine almost drowning out the moans and growls filling the street. The

Infected fell to the ground with a crunch. I hooked my foot in the door handle and tugged it shut, landing on top of them all, gasping and shuddering. I shut my eyes and covered my face with my hands. The silence that followed was drawn-out and full, squashing my ears. I concentrated on every bump in the road, every breath I could hear being taken, until I felt strong enough to sit up, squeezing into the gap between Gemma and the door.

No one spoke until Michael pulled up at a petrol station at the edge of the village. We sat and stared out the windscreen a moment before Michael turned around to face us.

"Where do we go?"

"As far away from people as we can," Jay said. "Somewhere without Infected."

"Short of driving into the middle of a field, I don't know what to suggest."

"A field would be great right about now."

Michael eyed us all. "Who's going to come and get supplies?"

We all looked to each other and nodded, climbing out of the car. I felt like a baby deer as my feet hit the ground. It took a minute to find my feet as Gemma and Jay, weapons raised, tried to enter the shop.

"What?" Gemma tapped on the glass as I joined them. "Oh. Duh." She slapped herself on the forehead. "How stupid can you get? The electricity's out."

"We're going to have to smash it?" I asked.

She nodded. "I can't believe it hasn't been smashed already." She smirked, readying her swing. "Might as well enjoy this."

My hands jumped to cover my ears as the almighty crash shook the world we stood on for a few seconds. We watched as thousands of pieces showered to the ground.

"Now *that* was the most fun I've had in ages." Gemma's grin was wider than it had been for days. "You two have to try it."

"No," Jay hissed. "There could be Infected everywhere just out of sight. We can't draw them here."

Gemma crossed her arms and looked around. "I see zero disturbance."

"Yeah. Now." Jay pushed past her and crossed the threshold, the glass crunching under his feet.

Gemma and I snuck in behind him, listening. Jay beckoned us further into the shop, scouting the two aisles they had.

"It's safe." Jay threw a basket my way. "Pick up everything."

"Everything? But we don't—"

"I said everything!"

I took a step back and kept my eyes on him as he went to the other side of the shop. Trying to shrug it off, I surveyed the shelves.

They were cluttered with knocked over bits of everything. I put my hand to the back of the shelf and swept the whole lot into the basket. A chill passed through me at the image of the supermarket. However many days ago that had been, I couldn't say. From arms everywhere and the swell of panicked voices to silence, emptiness, and dimness.

I threw packets of chewing gum, air fresheners, and hand fans on the floor as I sorted through my basket, hoping Jay wasn't about to appear and scold me. There were few food products left on the shelves at all. A few bizarre bars of chocolate and open bags of crisps. I stocked up anyway and grabbed what was left in the warm fridge behind me.

A rasping cry came from somewhere behind the counter. My trainers squeaked as I dropped my basket and sped towards the sound, heart thundering in my ears. I knocked over a stand of postcards and key rings as I went, straining my ears to hear what was going on. A quick look above the shelves had my breath pulsing hard. I couldn't see Gemma or Jay anywhere.

As I skidded to a stop in the office behind the counter, there was a squelch. Gemma was standing over the wrinkled-looking Infected. Jay was behind her with his head cocked to the side.

"Wonder how long she's been in here." Gemma jumped over the corpse and started rooting through the drawers.

Jay did the same "Find anything good, Gem?"

"Not really. It looks like this place got mobbed before the Infected got to it. There's no blood or anything in here, just stuff everywhere."

I left them to it and made my way to the front of the shop, Jay's back letting me know I was unwanted. I came across a stand holding hats and scarves. The one next to it had Halloween masks glaring at me. Had we missed Halloween yet? I spun the stand round, gazing at the hats.

Gemma came to join me when she was finished. Pulling a zombie mask off the stand, she turned it around in her hands. "Is it weird I find this offensive now?"

I chuckled, still spinning the hats and scarves around and around.

"Oh yeah. This is more like it." She pulled on a werewolf mask and pointed her nails towards me like claws. "Are you terrified yet?"

"Nah." I looked away, trying not to laugh. "Not even a little bit."

"Okay." She went back to the stand. "How about now?"

This time she was wearing a green witch's nose and a pointy black hat.

I pressed my lips together. "Suits you actually."

She smacked my arm and pulled the stuff off, smirking. "You wouldn't know fabulous if it hit you round the face,

Carlisle. And why can't a girl enjoy Halloween in the Zombie Armageddon?"

I turned to face her. "It's not Halloween."

"So? And anyway, how do you know? Could be. Could be New Year for all we know."

"It's not New Year. No way has that much time passed."

"I was using it to mock you." She rolled her eyes. "But it could be Halloween."

I shrugged, feeling stupid. "Doesn't feel like Halloween."

Gemma pointed to the pumpkin banners around the place as though that was argument enough. The one in the corner had fallen down and was looking sad in a heap. "You'd think we'd be better at marking the days. I'm sure Jay knows what day it is."

I grabbed her wrist and shook my head, stomach knotting tight.

She looked at me for a moment with those stormy-grey eyes.

"It's going to be Halloween forever," I said because I needed to say something to make her stop looking at me like that.

Gemma's mouth opened and closed again before she chucked a Santa hat my way. "Merry Christmas, Mr Positive."

We went back to our stands, Jay joining us in time to see Gemma in a cape, plastic fangs hanging out her mouth.

He looked at her and raised his eyebrows. "Really?"

"What?" She went for a pair of devil horns.

"Do you not realise the seriousness of the situation we're in?"

She pushed the witch's hat onto his head. "Do you not realise we're still alive and that's wonderful?"

He threw the hat to the ground. "We have to go, come on." He stomped off before she could say another word.

Gemma chewed on her lip. "I wish I knew what to say to him, but I can't imagine. I don't know what he wants to hear."

After all the spinning, I decided on the black and white hat with the bobble on the end and the matching scarf and gloves. "I don't know if he wants to hear anything so much as just wants to get on with things. I think he's trying to keep busy."

"Hmm." She looked outside. "I just wish there was some way I could make him feel better."

I wrapped a pink, fluffy scarf around her. "You'll think of something."

She yanked it off and cast it aside, going instead for a rainbow one. "What d'ya think?"

"Stunning." I laughed, covering my mouth and getting fluff on my tongue from the gloves. "I think you should wear it always."

"Maybe I will." She grabbed the matching rainbow hat, shoving it onto her head, before pulling items off the stand and into her basket.

Outside it had started raining. Even though she was now wearing a hat, Gemma used her basket as an umbrella as she raced back to the car. I stood and listened to the gentle pitter-patter for a moment.

I picked up the few garments on the floor, along with the witch's hat. Maybe at some point soon it would be able to make someone smile.

TWENTY-SEVEN

"Hey, Mick?" Gemma pulled herself forward between Lisa and Michael. "Before we leave town, can we check my house?"

No one said a word. I didn't dare meet anyone's eye in case Gemma saw.

"I know it's ridiculous and totally unlikely and not knowing might be better, I know. But I have to know. Please?"

Michael cleared his throat. "We take votes in this team, right?"

"Obviously I vote yes let's go and check." She looked around at each of us, holding her hand up in the air. "Just for five minutes. Quick sweep. Promise."

Mum raised her hand first, followed by Lisa. There was something sparkling in Gemma's eyes that I'd never seen before that made me raise my hand too.

"Right." Michael nodded. "Next stop Gem's."

Gemma sat back in her seat, crossing her arms. The grin I'd imagined lighting up her face was nowhere to be seen.

The car fell back into silence, everyone staring forwards except Jay. He was leaning his head against the window, somewhere else.

A few Infected were on the streets to meet us when we turned down Gemma's road. In the moment it took us to pull up next to her house, no one took a breath. I grabbed Gemma's hand, giving it a quick pulse of strength. She didn't look at me, just the house. Her face was pale, her eyes wide, and she was taking short, shallow breaths.

The house was white and about half the size of Ashford House. Even so, it was bigger than the one Mum and I shared.

There were a pair of square bushes either side of the front door and a path leading up to it. The flowers in the hanging baskets were limp and brown. A petal drifted to the ground like a tear.

No one made a sound.

After another huge minute, I opened my door and climbed out, jogging to meet the Infected on the lawn. I heaved the golf club into the side of her face and continued to smash down until her squirming stopped. I jogged up and down for a moment, checking the perimeter before going back to the car.

"Looks all clear." I stuck my head in, offering my hand to Gemma. After a moment of hesitation, she took it. I smiled at her, throwing all my hope into it.

She looked back at me, saying nothing.

Something alive and real squashed my stomach as we made our way up the path. I tensed my shoulders and held my breath as Gemma slipped her key into the lock and clicked open the door.

We watched as it fell open, revealing the silent house. We stood for a good few minutes, listening for any sounds. My heart was too loud. I held my breath. We waited.

Nothing.

I stepped through the door first, tugging Gemma with me. Her expression hadn't changed, but her eyes were glassy.

"Mr and Mrs Stuart," I called, feeling like a complete idiot but having no idea of their names. "It's Zane Carlisle. I'm Gemma's friend. I've got her right here with me. If you're hiding, you can come out. It's safe. There aren't any Infected around here."

There was a crunch outside. I spun round, golf club raised. I blew out a lungful of air and lowered it when Mum and Michael raised their hands in surrender.

"Any luck?" Mum looked around the hall.

"Not yet. No noise though, so that's something. I guess we check the rooms?"

Mum and Michael nodded. We crept through the first door, returning to full height when we were sure we were still alone. A blue L-shaped sofa dominated the room, its cushions all neat and in line. The wooden floor wasn't scuffed or marked. The picture frames were straight, displaying Gemma, her parents, and her older sister all smiling too wide. The whole place was spotless except for the coffee table. A single magazine was resting there, looking out of place.

I picked it up, staring at the beautiful woman on the front. It was dated the seventeenth of October. I couldn't help but wonder if this woman was still alive. A sick feeling leapt into my mouth, and I threw the magazine back down on the table.

"It looks like they left before things got desperate." Michael was looking at the pictures on the dresser in the adjoining dining room. "There doesn't seem to be any evidence of a struggle."

We snuck into the kitchen, which was also empty and free of any clutter. Mum and I started flinging the white cupboards open. Everything seemed to be in place. I pulled the bread down and shut it quick once I'd opened the wrapper. It was blue and green and growing stuff.

"I don't think they've been here for a while." I closed the cupboard and leant back on the counter.

Gemma was staring ahead with that same expression.

"Oh." Michael picked up a piece of paper left on the breakfast bar. "They went up north."

Gemma's head snapped round at the sound of his voice. She cleared her throat. "What?"

"They left you a note." He handed it to her. "They've gone to your uncle's."

Gemma's eyes devoured the page. I watched them flicker up and down, up and down, up and down. I calmed when her shoulders relaxed. She looked up at us, brain awake again. "They're okay."

Mum put her arm around her. "Exactly."

I bit my lip, hiding the words where they would forever stay in my mind.

"They probably don't have signal," Gemma said. "That's why their phones don't ring. I mean, they won't have battery now, but maybe they didn't pick up because they were driving and then because they had no signal."

Mum rubbed her hand up and down Gemma's arm. "It's all okay."

"Gem?" Michael was looking through the cupboards now. "Do you think they'd mind if we took their food? When this is all over I'll replace it, but they're not going to come back for it now."

Gemma handed the note to Mum, who was trying to read it over her shoulder. "I guess that'll be fine. Like you said, they won't come back for it. They won't need it. All right." She pulled carrier bags out from under the sink.

Mum handed me the note and started filling bags.

Gee,

We're heading north to Uncle Rob's. You were right, something terrible is happening. We need to run. We are safe. I pray you are too. I know the Ashfords will look after you. I'll call as soon as we get there. I promise.

I am so very sorry.

Be strong, Gem. I know you are. We love you so much. Stay safe. Stay hidden. If they come, run. Fast.

I can only hope this will all be over before you read this, but in case you're looking for us, I had to leave you something.

Stop looking. We are fine. Concentrate all your energy on staying safe. That's all that matters.

We love you to the moon and the stars and the sun and back, Gee.

Please be safe.

We love you.

Mum, Dad, and Kay x

I held the note in my hands, watching as they cleared out the kitchen. No one mentioned the call that never came. It didn't matter. Hope was stronger than fear.

"Zane?" Gemma hauled her bags into the hall where Michael was filling the car. "Will you come upstairs with me? There's something I want to get."

"Of course." I followed her up the stairs as Mum and Michael went to explore the shed.

We stopped at her parents' room for a moment and watched the way the light was catching the dust in the air. Without a sound, we moved on to a pink bedroom I couldn't believe belonged to Gemma.

"It's so pink."

"It's Katie's."

"Oh." I rubbed the back of my neck, unsure whether to smirk or not. "That makes more sense."

The top half of her body disappeared under the bed and returned with a pink, sparkly book. A photo album. Gemma sat cross-legged on the floor and flicked through it, not stopping on any image in particular.

"Come on." She jumped up. "One more stop."

The next door along held a much smaller room with posters and photos and notes and drawings on every wall. There was a guitar leaning in the corner.

"Now *this* looks like your bedroom."

"I'm a little disappointed that I'm so predictable."

She picked up the old, worn cuddly duck on her pillow and put it to her nose, breathing it in. A true smile pulled at her lips. Tears welled in her eyes. I wanted to put my arm around her, but I wasn't sure if she would shrug me off. So instead of doing anything useful, I stood there shuffling my feet.

"You're gonna think this is so stupid." She wiped her eyes.

"I don't think it's stupid at all."

"Yeah, right. Like you would grab your cuddly toy from your house."

I put my hand out, and she passed the duck to me. It was bobbled with age but soft in that way only old cuddly toys were. "Of course I would."

"Stop trying to be nice to me."

"I'm not being nice. I'm being honest."

"Oh yeah?" She took the duck back. "What would you go back for?"

I bit my lip, part of me wanting to hold back more than anything. "Elle." I gave in.

She put one hand on her hip. "Elle?"

"Yeah." I went to walk back onto the landing.

"That's it? That's all I get?" She nudged her way in front and blocked the stairs. "Come on."

"What?"

"Well?" She stomped her feet. "What the hell is Elle?"

I looked at the ceiling for strength. "A cuddly elephant."

She let out a hoot of a laugh.

"Hey! I didn't laugh at you and that thing."

"Puddle." She chuckled and made her way downstairs. "You know, I would've imagined you as a blanket sort of guy."

"Well, at least I'm not so predictable."

She passed me Puddle and the photo album when we reached the bottom. I pressed the note—which I still seemed to be holding—between the front cover and the first page.

"One sec," she called behind her. "I'm just gonna leave a note."

I wandered into the kitchen and watched her hand glide across the ripped out page.

> *Mum, Dad, and Kay,*
>
> *I've taken your note and Katie's photo album. And loads of food.*
>
> *I am safe. I'm going with the Ashfords some place safer. Do not go to Ashford House for anything. It is surrounded.*
>
> *But I'm fine. Everything is fine.*
>
> *I hope I see you before you read this note.*
>
> *I love you to the moon and stars and sun and back.*
>
> *Gee, the Ashfords, Zane and Jen Carlisle, and Puddle x*

TWENTY-EIGHT

We slept in the car in a turning for a field. I wasn't sure if anyone found any sleep though. The seats were uncomfortable, and there wasn't enough room for four people, let alone six.

My neck ached when I decided enough was enough, and I was going to wait for the rest of them to give up. Gemma curled up, putting her pillow behind where I was sitting, pushing me closer into the seat in front. I let her without a word, checking outside for Infected.

When I looked back round, Jay was awake, leaning his head on the window, drawing patterns where he'd breathed on it.

"Jay?" I wet my lips. "Are you okay?"

He didn't look at me, just continued to stare out the window.

"Jay?"

He didn't flinch or blink.

"Jay? Please talk to me."

He sighed, opening the car door and shutting it as quiet as possible. I flung my own door open and fell out, jogging to his side after easing the door shut.

"Jay?"

He shook his head.

"Jay?" I skidded to a halt in front of him.

"What?" he hissed.

Now he was looking at me with those soft baby-blue eyes, I found my mouth dry. It felt like my tongue had swollen to twice its normal size. He glared at me, daring me to say something.

I dropped my shoulders and scuffed my shoe into the ground. "I'm worried about you."

He threw his arms out wide. "Well, don't be." He turned away and watched the shadow of an Infected appear in the distance.

"You know?" I wandered to his side. "You can always talk to me. About anything."

"No thanks." He snarled the words, and my heart jumped.

"Jay, please? Don't be like this. I'm sorry for whatever it is I did. Please don't be angry at me."

He turned, slow, eyes like blades. "Whatever you did? Are you kidding me?"

I felt the overwhelming desire to take a step back, but I held my ground. "I don't want you to be angry with me."

"Well, tough luck. I don't want to speak to you. I don't even want to look at you."

"Can you at least tell me what I did wrong?"

"The fact that you don't even know is—there's not even a word for it!"

I looked at him, my heart growing heavier every second that ticked by.

When he spoke again, the words were dark and dripping with menace. "You killed my sister."

My mouth dropped open. Tears sprang to my eyes before I could stop them. My heart was replaced by a cold, lifeless rock. "I had to. She was going to kill all of us."

"No!" He swiped it away. "Not that! You think *that* is what I'm upset about?"

I had to swallow past my tight throat. "I didn't do it on purpose. I would never hurt anyone, let alone the love of my life!" I was shouting before I even realised. "You think I *wanted* that?"

"Do you realise I loved her too? She's my sister. *Was.* My only sister. My only sibling. You have no idea what it's like to have that taken away. She was always there for me, and now she's gone. If it weren't for you, she'd still be here."

I blinked past the tears. "I'm sorry. I don't know what more I can say. I would've done anything to save her. Anything."

"It shouldn't have happened in the first place. What stupid seventeen-year-old gets pregnant?"

"Hey!" I pointed my finger at him. "That is *not* fair."

"Isn't it? How difficult is it, Zane? How did she even...? She was the sensible one. Look what you did to her. You mushed her brain."

I grimaced at his choice of words.

"She changed when she met you. You ruined her."

All my fight drained. "I loved her. Love her," I corrected.

"And she loved you back." He shook his head. "Why couldn't you be like all of the other guys she knew, stupid and pointless?"

"I love her," I repeated.

"You ruined her life. You ruined my life. You ruined everything." He looked back to the Infected that had become five since we'd been talking. They were getting closer. "I wish you weren't here."

The malice was gone, but all at once I was wishing it back. The brutal honesty would kill me faster.

"I don't know how to forgive you."

"I don't know how to forgive myself." I put my hands in my pockets, feeling the cold at last. "You can hate me. I hate myself. You can blame me too. I definitely do. You don't have to like me, Jay. You just have to let me help. I promised. I promised Callie."

He faced me again. "Why?"

"Because up until this morning I thought I was a part of your family. I don't let my family down. But most of all, because she asked me to. She made me promise I'd look after you."

He pulled his hat off and ran his hand through his hair.

"Maybe it would be better if we didn't talk any more."

"Okay. I'm sorry." I watched him, waiting for him to make the next move.

He stood there for a moment before storming back to the car and grabbing for the baseball bat, nudging Mum and Gemma in the process. I tensed and covered my head as he came towards me, but he shot right by, heading for the Infected.

"Jay!"

Mum and Gemma were climbing out of the car, and Michael and Lisa were stirring.

"What's going on?" Mum called.

I ran back to the car. "Get the weapons."

"What's happening?" Gemma was squinting her eyes as she spotted Jay. "What the hell is he doing?" She grabbed the golf clubs and threw one to me before sprinting in Jay's direction.

Mum raced after her. Michael grabbed my arm before I could join them.

"What's this?" His eyes widened as he spotted Jay. "What is he doing? What's going on?"

"I'll explain later." I shrugged him off and dashed to catch up with Gemma.

Jay had taken down two of the five Infected and was wheezing, unable to catch his breath. Gemma swung the golf club round so hard it bent on impact, carving a dent in the Infected's skull. She couldn't pull it out so left it there like a hat as the thing dropped to the ground, motionless. She kicked another in the stomach. I brought my golf club down on its head until it cracked open and spilt brains on my shoes.

Jay was pushing an Infected back with the baseball bat but didn't seem to have enough energy to hold it off. Gemma flew to his side and pushed with him until the Infected toppled over onto the hedge clippers Mum held out ready. The thing still grabbed for us, clippers protruding out of its stomach.

160

Mum cringed as she pulled them out and took a step back. They were black with blood and dripping onto the grass.

The Infected looked between all of us, not sure who to go for, as Michael and Lisa caught up. Lisa threw herself in front of Jay, axe raised. Michael went to take it out with the cricket bat he'd found in Gemma's shed, but Jay put his hand out, stopping him.

"Wait."

Michael blinked and dropped the bat back down.

Jay took a step forward, watching as the Infected turned to him. He pulled a giant breath into his lungs and powered the bat down again and again and again, knocking it over and killing it. But that didn't stop him. He drove the weapon into its skull until there was nothing left to aim for.

Michael pulled him back. "Jay, Jay, Jay. Stop. It's all right."

Jay barged out of his grip, dropping the bat. "I didn't need your help!"

"Are you mad?" Gemma crossed her arms. "What the hell were you thinking, Jay? There were five of them."

"I said I didn't need help."

"What did you expect us to do? Not help? Watch you struggle and get hurt?"

Mum let the blade of the hedge clippers drop to the ground. "We just wanted to make sure you were okay."

"I can do it by myself. I'm not a little kid."

"We never said you were." Michael tried to make contact again, but Jay jumped out of his way.

"You all look at me like I'm a baby. Like I need your help. Like I need protecting. I don't need protecting. I can look after myself. If anything, you lot need me."

Lisa took a step forward. The axe looked awkward in her hand now. "We love you. What would we do if we lost you? We just want to make sure you're safe."

"Don't bother." He marched back to the car, leaving us all staring.

Michael turned towards me. "I think now we deserve that explanation. What on earth did you say to him to make him act like that?"

"Nothing!" I threw my arms wide, jumping on the defensive, heart rate still not back to normal. "I asked him what was wrong, and he told me he hated me. He blames me for Callie." I had to force her name out. It sounded wrong now in the air. It used to bring love and joy to my chest to say it. Now it brought nothing but misery and dread. I had to fight back against the thousand thoughts threatening to bombard me. I didn't have time for them now.

"Zane, how many times do I have to tell you it's not your fault?" Gemma wiped the blood from her hands down her combat trousers. "No one here blames you. After all, like I said, it's probably my fault. I'm probably the one who infected her. It's done now anyway. There's nothing we can do."

I dropped my head. "He doesn't even want me here."

"Nonsense." I was surprised to hear Lisa's voice. "He might be angry with you, but he doesn't mean that. He loves you, Zane. Even if he won't say it." She lifted my head up with her finger. "We all love you." Her arms were around me, and tears dripped onto my cheeks.

"Thank you." I choked out the words.

"You're welcome." She squeezed tight. "We don't want you going anywhere. We need you. And Jen. We're stronger together." She whispered the next part so only I could hear it. "It's not your fault."

TWENTY-NINE

The complete human noiselessness in the car was baffling. Even Gemma didn't try and lighten the mood. I stared out the window, trying not to think. Cars had been abandoned, all their doors open. Other than that, there were only trees to look at. When a moving car came into view, I sat up straight, holding my breath.

Michael slowed the car, and Gemma tried to sit on top of me to take a look at the passengers. I rolled down the window and squeezed the door handle, waiting. But they only glanced at us, passed, and were gone.

Gemma sat back in her seat. "At least we know we're not the only ones left."

Fields rolled by and blurred into one as we drove to nowhere. Hours passed in the blink of an eye. Sometimes a minute lasted just as long.

"What's that?"

I shook myself out of my daze and turned round to see Lisa pointing to a plume of smoke in the sky.

"Is someone having a fire?"

Gemma and I leant forward to get a better look. When the trees thinned out, a tent appeared in the middle of a field.

"People!" Gemma cried. "We have to stop."

"What?" Jay spoke for the first time in hours as Michael slowed the car. "You think we should just mosey on over?"

"Well, yeah. Why not?"

"We shouldn't stop for anyone. We don't know them. What if they steal from us? They could take the car. What if they have a gun?"

Gemma touched her short hair. "Well, they probably don't."

"I'm not setting my hopes on probably. Why do you want to talk to them anyway?"

"Because we're stronger the more people we are. And they might need help."

"So?"

"*So?* I would hope someone would do the same for me if I was in trouble."

Jay crossed his arms. "I don't like this. I don't think we should stop for anyone."

"Well, tough luck. We vote around here. I say we go and say hi. Anyone else?"

The rest of us raised our hands.

"If we get robbed, I'm not even gonna say I told you so." Jay jumped out of the car and slammed the door behind him.

Gemma took a deep breath and blew it out. "If they steal from us, I'll never hear the end of it."

We grabbed our weapons and walked in a huddle up to the camp, no one making any sound. There were no Infected around yet, but I kept sweeping the field with my eyes to make sure.

We tiptoed closer and closer until we could hear voices. No words came to me, but there were definitely two voices—a man and a woman.

"Hello?" Michael called into the wind.

Three faces appeared above the tent, expressions hard until they clocked our being alive.

"Oh my gosh!" A tall woman grinned wide, tucking her long sunset-gold hair behind her ears. I mistook the pink on the ends of her hair for blood at first glance. "People!" She dashed round to greet us. "Hi! Come round, come round."

We all stuck close together as we edged round the tent. There was another young woman squeezing her hands tight together in front of her. She had dark, wavy hair and almond-coloured skin. Next to her stood a man of similar age with pale skin and a smattering of freckles over his cheeks, nose, and forehead. His auburn hair was short but looked thick even from a few footsteps away. He was taller than the girls, but the closer we grew, the shorter he seemed. When we stopped in front of the fire, I noticed he was the same height as Gemma. All three of them had dried blood splashes on their clothes.

"I'm Savannah." The blonde woman offered her hand to each of us in turn, beaming. Her lipstick was the same colour as the pink in her hair. "Savannah Clements, am-dram actress and beauty consultant. And this is Aniya and Ollie."

We moved on to shake their hands also. Neither of them had a handshake as strong as Savannah's.

"Ah-nee-yah," Aniya said, sounding it out for each of us like we were idiots.

"Michael Ashford, Mick." Michael nodded his head. "This is my wife, Lisa." Lisa gave her tiny closed mouth smile. "And our son, Jay." Jay gave nothing.

"Gemma." Gemma waved before Michael could introduce her. "But call me Gem. People only call me Gemma when I've done something wrong."

"Zane Carlisle," I answered when Gemma looked to me. "And this is my mum."

"Jennifer." Mum nodded. "Jen."

Savannah laughed. "Gem and Jen, eh? Fantastic. Sit down, sit down. Make yourselves comfortable."

She sat almost on top of Aniya, making room for us. We all exchanged looks before we, one by one, gave in to Savannah's hospitality and joined them cross-legged on the ground.

"So how do you guys all know each other?"

"Old friends," Gemma cut in before any more could be said. "We had to abandon the house we were staying at before we got completely trapped. What about you three?"

"Old friends," Savannah said. "We were going on a road trip. Got stuck in traffic when weird stuff started happening. The Corpses just kept coming and coming. Chasing all the people who got out of their cars. We escaped and haven't stopped moving since. Well, except to build a fire and sleep for the night. The most we've stayed in one spot is probably seventy-two hours."

"Corpses?" Gemma brought her eyebrows together. "Is that what you call them?"

"Yeah. That's what they are. Why? What do you guys call them?"

"Infected."

Savannah's mouth pulled up to one side. "What if you were still alive and infected? Would that not be confusing?"

"You'd be infected. The Corpses are capital I Infected. It's really not that hard."

"Whatever." Savannah swatted it to one side. "Same difference. So where you guys headed?"

Michael shrugged. "We don't really know. Just away from towns and cities. We're trying to find somewhere free of Infected."

She nodded. "Sounds like a good plan to me. Have you got enough food and stuff?"

"Savannah!" Ollie glared at her. "You can't just jump straight in and ask them that."

"Why not? I was getting to it anyway. What's wrong with cutting corners?"

"What's going on here?" Michael asked. "Are you running out of food?"

"Desperately," Aniya whispered.

"I wasn't being rude, Ollie. I was just asking. I wasn't saying, *give us your food, strangers*. I was just asking." Savannah looked at us. "You don't have to share unless you want to."

Michael looked to Gemma before they both looked to Jay.

Jay was shaking his head. "No." The three campmates stared at him. "I'm sorry, but it's all about survival. What would we do if we gave them some, went on our way, and ran out?"

"Wait, Jay?" Gemma went to touch where her hair used to be before dropping her hand. "What if they're part of the team?"

"What?" Jay stood up.

Gemma jumped up too. "Why not?"

"We don't know anything about them."

"Erm, guys?" Savannah was biting her thumb. "Not to make this awkward or anything, but we're just about going mad the three of us. If it's an open invitation, we'd love to join you guys. We don't care where you're going or what you're doing. Right?" She looked to Aniya and Ollie, who both nodded. "So if you'll have us, we'll share what little we've got. We can even all cram in the tent. What do you say?"

Gemma's eyes swept over the three of them before going back to Jay.

"You cannot be serious."

"Why not?"

"This is ridiculous."

"So what? We vote in this team." She looked to Savannah. "Give us a minute."

We all followed Gemma to the other side of the tent where we drew into the tightest huddle I'd ever been a part of.

"Obviously we know Jay's a big fat no, but I don't see any reason why we shouldn't be one big happy family."

"I think they've got good intentions," Mum said. "And they're only young, and they need our help. We've got plenty."

"For now." There was worry around Michael's eyes.

"We can always get more," Lisa said. "I don't like the idea of just walking away from these people. And Savannah seems nice."

"I dunno," Gemma added, "I think she's just trying to make us like her."

"Well, I'm in," Mum said, putting her hand in the middle.

Lisa put her hand over Mum's. "Me too."

"And me." Gemma was looking to us men. "Boys? Want to be social?"

I exchanged a look with Michael, trying to read what he was thinking. I knew where Jay was coming from. There was a chance this was what Savannah did. Made you feel sorry for her, share your supplies, and then she killed you. But I didn't buy it. All I'd heard was the desperation in her voice. All I'd seen was the fear in Aniya's face, the hopelessness in Ollie's eyes.

They needed all the help they could get, and there was a certain comfort and strength in numbers.

"All right." I put my hand on top of the pile. "I'm in."

THIRTY

Savannah, Aniya, and Ollie polished off the food we gave them like they couldn't slow themselves. I was only halfway through my portion by the time Ollie had finished clearing every last drop of his own. The lazy smiles on their faces were too casual. I felt like I had a rod up my spine, scanning the area over and over again for Infected.

"When's the last time you ate?" Mum asked.

The three of them looked to each other. "Day before yesterday," Savannah said. "But it wasn't much of anything. We're trying to stay away from the Corpses, but that means staying away from the food. This whole thing feels like a losing battle."

Gemma nodded. "We've got enough for now."

Savannah stood—distracting me from our surroundings for a moment—and put her arms around Gemma. "Thank you," she said.

Gemma's eyes were wide, and it took a few seconds for her to pat Savannah's back in response. "It's all right. We're a team. We vote in a team. This wasn't my doing."

Savannah moved along the line to Mum and then me. Her frame was skinnier than I'd ever hugged before. I didn't want to squeeze her too hard in case she broke. She smelt like damp and sweat.

Lisa and Michael gave a reluctant hug back. Jay sat there and let it happen. The expression on his face was set. He hadn't looked my way since this morning.

"We are so grateful." Savannah's huge grin was back. "I can't even express how grateful we are. Thank you so much. We wouldn't have lasted much longer."

"So?" Gemma put her can down. "In all your walking you haven't met any other survivors yet?"

"Well, there were people in the traffic jam," Ollie said. "And we saw a couple once in the distance, but we haven't spoken to anyone since the outbreak." There was something in his eyes. I didn't trust the way his mouth was pressed tight.

"Us neither." Gemma didn't mention the man on the street we didn't save or the car that didn't stop.

A cold wind stirred the camp, and I tensed against it, pulling my blanket further around myself. Ollie shuffled closer to Aniya and Savannah, who were sharing a blanket.

"Hey." I stood, pulling my blanket off and bracing against the chill. "You're freezing."

He shook his head and tried to pass it back to me. "I can't do that. You need it."

I took a step back, holding my hands up so he couldn't give it back. "I can share."

Mum budged up, and I snuggled close. Her arm found its way around my shoulder, and she rested her head on me. "You are a sweetie, aren't you?"

Gemma stood up. "A sweetie that makes the rest of us look bad." She sat next to Savannah and offered her the other half of her blanket.

"You guys are too nice." Savannah took it, and the three of them huddled together under the two blankets like they were the best friends in the world. "I can't believe how lucky we were to find you. If there's anything we can do to help, just let us know."

"Can you kill them?" Jay looked up for the first time.

"The Corpses?" Savannah didn't miss a beat, Jay's tone of voice not throwing her off. "Yeah. We're still alive, aren't we?"

He looked down at his can and continued to stay quiet.

Savannah watched him for a moment before moving on. Her mouth was open like she was about to spout another long story where she talked and we listened, but her eyes hardened, and she stood up, grabbing for what looked like a thin pole.

I turned round to find an Infected stumbling this way on a foot that was almost falling off, dried blood all round its mouth and chin. I felt sick to my stomach that I'd missed it in my scanning. How vulnerable were we out in the open like this? How easy was it for the Infected to take advantage of us?

The look of decision on Savannah's face was harder than any expression I'd seen on her so far. She walked up to the Infected like she had all the time in the world. She smashed the pole into its forehead and jammed the end into its eye. The squelch had Mum flinching, squeezing my shoulder tight.

Savannah pulled the weapon out and wiped it on the grass. The thin pole looked like something you'd tighten screws with on a car tyre. Returning to us, Savannah sat back down like nothing had happened.

Gemma was smirking. "Hey, Jay?"

Jay looked up for the briefest of moments.

"I think that answers your question."

Savannah wiped her hands on her ripped jeans and flicked her hair. "It's nothing. Ollie got the last one."

Gemma chuckled. "You take it in turns?"

Ollie shrugged. "Depends who's got the energy to get up."

"So you've all killed one then?"

"Yeah." Ollie gave a quick look to Aniya. "One or two."

Aniya shut her eyes and grabbed her necklace tight. "Never again." She said it almost to herself, and Savannah wouldn't take her eyes off her.

Gemma cocked her head to the side. "What if there were a group of them and you were getting swamped?"

"Leave it." Savannah's face was taut, smile gone. She glared at Gemma for a second, putting her arm around Aniya and pulling her close. "Anyway, what about you guys?" She slapped a grin back on her face.

"We do okay," Michael said. "We all protect each other. We're family now."

I used this as an excuse to survey the camp again, not wanting to meet anyone's eye.

"Quite a team you've got there."

"We do our best." Gemma was smiling at all of us.

Her smile hit me harder than Savannah's. When Savannah smiled, it was like she was trying to invite you into her world. Like she wanted everyone to be smiling even if they didn't want to. Like no one had a choice in the matter. But when Gemma smiled, it lit the world behind her. There was always a sarcastic edge about her mouth she couldn't seem to help, but that always had me smirking back.

Michael brought the car into the field to shield us from the wind, and the eight of us sat chatting until the sun went down. I sat like a meerkat, unwilling to let my guard down for a single second. The one person who didn't join our merry band of survivors was Jay. The moment the sky went from purple to black, he shut himself in the car. Lisa and Michael looked to each other, but no words were said. What could they say? What could any of us say?

After a few minutes, Savannah brought her knees up to her chest. "Is he all right?"

"Yeah," Lisa said. "He's just having a rough time. He'll be okay."

"I'm sorry that we've disrupted everything." She pursed her lips. "It must be hard."

"It's really all right." Lisa waved it away. "It's not you. It's really not you. I think once he comes around, meeting new people will be good for him." She looked at Michael. If I wasn't mistaken, there was a tear in his eye as he nodded.

I had to hold my breath as thoughts of Callie whirled through my head. Her delicate beauty. Her closed mouth smile. Her light-golden hair. Her sea-green eyes. Her soft, peach lips. Her slender fingers. Her sweet, floral smell.

I couldn't miss her more than I did in that moment. Because I missed everything. I could have spent all night listing the things I loved about her.

Instead, I let out a wobbly breath and watched Savannah's eyes flicker between Lisa, Michael, and me. She tucked a strand of hair behind her ear and cleared her throat.

"We lost someone too." She looked to the ground before meeting my eyes. "At the beginning. In the traffic jam. He wanted to run. We couldn't stop him. There were more and more Corpses each minute." She shook her head. "He wouldn't listen to us."

"I'm sorry." Mum found her voice first. "I know that doesn't help."

Savannah nodded and tried to smile, but it was twisted and wrong on her face. "I'm guessing it hasn't been long for you guys?"

We shook our heads.

"I'm sorry too. It sucks, doesn't it? This world we live in?"

Mum pulled me closer and embraced me tight. "It's not so bad when we've got each other."

Savannah's smile found traction, and she grabbed for Aniya's hand, their eyes meeting. "I guess that's true."

Gemma's eyes found mine across the flickering fire. She gave a small smirk, darting her eyes to Savannah and back to me. My eyebrows came together, and I looked to Savannah and Aniya and the way their heads were resting up against each other and the way their hands were entwined.

I widened my eyes when I looked to Gemma, giving a quick nod. She pressed her lips together and tried not to laugh, but I couldn't take my eyes off them. I wanted everything they had in a touch of a hand. The jealousy that fired to life in my chest was hotter than any love I would feel ever again.

THIRTY-ONE

The ground was hard, and the air was bitter, but I slept better in the tent than in the car. I felt both sweaty and cold when I woke up. I had to jog around the camp a few times to stretch my muscles and feel human again.

Aniya had the final watch, and she and Mum were the only ones awake and out in the open when I appeared. Aniya watched me as I jogged back and forth. I pretended I didn't notice, but I could almost feel her stare on my back. Lisa and Michael joined them round the fire, hand in hand. Lisa's hair looked lank and dead. Michael's chin was dotted with stubble. They almost didn't look like the Ashfords any more.

I sat down when they did. "How's Jay?"

Lisa cringed. "The same. He's awake. I tried talking to him but…"

I looked at my hands, picking at my gloves.

"It's not your fault, Zane." Michael spoke before I had a chance to blame myself. "He just needs some time and space to think."

I nodded, watching the single Infected in the distance stumble this way. "Infected."

Everyone gave it a quick glance before going back to their conversations. I wasn't sure when the ZA had become about anything but the Infected, but I decided it didn't matter. It wasn't about the Zombie Armageddon any more. It was about survival. That's all it had ever been about.

I jumped up, dragging my golf club off the ground to greet the Infected.

The thing was missing half its face. The flesh of its right cheek had been ripped off to show white bone underneath.

The jaw didn't look attached, and its nose was hanging in such a way that made my stomach turn. What disturbed me more than the shape of its face, was the fact the Infected didn't seem to care one bit. Juvenile Virus didn't care what state its host was in. All that mattered was passing the infection on to as many humans as possible, thriving.

Well, not today.

I planted my feet shoulder width apart and readied my club, bending my knees and eyeing the monster. A swell of something sparked in my stomach a few seconds before I swung and knocked the thing to one side. It didn't take a lot to finish it off. Wiping the club on the grass and making my way back to camp, I realised what that feeling had been.

Anticipation.

I shuddered and sat next to Mum as she shared out rations. Everyone had surfaced for breakfast except Jay. Ollie was already tucking into his portion. Savannah was applying her lipstick for some reason. Gemma was sat next to them, trying to make coffee in a saucepan. She shot me a look as I sat down. Ignoring it, I made a hair flattening gesture, and her hand jumped to a clump that was sticking up like a candle in a cake. She shook her head and licked her hand, trying to flatten it.

"So what's the plan?" Michael asked when we all tucked in to half a can of whatever was open.

"Whatever." Savannah shrugged. "We weren't heading in any direction in particular. We'll just follow you."

"What about the car?" Mum asked. "We can't all cram in there."

"We can keep the supplies in the car and walk either behind or in front of it," Michael said. "I definitely don't want to leave it behind. I suppose some of us could go ahead in the car and scout the area."

"And leave some of us behind?" Lisa was shaking her head. "No. We have to stick together."

"Whatever works for you guys," Savannah said. "We're just thrilled to be a part of it."

When everyone was finished, we packed up the tent and blankets and piled everything in the car. Lisa kept Michael company in the passenger seat, and the rest of us trekked on in front. It felt freeing to walk without a rucksack, and my legs were grateful for the exercise. Jay walked alongside us and didn't say a word, but at least he was out of the car.

"So what's everyone looking forward to?" Savannah asked. "After all this, I mean."

"Safety." Mum wrapped her arms around herself. "And not being freezing all the time."

"A bed." Gemma was smiling. "One I don't have to share. An actual bed with a mattress. Is that really what this has come down to?"

"A shower," I said. It'd been about a week since my lukewarm bath, and I was dreaming of steaming hot water and a bucket-load of shampoo. I knew my hair couldn't be that dirty, but it felt slick in my hand and greasy every time it touched my forehead.

"Normality." Aniya was playing with her necklace. "People being on the streets. Belongings not being all over the road. Cars not being abandoned all over the place."

"Burger," Ollie answered. "Chips. Pizza. Chocolate. Pubs. Gaming."

Jay looked up and nodded. "Gaming," he agreed.

Gemma nudged my arm but continued like it wasn't a huge deal to hear Jay's voice. "What about you, Savannah?"

"Mine's stupid."

"Come on. What could be that stupid?"

She chewed on her lip. "Makeup."

Gemma raised her eyebrows. "Are you serious?"

"I told you." She laughed. "Nail varnish. Eyeliner. Different lipsticks. I worked on a makeup counter. I was surrounded by the stuff, and now I've only got a few bits." She shook her head. "It's stupid, the things you miss."

Not one of us mentioned the people we'd miss most of all. We didn't have to. I was sure the ghost of whoever they'd lost was hanging above their heads as much as the ghost of Callie was hanging over ours.

There were vehicles littering the roads in random positions. Some were crashed into lamp posts, others had collided with each other. But there were also a few sitting lonely by themselves with the doors open.

Gemma and I scouted each one, but with no knowledge of how to hot-wire a car, we were wasting our energy. It always looked so easy in the films. There were vehicles in abundance but no keys with which to start them. And all their engines were cold, owners long gone.

I watched Jay as we continued to walk, Ollie chatting to him about gaming. He became more animated by the hour. I even heard him chuckle. Gemma met my eye again and smiled. Somewhere on the road, they'd found an empty can to kick along with them as they spoke, neither of them letting it fall behind.

"Oh damn," Ollie said as his kick sent the can across the road and almost into the tree line. "My fault."

"What the hell were you aiming for?" Jay smirked as he went to retrieve the can.

The light in my heart was growing warmer and warmer, and I couldn't take my eyes off Jay. It didn't matter that he was pretending I didn't exist. All that mattered was his happiness. What little of it he had left.

Jay cried out as a hand snatched his arm. Two Infected emerged from the trees, teeth sinking closer to Jay. He yanked his arm but couldn't escape their grip.

My heart leapt out of my mouth. My legs were sprinting before I had time to think. I shot by Ollie and kept going, almost landing on top of the second Infected. I kicked it to one side, driving my golf club into the head of the one holding Jay. It stumbled back but didn't let go of him. Ollie took down the second one while I bashed the head of the one holding Jay until black blood splattered on both our coats and faces.

When the brain ceased to work, the hand let go of Jay. He fell back, landing on the road, shuffling back into the centre to safety.

"Jay?" I wheezed, having to lean my hands on my knees to catch my breath. My brain was struggling to work out what'd happened. "Are you all right?"

He stared at the Infected as Gemma and Mum bundled him up in a hug, asking him again and again if he was okay or hurt. Savannah rushed to Ollie's side. Aniya put her hand on my shoulder, making me leap out of my skin at the contact.

"Zane? All right?"

Her chocolate-brown eyes grounded me, and I nodded. "Yeah. Thanks."

She gave me a nod as I went to Jay.

"Jay?"

His eyes met mine without hatred for the first time in days. He stumbled out of Gemma and Mum's arms and stood in front of me, his baby-blue eyes soft and alert.

It was all I could do to stare back, not wanting to make the first move and say something wrong again. The seconds dragged on, and I was afraid we'd be stuck there for decades.

No one made a sound.

"Thank you." His voice was quiet, but it stirred something in my heart.

"I'm not going to let anything happen to you."

Before I was ready for it, his arms were around my neck, and tears were in my eyes. He squeezed me so tight I couldn't breathe, but I didn't care. I would do anything to keep the hug alive forever.

THIRTY-TWO

We walked until the sun started to go down, taking it in turns to finish off the Infected we came across. No one went anywhere near the trees.

"What's that?" Savannah's voice was shrill with excitement.

I had to squint my eyes to see what she was pointing at. It was some sort of building in the distance.

"Shelter!" She banged on the bonnet of Michael's car and rushed to the window.

Jay was shaking his head. "It's too far," he said to no one in particular. "It's almost dark."

Gemma had her hands on her hips. "Agreed."

Ollie grinned. "Would be nice to have something sturdier over our heads though."

Aniya was watching the skyline. "I think it'd be worth a shot. We can always make the tent in the dark if we have to. We've done it before."

Savannah returned to the group with Lisa. "I've been told a vote is required?"

Gemma sighed. "Feels like as the days go by we start to vote on stuff more and more."

"All in favour of finding the shelter before stopping for the night?" Savannah raised her hand.

Aniya, Ollie, Mum, and Lisa all raised their hands.

"Great." Savannah's trademark smile was back. "On we go then."

Gemma's mouth was twisted in disgust. "I will not be happy if it starts snowing or something. We don't even have a fire."

I looked up at the greying sky. There were a few stars waking up and glinting. "We'll be all right."

Gemma looked around and took a step closer to me. "First impression time is over. What do you think of our new team members?"

I shrugged. "They seem fine. It's nice to have someone else to talk to."

"You saying you're sick of me?"

I laughed and pushed her to one side. "Like a week ago."

She nudged me back, smirking. "You love it."

"Anyway, what do you think?"

"No complaints so far. I just hope we can continue playing happy families like there isn't a huge divide between us."

I shook my head. "I don't think there is."

"How so?"

I nodded in front of us where Jay was walking alongside Ollie, Savannah, and Aniya. A few times I'd even caught him smiling. "Jay seems to be fitting right in."

Gemma nodded. "He's probably sick of us by now. I'm glad he's got something new to occupy him."

We walked for another hour or so. The grey light became black. It was getting harder and harder to see the four of them in the lead, almost out of reach of the car headlights.

"Wait!" Gemma called, halting them as we caught up. "This is ridiculous. How can we watch for Infected if we can't even see each other?"

"But we're so close," Savannah begged. "It's got to be a barn or something. There'll be loads of room. It'll be great. We could scout on ahead in the car?"

"No." Gemma shook her head. "You are not abandoning us here in the dark. It'll still be there in the morning. We've gotta stop. Now."

Savannah's eyes narrowed. "It's right there. You can't seriously suggest we give up now?"

"You can't seriously suggest we keep going? Did you not hear me? We can't even see you."

"Well, I wanna keep moving."

"I definitely do not. Jay?" Gemma's eyes met Jay's. "You wanna stop, don't you?"

Jay was biting his lip. "Actually, Gem, I think we can make it in the next fifteen minutes or so."

She dropped her arms from her hips. "Really?"

He nodded, pressing his lips together.

"Fine." She waved them on. "Go. Don't come crying to me if you fall down a hole. Don't even think about taking the car."

The four of them walked ahead without another word.

"Stupid," she muttered to herself. "Bloody ridiculous."

"What's the big deal?" I asked once I decided it was safe. "Either we get there and have a night all stretched out, or they're wrong, and you get to say I told you so?"

"It's not even that. It's the way he sided with them so quickly."

"I think you're reading too much into this."

"Really? You think it was like Jay to go for the less cautious option? He didn't even want to let Callie leave her room."

The reply died in my throat, and I had to gather my thoughts. "You said it was better that he had new people to talk to. What happened to that?"

"I changed my mind."

"Just like that?"

She looked at me. "Yes. My mind is subject to change. Always has been. Problem?"

"No. Definitely not."

"Changed my mind about you, didn't I?"

My eyebrows came together. "What do you mean?"

She shook her head and picked up her pace. "Nothing."

I grabbed her arm. "No. What?"

"It was stupid. I shouldn't have said that."

"But you did. What were you going to say?"

She tugged her arm out of my grip. "It's nothing. It's just that maybe, before all this, I didn't exactly like you very much."

I blinked at her. "You didn't?"

"Not really."

"Why?"

She shrugged. "Just got this vibe off you."

We walked in silence for a minute before her words sank in. "What vibe?"

She chuckled. "Obviously one that told me how irritating you are."

"You really didn't like me?"

"And you liked me?"

"Of course I did."

"No, you didn't."

"I liked you, didn't mean I knew how to talk to you. What did I ever do to you?" I couldn't think of anything. Gemma and I had only spoken a few times before this mess.

"Nothing. Can we please drop it now?"

"No. Come on. Please."

"Bloody hell, you are irritating."

"Gem?" I tried to look into her eyes, but she was staring straight ahead. "Please."

She shook her head. "You were all she ever talked about. She would go on and on and on about how amazing you were, and I couldn't buy it. No one could be as incredible as she thought you were. I guess maybe I was a little jealous."

It took a second for me to find my tongue again. "You were jealous of me?"

"Well, yeah. She'd been my best friend forever, and you just swooped in and took all of her attention."

I shook my head. "I was always intimidated by you."

"As you should be." She was grinning again. "When I met you, I was blown away by how goddamn *normal* you were."

"Well, I am."

"I couldn't believe she was so crazy about you. You were just this guy. I didn't get it. I still don't, to be honest. But she really did think you were great, like you had superpowers or something."

"I guess I feel the same about her." Something was niggling about her confession. Something didn't add up. "If that's what you thought of me before all of this, why did you want to make friends? Just before all this happened, the day before we went to the seafront?"

She looked at me. "I wanted to be a good friend. A better one than I had been."

"That doesn't... There's got to be more."

She was chewing on her lip. "You're gonna make me say it, aren't you?"

"What? I really don't know why you did that. It baffled me then, and it still does now."

"It was because of the baby."

My stomach dropped to the pavement.

"Before she told me, I could pretend you were gonna go away at some point. The two of you would drift apart, and it would be finished. I felt terrible for thinking it, but there it was. When she told me she was pregnant, I realised that— even if you did break up—I would have to hear about Zane freaking Carlisle for the rest of my life." She ran her hand over her hair. "So I decided to just deal with it. I wanted to be the bigger person. That's what I was trying to do."

"For Callie?"

"Of course. It was never about you. Not really. I was just stupid."

"Nah." I put my arm around her and squeezed her tight. "I won't believe you were ever stupid."

She smirked. "You're actually pretty nice."

"So you like me now?"

"I can stand you."

THIRTY-THREE

I awoke to the sound of laughter and forgot for a minute where I was. The crisp rustle as I sat up put everything in place. Everyone was gathered on various bales of hay, grins on their faces and joy filling the barn.

"Morning, sleeping beauty." Gemma smirked.

I rubbed my eyes as I joined them, nodding to each of them, not quite ready to talk yet.

"So what's today's plan then?" Gemma was twirling a piece of straw around in her fingers. "Do we stay here a little longer, or do we head out?"

"Head out." Jay's voice was sure. "Where there's a barn, there's a farm, and where there's a farm, there's a farm*house*."

There was a wave of nods as everyone agreed, excited by the prospect of sturdier walls. They chattered away about what the farmhouse might bring, and Gemma jumped up as something caught her eye. She dashed into the corner and knelt down.

I wandered over to her, peering over her shoulder at her cupped hands.

"Look." She opened them, and a pair of beady eyes stared up at me, trembling in fear.

"It's a mouse."

"Yeah." She was smiling.

I just looked at her.

"He's still alive," she said.

"He won't be in a minute if you don't let him go."

We made our way to the door of the barn, and she put her hands to the floor, watching the mouse scurry out of them and into the grass.

"The mice have no idea what's going on."

"How do you know?"

"Did he look like an Infected to you?"

I shrugged. "I guess not. Are you suggesting all the mice are fine and healthy?"

"Well, this seems to be a human thing, doesn't it? I haven't seen any Infected cats or dogs strolling around the place. Look."

She pointed up at two birds ducking and diving around each other, singing as they went. It was the most innocent and beautiful thing I'd seen for a long time.

"They're not Infected. They're just leaving us to do our usual human thing and kill each other." She shook her head. "It's pretty depressing, isn't it?"

"Just a little. But I guess it's good that the whole of nature isn't suffering."

"That's true. That's very loving of you."

"I was thinking more that I can outrun an Infected human but not so much an Infected horse."

She pushed me to one side, chuckling. "And there I thought we were having a meaningful conversation."

As we walked, we put our faces up to the sun, trying to heat our forever frozen bodies. I even tried taking my hat off, but the air itself was too cold to ever warm up for real.

Jay stopped ahead, and Gemma and I hurried to his side. We stood there for at least a whole minute, staring.

"Told ya," Jay said. "Farmhouse."

On the edge of a field, in the middle of nowhere, stood a huge modern house. Bigger even than Ashford House. In fact, it looked more than five times the size.

"Wow." Mum appeared next to me. "It's beautiful."

The cream brick house was no less than ten windows across. The extension reaching out towards us was bigger than the house Mum and I shared. There was an expensive-looking estate car on the drive.

"What are we waiting for?" Savannah was jumping up and down.

Before we could say anything more, a bloodcurdling scream shot through the air, coming from the farmhouse. We all flinched, knuckles white as we gripped our weapons, jaws clenched. Gemma and I exchanged a quick look before sprinting to the front door.

I went for the handle, and Gemma leapt in front of me, blocking the door.

"It's stupid." She was shaking her head. "We can't."

Savannah, Aniya, Ollie, and Jay met us at the door.

"Why aren't we in there helping?" Savannah's eyes were wide. "We need to help them."

"We don't know how many are in there." Gemma had her arms stretched across the entrance.

"So? There are nine of us. We've got to save them."

"We don't have to do anything."

Mum jogged to my side as Michael's car parked on the giant gravel drive. "What's going on?"

"We *have* to go in." Savannah grabbed Gemma's arm and tried to throw her aside, but Gemma held her ground and was too strong to be moved. "Urgh!" Savannah swept her hair behind her ears. "Who are you to stop me? You don't have to go in. Let me pass."

"No," Gemma hissed. "I'm not letting you kill yourself for being stupid."

Savannah growled and launched herself at Gemma, both of them tumbling to the ground.

"Hey!" I yelled.

"Stop it!" Jay rushed to pull Savannah off Gemma, and I helped Gemma up.

"What on earth is going on?" Michael asked as he and Lisa joined us.

"This moron's going to get herself killed," Gemma said, wiping gravel off her coat.

Savannah went to open the front door, and Ollie grabbed her wrist.

"You're not going to stop me." She gave him a glare that made his eyes widen.

"Just wait a minute. Catch your breath."

Lisa was staring up at the house. "It's so beautiful. And big. And in the middle of nowhere. It's perfect." She looked to Michael.

"You can't be serious?" Gemma marched further into the group. "There was a scream in there. That means there's an Infected in there. And that's if we're lucky. A whole group might be in there."

"They'd be coming out here by now." Savannah flicked her hair. "And because of you, the screaming's stopped. Whoever needed our help is dead."

"Because of *me*?" Gemma squared her shoulders. "What could you have possibly done to help? How fast do you think you can run?"

"Shut up!" Michael's voice silenced them. "This is ridiculous. Now, I don't know about the rest of you, but this is an opportunity too good to just walk by. We'll go in, but we'll be quiet. We're not rushing in there and getting ourselves trapped. Everyone agreed?"

There were nods around the group, but Gemma crossed her arms.

"Okay then." Michael stepped to the front door, Ollie and Savannah by his side, the rest of us following behind. Mum grabbed hold of my arm and squeezed so tight it started to tingle.

As Michael's hand touched the door handle, we all took a deep breath, holding it. I clenched my hand round the golf club. With sharp decisive movements, the door was open, and no one made a sound.

We all stood still, listening. We listened until the utter lack of sound swallowed us up. Michael stepped inside, Ollie and Savannah less than a step behind him. We piled in, all as silent as practised serial killers.

My eyes fell on everything, sweeping the gigantic room. The ceiling stretched up to the sky, and we were faced with a hand-carved wooden staircase. There was a giant wooden doorframe to our left and a dining room within. Savannah, Ollie, and Jay stuck their heads in to make sure it was safe.

I went to the right with Gemma and Mum and checked the most massive living room I'd ever seen. It had three sofas surrounding a coffee table and a fireplace. In the back, there was a huge bookcase and a few armchairs, almost like a small library. Blankets were folded on the sofa, and there was a hairbrush on the coffee table. We edged round the furniture to look into the next room.

To our left was a room with the biggest sofa I'd ever seen pointed at the biggest TV I'd ever seen. That room was darker than the rest, and the stark opposite of the room to our right.

The extension was filled with yet more sofas. Between each window was a painting, and at the end stood an easel. A paintbrush balanced on a table to the side. There was also a jar of faded-blue water. The painting appeared to be of a village scene, but only a small portion of it had colour. There were faint outlines of pencil strokes. I shivered as we backed out, gripping the club ever tighter.

There were rooms after rooms after rooms. A whole list of halls and sitting rooms and drawing rooms and game rooms and rooms I didn't have names for. Rooms that didn't even seem to have a purpose. I couldn't comprehend having this much space. I wouldn't know what to do with it all.

As we rejoined the group, Gemma nudged my arm and flicked her eyes to the baseball bat leaning against the bottom of the stairs. I swallowed as I looked at it and followed the rest of them up the steps.

The landing was surrounded by a host of doors, but it was the one straight ahead that had a scuffling sound coming from it. One by one, we raised our weapons and crept closer.

Gemma was shaking her head when Michael threw open the door. I didn't breathe. On the ground a few metres away, kneeling over its prey, was an Infected. He didn't look more than a year or so older than Jay. The thing between its teeth looked as though it had been breathing not that long ago. As air shot into my lungs, I gagged at the stench of death and had to cover my mouth with my hand.

The survivor's stomach was almost all gone, and parts of it now covered the floor and were smeared all over the Infected's lips. It was wrong to call her a survivor now, but I didn't have another word to use.

There was an Infected in the corner, a still human-looking body entwined with it. The more my eyes swept the room, the more dead people I came across. There must have been at least another three to the right.

The moment before anything happened dragged on, and yet took no time at all. Before I could ready my stomach or my mind, the Infected's head snapped up, milky eyes glaring at us. It jumped up without issue and shot towards us.

I held my golf club out, blind, trying not to see Callie in its face. It jumped on top of Savannah, Ollie screaming and bringing a hammer down on top of its head. The skull caved in, but the thing wouldn't die until Ollie brought it down again, showering the room with even more gore.

Before anyone could rush to Savannah's aid, there was a groan from the left followed by one from the right as the bodies of the ex-survivors stood. Gemma held up her baseball bat and faced the one on the right. I stood next to her, raising my golf club, only getting half a second to breathe before it was on top of us.

Gemma's whack knocked it sideways into the four-poster bed but didn't slow it down. It roared at us, blood pouring from the gash in its stomach and bite marks up and down its arms. There was no time for sympathy as the thing struck again. I rammed my golf club into its head. Jay pulled a kitchen knife from his belt, skidding to a halt beside Gemma to help us.

Gemma used her baseball bat as a shield, and I shoved along with her until the thing tripped on a cricket bat lying next to the dead Infected. Before we could plunge anything into its head, it leapt up again, gnashing its teeth and letting out a screech.

I brought my golf club down on top of its head and was rewarded with a crack. Gemma's bat was a few seconds behind, and this time as the thing dropped to the ground, Jay was there with the knife, plunging it straight in the eye. The squelch didn't turn my stomach. I was immune to sounds now.

My head felt like it was spinning as we turned to the others, Jay darting behind us to put the knife in the other two dead Infected just in case.

Aniya was still by the door, holding onto her necklace with wide eyes. With a grunt, Savannah finished off the ex-survivor in the corner with the torn out throat, and beside her, panting, were Ollie, Michael, Lisa, and Mum.

The relief that no one looked hurt almost took my feet from underneath me.

But then the ex-survivor by the door leapt up. She was short, blonde, and fierce. What made my heart try and claw its way out of my body was her age. She must have been younger than Jay. It fixed its eyes on Aniya. Then it was sprinting towards her.

Without a thought, I dashed over to Aniya, throwing my body on top of her and shoving her out the way, the two of us falling to the ground. The Infected went flying out onto the landing, only milliseconds behind us. But I knew the difference a few milliseconds could make. Gemma stood in front of Jay as the thing appeared again.

It shot to the biggest group. Mum swung her golf club but missed. The rest of them were trapped behind her. There was a blur of movement, and Michael was on the floor. Lisa was screaming. Ollie tried to pull the thing off him.

Michael was wrestling, arms tensed as he howled. Ollie broke the new Infected's face with his hammer, red blood in his red hair. Savannah appeared like a tornado, throwing her weight into the wheel brace and burying it in the dead thing's skull.

All I could do was blink.

Lisa kept screaming. Jay dropped to his knees. Mum was lifting Michael's head as he pulled in a breath through his teeth, grasping his shoulder. Savannah had, sobbing, thrown herself into Ollie's arms. Aniya hadn't moved from her place on the floor, staring at me.

Gemma's steps were slow as she made her way over to the Infected with the caved in face. She eyed it for a moment, cocking her head to the side, before she smashed her baseball bat into its skull until it was unrecognisable as a head.

"Gem?" Not enough sound came out. My throat was all thick and closed. I coughed through it as I stood up. "Gem?"

She either didn't hear me or ignored me, continuing to pound the weapon into the flattened brains. Her breathing was hard as she huffed and gasped.

"Gemma?" My stomach was curling in on itself as I watched her and edged closer. "Gemma!" I grabbed her round the waist and spun her to face me.

The second her eyes connected with mine, she dropped the bat and crumpled into my arms, shuddering. I held her close and stroked her dirty, bloodstained hair.

When my brain allowed me to take in more information, I looked over at Michael. Mum's hands were pressing down on his shoulder. Blood covered every inch of her skin. She was slick with it as though she'd been swimming. Lisa was kneeling beside her husband, tears cascading down her face. Aniya rushed over to them with the first aid kit.

Hopelessness drowned me as I watched them. Sounds didn't reach my ears. I glanced at Jay. He was still on his knees by the four-poster bed, shaking his head back and forth.

They tried to stop the bleeding, but for what? Michael had been bitten. Michael was infected.

THIRTY-FOUR

After a stretch of time—I couldn't figure out how long—Savannah bustled Gemma and I out of the room, saying something about leaving the Ashfords with Michael and leaving Mum and Aniya to help. Ollie's face was paler than usual as he followed behind.

They left us on the landing as they went to check the other rooms. Neither of us said a word, but I offered my hand to Gemma, and she took it.

"There are another five bedrooms," Savannah said as they finished their sweep. "All of them have bathrooms. There's also a study with a balcony."

We made our way downstairs, Gemma and I slumping down at the breakfast bar. Savannah and Ollie disappeared into what seemed to be a pantry or larder—I wasn't sure what the difference was—leaving us to try and figure out what on earth had happened.

Gemma shook her head and rested her hand on her forehead. "This can't be happening. What are we gonna do?"

"I don't know."

"What is going on?"

"I don't know."

"What's happening to us?"

"I don't know."

"How long do you think?" She whispered the words.

All I could do was shake my head and repeat myself. "I don't know."

"We need to be able to protect each other. Without that, what do we have?" She shut her eyes. "I feel like there's a hole in our force. It's like we're a thousand times weaker than when we woke up this morning."

"We are."

Savannah appeared again, waving a bottle of red wine. "Expensive wine, anyone?" She pulled a corkscrew from a drawer as though she knew where to look, a satisfying pop filling the air as she released the cork. Placing the bottle on the breakfast bar, she went to look for something.

The second her back was turned, Gemma grabbed the bottle and took a huge swig, offering the bottle to me as an afterthought. When I declined, she took another gulp and set the thing back on the breakfast bar before Savannah turned round.

"There's loads of wine in there." Savannah placed two glasses on the table and tapped the two left in her hands together. The ding rang throughout the room and made her smile. "Expensive glasses for expensive wine. Amazing."

Gemma was pressing her lips together as she watched her. She threw back the glass of wine she was poured before Savannah even sat down.

"Careful." Savannah eyed her. "You're not your usual body weight. That'll go straight to your head."

"Good." Gemma grabbed for my glass and finished that too.

"Are you even legal?"

Gemma gave a dark chuckle. "Like that matters now."

Savannah picked up her glass. "I guess you're right. But for curiosity's sake, how old are you?"

"Seventeen. Me and him both." Gemma went for Ollie's glass, but Savannah moved it out of her reach. "What are you, my mum?"

"Lucky for you, I'm not old enough to be."

Ollie emerged and took his seat. "There's maybe enough

food to last us two weeks. At least we'll be all right for a little while. There's enough wine to last for months though."

"Not with *some* people in the house." Savannah pointed to Gemma.

"What about water?" I asked before Gemma could say anything.

"Not that much. There are a few pans and bits and bobs that are filled with water, which I thought was weird."

"Jay did that where we were before. He had every spare container filled with water." I jumped up and fiddled with the tap, but nothing happened. There wasn't any pressure behind the movement. "I guess the water's stopped too."

"I guess we'll have to drink wine," Ollie said, shrugging off his coat and revealing a monochrome tattoo sleeve.

Savannah twisted her glass around in her fingers. "How long do we wait before going back up there?"

Ollie cringed. "Do we really have to go back?"

"Well, yeah. I'm not leaving Aniya up there. He's not just going to die, Ollie."

I flinched at the word, trying to hide it somewhere I couldn't find it again.

"It's too dangerous," Savannah said. "We're not putting them at risk. It didn't look good. It won't take long."

We sat in silence until the glasses were empty—a silence so intense I couldn't comprehend it. All the background noise of modern life had gone. No cars rushed by. No hot water tanks ticked. No computers buzzed. We sat there, letting time pass, letting the silence consume us. Relaxing into our new surroundings. Letting Juvenile Virus pulse round Michael Ashford's veins until everything we knew and loved of him was gone.

When we stood to make our way upstairs, I noticed for the first time that there were smashed plates and jars on the floor.

At least the survivors went down fighting. I couldn't help but wonder what they'd think if they knew we were sitting in their house, drinking their wine, before their bodies were even cold.

If survivors found themselves in our house, I wouldn't mind. The only thing I wanted from there was Mum, and she was safe. But when I thought of survivors stumbling across Ashford House, it made my hands clench into fists. I didn't want anyone touching Callie's things. I didn't want anyone erasing her smell. I didn't want anyone to see the way we'd just left her there.

Gemma's hand slipped into mine as we left the kitchen, and Savannah took Ollie's before offering me her other one, which I clasped tight. Hand in hand, the four of us crept up the stairs like we were tiptoeing our way through a haunted house.

We were.

My eyes found Michael before they found anything else. They'd moved him onto the huge four-poster bed. He was writhing, twisting, and shivering as he fought whatever battle was raging inside him. Sweat was dripping off his forehead, and he looked hot to the touch.

It was the virus all right.

He was holding onto what looked like one of the pillowcases and pressing it against his shoulder. It was soaked with his blood. Mum was standing next to the bed, hand pressed over the top of his. There was blood on her face and in her hair. Lisa was sitting on the other side of the bed and stroking her hand over Michael's hair, telling him everything was going to be okay. Jay was sitting on the end of the bed, watching his trainers like they had the answers. Aniya was leaning up against one of the posts, looking into the first aid kit as though something in there could help.

Michael cried out, shutting his eyes. The four of us snuck into the room and squeezed ourselves onto the chaise-longue.

I didn't know where to look. It didn't matter. I couldn't drag my eyes off Michael.

He grabbed Lisa's hand. "Don't let me." He puffed out a breath, gritting his teeth. "Don't let me hurt anyone."

She shuffled even closer. "I won't. You won't."

"Please."

"I won't let you."

"You promise you'll do something? Before it's too late?"

She nodded. I didn't believe her.

"You can't let me. Not like before…"

Gemma's hand tensed in mine.

"I can't…"

She shushed him, and tears started to roll off her face as she shuffled down the bed and clung to him. I couldn't breathe as I watched them. It was too painful. Too heartbreaking. Too familiar.

I wanted to run. I wanted to run until I couldn't feel my legs any more. Until I couldn't breathe. Until I couldn't think. Until it stopped hurting. But I couldn't. If I ran, who's to say I could stop?

"Leese?"

Lisa had her face centimetres from his at once.

"I'm sorry."

"It's not your fault." She had to squeak the words. "I'm sorry I couldn't do anything."

"It's okay."

"It isn't." She was shaking her head.

"I love you."

"I love you too."

"Jay?"

Jay lifted his head and crawled further up the bed so his father could see him. Jay took his hand.

"You can do this."

Jay was frozen. He didn't cry. He didn't scream. He didn't move.

"You can survive this. I know you can. You're strong. I love you."

Jay's words were croaky. "I love you too."

"I'm so proud of you."

Jay nodded but didn't speak a word. As the moments dragged on, Jay heaved himself off the bed and stood on the opposite side to Mum. She'd pulled away from Michael's wound, at last, giving up.

Michael began fluttering in and out of consciousness, and we knew it couldn't be long.

"I love you both," he said, voice just loud enough to make out. "So very much."

"I love you, Dad." Jay's voice was dead.

"I love you, Michael." Lisa was gulping her breaths. "Forever." Somewhere deep within her soul, she found a smile. And that, after everything that had passed between them, made the tears start falling onto my cheeks.

We watched Michael heave his last sigh, and there was silence apart from the beating of nine—*eight*—hearts.

Lisa let go of her husband and disappeared into Mum's awaiting arms. How could she walk away so soon? She was stronger than I was. Stronger than I'd ever imagined she could be. The strongest of us all.

With eyes as dark as those of the living dead, Jay walked over to one of the bodies lying on the floor, or what was left of it. He picked up something with a glint of silver and walked back over to Michael. His movements were slow, as if every footstep hurt. He took a breath and gulped, letting a single tear hit the ground.

The bang crackled in the air, sending a shock through my system. My whole body jumped. Every nerve twitched. Every muscle tensed. My heart was beating so damn fast and hard I thought it would kill me.

Jay dropped to the bloody carpet, gun sliding out of his hands. He'd done what he'd had to do. He'd put a bullet in Michael's head.

THIRTY-FIVE

As the first ones to wake in the morning, Mum and I took it upon ourselves to go into the garden and start digging holes. Neither of us said it in so many words, we just went out to a huge garage and found a couple of shovels behind an immaculate Aston Martin. Either it'd never been driven, or whoever owned it had been obsessive about the way it looked. We went to the back of the giant garden by a line of trees and started to dig.

I knew it was going to be hot, sweaty work, but I didn't realise how difficult it was going to be. My arms ached as the tiny patches of ground came away piece by piece. I threw my hat and coat off, the first time I'd been warm outside since we'd been running away from the pier all that time ago.

Aniya was the first to join us, reappearing from the garage with a big pitchfork. She gave us nothing other than a good morning nod. It was at least another hour before anyone else stirred in the house.

Savannah and Ollie were sitting at the breakfast bar when we went in for a break.

"Where've you guys been?" Savannah was holding her head with one hand, her hair in a messy bun.

"Outside. Digging," Aniya answered for us.

Savannah screwed up her face. "Ah."

She pushed a tin of pasta our way, and as no one else jumped at it, I picked it up and finished the bottom half. I threw the can down when I was done, and both Savannah and Ollie flinched, cringing.

"What's the matter?" I wiped my mouth with the back of

my hand even though I knew there was no wasted food round my face.

"No loud noises." Ollie's voice was quiet. "Please."

Mum crossed her arms and shook her head. "How much did you drink?"

Savannah gave a chuckle, and it sounded too low for her. "This is nothing. Ollie and I can usually drink all day and all night. We were careful, honest. Just hits a starving body hard."

"How much did Lisa drink?"

"Not much," Ollie said. "Maybe two glasses at the most. She went to bed not long after you did."

Mum nodded. "That's all right then."

"It's Gemma you should be worried about."

I groaned. "How much did she drink?"

Savannah and Ollie exchanged a look.

I leapt up. "How could you let her?"

They both put their hands on their heads and winced.

"I told you not to let her."

"And you should know better than anyone that you can't tell that girl what to do."

There was a moaning coming from the hallway, and I spun round to find Gemma shuffling towards us, eyes almost closed, face pale. She had to wet her mouth before any sound would come out. "I heard my name."

I looked at her for a minute. "You're an idiot."

"Yes."

"What the hell did you think you were doing?"

"Drowning my sorrows."

"Did it work?"

"No, of course it didn't. I feel awful, and Mick's still dead."

There was silence, and she wiped her hand over her face.

"I'm sorry. Lisa and Jay aren't here, are they?"

"Not yet."

"So what's the plan?" She eased herself onto a barstool. "What's the plan for today?"

I could only watch her.

She was shrinking in her seat. "I'm sorry, all right. I won't do it again."

There were a thousand things I wanted to say to her, but I couldn't bring myself to voice a single one of them. It wouldn't make a difference anyway. Who was I to tell her how weak it made our team when she was hungover? She was already aware of that. Who was I to tell her alcohol wasn't worth the fuss? Who was I to tell her anything?

I exhaled to steady myself. "You better not do it again. I might not be so kind next time."

She gave me a wonky smile. "So what's the plan?"

"We're in the garden, digging. Come find us when you can deal with the sunlight."

It wasn't until the sun started to go down that Gemma wandered her way into the garden.

I leant on my shovel, drenched in sweat.

"Looking good," she said. "Need any help?"

"Really? Don't you think it's a bit late for that?"

"Look. I said I was sorry. I'm here now, and I want to help. How many more do you have to dig?"

I looked to Mum, Aniya, and Ollie, who'd joined us after lunch. They all shrugged, throwing glances at one another.

"We don't know," Mum said. "I don't know about anyone else, but I don't really want to go back up there."

Gemma held up her hand. "I can go."

I shook my head. "No. You don't have to—"

"Yes, I do. You've been working all day. I need to do something. I can go and count them. No problem." She went to turn back into the house, but I grabbed her arm tight.

"I'm not letting you go by yourself."

She spun, eyes narrowed. "What?"

"I'll come with you."

"They're all dead, Zane. You saw yourself. I'm just gonna count them. I won't even touch them, I promise."

"I'm still coming with you."

She shook me off. "What *is* this? You don't think I can handle it? You think I need protecting? What is your problem? I've saved your life, Carlisle. Don't you *dare*."

"Gemma." I went for her arm again.

"Let. Me. Go!"

"Listen to me! I know you can handle yourself. I know that without you I'd be long dead, but please just listen." My heart was drumming against my ribcage. I was aware of the eyes watching behind me.

Gemma clicked her tongue. "What's your issue?"

"I can't lose you. Okay? I can't. Just let me come up there with you. Please."

Her eyes seemed big as she looked at me, quiet for a moment. "It'll take a few seconds."

"I don't care."

She watched me, eyes travelling up and down my sweaty— and no doubt red—face. She gave a quick nod, and I followed her into the house. We didn't say a word as we stuck our heads in the living room to find Lisa, Jay, and Savannah playing cards. Not one of them smiled when they looked up at us, not even Savannah.

Gemma stopped at the top of the landing while I was still two steps down. I had to look slightly up at her.

"I didn't mean to be a jerk," she said. "I didn't think that's what you meant."

"I know. I'm sorry. I didn't mean to..." I didn't know how to finish that sentence. I didn't mean to make her angry? I didn't mean to snap at her? I didn't mean to care about her?

She nodded. "I know. I appreciate the gesture even though executed poorly." She was smirking again, and everything fell back into place.

I stood in the doorframe of the master bedroom as she counted and double counted and triple counted the bodies, holding her nose. The way their eyes were open and staring at the ceiling wide in horror made me shudder. I tried not to see anything. Michael was wrapped in a sheet, and I was glad Aniya had the good sense to cover him.

My lips were pressed tight together, and every time I needed to breathe, I faced back onto the landing. Though I still caught a whiff. I still gagged. I could still almost taste it.

"Eight." Gemma opened the windows and shut the door behind her. "How many holes we got?"

"Four. And two that aren't done."

"Fantastic." She blew out a breath. "I'll help carry them downstairs and that when it's time. I feel terrible about being such a waste of space this morning."

"S'all right. I was just worried about if something happened or if we had to run or whatever. I don't care that you have a hangover and didn't want to dig in the garden all day."

She gave me a smile almost absent of humour. "This is pretty good you know?"

"What is?"

"Being cared about."

My eyebrows came together. "Everyone cares about you. We're a team."

She dug her toe into the carpet. "I know that. But you've got your mum. Jay's got his mum. Savannah and Aniya have each other, and Ollie's their best mate. I've lost all those things. My mum's who knows where. My best mate's gone. And I never had a boyfriend to begin with. It's just good to know someone's looking out for me."

I pulled her into my arms. "Well, you've made a new best friend now."

She laughed. "I certainly have. How about that?"

"And you're never getting rid of me."

THIRTY-SIX

Ollie was staring into space, and Savannah nudged him. "Ollie? You on this planet?"

He shook his head and dropped his eyes to his cards. "I fold." He pulled himself up and left the room without another word.

Gemma shot me a glance.

Savannah was chewing on her lip. "I think it's hitting him more and more, you know? Especially after yesterday."

We'd dug until we couldn't see our hands in front of our faces and awoken at first light to bury the dead. We even buried the Infected. They may have killed the previous survivors—and one of them may have killed Michael—but they were people once too. Gemma and I scavenged some flowers for Callie. Savannah found some more for whoever they'd lost. They may not have been anywhere nearby, but they deserved something. Even if that something was a flower that would blow away in the wind.

Afterwards, we'd trekked out to the barn and collected as much wood as we could to board the windows. The farmhouse was darker but safer, like a human nest. But we were going to have to make another trip if we wanted to board all the windows. That was the only downside to this enormous house.

I threw my cards down on the table. "I fold too."

Watching the space where Ollie had been sitting was making me think of Callie. I crossed my arms over my chest to block her out, but she was seeping into my soul. It became a little bit more real every day, and I wasn't ready to process it yet. She wasn't here with me, but did that mean she was gone?

When Gemma collected her winnings—a stack of coasters, pens, and cutlery—the front door opened, sending us on red alert. But it shut again, Ollie reappearing with an acoustic guitar. He placed it on the table. Savannah's eyes were wide as she ran her hand over the front.

"You play?" Gemma leant forward, inspecting the guitar.

"No." Savannah shook her head. "It's not ours. This is Joel's—the one we lost. He was phenomenal with it. Took it everywhere."

"I'm sorry." Gemma's voice was soft.

"Story of our lives now, right?" Savannah didn't look up as Ollie took his place next to her. "I'm just glad the rest of us are still here."

Gemma nodded. "All in all, we're surviving. Right, Zane?"

"Yeah." I had to clear my throat. "Yeah, surviving."

Gemma shuffled forward. "Can I?"

"Sure."

The guitar fell into Gemma's hands as though born to be there. Her face relaxed, and she shut her eyes for a moment. Her fingers skimmed the strings but made no sound. She opened her eyes and plucked the strings as soft as possible, turning the screws at the top to tune it.

"Incredible." She was smiling that big true smile, her usual hint of a smirk almost gone. "This is a fantastic guitar."

Savannah shrugged. "That makes sense. It was his pride and joy."

"I bet."

"We couldn't part with it. It would be like accepting he was gone." She tucked a strand of hair behind her ear. "You play?"

Gemma played a chord and tapped the strings to stop it. "What gave me away?"

"Your face. Same as Joel's was." Savannah sniffed back her tears. "You would've really liked him."

"He sounds like a great guy." I had to force the words through my tight throat.

"He was. The best. He was my best friend. Obviously I love this loser." She put her hand on Ollie's knee. "But I'd known Joel since I was eleven. We were so close. People at school thought we were a couple. It didn't matter how many times we'd say we were just friends. He was... There was something about him. I miss him every minute of every day."

I nodded and looked to Gemma.

She was watching us, guitar paused, ready to burst into song. She pressed her lips together. "We all know that feeling."

Before Savannah could ask any questions about Callie, Gemma started picking the strings in a beautiful, complex tune I recognised from somewhere. Her face was deep with concentration, but her eyes weren't always on the strings. The instrument was an extension of her arm and she an extension of it. Though I'd never given it any thought, she belonged in its presence.

I wasn't shocked by this burst of talent, but I was surprised when she opened her mouth and began to sing. The lyrics, like the tune, rang a bell, and I found myself staring like I was seeing her for the first time. She was gentle with the words, unlike her speaking voice. I leant forward as the song went on, wanting to be closer to her voice. It wasn't as stunning as other voices, but she had a passion in her delivery the music industry couldn't hope to reproduce. The music took me in and swallowed me whole and pinned me in my place.

As the song went on, all I could recognise in the lyrics was Callie. No matter how hard I fought, the tears took over. I gave in and let them fall down my cheeks in silence as Gemma finished her song.

No one said a word for a few minutes as Gemma laid the guitar down in her lap. Her lip wobbled, and she buried her face in her hands, shoulders moving up and down as she cried.

Savannah was playing with her nails and not making eye contact with either of us. For the first time since we'd met her, she didn't feel the need to break the silence. Ollie wasn't taking his eyes off the guitar.

When Gemma wiped her eyes with her hoodie sleeve, Savannah looked up again, smile fixed back in place but not as comfortable as before.

"That was beautiful. You really can play."

"Yeah." Gemma gave a sad chuckle. "Been playing since I can remember. Not that it means anything now of course."

"It does," I found myself saying. "Of course it does."

Savannah was nodding. "It's not easy, is it?"

Gemma ran her hand through her short hair before dropping it into her lap. "No. It isn't."

"Who did you lose?"

Gemma's eyes welled up again, and she looked to me.

I squared my shoulders and took in a huge breath. "Callie Ashford."

"Ashford? Lisa and Mick's…"

"Daughter." I let the tears fill my eyes again. There was no fighting them back. And maybe I didn't want to fight them any more. "Jay's older sister. Gem's best friend."

Savannah was looking at me, waiting for more like she knew what was coming.

"And my entire world."

Savannah wet her lips and shuffled forward to put her hand on my knee. "Zane, I'm so sorry. I don't know what I would do if I lost Aniya."

"You carry on." Gemma's voice sounded harder than usual. "It's what we've got to do. We lose people, and we carry on. We have to."

Savannah nodded and then shook her head. "It's my fault, isn't it?" She sucked in a breath. "That Mick's gone?"

"No," I said, before anyone else had a chance to answer. "No, it isn't. How can you think that? You were in there helping like the rest of us. It isn't anyone's fault." But even as I said it, a terrible part of me wanted to blame her too. I wanted to blame someone, anyone. Because if it was someone's fault, it might start to make more sense.

"I was the one who wanted to go in the house in the first place."

"You're not the only one," Ollie said. "If the rest of us didn't want to go in, we would've walked away. We all wanted to go in. Mick wanted to go in. He led us in. It's not your fault."

"We didn't all want to go in," she muttered and glanced at Gemma.

Gemma shook her head. "Savannah, it isn't your fault."

Savannah looked at her.

"It isn't. No one's blaming you. Like Ollie said, you all wanted to go in. It wasn't just you."

"Thank you." Savannah sniffed and nodded. "I still feel awful. I can't push the guilt away."

"Same for all of us," I said. I knew too well what that felt like. Callie's death would be hovering over me for the rest of my life. It was all I could do to try and forget about it. *I just need to survive*, I kept telling myself. Over and over again.

It's all about survival.

"I don't think Jay will ever forgive me. It's because of us he lost his dad. How can you forgive a thing like that?"

Ollie shrugged. "I dunno. I dunno what it's like to lose a dad."

Savannah looked at him for a minute. "We've all lost that. Do you see any father figures around here?"

"Hey, wait." Gemma jumped forward in her seat. "Just because our parents aren't here doesn't mean anything bad's happened to them."

Savannah pressed her lips together. "All right, whatever you say, Gem."

"What's wrong with having a little hope? It's not hurting anyone. So what if I believe my parents made it up north to my uncle's house? That they're safe? Am I hurting you, Savannah?"

Savannah smiled, but it was too sweet, too fake. "Course not. I didn't mean it like that. I just... My dad and step-mum were in London on that Saturday when everything went to hell. And I never heard from my mum. Not even before Joel. She was out shopping. I'm not saying anything about any of your parents." She looked to each of us. "Just that it'd be a miracle if mine were still alive."

We all looked at Ollie as he started speaking. There was something off about the sound of his voice. Something far too serious about it. "Mine were on holiday because I was away on the road trip. They were in Cornwall. They kept sending me and my brothers these cheesy photos in a group message. I know it's like on the edge of the country and everything, but how many other people were there too?" He shook his head. "I think I'm with Savannah on this one. As soon as we hit that traffic jam, their photos stopped."

Savannah rubbed his arm, trying to offer him a smile.

Ollie put his hand over his face as he continued. "Then my oldest brother, Andy, stopped replying. George said he was gonna go over and make sure he was okay, but we never heard from him again. I was in contact with Chris until my phone died, but now I have no way to know if he's all right."

Savannah put her arm around Ollie, pulling him closer. "You don't know. He could be all right. After all, you're still here."

He tightened in her embrace, like he didn't want to let go of himself. He took a huge breath, cramming all his emotions inside.

They looked to me next, eyes big.

"What?"

"Don't you want to share?" Savannah asked. "We know your mum's safe, but what about your dad?"

I clenched my hands into fists. "Nope."

"Don't look at me." Gemma shrugged as Savannah met her eye. "I don't know his entire life story."

"If there's anything you wanna say, Zane, you're safe here with us," Savannah said.

I nodded, blowing out a great big puff of air. "I don't care what happened to my father. I don't care if he's alive or dead or an Infected. It makes absolutely no difference to me whatsoever. Sorry."

"You don't have to be sorry. I guess in this weird world you're lucky. You've got one less person to worry about. To mourn."

I shook my head. "He doesn't exist. I have no father."

Savannah let go of Ollie and squeezed between me and Gemma, putting her arm around me. "I'm sorry."

I shook her off. "Don't be. It doesn't matter. It's never mattered. I don't care. I don't need him. I never have. Mum was always enough."

Savannah was biting her thumbnail as she watched me. "It's okay to talk about this stuff."

"No, it isn't." I was almost shouting. I couldn't calm the rage inside my chest. I never had been able to. Not when people brought him up. "I told you. It doesn't matter."

"You might feel better?"

"There's nothing you can say that I haven't heard before.

Why are people obsessed with this?"

"I'm sorry, Zane. I'm just trying to understand. I just wanna understand."

"Why?" I had to stand. I had to move before I exploded. "We're all the same now, right? You said so yourself. Why does it matter?"

"He hurt you." Savannah's voice was quiet and seemed to ring out after my volume. "Didn't he?"

"No." I rubbed my hand over the back of my neck. "I couldn't care less. It's Mum, it's... How could he do that to her? He ran off before I was even born. How can I forgive him for that?"

"I don't know whether this will make it better or worse, but I'm going to say it anyway."

I met Savannah's honey-brown eyes.

"It wasn't her he was running away from. It was you."

I stared at her. "But he didn't hurt me. I never knew him. He hurt her. She's spent the last seventeen—eighteen—years of her life looking after me. Alone. She was seventeen." Before I even realised, I was looking to Gemma. Her mouth was curved down in a small frown, and there were tears in her eyes.

Callie. Callie was seventeen. Had been. Lisa was right after all. Like father, like son.

I sniffed the tears back into my heart and went over to the window, peeking through the boards, trying to forget. I had no face for the man Mum had been in love with. He was just a name to me. A reason to hate my middle name. A reason to hate my hair and eye colour. But the reason I was alive at all. I wasn't grateful for that. Mum's life would have been easier if I hadn't been in it. The same went for Callie. She would still be here, standing next to Gemma.

I used to want my father, my dad. I used to want him to appear at our front door. I wanted us to be a normal family.

I wanted to ride my bike with him, play football with him, catch, cards, board games, the whole lot. I wanted him to tuck me in at night. I wanted him to be proud of me. To love me the way Mum did.

Not any more. Now all I wanted was to forget him. To forget I'd ever wanted him. To forget he even existed at all. I'd meant what I'd said before.

I had no father.

Savannah crept over to me and kissed my cheek. Heat flared up the back of my neck.

"It doesn't matter." She gave me a squeeze, and I hugged her back. "We're your family now."

THIRTY-SEVEN

I found Mum curled up on the sofa under a duvet in one of the sitting rooms, out of breath, face pale.

"What is it?" I asked, trying to read her face.

"Oh, it's nothing." She waved it away. "Just reading…a scary book."

It looked nothing like a novel. It looked more like a notebook. It was pink with smiling fruit on the cover.

"What is that?" I sat next to her and buried myself in the duvet.

"A diary."

"Whose?"

"A girl who lived here. The one who…"

"Oh." I shuddered. "What does she say?"

"Lots of stuff. About her family's problems. About being shut in the house."

"So do you know who all the people were?"

"I think so. According to this, there were seven people living in this house after the outbreak and…"

"Seven bodies upstairs." My stomach rolled over. "So that means they weren't overrun?"

Mum looked at me for a moment before dragging her knees up closer as she read. I watched her as she turned the pages. When she reached the end, she flicked through to the back, looking for more words. She swallowed and passed it to me. Her hands were freezing as she touched mine.

"It's horrible." Her eyes were filling with tears.

I went to open the book, and she put her hand on top of mine, looking into my eyes for a moment.

"Are you sure you want to read that?"

I pressed my lips together, heart picking up pace. "I want to know what happened."

She nodded and kissed me on the forehead before standing. "I'll go and help them with the boards."

I watched her until she left, a shiver shooting up my spine. With a moment of hesitation, I turned the front page. The handwriting was neater than any I'd ever seen. It was curled, joined up, and slanted to one side. After flicking through the pages about school and her friends, I found what I was looking for.

Saturday, 4:30pm

This afternoon Mum and Dad made me go and sit in my room as they watched the news and listened to the radio. I know they're only trying to protect me, but it's no use. I know about Juvenile Virus, of course I do. It's all over the internet. People are posting videos of infected people taking down others and biting them. At first I didn't believe it, but they're everywhere.

I'm scared. What if one of them came to the house? What if one of them broke in? What if they bite me or Mum or Dad? I wouldn't know what to do without them.

Before they told me to go to my room, they told me they loved me. They told me everything was going to be okay. They told me not to worry.

But I can't think of anything they could have said to terrify me more.

*

7pm

Mum came to get me before dinner. Not one of us

ate even half our food. I wanted to ask about the virus, but I was too afraid. What if they told me everything I was terrified of hearing?

Dad told me I wouldn't be going to school on Monday. He said he wanted to make sure this was all over before we go anywhere near people.

I don't like this. There are always terrible diseases ravaging the country, but this one's different. This is the first time Mum and Dad have looked so pale. This is the first time they haven't made a joke about it.

The farmhouse is in the middle of nowhere. You have to drive over fifteen minutes to get anywhere. They're always complaining about it and then celebrating the fact we don't have to deal with irritating neighbours.

Usually we don't worry about epidemics. We don't live in a city, or anywhere near a city, but this is different.

Mum keeps looking out the window. At every noise, she jumps up.

I'm in the sitting room, watching their every move. Dad's calling Aunt Julie. He's trying to get them to come here.

Why?

Mum's so terrified someone's going to come up to the house. I want Aunt Julie, Uncle Owen, and Cousin Henry to be safe, but do they really have to come to the farmhouse? If Mum's so scared here, does that mean there's somewhere safer?

I don't know whether there'll be a safe place out there somewhere where they've prepared for a thing like this. There must be somewhere the Prime Minister will go. And the Queen. Would they let us in too? Would it be worth a try?

Or are we waiting for Aunt Julie, Uncle Owen, and Cousin Henry to head anywhere? Is Dad just making sure his sister's safe?

But are we any safer here than we would be anywhere else?

Maybe all this fuss is for nothing. Maybe we're just being those people Mum and Dad usually laugh at. We could be panicking for nothing.

I hope we are.

Either way, I won't sleep tonight.

Hollie Lucinda Mandeville.

Sunday, 6pm

Mum and Dad have seldom let me out of their sight all day. We even played board games together without Mum checking her phone or Dad getting an important call. It was almost nice.

It would have been if not for all the news reports.

I thought when I woke up that maybe it'd all been a bad dream. I don't want people to be rising from the dead like in some sort of horror film. But there's no escaping it. The dead are walking, groaning, coming to get us.

Mum still keeps checking the windows, but we haven't seen anyone yet. I hope we're too far removed. I hope we can hide out here until it's over.

If I wish it hard enough, will it happen?

Hollie Lucinda Mandeville.

Monday, 9pm

Cressida still hasn't called me back. I've left her phone calls and messages and emails and everything, but she hasn't replied to me. She usually takes all of five seconds to respond, but now there's silence.

I'm hoping her phone died or she dropped it or lost it or something. I can't think about what the alternative is. It's too scary.

I can't believe this is truly happening. It doesn't make sense.

How can the world have ended?

And so fast?

Hollie Lucinda Mandeville.

Tuesday, 1pm

Dad's trying to convince Aunt Julie to come here again. He said he doesn't know how long the power will stay on and how long they can remain in contact.

The power can't go out.

Can it?

Then what would we do?

Hollie Lucinda Mandeville.

Wednesday, 3pm

Aunt Julie was screeching when she arrived, towel wrapped around her arm, just below her elbow. She screamed about an 'Unpure' touching her. He had the nerve to bite her, that's how she put it. She wailed and cried about how she couldn't go to the hospital because they were overrun with 'Unpures'.

Uncle Owen, Cousin Henry, and Isla—Uncle Owen's sister—all piled in behind her. The only one who took any notice of me was Isla, who winked and ruffled my hair as she followed the rest of them upstairs.

Nothing Dad or Uncle Owen could say calmed Aunt Julie down. She just wouldn't be quiet. I stood against the wall, watching them rush around her like she was so used to. I don't know how Dad grew up with her. I don't know how anyone could live with her. I don't know how one person can view herself so highly above all others.

All others except Cousin Henry.

Cousin Henry had his normal face of disgust on as he leant in the doorframe, crossing his arms, observing the situation as though it was beneath him. As if it didn't matter to him one jot that his mother had been bitten by what I suppose we're calling an '*Unpure*'.

Did it not dawn on him that she was going to die? No one had survived the virus from what I knew. Did it not bother him? Not even a little?

I've never really liked Aunt Julie, but I can't imagine a world without her in it. Who else will boss everyone around? Who else will Dad make fun of to cheer the house up?

How can she be dying?

It doesn't make any sense.

Hollie Lucinda Mandeville.

Thursday, 11am

I can hear Isla snoring from the next room. It's almost like she's here in bed with me. And when she wakes up, she feels no need to be quiet. This morning she was humming to herself and singing with no regard for how little sleep I got last night. Then, just when I thought everything was going to stay quiet, she fell asleep and started snoring again.

I always dreamt of having a sister, but now I take it back.

*

8:30pm

I was wrong. The electric can go out. Now I have to write by candlelight.

I would write more but I can't seem to stop crying.

Hollie Lucinda Mandeville.

Friday, 5:45pm

An Unpure came up to the house this afternoon. I'd never seen one in real life until now. Its skin was falling away and ripped and blue and black and red. It had blood dribbling down its mouth, and it growled like an animal, lashing out at the windows.

Dad, Uncle Owen, and Isla grabbed baseball bats and cricket bats and other 'weapons' from the garage. Their faces were grave when they rushed out there.

I couldn't look. But I could hear.

I heard the crunch, the crack, the squelch.

And I only just held my stomach.

Hollie Lucinda Mandeville.

Saturday, 9:30pm

Aunt Julie called me a fool today. And a stupid girl. And a waste of space.

All I did was bring her a glass of water. I was just going to keep her company. It's not my fault Cousin Henry tripped me as I made my way into the biggest guest bedroom.

She wouldn't listen to me of course.

As if Henry Owen Bartholomew Pennington could do wrong.

She's blind if she thinks her son has any redeeming qualities whatsoever.

So far, the worst thing that's happened in this so called zombie apocalypse is the Penningtons coming to the farmhouse. At least the Unpures don't call me names.

Hollie Lucinda Mandeville.

Sunday, 8:45pm

Cressida used to joke about making a hit list, but I'm considering making one in her honour. First up, Henry Pennington. Second, Julie Pennington.

Today Henry told me my hair looked stupid and gross. Not that his looked any better. I thought my hair looked pretty today considering there was no hot water to wash it, but now every time I catch a look in the mirror, I hate myself.

I know it shouldn't matter, especially now. I know it's stupid. I know I shouldn't care what he thinks, but I can't help myself.

I spent the rest of the day thinking of something to hurt him back, but he doesn't care about anything enough to get hurt. Not his parents, not his looks, not his friends. I've never seen him get emotional about anything.

It shouldn't surprise me that to live with Aunt Julie you have to be a robot.

Hollie Lucinda Mandeville.

Wednesday, 10pm

I'm sorry I haven't written anything for a while. Everyone's been watching Aunt Julie. They were kidding themselves it wasn't the virus, but of course it is. She was bitten. The man on the news had said that if you get bitten you get the virus one hundred percent of the time. How can you argue with one hundred percent?

Well, now she's shivering and vomiting and has an outrageous fever, they finally believe that this is it. This truly is it.

Uncle Owen won't leave her side. Cousin Henry seems unruffled about the whole thing. But the more I watch him, the more he seems to be twitching. He can't hold that sarcastic smile as long. Or maybe I've stopped believing it.

He snaps at me if I bring up the virus or the Unpures.

He's cracking. And I feel like an awful person because I'm pleased.

Hollie Lucinda Mandeville.

Friday, 7:15pm

Today Aunt Julie has given up the will to fight. She can't sit up any more. She's lost all energy to scold.

That scares me more than the Unpure that came to the window to see what all the fuss was about.

They moved her into the master bedroom today as that was one of the things she'd been complaining about. Not that she seemed to care any more anyway. Why would what room she was in matter to her? Why would anything matter to her any more?

I feel like I should be writing more. Like I should be attempting to make a note of every little thing that's happening. It seems the world is stuck in this horrific apocalypse, and someone should know what happened.

But who?

Is it stupid of me to think that writing in my journal could help future generations? Who would I help exactly? Everyone would know about the Unpures. They would know people got bitten, got sick, and died. I wouldn't be telling anyone anything they didn't already know.

So why am I bothering to write at all? Because I always have? Seems stupid now. I used to write about Cressida and Mum and Dad and school and stupid things. Things that didn't actually matter.

The truth is, I'm writing this to stay alive. If someone picks up my words and reads them, I'll be alive somewhere, whatever happens.

I am Hollie Lucinda Mandeville. I'm thirteen years old. I'm an only child. My best friend is Cressida Atwood-Jenson. I hate most of my family. I love my parents more than anyone. I'm the daughter of Andrew Laurence Mandeville, heir of Mandeville Farmhouse. My mother, Nicole Johanna Parker, met my father at university. She didn't know he was rich. He didn't know she grew up on a council estate. They fell in love in a month. Were married the year after. My paternal grandparents have never liked my mother and by extension, me. My maternal grandparents treat me like a princess. My Aunt Julie and Uncle Owen don't care I exist. I've seldom ever seen all the cousins on my mother's side. She's one of five brothers and sisters.

Mandeville Farmhouse is the only place I have ever lived. I know if the apocalypse hadn't struck, I would have most likely continued to live here my whole life. Unless I married a man who already had a big house. Not that my parents encouraged such things. My dream life included moving in a boyfriend here and all living under one roof together until my parents wanted to move on, which I knew they did.

My children would have inherited the farmhouse after me, and our reign of rich-common Englishmen would have continued forever and ever.

I can't see that happening now. The best I can hope for is not having to leave my home. I've still got my fingers crossed this all goes away. Every night, I climb into bed convincing myself it will all be over when I wake up.

One of these days, that might happen.

Or one of these days, we'll all be dead.

Hollie x

Saturday, 7:30am

It's happening. She's dying. Mum shouted us from downstairs, and Cousin Henry threw plates and mugs and things, yelling obscenities like I'd never heard before.

I guess he does care after all.

We're all standing round, watching her. She hasn't been conscious all day, and her breaths are getting shallower. I don't know why everyone's adamant we all watch.

I don't want to watch someone die.

Henry's on the bed, crying into his mother's arms. Uncle Owen is on her other side, stroking her hair. Isla's standing next to her brother, watching him more than her sister-in-law. She's got a cricket bat in her hand, and no one seems to be questioning her. I know Henry has a gun. He's pointed at me sixteen times since he's been here, but I can't see it now. Maybe it wasn't real.

Mum and Dad are sitting with me on the chaise-longue. Mum's gripping my left hand tighter and tighter. Dad's telling me to put my journal away.

I've escaped the room for now. I'm going to have to take big deep breaths before I go back in there. I'm going to have to hold back my tears.

I'm going to have to… Oh gosh, I don't even know.

Wish me luck.

Hollie x

I did what Mum did, flicking through the back pages, longing for more of Hollie Mandeville's words. It was trickling into my consciousness bit by bit that the people in the diary had been the ones lying on the floor in that room. I'd seen each of their faces. I'd heard one of them scream.

My entire body was cold as my eyes swept the room. I was sitting on one of her sofas in one of her sitting rooms reading her diary. A diary that she'd written in just two days ago.

And this morning I'd helped bury her corpse.

THIRTY-EIGHT

It took another whole day to cover the windows of Mandeville Farmhouse, and then we found ourselves idle for the first time since leaving Ashford House. I left everyone in the living room playing cards and explored the rooms upstairs.

The room Savannah and Aniya were sharing had white furniture and pistachio-coloured walls. I assumed it was the guest bedroom Hollie had mentioned in her diary. It didn't make sense that her aunt and uncle had been sleeping in this room only a few days ago, and now they were dead. As I walked across the landing, I felt ghosts whispering, and I hugged my arms tighter over my chest.

I let myself into the room Mum was sleeping in, shutting the door behind me. The walls were a light pink colour and again, the furniture was white. The bed was a four-poster with pink, sparkly, delicate curtains draped from the corners. There was a jewellery box on the dressing table, the diary sitting on top of it. On the wall above the bed were white letters spelling out *PRINCESS HOLLIE*.

I sat down and watched myself in the mirror, wondering how many times Hollie had sat there. As I went to open one of the drawers, the bracelet Callie made me got caught. I swore, jumping back, rubbing my wrist.

Before I could think, tears were blurring my eyes, and I fell down onto Hollie's bed, sobbing. I pulled the pillow closer to drown out my howling. I couldn't hold it in any longer.

Callie.

Her name went round and round in my head until I was dizzy.

Callie, Callie, Callie, Callie, Callie.

Why was I still here and she gone? What made me so special that I was still fighting? What was I even supposed to do now? Keep moving from place to place, meeting survivors, and watching people die? Why? For what?

I sniffed and pulled the pillow closer, trying to regain control. I held my breaths until my lungs stopped stuttering, and my head cleared.

She'd told me once that nothing could be created and nothing could be destroyed. Everything in the universe was made up of all the things there have ever been. Nothing's new and nothing's gone forever. Then where did she go? If nothing's gone forever?

But something dark inside told me that no matter what people said—she's in the flowers, the breeze, the sunlight— she was gone forever. And I was still here. Alone.

I wiped my eyes and sat up, leaning my back against the headboard, pulling my knees up to my chest.

"What would you do?" I whispered the words, not trusting my voice and feeling stupid. "If you were me and I was you, what would you do now?"

I shook my head and shut my eyes. But all I could see was her face, and it killed me. But for some reason, I couldn't wrench open my eyes again. Maybe if I believed it hard enough she'd reappear. Maybe if I wished hard enough. Maybe...

Another wave of tears took me by surprise, and I choked, gagging on my own sorrow. I had to take a few panicked breaths to steady myself.

I didn't want this to still be real. I was done. Wrung out. Used. Defeated. I wanted someone to take it back. *Please, please take it back. Please stop.* Why wouldn't it stop?

I had to hold my breaths and count them in and out to calm the raging of my heart. I didn't want downstairs to hear.

I didn't want their sympathy. I didn't want to hear one more time that it wasn't my fault. Because it was.

"Zane?"

I rubbed my eyes and cleared my throat as Aniya opened the door. She sat next to me on the bed, watching me for a moment.

"Are you all right?"

"Yeah." My voice scratched in my throat, and there was no bigger lie in the universe.

"Savannah said she told you about Joel?"

It was all I could do to nod.

"And she told me about Callie."

Her name sounded so wrong coming out of Aniya's lips, so soft and gentle, like she was a child.

"I'm so sorry."

I had to cough past what was left of the tears in my mouth. "S'all right." It was anything but, and she knew it.

"I..." She fiddled with her necklace. "I know what it feels like." She looked to the ceiling like she was waiting for some eternal knowledge to fall on her head.

"It's okay. You don't have to say anything. I was just..." Just what? I didn't even know. "Just losing it. I didn't mean for anyone to come looking for me."

"I came up for something, and I heard you." She looked straight into my eyes, searching for something there instead of the ceiling. What she could want from me, I couldn't imagine. "I couldn't leave you."

"I'm all right." Maybe if I kept saying it out loud it would become true.

"It's okay not be all right. No one's asking you to be perfectly happy. You don't have to hide up here."

"I don't want them to see."

She nodded. "Me neither." She wiped away a tear on her face so fast I wondered if I'd made it up.

"Were you close to him? Joel?"

"No. He was Savannah's best friend. Everyone was Savannah's best friend." She gave a tiny smile and unfastened her necklace, squeezing it tight in her fingers, before passing it to me.

The metal was hot in my hands, and I just looked at it.

Aniya watched me for a few long seconds before explaining. "It's a locket."

Inside were two of the smallest photos I'd ever seen. On the left-hand side, there were two boys with the same almond skin as Aniya, their arms around each other. The taller one looked about my age, and the smaller one looked to be maybe ten. On the other side, there was a handsome man with perfect stubble. My hand brushed against my chin to feel the nothingness there. It'd been more than a week since I'd thought about it, and even so, there wasn't much going on. In the old world, I'd shaved because I'd felt it was something I was supposed to do. In the ZA, it felt like a waste of time.

When I looked up, Aniya was pressing her mouth shut so tight her lips were going pale. She pulled in a breath that caught on the way in.

"Are they your family?"

Her eyes dropped to the locket, and I felt like I could breathe again. "These two are my brothers. Samien and Nasir." She rubbed over the photo like she could still reach them. "They were everything."

I gazed at the locket again, unsure what she wanted me to say.

"If Savannah hadn't been there, I don't think I would've had the strength to leave."

"I'm so sorry," I said, because that's what we all said to each other.

"It's terrible, isn't it? Not being able to do anything for them?"

I put my arm around her. She squeezed me back with a strength I didn't think she possessed. Her tears soaked into my T-shirt, and she clung to me tighter and tighter. Sitting there like that, stroking her hair, I could almost pretend she was Callie. Almost.

When her chest stopped juddering up and down, she didn't let go. She sat curled in my arms like we were more to each other than we were. It didn't matter. Stuff like that didn't matter in this new world.

"You remind me of him," she said, breaking the comfortable silence. "Sam. I would do anything to have him back. He was my best friend. We did everything together. And when I look at you, a part of me hopes it's him."

I continued to hold her, letting her pretend whatever it was she wanted to pretend. Who was I to tell her he was gone? Who was I to tell her how to grieve?

"The other one's Khalil." She pulled away to look at the locket again, this time at the man with the impeccable stubble. "My fiancé."

I nodded past all the questions that popped into my head, biting my tongue.

"My parents gave me the locket. They chose the pictures. They didn't know about Savannah. Nobody did. I don't know what happened to Khalil. I can only hope he's all right."

"Maybe he is."

She nodded and closed the locket, bringing it close to her heart.

"You're lucky you have the photos."

She shook her head. "It's stupid. I was so worried about making a decision. So worried about whose heart I was going to break and now…"

"Everything's different now."

She was looking deep into my eyes. "Don't tell Savannah. About the picture, I mean. She'd take it the wrong way. I didn't love him like that. He's one of my oldest friends. But she doesn't know what it's like. She wouldn't understand."

234

"Of course. I won't say a word."

We sat in silence again until something bubbled up inside my chest. I didn't know whether it was the room, or the company I was keeping, or the talk of the dead, but I had to let it out.

"Callie was pregnant."

Aniya only stared at me.

"And she didn't tell me. Not until it was too late."

"Oh, Zane."

"And I hate myself because I'm so *angry*."

"It's okay to be angry."

"How could she hide something like that from me? If things had been different and the world hadn't ended, we would be expecting a baby. A *baby*." My heart was doing great powerful leaps, making it hard to breathe.

Aniya only repeated herself. "It's okay."

"Before, before she…" I couldn't say it. "She told me about the future we were supposed to have. Why would she tell me that? I have to live with knowing what I could've had. Instead, the world ended, the dead are walking the streets, and every day I blame myself. I must be in hell."

I didn't realise I was crying until I couldn't see through my tears. I didn't want to see. I rubbed the bracelet back and forth over my wrist, concentrating only on the graze of it against my skin. But even so, I couldn't fight the images that pounced on top of me.

Callie's gorgeous smile. The way her hair danced in the light. When she kissed me and made me feel like the luckiest man in the world.

And now I was half a man, and she was gone. And I had to realise what that meant every day.

"It's okay to feel like that. At least you didn't have to… finish it."

"But I did."

Her chocolate-brown eyes devoured me. "You had to…?"

I swallowed. "Yeah."

"Me too."

She threw herself into my arms again, and just like that we were both crying, she filling Callie's space and me filling Sam's.

For now, all we had to do was survive the ZA. But then… then what? Part of me wanted all this to end so I could put effort in to mourning Callie. I could look through photos and listen to songs she'd loved and watch films she'd loved. I could read her schoolwork and run my hand over the pages where her hand had sat. I could go through her wardrobe and cuddle with her jumpers and lose myself in her smell. I could think back on every memory we'd shared together.

But the other half of me was too terrified. If this thing ended, I would have to come face to face with my worst fear: a life without her. I would have to learn to carry on. I would have to learn to live and breathe knowing she was gone. I would have to figure it out somehow. I would have to work out how to live with myself, knowing I'd fought monsters and demons. I would have to learn how to fall asleep and stay asleep at night. I would have to teach myself to sleep alone, without Gemma on the sofa opposite me. I would have to live with my own thoughts.

But I knew what was expected in this new life. We needed shelter, food, and weapons, and that was all. Surviving was easy if all you had to think about was survival. This world was starting to make sense to me, but the old world was becoming a mystery.

Even with the dangers we faced every day, I wasn't sure I was ready for this to be over. I wasn't sure I was ready to have a comfy bed, a hot meal in front of me, running water, and electricity. If I had all that, it meant the world had turned itself around. And I wasn't sure I was ready to learn how to live with myself after the ZA.

THIRTY-NINE

Gemma leant up against the kitchen counter and shut her eyes, the smell of coffee hanging in the air. "You know, the day the coffee runs out is the day the apocalypse really starts."

"Armageddon."

She rolled her eyes. "Armageddon then."

"You know Jay would kill you if he saw you using water like that?"

"I can do whatever I like with my water rations. This is about the only thing that makes me feel normal any more. I've already decided that when the gas eventually stops, I'll mourn."

"You'll just have to make a fire."

The moment the word escaped my lips, there was a squeal of delight from the garden, and the two of us rushed to the window to take a look. Jay, Ollie, Savannah, and Aniya were all gathering round a small bundle of smoking sticks and leaves.

"What are they doing out there?"

I shook my head. Gemma went back to her saucepan of coffee.

Outside, Ollie was lying on the ground, face far too close to the would-be fire. After a few long seconds of them all standing still, the fire caught, and they jumped up and hugged each other.

"Why are they making a fire?" I asked.

"Why do they do anything? They're just gonna have to put it out before dark. We don't want the house burning down. I'm not sure I could handle another disaster right now. The Infected are enough."

When Gemma had poured her coffee into a mug, we shrugged our coats on and headed outside to see what all the fuss was about.

They'd stopped hugging each other and were all crowded round the fire like it was a toddler taking its first steps.

"Hey, guys." Savannah spotted us first. "Look what we've made."

"A mess," Gemma said. "Congrats."

"We've moved up a rung in history. We are now equal to cavemen."

"Great. What's next? A pyramid?"

"Why did you make a fire?" I cut in before Savannah could think of a response.

"Gotta know how," Ollie said. "It's a basic survival skill. We were just showing Jay."

"How hard is it?" Gemma scoffed. "We had fire when we were at your camp. Anyway, we've got matches. Are we expecting the ZA to bring us another blow, the famine of lighters?"

"Well, *Gemma*, it pays to be prepared."

Gemma narrowed her eyes at Savannah and continued to drink her coffee.

"Anyway, we might attract other survivors."

"Or the Infected."

"No," Jay said. "I don't think so. In all my research, I never found anything to suggest the Infected follow smoke to find people. The Infected rely on their hearing. The only thing they seem to follow with their eyes are humans."

"Are you telling me that if I stood still, an Infected would walk right by me?" Gemma asked.

"Well, no. I don't think they're that stupid."

"Hey!"

We all turned at the sound of Aniya's voice. She whacked Ollie's arm, and a cigarette jumped to the ground.

"You said you'd given up."

"I did."

Savannah picked it up off the ground. "What's this then?"

"A celebration."

"Are you serious? You're such a liar, Oliver."

"Don't 'Oliver' me. I gave up. But what the hell's the worst that could happen now?" He took out another and tried to light it over the fire without burning his fingers before giving up and pulling out a lighter. He offered the packet to Gemma when he was done.

"I'm offended."

"Just being polite." He blew smoke away from the group and offered the packet to me.

"No thanks. I sort of need my lungs to run."

He rolled his eyes. "It's the—what is it?"

"ZA," Jay finished for him.

"Yeah. ZA. None of that stuff matters now."

"Still rather die of an Armageddon caused death rather than some lung disease," Gemma said.

"Suit yourself."

"I'm disappointed in you, Oliver." Savannah put her hands on her hips.

"Fine." He moved a few footsteps away. We all watched as he finished his cigarette and stamped it into the ground. "Your wish is my command, Miss Clements." Without another word, he turned and disappeared into the house.

For some reason, Savannah had a smirk on her lips. "I knew it. Such a liar."

We stood round the fire for a while, Savannah chatting about how she wished she'd never taken her job at the makeup counter. How she wished she'd gone for it with her acting career. I wasn't sure anyone was listening. Gemma drank her coffee, Jay played with the fire, Aniya looked at me, and I tried not to be too awkward.

"I mean," she said after an immeasurable stretch of time. "The idea of not being something is terrifying. Is that stupid?"

I blinked and looked up from the fire, breaking its hypnotic hold over me, feeling the chill of the air for the first time. "No. It's not stupid. I know what you mean."

Savannah looked to Aniya. "See. He gets me."

"Shut up!" The sound exploded out of Jay, and my body jumped up. "Listen!"

I strained my ears, but all I could hear was the crackling of the fire, which was dying a slow but dignified death. But then I heard it. Footsteps.

"People!" Savannah's smile was big and wide and identical to the one she'd given us when we'd first met. That felt like a lifetime ago now.

"I don't know about this," Jay said.

"You weren't sure about us."

"I stand by it."

Savannah wandered over to the end of the garden and peeked through the conifer trees. Aniya followed after her, and it wasn't long before my curiosity convinced me to take a look too.

"This is stupid," Jay whispered as he appeared behind me. "We can't just invite any old nobody in."

"Exactly," Savannah said. "I reiterate. The idea of not being something is terrifying."

It was difficult to see through the dense branches, but there, in the distance, were three figures walking this way.

Gemma pulled her face out of the tree. "They're not human."

"How can you tell?"

A voice sounded from behind us. "What the hell are you all doing now?"

I removed my head from the branches to face Ollie as he walked this way, holding a baseball bat and a tennis ball. There was something off about the hard line of his mouth.

"There are people out there," Savannah said.

He grabbed her arm and yanked her out of the tree. "Are you mad?"

She snatched her arm back. "What? We've got strength in numbers."

He shook his head. "No, we don't. People are stupid and dangerous."

"No, they're not. And what if they need rescuing?"

"And what if they do?"

She took a step back. "Well, we got rescued."

"That wasn't our mistake."

The silence of voices swallowed us up. All that filled the void was the fire crackling and the trees creaking in the breeze.

Ollie spoke first, staring hard at Savannah. "I'm not trusting total strangers. You never know what people's real objectives are."

She stared right back. "Sometimes people are only trying to do what's best."

"And other times they're not."

"Hey." Gemma stood between them. "Is there something going on here?"

They both ignored her, neither breaking eye contact.

"Savannah?" Aniya slipped her hand into Savannah's. "Come on. Stop it."

Savannah shook her head. "You're not the boss of everyone, Ollie."

Ollie let out one big, loud hoot, and then there was silence again. "You can talk."

"Right." Gemma stepped in again. "Whatever the hell is going on here between you two needs to stop right now."

They still didn't take their eyes off each other.

"I'm pretty sure it's just a few Infected, and we're drawing them here by talking. End of discussion. Anyway, we're a democracy. We would've voted on the matter."

Ollie switched his gaze to Gemma. "And what if we hadn't had enough time to vote? What if they'd had guns? What if they'd wanted to steal from us? Or worse?"

Gemma crossed her arms. "What TV show do you live in? I believe in the human spirit. There are plenty of Infected and not a lot of us. We've got to fight this together. And what guns?" She chuckled. It sounded wrong in the air.

Ollie stared at Gemma for a few seconds more, before he made a sort of growling noise, turned, and raced for the gate in the corner of the garden. Jay went to take off after him, but Savannah grabbed his shoulder.

"Don't."

We all pressed our faces into the trees again as Ollie exploded into the field, sprinting towards the Infected. He flung his baseball bat back and smashed it into the nearest one's head, knocking it straight to the floor. At once he was on the next one, and I could hear him grunting every time he made impact. In a matter of minutes, all three Infected were dead, and Ollie stormed back into the garden covered in blood. He didn't look at us as he marched inside.

FORTY

Life in Mandeville Farmhouse took on a bizarre routine I hadn't expected from the ZA. We started each day by sitting round the huge dining table, eating half a can of whatever we were lucky enough to have for breakfast. Then we checked our boards and weapons and rucksacks, making sure everything was in its place. Once everything was as it should be, we played a game we invented. It involved balancing a cricket ball on a platform and whacking it as far as possible. When it wasn't my turn, I jogged back and forth, stretching my legs. I felt more human for it, more alive.

When it rained, we had to occupy ourselves inside. Jay tried to make sense of maps he found in the study. Savannah tested out Hollie's makeup, painting the girls' nails. They all scavenged the bookcases for something to read. I read nothing but Hollie's diary, reaching the end only to go back to the first page and continue.

We talked about our lives before like they didn't belong to us. Gemma complained about stupid things that didn't matter any more. Ollie talked about his older brothers as though they were someplace safe. Savannah talked about her acting career like she was weeks away from a big break. Aniya spoke of her family as though they were waiting for her back home, but she never mentioned her fiancé. Jay never joined us for these talks. He just listened in, head in a list or a map or a plan.

As the sun went down, we gathered in the living room under blankets and duvets and told jokes and stories. On the menu for dinner was another half a can of food. After that, we played cards until we disappeared, one by one, off to bed. Or sofa in the case of Gemma and I. Mum and Lisa had offered to share to free up a bed, but that would leave one of us down here by ourselves. I didn't know about Gemma, but I didn't know how to be by myself any more.

Life was simple. Not easy, but better. It even brought a little bit of light back into Jay's eyes.

I pulled my hood up as I shuffled into the kitchen one morning, dropping my head into my arms and shutting my eyes again.

"Just over a week," Mum's voice said from the pantry. "But that's it? There's nothing else?"

"Nope," Savannah said. "That's it. Aniya's looked everywhere. They don't seem to have a secret stash unfortunately."

"What are we going to do? There's nothing for miles. Not unless we go back towards the sea."

"Where there are thousands of Corpses."

"But." I picked Lisa's voice out too. "We need to move on. We can't stay here just because it's safe. We'll starve to death."

"Unless some of us go?" Savannah suggested. "And some stay?"

"No." Mum's voice was strong. "No. We can't split up. We're only strong in numbers. We can't have half go off and maybe never come back. The others would never know what happened. No. We can't do that. I couldn't..."

"I agree," Lisa said. "We all go together. We're a team. We don't split up."

I lifted my head and stared at the doorframe of the pantry.

"Shouldn't we, I dunno, have a vote on this? That's what we do, right?" When there was no answer, Savannah spoke again. "Right. I'll rally the troops." She grinned as she appeared out of the pantry and spotted me. "Morning, Zaney. Gem in the land of the living yet?"

"Yeah, you wish."

"Well, I guess I'll go wake her up. We're having a vote in the living room."

"I heard."

But she was already gone, singsonging as she went. I could hear Gemma groaning.

I shoved her up when I made my way into the living room. She gave me a death glare before shuffling closer to the arm of the sofa, hiding Puddle under the duvet. Pulling the covers round my shoulders, I shot her a grin. Jay collapsed onto one of the sofas, cocooned in his duvet, and refused to budge up when Ollie went to sit next to him. Aniya, Mum, and Lisa entered the room and sat themselves down, Savannah standing between two of the sofas, looking at each of us.

"So it turns out we have a situation, guys. We knew it was going to happen at some point, and that time is upon us. We think we have about a week's worth of food left. Now no one wants to leave here. It's safe and warm and familiar now. But we need more food. And I suggest now's the time to move. If we leave it any longer, we won't have enough to travel with. We've got the cars now, so it should be easier. We can always come back here. So we need a vote. Who wants to go find food?"

Everyone raised their hands without question.

"The bigger problem is where?" Savannah sat on the arm of one of the sofas. "The seafront will likely have more food but more Corpses. But we can't guarantee finding food if we head in any other direction."

"There'll be shops or restaurants or something," Gemma cut in. "We may be in the middle of nowhere, but we don't need to find somewhere tomorrow, just before the week's out."

"Do we want to die of starvation or infection?" Jay's voice was dark, and I struggled to drag my eyes off him.

"Or..." Ollie ruffled Jay's hair. "Do we want to fight the

Corpses or fight to find food? I know I'd rather move *away* from the busy areas."

"Me too." I put my hand up.

Mum nodded. "And me."

Lisa and Aniya looked to each other and raised their hands also.

Gemma ran her hand through her hair. "Good shout. Away from the Infected is always the best plan. So when are we off then?"

"Today." Savannah tied up her long hair. She'd laughed at Gemma's suggestion to cut it. "Whenever you're ready."

Everyone dispersed to gather their things, and when Gemma returned, fully dressed, she ran her hand over the back of the sofa she'd been sleeping on.

"I'm gonna miss this house. I know it wasn't as perfect as it could've been, but it was pretty great. I've never seen a place like this."

"I didn't know people living in these places really existed," I said.

"This is what we're going to get, a place like this."

"What do you mean?"

"When we survive this. Our reward will be fantastic houses we wouldn't have owned in our wildest dreams. I mean, it's only fair really."

We each did a sweep of the house before gathering on the driveway, shuffling our feet backwards and forwards against the gravel, waiting for Ollie and Jay to make their way round the front in the Aston Martin.

"I'd rather not drive if that's all right?" Lisa was holding out the keys to Michael's car. "I'll go with Jen."

My heart jumped, and I raised my hand. "I'll drive it." A thrill was pulsing round my blood at the notion. I hadn't realised I'd missed driving.

Lisa gave me a small closed mouth smile and passed them over. I hooked the key ring around my finger and squeezed the keys in my hand over and over again.

"I'll keep him company." Gemma elbowed me in the ribs as we made our way over to the car.

Mum, Lisa, Savannah, and Aniya headed over to what I assumed was the Penningtons' red Jaguar.

Savannah had the cricket bat resting on her shoulder. "Farewell, farmhouse. Hope to meet again."

They all climbed in and shut the doors, Gemma and I jumping into Michael's car. I ran my hand over the steering wheel for a moment, taking a long, slow breath, before putting the key in the ignition and feeling the roar of the engine as I pressed my foot on the accelerator. I grinned big and wide. I couldn't help it.

Gemma was smirking at me when I turned to her.

"What?"

"Nothing. I just wouldn't have pegged you as an adrenaline junkie."

I shrugged. "What can I say? I'm afraid it comes with the job description."

Her eyebrows came together.

"A hundred metre sprinter."

"Oh right." She sat back in her seat as we watched Ollie and Jay take the lead.

"Anyway, what were your plans?"

"Plans?" she scoffed. "I didn't have plans. Not like you did. Which I guess sucks for you but not so much for me. None of my plans have been ruined, and now I don't have to think about them."

"You're talking as if this is never gonna be over."

Her eyes met mine, and silence filled the car for a moment. "We've got to consider the fact that maybe this is all there is."

I shook my head.

"It might be. We don't know. How much effort will it take to clear this mess up, and how many hands do we have left to do it? I'm not saying for certain we're doomed to travel round the country searching for food and killing the Infected, but it's a possibility, and I'm not just gonna pretend it's not there."

After another bout of silence, she continued.

"And anyway, who's to say it has to be all bad?"

"Not all bad? There are dead bodies getting up and walking about. We're having to hunt for food. TV and the internet and our phones are all gone."

"But you know what else is gone? Homework. Exams. Stupid bus timetables. Rush hour. Busy supermarkets." She chuckled. "Bad signal or lack of Wi-Fi will never be a problem ever again. That's pretty special."

"Whatever happened to *'I'm not saying for certain we're doomed'*?"

"You think the first thing we'll set up is fantastic phone service? What about hospitals and farms?"

My stomach squeezed at my evil thought, but my heart gave a sick kick. "You know what'll be easier when the world starts again?"

"What's that?"

"Getting into the Olympics."

"That's the spirit." She clutched her stomach as she giggled. "And who knows, maybe I'll get in."

Gemma tapped her fingers on the window and drew patterns where her breath had steamed it up. Outside it had started raining, and the wipers were creating a gentle beat.

"I'm bored now." She turned to me.

"You don't have to stay here. You can go squeeze between Savannah and Aniya."

"No thanks." She stretched her arms above her head and fell back into the seat. "I'm not sure I can stand many more of Savannah's stories." She snapped her fingers and sat up again. "I have a game."

I raised my eyebrows at her. "I don't know if I like the sound of it already."

"Oh, come on. You'll love it. It's fun."

"All right, fine. What is it?"

"Snog, marry, avoid."

"No." I laughed. "No way. We are *not* playing that."

"Why not? It'll be great. Snog, marry, avoid is always entertaining. Even now. Come on. You can go first."

"No."

"What? You're saying you want to play the other version instead? I was going for light-hearted but…"

"All right, all right."

"Excellent. You're going first."

"Oh yay."

"Savannah, Aniya, and Lisa."

I rolled my eyes. "I'm shocked."

"Come on. Play the game."

I pressed my lips together as I considered it.

"I already know who you're gonna pick," she said.

"How?"

"Duh. I know you."

"You think you know me that well?"

"I think I know you too well. Now pick."

"All right," I said. "I'd avoid Lisa."

"Knew it."

"Snog Aniya."

"Yep."

"And marry Savannah."

"Course you would. You're all about blondes, aren't you?"

I grinned. "Not necessarily."

"Are you sure you could put up with her big mouth?"

"I put up with you, don't I?"

"Oh burn. I'm so hurt. You guys would be divorced in like two weeks."

"Considering I'm not exactly Savannah's type, I don't think she'd marry me at all."

Gemma sniggered. "Come on. My go."

"Jay, Ollie, and I guess me."

She stuck out her tongue. "You cannot be serious. Jay's fourteen."

"Just play the damn game."

"All right, all right. On the basis of yuck, I'd avoid Jay."

I nodded. "Good choice."

"And now I'm not sure. I mean, on the one hand, you're extremely irritating, and I could never marry you. But on the other hand, if you think you can put up with Savannah's big mouth, you could definitely put up with mine so…" She tipped her hands like scales. "Yeah. I'd marry you and snog Ollie."

I couldn't help the smirk that fell on my lips. Something in me was pleased, but I wasn't sure why. "Why wouldn't you marry Ollie?"

"I don't think he could handle me." She winked. "Now if we're playing *this* game, I ask you the same question as before but with Lisa replaced with me."

I shook my head at her.

"Changes everything, right? I knew it."

"Do you know what I'm gonna pick now?"

"Not a clue. Surprise me."

Something tight and hot gripped my insides. I tried to ignore it with a joke. "If I avoid you, will you still keep me company?"

She crossed her arms. "That depends if you really mean it."

Her mouth had a crooked edge to it that was making the

squeezing worse. She watched me for a few minutes, and I was aware of nothing but her eyes on me.

"Come on then. Make your choice."

"I'd avoid Aniya."

"Why?"

"She's so quiet. I don't know what she's thinking." And I was afraid our combined grief would swallow us whole.

"Too afraid of the silent treatment?"

"I guess."

"Maybe that's why you'd go for Savannah."

My mouth didn't so much as twitch. "I'd snog…"

"The suspense is *killing* me."

I sighed. "Savannah. And marry you." I met her eyes, and her face wasn't as sarcastic as I'd imagined and hoped.

"Really?" Her voice was too quiet. "Why?"

I looked away. "You're my best friend. I don't know what I'd do without you any more. I don't want you to go anywhere. I guess it makes sense. If I had to condemn anyone to a life by my side, I think it'd have to be you."

She chewed on her lip. "The world really is different now, huh? Nothing's the same as it was before. Everything, *everything* is different now."

"I'm sorry." I tried to shake the unease away. "This was supposed to be fun."

"Such a buzzkill." She was smirking again, and the heavy air in the car vanished. "It's your go again. We've kinda run out of people here. What about mine? Answer that."

"Jay, Ollie, and myself? Really?"

"Come on, Carlisle. It's just a game."

"Well, I can't choose Jay, can I?"

"Because yuck."

"Exactly. So I'm gonna have to avoid him and—this is nasty."

"It's supposed to be. Come on, admit it. You want to marry yourself, don't you?"

I pressed my lips together. "A little bit. I'm not sure I could spend my whole life with Ollie."

"Just for a little snogging." She was grinning big and wide. When our eyes met, she burst into a wave of giggling that came around again every time I thought it was over.

"Why's this so hilarious?"

She wiped her eyes, shaking her head. "I have no idea."

"All right, your turn. Savannah, Aniya, and yourself."

She ran her tongue over her teeth. "You know, I think I'd marry Aniya."

"Yeah?"

"Yeah. She's harmless and sweet. Savannah and I would definitely end up killing each other."

"Shame. You two have chemistry."

She whacked me on the arm. "That being said, I'd snog her. I could probably do it on a dare. There's no denying that girl's hot."

"Wait." My eyebrows came together. "You'd avoid yourself?"

"Yeah."

"Why?"

"Just because you'd marry me doesn't mean I'd want to. And we can't all be as self-obsessed as you are."

"Gem?" When I looked over, her mouth was drooping down.

"I couldn't spend eternity in my own presence. I just couldn't. I don't think I'm all that."

"Shut up." I shot a smirk her way. "You're great. You know you are."

"Do I?" Her voice was low and sad. Where had the laughter gone?

"What's not to like?"

"I'm loud and bossy, and I'm not very nice."

"You're plenty nice," I said.

"Not like you. You're a freaking saint."

"No, I'm not. I just stay quiet, that's all. Doesn't mean I'm not sitting on an opinion."

"But you don't have to give it. How?"

I shrugged.

"That's why people like you. You're a listener."

"Well, I like you, Gemma Stuart."

Her mouth curved up a little. "All right then."

"I do. You're funny and strong and secretly caring."

"Secretly?"

"You care about everyone and everything. Don't you?"

She puffed out a breath. "When did we get here?"

"Where?"

"Knowing everything about each other?"

I shook my head. "I have no idea." I put my hand on hers. "The more I learn about you, Gem, the more I love you. Honest. I couldn't ask for a better best friend—or wife." I winked at her and the laugher escaped.

"We really are in a pickle now." She rubbed her hand over her hair. "There's no way I'd take your name. We can leave that silly, sexist tradition on the other side of the ZA."

"All right, wifey."

Her smile was one of the few true smiles that crept onto her lips. "What would Callie think of us now?"

FORTY-ONE

The next day, Savannah drove the Jaguar, and Mum joined Gemma and I. Every mile dragged as we dodged pile-ups and debris. The speed was infuriating. I hadn't driven so slow since my first driving lesson.

We started in good spirits, but our voices grew quieter and quieter with every hour that passed. The nearer we grew to the built-up area we were heading for, the more signs of life we saw. And death.

The closer we became, the more blood there was on the ground. It wasn't just old, dried stuff. There was crimson sludge that looked only hours old. With every metre there were more guts and brains and whatever else splattering the floor. There were bodies too. Bodies I drove over, making sure they were dead and not about to jump up like at Mandeville Farmhouse.

What gripped my heart tighter were the possessions of the dead littering the ground. There were phones and wallets and photos scattered around where they were dropped, never to be remembered again. The photos bothered me the most, turning my stomach. These people had meant something to someone once, and now they were chewing on someone else's flesh without care or love or the ability to feel again.

My body stiffened every time I spied something. With each item, my hands clenched tight around the steering wheel. I bit my lip and took a breath, almost as though I was holding my body together.

"Wait." Mum's eyes were wide in the rear-view mirror. "Do you hear that?"

I strained my ears and felt the blood drain from my face. It was a groaning. But not from one Infected. Every pitch was covered, and it was in varying volumes. A constant buzz of moans vibrating my lungs like a bass guitar. It was not the groan of a single Infected but a *horde* of Infected.

We exchanged frightened looks before creeping the car forward in silence.

An Infected stumbled onto the road in front of us, skin grizzled and missing in places. The bone on its right arm was sticking out of the rotting flesh that'd been ripped away, purple to almost black underneath but shining pink and red and wet on top. It stumbled towards us on what appeared to be a broken ankle. It looked as though it wouldn't be able to stand back up again if it fell over.

I mowed it down. But when I looked out my window, it was still twitching on the ground. Its head was dripping with dark blood that matted its straggly hair and dribbled into its eyes. It didn't even try and wipe it away. It bared its teeth, trying to reach us and rip chunks out of our flesh.

We passed through a village in distress not long after. Front doors were open. Windows were shattered. There were words written on walls and cars and lamp posts. Houses with cracks and holes had been boarded up. Cars were abandoned in forgotten collisions. Random objects were dotted around the street. Weapons. Cans. Wrappers.

And of course there were bodies. And the gut-yanking odour of death.

After scouting the houses, we headed for the main road, more Infected flinging themselves out at us by the minute. When we reached the end of the abandoned traffic jam, the cars were covered in blood.

"Well, now what?" Ollie asked, leaning out of the window.

Jay pulled himself out of the passenger window to look at the rest of us. "We have to keep going. We can't just turn around."

Gemma wound down her window. "We leave the cars? Really? They've got all our stuff in them."

"We can always come back for them."

"You really want to abandon our fastest escape? Why can't we turn around?"

"We need to find food. The cars won't save us from starvation."

"Whatever we do, we need to do it fast." Mum whispered the words, and I turned around to see what she was looking at.

Out the back window, there were a line of Infected creeping towards us, hands out, grabbing, though we weren't in reaching distance. Yet.

"Leave the cars!" Lisa squeaked as she flung herself out the door and hurried towards the traffic.

Gemma leapt out the car. "I'm not going anywhere without my rucksack."

I almost tripped over my feet as they hit the pavement, heart thrashing, breath firing. Everyone was grabbing rucksacks and snatching up the spare weapons we'd found at Mandeville Farmhouse. We had to leave Gemma's photo album, the witch's hat, and Joel's guitar behind.

Without bothering to shut the boot, we dodged between cars, whacking the stray Infected that fell through the gaps. Savannah and Ollie led, with Lisa and Aniya no more than a few steps behind. Mum and Jay watched their backs. Gemma and I brought up the rear. No one spoke. We listened to the pounding of each other's feet and the erratic flow of our breaths.

We darted around open doors and arms trying to reach us through open windows, Infected trapped behind steel and glass and seatbelts. Cars were empty or acting as coffins for those dead or undead inside. Blood was sprayed on windows, and glass was shattered everywhere.

"This is getting ridiculous," Gemma hissed as she cracked

a skull against a car bonnet with her baseball bat. "Where are we even going?"

"We can't go back now." I chanced a look behind, and the Infected were further away but bigger in number than the last time I'd looked. "No other choice but to keep going. Wherever that is."

"There's another choice."

"What's that?"

"Give in."

"I think I pick life."

She gave a smirk, cheeks red and face beginning to glisten with sweat. "Me too."

She slowed, and I matched her as the others started flagging. My legs were grateful for the workout. My lungs were gulping down air. The further we walked, the more alive I felt, but that seemed to be the opposite for everyone else.

"There's got to be a petrol station around here somewhere," Jay yelled to us. "And there's got to be something in at least one of them."

There was a cry from up ahead, and fight flared through my body as we sped to where Savannah was clutching her ankle on the ground. She was gritting her teeth and squeezing her eyes shut.

"What happened?" Mum dropped down into a crouch next to Aniya.

"I tripped on that bloody thing!" Savannah shrieked, pointing at a tool box obscured by an open door.

"Let me see." Aniya had to prise Savannah's hand away before she could push up her jeans to reveal a red welt where something had scratched her. Blood was beading to the surface.

Gemma, Jay, and I turned to face the Infected as Aniya fiddled around with the first aid kit.

"I don't like this," Gemma whispered. "They're too close."

"Far too close," Jay breathed.

I couldn't calm my heart as we waited. Blood pulsed its way around my body in a fury, and my limbs were itching to move. To run. Now.

"Can you walk?" Aniya went to offer her hand to Savannah, when an Infected broke out of the car behind her and grabbed her hair.

"Aniya!" Savannah's screech turned every head, dead or alive.

Aniya tried to free herself, but she was trapped in the iron fist of the Infected. She yelped as its other hand brushed against her, and she struck out with her fists as its teeth moved ever closer.

Savannah tried to pick up her cricket bat, but Mum was there, flinging her golf club down on the Infected's arms. I didn't flinch at this crack, just raised my own golf club, ready.

Jay muttered under his breath, turning his head from the Infected behind and the scuffle in front. "Hurry, hurry, hurry!"

Mum finished off the Infected, and Lisa steadied Aniya as Ollie helped Savannah up.

"Ready?" Gemma asked. "Go, go, go!" She pushed them forward, and I almost tripped over her as she stopped. Frozen.

I went to shove her onwards, but she was stuck to the ground.

"Gem?"

She'd lost all colour from her face, and she was shuddering. There were tears in her eyes. I tried to take a breath but nothing happened.

"What? What is it?"

With a shaking finger, she pointed at something in the distance. "That's my car."

FORTY-TWO

My legs wanted to collapse from the fear. The noise pressing down on us was making my limbs shake and my heart leap.

Gemma raced towards the car. Towards the Infected.

"Gemma, no!"

Before any thought could stop me, I threw myself after her. She halted a metre or so away from the car and remained frozen.

I shook her shoulders, but she didn't seem to notice me. "Gem? Gemma?" One look at the car told me everything I needed to know.

The doors were flung open. In the passenger seat was a woman. But she was still. She was alone. Her skin had lost colour. She was covered in blood. Her head had caved in. And her remaining eye was open. Unblinking.

I fought down the nausea and looked away, standing between Gemma and the car, shaking her again.

Mum skidded to my side. "What is it? Gem? Gemma?" She tried to drag her away, but she wouldn't budge.

The first Infected reached us, and I powered my golf club down on top of it, channelling all my fear and anxiety into one strike.

"Gemma!" I growled her name. "You'll kill us!"

"Zane!" Mum was pushing an Infected away from her as two more joined the party. Its mouth was so close to her face, saliva flung everywhere as it tried to reach her.

"Duck!"

I cracked the Infected's skull, and Mum was up and fighting like she hadn't been seconds away from infection.

"Run!" It was Jay's voice from up ahead. "Run now!"

If Gemma didn't wake up in the next three seconds, we were all going to die.

Something primal and furious exploded out of my mouth as I screamed her name. "Gemma Stuart! Snap out of it. Now!" My throat was raw and scratchy when I was done. We were a second away from infection. Two at most.

Gemma blinked and stumbled back a step as the situation fell on her. Mum and I grabbed her arms and hauled her forward. But we weren't fast enough. Some of the Infected could still run.

We caught up with the others, who were supporting a limping Savannah. They weren't moving fast enough.

We weren't going to make it.

"I'm sorry." Gemma was taking in huge breaths. Her face was whiter than I'd ever seen it. "I'm so sorry. You should've left me there."

"Shut up!" Jay snapped. "I'm trying to think."

"You better be quick, Jay." There was a wobble in my voice.

"That's not helping, smart-arse!"

Lisa was whimpering, Savannah was swearing, Aniya was crying.

"Zane." Jay's baby-blue eyes fixed on me. "Run!"

"What?" I had to strain to hear him over the roar of the blood pulsing in my ears and the rumble of the Infected behind us.

"Away from here! Make noise and run!"

"But—"

"Now!"

Without another word, I took off to the left, banging on car bonnets and yelling at the top of my voice.

"No!" Mum's shriek cut through to my heart, and I had to force myself on without looking back.

I was not ready. My heart was pulsing blood through my

body, fierce and alive. I could feel it in my ears, behind my eyes. Every muscle was coiled and tense. But not ready.

Go!

I launched my way through the cars. The wind fired in my ears. Ignoring the rush of fear, I pumped my arms and drove my legs faster. Snarls were catching on the wind as all mouths opened to jeer, waiting for me to fail. I was aware of the eyes on me, ogling my performance.

But this was nothing like athletics.

I checked back over my shoulder every few seconds. All the Infected were looking in my direction except a stray few heading towards the others. The runners were fast, but not as fast as me. All my training had amounted to something. At last.

Fear had gripped my heart though, and my breaths weren't in their steady rhythm of sprinting, or even long-distance running. They were erratic and panicked. A stitch so vicious I thought I would collapse tried to break its way out of my side.

But I didn't stop. Didn't even slow. If this was how I was going to go down, I wasn't going down without a fight.

When the only people I loved in the universe disappeared from my sight, I dropped back into a jog, making sure the Infected weren't turning around. It felt as though the whole of the human race—or the ex-human race—were following me. Thousands of eyes fixed on me as they drooled, reaching their hands out to grab pieces of my flesh. I swallowed and suppressed a shudder as I pushed on.

All I could hope for was the survival of the group. Even if that didn't include me.

I had no idea how I was going to evade the Infected now their attention was focused on me. I couldn't even outrun them because they'd follow me wherever I went. Unless a new target showed itself, but I didn't hold out much hope of that happening.

The terror struck me hard, and I almost tripped. It wasn't the fear of death. It wasn't the fear of infection. But the fear of being alone.

Forever.

I tried not to let my emotions engulf me as I marched on. On and on and on.

As time passed, it became more and more difficult to focus. What if it got dark? It wouldn't take long. How would I see where I was going? What if I found myself surrounded?

What if I fell over? What if I hurt myself like Savannah or worse? How would I get back up? How would I carry on? Would I have to lie there and wait for my guts to be ripped out?

What if I needed to eat? What if I needed to sleep? What if, what if, what if?

I imagined my peers calling my name, egging me on, sending all the goodwill in the world my way. I let it fill me up and carry me forward, but it didn't last long. My imagination wasn't as strong a force as I hoped.

As the sun started to set, I started to panic.

"Keep going. Keep going. Keep going." I breathed it to myself over and over for something else to do. Something else to think about.

The Infected were still following me, but not so close I couldn't slow to an almost-walking jog. I needed to find somewhere to rest. Somewhere to regroup, to figure out what on earth I was going to do next.

As the sun ducked behind the horizon, I approached a small town. The welcome sign was so welcome indeed I almost shed a tear. There was chaos here as in every place we'd passed. Infected wandered the streets without much purpose.

The road I picked happened to be a dead end. I cursed as I pounded to the end, throwing myself at the front door of one of the houses that wasn't smashed and open. But the door didn't budge.

I made a decision without thinking and jumped onto the car on the drive, scrabbling onto the lower roof of the garage and throwing my golf club down over the other side. I wanted to stop there and catch my breath for a few minutes, but the longer I stopped, or even if I stopped for a second, that'd be the second they'd gain. So I slid down the other side into the garden, bending my knees on impact as not to break my legs.

That'd be game over.

The back door was unlocked, and I thanked every greater power I could think of as I flew inside and locked the door. I waited for a full minute, listening for noise inside the house. I pressed my back on the door and slipped down until I was on the floor, resting my head on my knees. Panting, hearing each intake of breath like gunfire. I was alive.

I was alive.

As soon as I'd recovered, I did a sweep of the house, making sure it was clear of Infected. *The Game of Life* was open on the kitchen table, pieces halfway round, not one of them ready to cross the finish line into retirement. Upstairs there were two bedrooms. One had a baby's cot with cuddly toys piled at the end in soft, muted colours. It made my heart ache. I had to turn away.

I fell down onto the double bed in the other bedroom and thought about getting up and figuring out what I was going to do next, but I couldn't lift my iron limbs. And I couldn't stop my eyelids from closing.

FORTY-THREE

I awoke to sunlight beaming through the windows, and it took me a full minute to remember where I was and how I came to be there. My back and shoulders screamed as I sat up and rubbed my hand over my hair and neck. My arms ached too. As did my stomach muscles and of course, my legs.

I hobbled into the bathroom to check the water situation and like at Mandeville Farmhouse, nothing happened. In the kitchen, I looked through every cupboard and drawer, taking out everything and anything that was food and placing it on the worktops. I filled my rucksack and another I found in the bottom of a wardrobe. What I couldn't fit in, I sat and ate.

Soft biscuits and cereal and the middle part of a block of cheese that didn't have mould on it. I treated myself to the dregs of some flat orangeade too. It wasn't much, but it was the biggest feast I'd had in weeks, and I felt bloated and unbalanced.

My legs cried out in pain as I made my way up the stairs, so I trekked down and back up and down and back up again until the pain was bearable. I threw my old, ripped, bloodstained, and stinking clothes onto the carpet and went through the wardrobe until I found the softest black T-shirt in the world, some tight running trousers, and combats. The only thing I bothered to keep were my Nikes. I pulled the combats over the top of the running trousers and felt snug and warm and—though it seemed stupid—safe. After more searching, I found a brown hoodie a few sizes too big for me and tested to see whether I could fit my coat on over the top.

As I explored, I found a smartphone attached to some hub that wasn't connected to anything. I pulled the phone off the stand and it shone to life, letting me know it was fully charged. If we'd kept any of our phones, I would have made space for the hub in my rucksack, but it was useless without a phone, even if I kept this one. There was no point.

I scrolled through the contacts for something to do, reading the names of all the people in this person's life. The thought shot to mind before I could stop it. What percentage of these people were dead?

Moving on to the messages, I flicked through only to return to the one at the top.

I love you xxx

There was nothing more to the message, but did there have to be anything more? I stood and stared at the words for a long time, convincing myself this was my own phone and those were Callie's words.

What had my last message to her said? Was it something about the zombie walk or athletics or being on the bus? There was a high chance the last message was just a stream of kisses, and I found myself wishing I'd said something more.

I spent the next however many minutes trying to remember any phone numbers that could be useful. When I couldn't recall even a single one, I flung the thing down on the bed and stormed out the room.

Who would I even call anyway?

I had to come to terms with the fact that I was stranded with no way of telling Mum and Gemma and Jay I was alive.

What were they doing right now? Where were they? Were they all safe? Were they thinking about me? Were they voting on waiting for me? Were they arguing about whether or not I was alive?

"I'm alive," I whispered to myself. "I made it. Did you?"

Attempting to hold the tears in, burying my head in the stranger's pillow, I tried not to sob too loud.

I awoke, realising I'd been asleep, and traipsed back downstairs to eat more of the food I couldn't fit into the rucksacks. With every hour that passed, I was finding it more difficult to smile.

"Come on, Zane." I jumped up and paced the kitchen, pulling my tired legs into submission. "Stop being a baby. You can do this. You can carry on. You're fine." I shook my head. "You're fine."

Chancing a look out the window, I found a group of Infected standing out there waiting for me. Somehow I hadn't noticed their groaning.

I couldn't sit still any longer. I needed to move. I needed to do something.

I pulled my coat and the two rucksacks on but paused with my hand on the handle. What would Gemma do? Would she think this was a good idea? Would she stay where it was relatively safe? She would wait until morning. I wasn't sure how much daylight was left.

Trying not to make a sound, I eased open the door and shut it behind me. The freezing gust of wind took my breath away as I slipped out the back gate and onto another street.

It didn't matter what Gemma would do. Gemma wasn't here.

Wandering through the town, I soon came to the conclusion that all the streets looked identical. Especially with the lamp posts out. The light started to fade a lot sooner than I expected, and I jogged from street to street, blind with panic, looking for something, anything at all.

The Infected came in waves, nothing more than I could handle. A lone one here, a pair over there. But the darker it got, the more terrifying they became. They could appear as if from nowhere, groaning in my face. It was harder to pick them out as my heart sped, my breath huffing in a loud rhythm. It was one thing being chased by a horde of Infected, but it was quite another having them jump out.

My die-hard fans found me once again, and I started building up a crowd. I didn't bother to sprint. I didn't have anywhere to sprint to. My sense of direction had disappeared. I might have been running around in circles for all I knew.

All I could do was keep going. Try not to trip. Try not to give in. Try not to die.

I was prepared to dart off at any second if something caught my fancy, then I could break away from them. If I was lucky.

As I scanned the houses, I noticed a few of them boarded up like Ashford House. I narrowed my eyes, but I couldn't see candlelight emitting from any of them. But there had to be some people left somewhere. It couldn't just be the eight of us. The virus couldn't have wiped out the entire country? Could it?

I ran. I kept on running. The light faded. I kept on.

My muscles started to tense as the panic bit down harder and harder. I couldn't fight the terror that swirled around in my head. I was becoming breathless with each street, each step, each thought.

I threw myself down an alley, checking back over my shoulder every few seconds, hoping I wasn't going to come across a swarm of them around the next corner. But when I turned my head back, it was worse.

A brick wall. A dead end.

I was trapped.

I gave a cry and spun round, facing the crowd of Infected. They were squashing themselves into the alley, each dying to be the one to reach me first. I ran my shaking hands over the wall behind me, searching for a way out. I threw myself at the wall, jumping as high as I could to try and grab the top, but my palms scraped against the brick, tearing through my gloves and my skin. I jumped again, yelling out with pain as another layer of skin was ripped from my palms. My hands felt wet with blood.

I looked for a window instead. There was one to my right, but it was up a storey. With a jump I could brush the windowsill, but there was no chance of getting a good enough grip to pull myself up. And anyway, it was closed.

I turned my head around and around, looking for my salvation, moving almost too fast for my brain to keep up.

No.

My breaths were so loud they were almost drowning out the roar of the Infected. "No."

My head snapped from side to side, looking from the Infected to the wall, having no idea what to do. I was out of ideas. Out of time.

The dread was all-consuming. My heart felt like it was doing all its beating at once. It was so furious it was a struggle to pull any air into my lungs whatsoever.

My entire body was trembling. I wanted to fight, but it was hard to engage in a battle I knew I would lose. Half of me wanted to curl up, and the other half wanted to fling myself into the fray and get this over with, but I couldn't.

They grew closer, crazed at the sight of my blood-soaked gloves. Sweat dripped down my face. I couldn't breathe.

I was going to die.

Not only that, I was going to be bitten. Eaten. Chewed on while still screaming.

I wished I had Jay's gun.

They were so close. Only a few seconds left. Their rancid breath was on my skin.

"Here I come, Callie."

I breathed my last breath.

I shut my eyes.

I tried not to scream.

FORTY-FOUR

Hands were all around me, engulfing me. I had to bite my lip to stop from squealing. I wasn't going to yell. I wasn't going to cry.

As the first pair grabbed me, I let out a terrific shriek like I'd never heard. Never would hear again. Never see. Never know.

My brain was in override but also in shut down. The sound of hissing consumed me. I felt saliva flung onto my face. Only a few seconds and teeth would be tearing my flesh.

Please let it be quick. Please let it be over in a second. Please just kill me. Please.

The first pair of hands gripped tighter. So tight it felt as though my skin was being punctured. The hands pulled me upwards.

Upwards?

I wasn't being ripped apart, just hauled towards the sky. Looking to the heavens, I found a man hanging out of a window, trying to yank me inside.

"Little help, mate?"

I kicked off the floor and the Infected's skulls and propelled myself into the stranger's arms by some feat of immense strength.

A miracle.

I grazed my stomach on the window frame, but when I rolled onto the carpet, I was still breathing. Still thinking. My heart was still beating.

I was alive.

Still.

"Were you bitten?" my saviour asked.

I couldn't speak. My tongue was all knotted up in my mouth. I couldn't figure out how to make it work again.

"Were you bitten?" His voice was firmer this time.

I patted myself down, unsure. How stupid that I didn't know whether I'd been bitten. My bare skin seemed fine, but I took my coat off to double-check.

The saviour was staring at my bloody hands.

"No." The word came out as a squeak, and I cleared my throat. "No. I think I'm all right." I rested my head back on the wall and let out a long breath, tears beading to my eyes. "I'm alive."

"Just." The saviour dropped down beside me.

We didn't speak for the few minutes we sat catching our breath. I was less concerned with breathing and more amazed by the all-consuming beauty of being alive. After all, this wasn't a video game. We only had one life each.

"Are you all right, mate?" He turned to me. His hair was dark and short. It looked as though he'd cut it himself. It had jagged, fluffy ends like Gemma's when she'd gone for the scissors. His face was young but haggard. I guessed he was in his thirties. There was a sadness swimming in his brown eyes as they burrowed into mine. Broken.

"Yeah. I think I'm all right."

"What were you doing out there?"

"Trying to find my group. We got separated, but I have no idea where I am." I peeled off my gloves and wiped as much blood off my hands as I could. The scrapes weren't bad underneath, just raw and sore.

"I almost didn't save you." He was watching me smear blood over my new combats. "I thought you might be infected."

"I just tried to climb that wall, that's all." I looked at him again. "I wouldn't have blamed you. For leaving me, I mean. I don't know what I would've done. But thank you. For saving my life. I have no idea how I can ever repay you."

"S'all right." He pulled himself up and went into another room before returning with a roll of bandages, cream, and wet wipes.

I went to take the roll off him, but he moved it out of my reach.

"Let me help you."

"It's okay. I can do it," I said.

He waved it away. "Oh, come on. Let me help."

"Why're you being so nice to me?"

He shrugged. "You're the first person I've spoken to in...I don't know how many days. I'm starting to lose my mind. I'd forgotten what my voice sounded like." He was gentle as he cleaned my hands. I tried not to flinch.

"How long've you been here?"

He smeared cream over my scrapes and wrapped the bandages around my hand. "Little over a week I think now."

"Were you travelling with people?"

He nodded. "My wife and boys."

"I'm sorry."

"What can you do? We've all lost someone, haven't we?"

"Yeah."

"Just been me for about two weeks now. It's nice to see someone else made it. How many of you are there?"

"If they all made it, eight. Including me."

"Eight?" His eyes bugged wide as he fastened the bandage. "Whoa."

"Met three on the road and just kept going. We were at a farmhouse for about a week but ran out of food. We were out searching for more. I think the plan is to go back there."

"Is that where you'll meet them?" He started on my other hand.

"I dunno. I was leading the Infected away when we got

separated. I dunno if they're waiting for me. They were going to check petrol stations and services. One of them is injured, so they won't be moving that fast, but I dunno how to get back there."

"I know how to get to the main road. If you want, I could show you?"

"No, you really don't have to do that. You've done so much already." I pulled my hand back, looking at them both bandaged and clean. "You don't have to put your life in danger for me."

"Maybe I'm asking for something in return?"

"What? Anything."

He ran his hand through his hair. "Maybe I don't want to be alone any more."

"You want to come with us?"

He gave a short, sharp nod.

"Of course. That's the least I can do. The more we are the stronger we are, right?"

"Yeah. I'm done with being alone anyway. You start thinking crazy things when you've got nothing to live for, mate."

"Zane." I offered him a smile.

"Tom." He held out his hand for me to shake.

I took it. "Thank you for saving my life, Tom."

"You're welcome. If you ever feel like repaying the favour, it would be appreciated."

"Noted."

"So what's your story?"

A knot crushed in my stomach. "What?"

"Your story? Everyone's got an apocalypse story. Where they were when it happened. What's gone on since."

"You don't want to hear it." I tried to wave it away. "It's long."

"I don't think we should set out until first light. And I'm not sure your legs have stopped shaking. We've got all night."

"I dunno."

He shook his head. "It's all right. You don't have to tell me if you don't want."

"I…" Something made me want to tell him. Maybe because he'd been alone for so long or because he'd saved my life, but I felt the desire to share with him. "I lost someone important to me, and I'm not sure I can tell it."

"That's okay." He went into the next room to put everything back.

"We were in Brighton, at the pier," I started. "We were on a zombie walk."

I told him everything. More than I thought I could tell. I didn't think I'd be able to explain it to anyone, but it flowed out of me in one stream of consciousness.

"And then we got separated, and I had this amazing idea that I could find them again in the middle of the afternoon when it was getting dark. And then this awesome guy saved my life."

He grinned. "Lucky I did with all those people relying on you."

"Have I said thank you in the last five minutes?"

He smirked. "Not this last five minutes."

"Thank you." I gave a small chuckle, and my chest felt lighter after baring my soul. That and I was still alive. "So what about you? What's your ZA story?"

His eyebrows came together. "Zed-ay?"

"Oh, Zombie Armageddon. Jay was calling it that before all this. I guess it stuck."

"Oh right." He ran his hand through his hair again and rested it on his neck. "We were coming back from football practice with the boys. Josh and Jack." He grinned, but his eyes were filling with tears. "Twins. Quite a shock, gotta admit."

I smiled too and felt a pull on my heart for the life he'd lost.

"We were in the car. Everything started getting crazy.

People were getting out and driving onto the pavement. It took us a lifetime to get home. A zombie nearly got at Jack, but my wife, Tori, pulled him back. We managed to bundle into the house to safety."

I cringed. "Zombie?"

His eyebrows came together. "Well, yeah. What do you call them?"

"Infected."

"Infected?" He considered me for a moment. "Okay, we were safe from the *Infected*, but we didn't know about the dormant virus. We didn't realise what it would do to children."

I shook my head.

"We didn't know what was happening and then… We had to get out of there. We needed to run. Tori she—she tripped, and she wasn't fast enough. I wasn't fast enough. I…I had to leave her behind."

"I'm so sorry."

"And now I'm here, and that's it." He turned away and wiped his eyes. "The only reason I'm here is because I'm stubborn, that's all."

I nodded. "That's not a bad thing."

"Sometimes I think it would've been better if I'd gone back to her and died by her side."

I couldn't meet his eye. "I know exactly what you mean."

FORTY-FIVE

"So, are you ready?" Tom asked as we stood at the window, though not the one he'd pulled me through. There were still loads of Infected milling around down there. We were minutes away from daybreak. "This is about as quiet as it gets."

"Straight to the main road?" I felt light on my feet and ready to do this. An air of positivity and confidence had made a home inside my chest, and I was determined to keep it there.

"Yep."

"I'll follow you."

"How fast can you run?"

I smirked. "Fast."

He nodded, grinning back. "Me too. Do you think you'll be able to keep up?"

"I'll try."

Tom threw his rucksack on his back and sheathed his machete before grabbing his cricket bat. I watched him with wide eyes.

"What?"

"Where'd you get that?"

"Oh. I'm sort of an enthusiast," he said. "It was on our wall at home."

"Is it any good?"

He nodded. "It's lethal."

We lowered ourselves down onto the ground and were off. I was shocked by the fact that Tom was by my side. I took a quick look at him, and he raised his eyebrows in question, his lip quirking up. So I did what any self-respecting athlete would do and quickened my pace.

Ducking and weaving through the hordes seemed to be working. They couldn't keep up, and they didn't have enough time to get their teeth anywhere near us. How much simpler everything would be if everyone could run like this.

When we came across a huge mob of Infected, Tom skidded to a halt. "Dammit. We're gonna have to go round. This way."

I followed after him, and we turned down a tiny road. Tom pointed to a side gate into someone's garden. It was swinging in the breeze and creaking. A shudder overtook me as we walked past it.

"We've got to climb these fences." He rested his hands on his knees to catch his breath. "The road's just down there."

I walked back and forth to slow my heart. "If this is your idea of a shortcut…"

"Well, this is the best I've got. Worth a shot, right? Unless you have any great plans?"

"Not one."

"Then climbing the fence it is."

We searched the garden for something to stand on and found an abandoned washing basket. Tom raised his eyebrows at me but rested it up against the fence anyway. I could hear the call of the Infected out on the street. It would only be a matter of moments before they found us.

"You go first."

I opened my mouth to argue, but he pushed me onto the basket before I could say anything.

"Just do it."

I jumped onto the washing basket, pleased it didn't break. My bandaged palms screamed in agony as I grabbed the fence and heaved myself over. My stomach ended up resting on top of the fence, sending stinging pain through my body. I tottered there for a moment before my heavy rucksacks tipped me over the edge. I fell in a heap on the other side. Lucky for me, I didn't land on my head, and there were no Infected to be seen. Yet.

Tom threw my golf club and his cricket bat over the fence and tumbled over after them. He groaned as he stood up. "This isn't going to be as easy as I'd hoped."

"Only..." I jumped up to look at the fences we had left. "About six to go."

The next two gardens were easier as they had slides to climb onto. But when I landed with a thump on the ground for the fourth time, I looked up to be greeted by a pair of milky eyes and a flap of rotting flesh.

I cried out and couldn't slap my hand over my mouth fast enough.

Every Infected within hearing distance was now looking and travelling in this direction. I scrabbled away from it on my hands and knees until I could jump up, only to realise my golf club was on the other side. My heart pounded so hard I could feel it in my ribs.

"Tom! Golf club!"

Three were coming towards me with a fourth crunching against the fence panel from the next garden across. I ran from side to side, trying to push them away by kicking out, but I was too afraid of being bitten, and they were not afraid of me at all.

"Tom!" I didn't care about yelling now. All I cared about was staying alive. "Where the hell are you?"

They were closing in, and there was nowhere for me to run. The golf club and cricket bat flew over and landed on the grass, too far away for me to reach. I'd backed myself into a corner.

"Tom!"

"Zane!" He flung himself over the fence and landed with a crash. He moaned as he looked up, clutching his chest.

"Help!" The word escaped me though I knew it was futile.

I ducked down and curled myself into a ball, protecting as much of my face as possible, not knowing whether Tom was going to pull himself up and save me or not. It hit me that I was resting my life in the hands of a total stranger.

There was a grunt and a whoosh of steel and nothing touched me. I prised open my eyes to see Tom beheading each Infected one by one, their heads dropping from their shoulders and their bodies slumping to the ground.

Tom offered his hand to me. "Told you. Lethal."

I took his hand and tried to uncoil my frozen body and stop trembling.

With audible effort, Tom dragged me to my feet and patted me on the back. "You okay?"

"Alive."

"Good. Next one?"

I shook my head, clearing my throat. "No way."

"Yes way."

I wrapped my arms around myself. "You can go first this time."

"How about we check it's safe, and then you can go over?"

"No. I'm not going over first."

He wiped the blood off his machete and sheathed it again. "Come on, Zane."

"No. You saw what happened. That's the second time you've had to save my life." I couldn't hide the shake in my voice.

"I didn't have to. I don't mind saving your life."

"What's the problem? Why can't you go first?"

"What if they swarmed here? You'd be safer on the other side."

"Why does it matter if I'm safe? What about you?"

He sighed. "You've got something to live for. They're waiting for you. They're counting on you."

It felt like my chest deflated. "We'll get through this together. We're both gonna survive this."

"As long as I keep saving your life."

"Exactly." Somewhere deep down, I found a smile.

"Please just go first."

I watched him for a minute as his brown eyes looked into mine. They seemed both too innocent and big, and too horrified all at once. I took a breath and nodded. "All right."

We continued the process until we reached a mesh fence and the main road. Cars had backed up on both sides, and belongings were scattered all over the place.

My whole body ached from fear and running and hitting the floor, but I stretched my shoulders and legs as I surveyed the scene. Tom was wheezing as he pulled himself off the ground one final time.

"Remind me never to climb a fence for as long as I live."

"Apart from that one." I pointed to the mesh fence in front.

"That's different. That's one I can actually climb." He held his hand to his side. "I feel like I've cracked a rib."

There weren't any live people wandering along the road, just a few Infected here and there. There wasn't a group of seven survivors marching along with purpose, and my heart dropped.

They wouldn't even know to look out for me. If I was in their situation, I would have assumed the person missing was long dead by this point. And I would have been if not for Tom. I didn't care what their reaction to him would be. I needed him by my side to keep me out of trouble, and if all he asked in return was some people to talk to, who was I to take that away? He was a gift as far as I was concerned. He knew what he was doing, could run fast, and had a machete. What better gift could I give to them? And he'd saved my life—twice.

Tom clapped a hand on my shoulder as he passed. "Onwards and upwards."

We walked for what felt like hours, dispatching any Infected we came across with one swipe of Tom's machete. When it was my turn, I was amazed by how light and deadly it was. The hot touch of jealousy flared at once. It was unlikely I'd ever get to own one, but I could fantasise about it all the same. It was strange the way your dreams changed in the ZA.

"Hey look." Tom pointed to a sign. "Services."

I chewed on my lip. "Won't it be crawling with Infected?"

"Are you telling me you don't even want to check it out?"

"I don't want to get eaten."

"But you want to find them. They would've taken a look in there, surely?"

"Yeah, I guess. Fine. We'll take a look."

Tom chuckled and shook his head. "Such a spoilsport."

The car park was jammed with dented cars and belongings like the road, but the Infected must have all been running after their prey because there were only around ten or fifteen in the whole car park.

We ducked low behind the cars and snuck our way to the front of the building where the automatic doors, of course, didn't open. I pressed my face against the window. Tom watched my back.

"Anything?"

"No. There don't seem to be any Infected in there though. Not that I can see." I squinted at a patch of red, and my stomach rolled over. "No, wait. There's a dead one on the floor in there."

"That means someone killed it. They might be in there."

My heart tried to jump out of my mouth. I wanted to cheer and let myself hope, but I couldn't. There was a huge chance I'd never see them again. I had to come to terms with that.

I pulled myself away from the window. "Let's see if there's a back door."

We crept round the side of the building until we came to a fire exit that belonged to the hotel attached to the services.

"Only one thing we can do." Tom leant on the handle and let himself in.

Before I could tell him to wait, before I could think about our next move, there was a wave of shouting and screaming, and a weapon was raised in our faces.

FORTY-SIX

"Hey, hey, hey!" Tom raised his cricket bat. "We're alive. We're alive."

I poked my head in the door to see a scowling face topped with thick auburn hair. His powder-blue eyes were glaring at Tom. He didn't notice me.

The joy that crushed me was so intense I thought I would pass out. I tried to speak his name, but no sound would come out my mouth. Instead, I pushed Tom to one side and stood in front of him.

Ollie's eyes bugged. "Z—Zane?"

I nodded. He flung his arms around me, squeezing me so tight I couldn't breathe. When I could take a breath, all I could smell was cigarette smoke.

A figure skidded to a halt, and I pried myself from Ollie to find Gemma's face pale and sunken. Her eyes brightened as they connected with mine.

She made no sound, but her lips moved to speak my name.

I didn't see her move, just stumbled backwards at the force of her body. She clambered into my arms so that her head was buried into my shoulder, legs wrapped around my waist. Her hands were all over my back, my neck, my face. Tears spilt onto my skin. I held her closer, slipping my hand into her dirty hair.

She pulled back to look at me again, stormy-grey eyes drinking in my face. Before I could say anything, her lips had mashed against mine in a kiss so fierce I almost fell over. I clung tight to her and kissed her back like I'd never live another moment again.

"I'm guessing these are your friends," Tom said as I broke away from Gemma and placed her back onto her feet.

Jay threw himself into my arms and hugged me as though I might disappear any second. I teared up at his embrace, but sniffed them back down into my heart as we parted.

"You saved us." Jay had a small but genuine smile on his face.

"Where's Mum?"

"I think they're just coming." Ollie had his head through the doorframe. "Guys! Come here!"

Lisa's face lit up as she saw me. "Zane!" Like the others before her, she made a beeline for me and squashed me tight against her.

"Who's this?" Jay walked up to Tom as Lisa let go of me.

"Oh, this is Tom." I grinned at him. "He saved my life. Twice."

Gemma hurled herself into Tom's arms, and his eyes went wide with shock. "Thank you," she said as she hugged him.

"It's really fine."

Jay went to shake his hand, but I no longer cared as Savannah entered the room, being supported on each side by Mum and Aniya.

This time I was the one off my feet. I didn't even feel them moving forward. I was propelled into Mum's arms and burying my face in her hair before I could think. The tears were falling off my face, and I couldn't breathe. But I didn't care because she was here, and she was alive, and so was I. I couldn't ask for anything more.

"Zane," she whispered into my ear. She was clinging to me so tight it hurt, but I didn't care. I never wanted to let go. "I knew you were alive. I knew it. I love you so much."

"I love you too."

Somewhere in the distance, Savannah and Aniya were saying hello to Tom, and Gemma was telling them he'd saved my life. I didn't care about any of that. Not in that moment.

Mum squeezed tighter for a second before letting go. "Who's this wonderful man then?"

As her eyes met Tom, her hand dropped from mine. She stared as though she'd seen a ghost. Tom's mouth popped open, and he gazed back. Silence fell upon the room, every pair of eyes watching between the two of them.

It took me a whole second to work out what was going on. Then it felt like my legs were going to collapse, but Gemma was there, ready, in case I fell.

Tom swallowed as he looked at Mum. "Jenny?"

She was shaking her head, and tears were filling her eyes. Her lip was wobbling. She took a shuddery breath.

When I found my feet, I went to stand in front of her.

"And, Zane? Are you…?"

"No." I glared at him.

"*Carlisle?* Zane Carlisle? I didn't…"

"Zane *Thomas* Carlisle." I growled the words at him, but they had no effect.

"I …"

"Why didn't you say anything?"

"Say anything?" He puffed out a huge breath. "I didn't know. You think I knew? Why would I have? The thought didn't even…"

"Of course it didn't. You don't know me. I don't know you. You didn't even know I existed. How would you ever jump there?"

"I…"

"Zane?" Gemma twisted her fingers with mine. "No offence, and not to make this *any more* awkward than it has to be—I think we've reached our limit there anyway—but, can't you see it?"

"What?"

"Look at him."

I did. Every last inch of him. He was my height, maybe an inch shorter. His hair was black, like mine. His eyes were deep-brown, like mine. His skin was a tanned-honey colour, like mine. The more I looked into his face, the more of myself I found there. That was my nose, my ears. Everything. I didn't look like Mum at all.

I had to avert my gaze.

"Tom?" Mum stepped closer until she was on his side of the room. "You—you're alive?"

He nodded.

She pressed her lips together. "I've imagined this moment in my head a thousand times, but you know what?"

He went to reach for her hand, but she snatched it away.

"I have nothing to say to you." She turned to leave.

"Jenny." Tom raced in front of Mum and blocked her exit. "I'm sorry. I was a kid. A stupid kid. I never wanted to hurt you. I was just scared."

Mum narrowed her eyes. "And what did you think I was feeling? Do you even realise what I went through?"

"I'm sorry."

"Sorry doesn't cut it. Sorry doesn't even *begin* to cover what you owe me."

"I'm sorry. I am. If we were in the old world, I'd offer you money or time or whatever you wanted, but we're here. The only thing I have to offer you is Zane. Our son."

"*My* son."

"Jen, I can't say anything else. I can't take back what I did, but I saved Zane's life. Twice. I'm not saying you owe me anything because you don't, but if that doesn't make up for it, I don't know what will."

Mum put her arm around me. "Thank you." It was fast and fleeting, but it was out in the open. "For saving his life. Of course I'm grateful for that. Zane is an incredible person.

He is the best man I know and have ever known, and he's by far the most amazing thing that's happened in my life. But that doesn't mean I don't blame you for everything bad that happened to me. Zane's the cause of all the goodness and you're the badness. I don't care that without you he wouldn't be here. That doesn't seem important. Because he was always going to be here. You weren't."

"You don't think I know the pain I've caused you? I've been sorry for what I've done for eighteen years. I've thought about you day in and day out. Both of you. I wanted to come and apologise a thousand times, but I couldn't. I was too scared."

"You didn't try, did you? My parents never moved house again. If we were in the old world, they'd still be there. They'd tell you where we lived or would've passed on the message that you were sorry, but you didn't say it. Didn't even try and say it. I'm not the one who ran away. That was you."

"I know. I was stupid. I didn't know what I was giving up. I didn't get it then. After I had my boys, I felt even guiltier. Then I knew exactly what you were going through and that you were going through it alone. I was going to find you, but I was too afraid of hurting my family. I had to do it right that time."

"What about Zane? Didn't he deserve your love and attention? Did he not deserve a father?"

I shook Mum off. "It doesn't matter. I didn't need one. I didn't want one. I wanted you. You were all I needed. I didn't need him. We didn't need him."

"You didn't always feel like that."

"But that's over. I might have felt like that, but I don't now. I'll be eighteen in two months. I'm practically an adult. I've lived this long without him. Who's to say I've got any interest whatsoever now?"

"But…" Tom moved forward. "I know you must hate me. But before we were almost friends. Can't we forget about this and go back to being friends? Please, Zane? I just want to know you."

"Is that right?"

"I can't promise to make it up to you. Ever. I'm not promising that. I'm just here to promise that I'll do my best to keep you alive. Nothing's changed between us. I'm still grateful you brought me here."

My voice was dark. I made no effort to hide it. "Maybe I want to take it back."

Jay jumped in front of us. "Erm, no. This guy saved your life more than once. He knows what he's doing. We are not letting him run away now. He's one of us. I don't care what you two think. That's old world stuff. It's the ZA now."

I raised my hand. "I vote he goes."

Everyone looked at me as though I'd brandished a knife.

"Zane?" Gemma took both my arms and turned me to the side so I could look nowhere but in her eyes. "Listen to yourself. You'll regret this."

I went to open my mouth, and she put her hand over it.

"I don't care. I'm done listening to this story. I thought you were dead. Do you understand that? Do you know what that's like? You're my ally, Carlisle, my best friend. I've lost one, and I'm not ready to lose any more. I don't care who this guy is. He left, I don't care. He could be some sort of drug lord, and I wouldn't care. He could've done anything at this point, and I would forgive it because you're here right now. And there is nothing more important to me in this universe." She shook me. "Understand that. You can hate him. Jen, you can hate him too. But you're just going to have to come to terms with the fact that I freaking love him, okay? I can guarantee some other people in this room feel the same way." She let go of me. "And you can hate me and never talk to me again, and that would be okay. Because your life is worth more to me than anything else on this stupid planet. And I, for one, am grateful you're still here."

She went up to Tom and shook his hand.

"Gemma, but you can call me Gem."

"Tom." He nodded. "And thank you."

She shook her head. "No. Thank you. If Zane had really been dead, I wouldn't know what to do next."

Mum went up to Tom again, letting her eyes wander up and down his face. "Gemma's right. You saved his life. That's worth being civil."

Tom pressed his lips together. "For what it's worth, I would take it back if I could. What I did to you, I mean."

Mum shook her head. "I don't care. That's old world stuff. It's not important now." She took a deep breath and held it. "Welcome to the team."

FORTY-SEVEN

"Come on." Gemma pulled me out of the room. "Let me show you the place."

Jay hurried after us, grabbing a cricket bat on the way out as we left the official adults together in one room. I couldn't look at Tom any more anyway.

Jay gave a nervous laugh when we were halfway down the corridor. "Well, that was intense."

"Yeah," Gemma agreed. "I mean, what are the chances that your—"

"Please." I rubbed my hand over my forehead. "Please, let's not talk about it."

Gemma and Jay exchanged a look I ignored as we went through a set of doors and into the heart of the service station. It was filled with tables and chairs and benches and sofas and around the outside were the shops. The tables were all still upright as they were screwed to the floor, but chairs were scattered here, there, and everywhere as panic took the place however many days and weeks ago that was. The sign declaring that these were '*Services*' didn't do it justice.

"Welcome to paradise." Gemma opened her arms out wide. "Filled with excitement and disappointment all at once."

"Are you sure it's clear of Infected?"

"Pretty sure. This place had some sort of panic attack and got locked up. There were a few strays but nothing like we imagined."

As my eyes took in the room, the possibilities filled me up. There was coffee, pizza, burgers, chicken, and some sort of healthy wrap place. I didn't know where to run first.

"Don't get your hopes up." Gemma walked us by the first

few places. "Most of the food was frozen and has defrosted and gone bad. All the fresh stuff looks pretty nasty too."

"Are you sure?"

I went behind one of the counters, and there were old chips dotted around. The instrument they used to scoop them with was upside down on the floor. I bent down to check the shelves under the counter, which were covered in grease and dirt. There were chips there too. From the corner of my eye, I spotted some packaging, and my heart leapt. I couldn't control the smile on my face when I pulled out the blueberry muffin, still in its packet.

"You should've checked more thoroughly." I waved the packet as I joined them back on the other side of the counter.

"Blueberry?" Gemma crossed her arms. "Come on."

"What? You're giving up a muffin?"

"I don't like blueberry."

"Even now?"

Jay shook his head. "Would it kill anyone to leave anything chocolate laying around?"

I offered it to him, and he looked at me for a moment.

"No. You have it, Zane. You deserve it."

I didn't argue as I ripped the packet off and took a bite of the out-of-date muffin. It wasn't as soft as it was supposed to be, but it was heaven down here in hell. If I hadn't been in company, I would have cried.

We walked by the other food places, and Gemma headed to a shop with books outside.

"Is there really nothing over there?" I pointed to the coffee shop.

"Nah. Trying to make anything remotely tasty without power is impossible. Unless you like eating coffee beans and doing shots of neat caramel syrup."

"What about the cakes and stuff?"

"Way ahead of you. There's some stuff over there, but it's hard and not particularly nice. They must have loads of preservatives in them to keep like that."

"There's nothing still in its wrapper?"

"Not that I could see." She smirked and shot a look at Jay. "He's come back a freaking scavenger."

"I thought the whole idea of this exercise was to find food?"

"Well, maybe there'll be some over here. We didn't get to these shops last night."

We made our way down the few aisles one by one. There was still a lot of stuff left in this shop. There were books and magazines and notebooks and pens and cuddly toys and all sorts.

Gemma pulled out one of the notebooks and a green, sparkly pen. She wrote *Gemma Alice Stuart, surviving the ZA* in the middle of the page, adding a little smiley face. Jay took a blue pen and jotted *Jay Michael Ashford, ZA Ready* underneath hers. I scribbled my name at the top in the pink glitter pen she handed me. Unlike them, I omitted my middle name.

"This is a bust, huh?" Gemma threw a cuddly horse my way.

I caught it before it hit me in the face. "Don't you want this?"

She brought her eyebrows together. "In what universe would I want that?"

I shrugged. "Friend for Puddle."

Her eyes narrowed. She looked to Jay, who had his lips pressed together. "That was supposed to be between you and me. But I guess I can tell him about Elle."

I chuckled. "I don't care."

She threw a cuddly elephant my way. "Here's a replacement."

Before I could think of anything clever to say, Gemma

squealed and brought us a pink packet of bubble gum, eyes bright.

Without a word, we each took a piece and were united in the greatest moment since the ZA began. We had stupid grins on our faces while we stood there chewing the tiny splat of flavour until it tasted of nothing but grey.

Gemma tried to blow a bubble, but it was a sorry excuse of a thing, and Jay sniggered.

"I'm kinda out of practice. Haven't done this since I was about twelve."

We each tried to blow a bubble, Jay almost choking on his piece. We ended up laughing our way into the supermarket next door, throwing the tasteless blubber into the bin in between.

"I'm not sure about Infected in here," Gemma whispered. "We didn't get this far yesterday. They should've shown themselves by now the amount of noise we were making though."

Like the previous shop, there were still lots of things untouched. DVDs and CDs had been knocked off the shelves, but it looked as if only a few had been taken. We crept between the aisles, my body tensed for a fight as the quiet overwhelmed me. There were no sounds except for the thud of our own feet hitting the still kind-of-clean floor. There wasn't even much dust hanging around. The place felt eerie and haunted.

We passed mouldy vegetables and fruit that were caving in on themselves and made our way to the back where bread and pastries were slumping. I tore open a packet of croissants to find that they too were solid. I threw the packet back and continued on.

Down the next aisle, I ripped open anything still in a sealed packet and wolfed it down as though I would never eat again. I shoved random items in my pockets and the carrier bags Jay had picked up in the entrance. He was doing the same, almost not stopping for breath. I looked to Gemma, but she wasn't beside me.

All at once I wasn't hungry any more. In fact, I felt sick.

"Where's Gem?"

"Don't call out for her," Jay hissed as he finished his mouthful.

Instead, I sprinted down the shop, trainers squeaking against the floor. I slid to a halt as I found her. A wave of relief washed over me so strong my legs almost buckled.

"Gem?"

She looked up and let the packet drop from her hands. It was chocolate. Of course it was chocolate. Her cheeks were blazing with colour.

"I nearly had a heart attack!"

"Sorry." She dug her toe into the ground. "You should have some chocolate, Zane. Can you even remember what it tastes like?"

My mouth filled with saliva at the mere thought.

Gemma handed me a bar of chocolate with an obscure brand name I'd never seen before. I pulled the packet apart and took a bite, savouring every millisecond. The smooth, sweet, luscious flavour was unlike anything I'd ever tasted. I'd never been a huge chocoholic, but this was by far the best thing I'd ever tasted in my entire life.

Jay found us when I took my last bite and shook his head, taking a bar from Gemma in silence.

"This is so ridiculous," he said when he'd finished. "Look at what food is doing to us."

Gemma shrugged. "Got to get excited about something. Can't just wander around feeling sorry for ourselves in this world. Otherwise we might as well be one of them."

Jay rolled his eyes. "You're one to talk."

She whacked him on the arm. "Well, I learnt my lesson, all right? We're all fine. Zane's back. There is chocolate in the world again. And no doubt I'll have a decent sleep on a bed tonight." She grinned wide. "This is the best day I've had in a *long* time."

FORTY-EIGHT

Gemma was right, I had the best sleep I'd had in what felt like an eternity. For the first time in the ZA, I was sleeping on a bed, with all the people in the world that mattered only a few doors away from me.

Jay and I shared a room, and he let me have the double bed. When sunlight streamed through the terrible curtains, I awoke with a smile on my face. Gemma was sitting on the end of Jay's bed. They both stopped chatting to look at me.

"Morning." Gemma had her usual smirk on her face.

"You should've woken me up." I rubbed my hair. "Don't wait on my account."

"Stop panicking. It's only just daylight."

"Then what are you doing here?"

"Nothing." She looked away from me. "Just talking to my good friend Jay."

He rolled his eyes. "She was checking you were really here."

"Jay!" She hit him. "I wasn't."

He rubbed his arm where she'd struck "You're a bloody liar, Gemma."

I pressed my lips together to stop from laughing.

She shook her head and jumped up. "Anyway, I'll leave you boys to sort yourselves out. We're probably going to leave in like ten minutes."

"She was," Jay said as soon as she shut the door. "She wanted to make sure you were really alive."

"I gathered as much. She must've hit you hard. You full Gemma'd her."

Jay pulled himself up and went to the mirror, brushing his

hair with his fingers. "Yeah, well, I dunno why she's being all bizarre."

I shrugged and something tight and squeezing nestled into my stomach. "I dunno. Anyway, what's the plan?"

The plan turned out to be another vote about staying or going now we'd collected all the food. Savannah said she'd felt cosier in the farmhouse, and her ankle was much better. Aniya agreed with whatever Savannah said, and Ollie wasn't far behind.

Mum suggested it was safe here for now, but she didn't mind going back to the farmhouse. Lisa agreed. Jay didn't seem to care. I said I didn't mind what we did. I didn't hear what Tom had to say. I was too busy ignoring his existence.

Gemma was the only one to oppose the idea, but once everyone had set their sights on the luxury of Mandeville Farmhouse, the decision was made.

We walked and walked and walked and walked, hauling all the food we could carry on our backs. If only we knew how to hot-wire a car.

Everyone wanted a go with Tom's machete when the Infected strolled up to us. All except myself, Mum, and Aniya.

"It's awesome," Jay said.

"So jealous." Ollie was shaking his head. "How much did this cost?"

"Not that much. The medieval swords are a lot more expensive, but they're more for show. I'm glad I ended up with this instead of one of the heavier ones. I didn't have the time to weigh up the pros and cons when I grabbed it."

Mum scoffed. "You had enough money to fritter away on swords?"

Tom just blinked.

"And you had weapons in the same house your children were in?"

"It was perfectly safe." Tom rubbed the back of his neck. "They were in displays, and they knew not to go anywhere near them."

"It's stupid and irresponsible."

I could almost feel Mum simmering next to me. Like her, I had a million things I wanted to say, a million insults I wanted to hurl at him. But I couldn't make my lips form a single one.

The world kept spinning. Our feet kept walking. Our hearts kept beating. But the boredom was never far behind us. I knew we'd hit rock bottom when we started to play I spy. People say talking to yourself is the first sign of madness. It's not. It's I bloody spy.

We stopped for the night in a boarded-up pub, Ollie hammering the way through the panel across the door. Gemma and I took the last watch before the sun came up, and she couldn't stop talking though she didn't seem to be saying anything. She talked about the old world, TV shows, books, and things that'd happened in her life. Not once did she mention anything to do with the ZA.

I watched her, nodding my head, wondering what had shaken her up so bad while I'd been gone. It was like something had flipped a switch, and she was more excitable and nervy than I'd ever seen.

We kept on trekking, and when I thought there was no way on earth we'd ever find the farmhouse again, Savannah spotted the barn in the distance, just like last time.

"Yes! We've made it." She was favouring her good leg but hadn't slowed all day. "I knew we could find it again."

We ran our hands over the wood of the barn as we passed, excitement buzzing through the group at the prospect of the farmhouse. The prospect of *home*.

I wanted to crash on my sofa. But it was the ZA. There was no way I was getting my wish.

"The roof," Savannah sung. "The roof, the roof, the roof, the roof!"

Laughter swelled in the air, and grins filled everyone's faces. But as we drew closer and closer, we noticed something wasn't right at all.

"It's not safe," Mum said.

We stopped at the end of the gravel drive and watched as the horde of Infected cried out, banging on the door, trying to claw their way in. The sea was a mass of grey, and the smell drifted over to us on the breeze. I had to hold my breath. It was insane. There were hundreds of them, and they were creating a ring around the house.

"What happened here?" Ollie was shaking his head.

"Look." Aniya pointed to a new car on the drive.

Savannah tried to hold her smile. "Someone else made it."

Jay let out a breath. "I don't think they made it."

We all stood there in a line, staring, gripping each other's hands.

"What now?" Gemma asked. "Back to the services?"

Before anyone could answer, Tom jumped round, brandishing his machete. "Watch your backs!"

A few Infected were stumbling behind us, mouths open and ready. Tom beheaded two in one go as two more appeared. Gemma squeezed my hand tight as the horde of Infected surrounding Mandeville Farmhouse started turning their heads and coming this way.

Aniya squealed and a whole row of Infected snapped their heads round, trundling this way.

"Aniya!" Gemma spun to face her. "What are you—look out!"

An Infected was centimetres away from her, and it grabbed onto her shoulders. Gemma and I jumped into action, but we were too far away. Jay and Mum were busy fighting the

298

Infected coming towards us. Tom and Ollie were busy fighting the Infected coming behind us. And Savannah was too busy screaming.

Aniya's fists circled round, having no effect whatsoever on the Infected. She'd already dropped the golf club we'd made her carry. All she was doing was yelping louder and louder, drawing them nearer and nearer.

The Infected opened its mouth wide and closed it over Aniya's throat. Blood poured all down her front, covering her hoodie and necklace. The shriek died mid-cry. The Infected wouldn't let her go as her eyes went dark forever.

And I couldn't do anything.

Lisa's arms clasped round Savannah, holding her back as the Infected took another bite out of Aniya for good measure. Tom sliced off the thing's head and moved over to Aniya.

"No!" Savannah's screech shook the world I stood on.

I'd never heard a sound like it, and I almost dropped my golf club.

"No! Don't! Please!"

Tom gave her a look of despair. "I'm sorry."

"No!"

His machete swung down and disconnected Aniya's head from her body. Vomit wanted to leap up my throat. Tears wanted to well in my eyes. My knees wanted to collapse. But I couldn't let any of those things happen.

"No! You killed her! You killed her!"

Mum and Jay backed up to Gemma and Ollie and I, and Tom moved closer too.

"Stop it," Lisa was saying. "Stop it, Savannah. Breathe."

The Infected were coming from all angles, and I had no time to think or process what was happening. In that moment, all I had to think about was killing. Which was all I did.

I drowned out Savannah's howling and pushed Aniya out

of my mind. There was no time for that now. No time for anything.

Skulls cracked. Blood was spilt. Guts stained my clothes. Sweat ran down my face. The Infected screamed.

"This is stupid!" Jay yelled. "We need to move."

"Back to the main road," Ollie agreed.

"The services," Gemma said. "Head back to the services."

"See you there." Lisa was pulling Savannah out the way, and Gemma and I covered their backs as best we could.

"Mum!" Jay called. "Mum, come back!"

I could still hear Savannah weeping in the distance.

"Jay!" Ollie was at his side. "They'll be fine. Come on."

"Be safe!" Mum shouted to them as Ollie and Jay made their escape.

"Freaking run!" Gemma shrieked, powering off in the opposite direction to Mum and Tom.

Without thought, I followed her. Without time to turn back, Mum was gone. Again.

No time for that now. I put my head down and ran, pumping my arms, listening to my heart gallop. Gemma was panting beside me, and although as the seconds wore into minutes her breath became more and more laboured, she didn't once ask to stop.

FORTY-NINE

When it started to get dark, Gemma and I ducked into a tiny terraced house with the door unlocked. There were unopened letters on the coffee table and dirty plates by the sink. We tiptoed up the creaking stairs to check the bathroom and bedroom, but all was silent.

Gemma threw her rucksack to the ground and dropped her head in her hands as she plonked down onto the bed. I sat beside her and put my arm around her shoulder.

I wasn't expecting the devastating sob that shook her body, and I jumped at the sound. I could do nothing but sit and shush her, pulling her close.

When she could breathe again, she watched her hands as she played with her nails. "This is horrendous. When's it gonna stop?" She sniffed. "I wasn't expecting... I never actually thought they'd get any of us and then..." She shook her head. "It was different with Mick and Callie. We were expecting it. We knew they had a certain amount of time left. But one minute she was totally fine and healthy and the next she was gone, and that was it."

I nodded, having nothing to add. I could still hear Savannah screaming in the back of my mind. I shut my eyes to try and hide from it, but if anything, that made it worse.

"Poor Savannah." Gemma snuggled closer to me and rested her head on my chest. "I swear I could hear her heart breaking."

We sat there until the last of the dying light disappeared. Gemma crawled to the head of the bed and from the sound of it, kicked off her shoes and discarded her coat before climbing under the covers.

I did the same until we were both sat there, staring at the blackness, listening to the other breathe.

"Do you think they made it?" Gemma whispered.

"Yeah. Of course. No one was alone. They'll be fine."

"Who're you most worried about?"

"Lisa and Savannah."

"Me too."

I turned to her though I still couldn't see a thing. "At least I know you're safe."

"Yeah." She said it so quiet I wouldn't have heard if not for the total silence surrounding us.

After an eternity, I broke it. "What's the matter, Gem?"

"What do you mean? We almost got killed today."

"No. I mean before that. You've been bizarre." I chose Jay's word. "What's going on?"

"Nothing. Nothing's going on."

"Gem. Come on. It's me. What can't you tell me?"

"It's stupid really."

"I don't care. I won't think it's stupid."

"You were dead."

"Is that all?"

"Zane, you have no idea what that's like. You know what it's like when people actually die, but you came back."

I couldn't think of anything to say, so I sat and let her continue.

"I'd convinced myself of it. I didn't want to be like your mum, clinging to this ridiculous hope. That horde was insane that followed you. I watched you sprint out of my life with no regard for your own safety. You were the biggest hero I'd ever known, and I was the one who'd killed you."

"It wouldn't have been your fault."

"Oh yeah? Did anyone else stop? Did anyone else freeze?

You refused to run away from me. You could've left me there and carried on and secured your own survival."

"Yeah," I scoffed. "Like I could just leave you there to die. Don't be stupid, Gem. I couldn't do that."

"Exactly! Exactly. You're a hero. And I was the reason you led them away."

"No. I led them away because Jay told me to, and we didn't have many other options. I didn't really think about it. I just did it."

"Again, exactly. Only you would've just listened to Jay and run off to die."

"I didn't think that was what I was doing until I was already doing it. Please stop acting like I wanted to make a martyr out of myself. I didn't."

"Then why did you do it?"

"Because I promised her. And that's all I've got left now."

"Exactly."

The quiet surrounded us but wasn't as heavy as I expected, and I sat in its safety for a moment before speaking again. "It wasn't your fault I ran. If anyone's, it was Jay's. But it really doesn't matter because everything turned out fine."

"Aniya's dead."

"And that has nothing to do with any of us. That's a totally different issue. That wasn't anyone's fault, and you know it."

"I'm sure Savannah doesn't see it that way."

"Who could she possibly have to blame?" I rubbed my hand over the back of my neck. "She probably blames herself."

"How?"

"She'll find a way. If she's anything like me, she'll need to blame herself."

"Callie was different."

"They all were." I chewed on my lip. "But you've got

nothing to blame yourself for anyway because I'm alive."

"That doesn't mean I can forget what it felt like when you were dead."

"I don't know how to make that go away." I took her hand, missing at first and touching her arm, making her jump. "I'm still alive. I promise." I pressed her hand to my chest. "See. My heart's beating and everything."

"I know." She didn't pull her hand away. "But that's just it. You'd turned into this incredible hero who sacrificed himself, and you're still just Zane Carlisle."

"I don't understand."

"You became this amazing legend as I watched you go. I can't undo that."

"What are you saying?"

"I'm saying I can't see you as that normal boy any more."

"I'm still him."

"And yet now you're something else too."

The tight thing in my stomach that'd shown itself when Jay had mentioned Gemma's behaviour was getting wild. It was hard to breathe. I didn't want to think too much about what was going on, so I changed the subject for better or worse. I didn't care. I needed to change it.

"Was it your parents' car that you saw?"

She dropped her hand from my heart but didn't let go. "Yeah."

"The others could still be all right."

"Now you're just lying to me."

"But Savannah and Ollie came from a traffic jam, and they're all right."

"They had stuff with them. There was loads of food at my house. They can't have taken much. They weren't killers, Zane. Not like we are."

"We aren't killers."

"I'm not saying it's a bad thing. It's a necessary thing. Aniya wasn't a killer either, and that can only take you so far."

I tried not to squirm as I pictured the brothers in Aniya's locket.

"I didn't want to believe they were dead. I was trying to think of a way they could still be alive. I didn't want to join the camp with the rest of them that believed their parents were dead. I didn't want to. And then you come back, and you've got both your parents. I mean, what the actual—"

"We're not talking about him."

"We can if you want to."

"I most definitely don't want to. Anyway, I was asking you what was wrong, not the other way around."

"Well, I thought I'd killed my best friend. My mum's... Things pretty much went to hell."

"But that doesn't make sense of..." I didn't want to bring it up. I wasn't even sure I could say it aloud. I cursed myself every time I thought about it, but I couldn't help myself.

"The kiss?" She said the words without fear in a way I never could. "I was glad you were alive. It felt like my heart had been ripped clean out of my chest, and then there you were, offering it back to me. I had a hole in my middle, that's what it felt like. I wasn't a full person any more, and then you came back and fixed it. I've never been so relieved of anything in my entire life. I've never felt anything like it. Not even close. Are you saying you wouldn't have done the same thing?"

"I dunno." I didn't want to admit that no, I would never have initiated a kiss. And now I was feeling guilty about Callie. Feeling guilty about a kiss I didn't even know was coming. A kiss I pulled away from. But even so, I couldn't lie to myself.

I enjoyed it. And that made me the worst person in the world.

"I…" She gave a nervous titter. "I would've done it to anyone."

We both knew that was a lie.

"I'm sorry. It won't happen again."

I wanted to crawl into a hole and die when the squeeze and drop of disappointment filled me up. What was wrong with me? I didn't want to kiss Gemma. Why was I feeling like this? I wanted things to stay the way they were.

"Don't apologise," I said.

She squeezed my hand. "Funny old world we live in now, huh?"

"Funny old world indeed."

FIFTY

Gemma fell asleep in my arms. When I awoke, I discovered I'd wrapped myself around her. Guilt was like a kick in the stomach, and I rolled over to face the other way and waited for the sun to rise. For weeks and weeks I'd dreamt about sleeping next to Callie, and here I was next to Gemma like it was the most normal and unexciting thing in the world.

She ended up snuggling into my back, but she jolted away when she awoke. "That's not awkward at all." She cleared her throat. "You could've moved me."

"You were warm." I didn't look at her.

We left the house and made our way to the motorway without many words. Gemma started kicking a stone. When it bounced in my direction, I kicked it too, but we didn't talk.

It wasn't until we found the motorway and gave it a quick sweep for survivors that Gemma spoke. "I'm sorry, okay? I feel awful."

"Awful about what?"

"Everything I said last night. I'm taking it back. You're just Zane. You're just as irritating as always."

"Why do you feel awful?"

"You haven't looked at me yet this morning."

I kicked an empty bottle.

"You're not looking at me now."

I found a huff building in my lungs as I made a point of looking her straight in the eye.

She shook her head. "I already said sorry. What more do you want me to do? I've taken it back. I've taken it all back."

I didn't have anything to say.

"Come on, Carlisle. What is it? I can't do anything unless I know what's wrong."

"It's nothing."

"Yeah."

"It isn't."

"I don't believe you."

"You don't have to."

"Zane, please. I can't stand this much longer."

"I said it's nothing."

"But it isn't nothing."

"But it is!" I didn't know where the shout came from, but it burst out of me, my hands clenched into fists.

Gemma stared at me.

"I'm sorry." I looked back to the ground.

She didn't try again until the turn-off for the services appeared in the distance. "It's Callie, isn't it?"

I didn't answer.

"I knew it. If that's what you're worried about, you can stop it, because I won't make that mistake again."

I watched as she scuffed her boots against the ground.

"I wasn't professing my love for you or anything. That's not what that was. All I was trying to say was I need you in my life, and I got kinda a little excited about the fact you weren't dead, and I'm sorry about that. I should've realised how oversensitive you would be about it."

I bit back an answer as we made our way to the fire exit. After a quick scan, we discovered we were the first ones back. Gemma grabbed a marker pen from the stationery shop and wrote *GEM AND ZANE MADE IT* in huge capital letters on the door.

And then it was a waiting game.

We dragged chairs from the food court into the back room and sat in front of the fire escape. Gemma pulled on tufts of her hair. It'd grown about an inch since she'd hacked it all off. It was beginning to suit her.

"Rockin' a pixie cut." She chuckled to herself. "Never thought that would happen."

"It suits you better than it first did."

"Hmm. Miss my hair though. I still go to play with it. It's so stupid."

We sat for another minute.

"I'm sorry about before," I said, looking at my still bandaged hands. When I took the original bandages off, I put more on out of comfort rather than necessity. I didn't notice last night that they were dirty and splattered with blood. "I didn't mean to shout at you."

"And I didn't mean to corner you."

I started unwinding the bandages.

"We're a mess, huh?"

"No. Just figuring out the ZA."

"Still. Bloody hard work this. I wish everything would go back to normal."

I didn't have a reply, so I watched the bandages float to the ground. My palms were scuffed but almost healed, and they didn't hurt any more. Another thing Tom had helped me with. The more I thought about it, the harder I was finding it to hate him.

"Who'd you think will be back first?" Gemma asked.

"Mum and Tom."

"Don't you mean *Mum and Dad*?"

I was about to make a fuss and let my rage loose when she smirked at me. I let it out in one big gust. "Shut up."

"You're too easy, Carlisle."

"Shut up."

It was over an hour later when there was a voice and a creak, and the fire door opened.

"You were right."

We jumped up, and I flung myself into Mum's arms, drinking her in, letting her scent overwhelm me.

"Thank goodness," she breathed, pulling back from me. "Let's not get separated again. I don't think I can handle it." She had tears in her eyes.

I took her hand. "Okay, deal."

"Are you both all right?" Tom asked.

"Fine." Gemma gave him a quick hug. "Everything's fine."

"Zane." Tom nodded to me and offered a smile. "Glad you're all right."

I nodded back, not quite able to reciprocate.

Gemma gave Mum a hug. "That's progress, right?"

We brought in two more chairs, decided to be optimistic, and brought a further four in after them. We swapped stories and waited and waited and waited.

"It'll be Jay next," Gemma said after we finished a crossword from the puzzle book Mum brought back from the food court. "It has to be."

"Why do you think it'll be Jay next?" Tom looked to her.

"It has to be. Jay knows what he's doing. He'll be here."

"Well, we shouldn't worry," Mum said, though there was a lack of conviction in her voice. "We were with the speedy twins, so of course we were here first. Savannah might be a little slower, and I doubt Jay and Ollie would get here quite so fast."

I passed the words *speedy twins* around and around in my head, wondering what she meant by that. The next time I looked up, the room seemed darker.

Gemma stuck her head out of the door. "It's getting dark out there."

"How long do we wait?" Tom asked.

I shot him a dirty look.

"I've never had to wait before." His voice jumped up a pitch. "I didn't mean any offence. I'm just asking."

I looked to Gemma. "How long did it take you to think I was dead?"

She pressed her lips together and leant back against the door. "All of five seconds. But that was different."

"Mum?"

"I didn't let myself think it." She put her hand on top of mine. "So I don't know either."

"The idea that you would stop waiting for me scared me like nothing else." I met Gemma's eye as I spoke. "I was so terrified of being left alone. I thought there would be no way you would think I was alive, and that thought was terrible. I didn't want to be dead to you. I say we give them more time. I'm not giving up on them yet."

My eyes were drooping by the time the door opened again. Everyone was on their feet in an instant. When I saw the long blonde hair with pink ends, I felt a sick disappointment I hated myself for.

Mum hugged Lisa first, and I went up to Savannah. The look in her eyes was dull and dead. She didn't even try her trademark smile. It looked as though she'd never smiled once in her life and never would.

I pulled her into my arms without a word, knowing nothing I could say could make it better. Nothing I could do could make it better. Even the fact I knew how she was feeling would mean nothing. If anything, she'd want to pretend she was the only one in the world who'd ever felt like this.

"I'm glad you're safe," was all I said when we parted.

"You too," she forced out. Her throat sounded scratchy.

"Where's Jay?" Lisa was looking over each of our faces like Jay was about to appear out of nowhere.

Gemma pulled Lisa close like she hadn't heard, and Lisa tried to push her off.

"Where is he? Where's Jay?"

"Leese." Mum took one of her hands. "He's not back yet. But I'm sure he will be. He'll be fine. We'll just wait a little longer."

"But it's almost dark."

My heart sank at her desperation.

"Don't worry," Mum was saying. "He'll be here."

I couldn't help but watch as Lisa's chest billowed up and down as she tried to hold her sobs in. "I can't. Not Jay. He's all I've got left. He can't."

"He'll be here," I said, trying to convince her as much as myself. "I know he will." Although even as I said it, I was having trouble believing it.

FIFTY-ONE

Lisa sat by the door all night, gripping a golf club tight in her hands. The only one who went back to the hotel to bed was Savannah, Mum trailing after her to make sure she was okay. Gemma's head kept bobbing up and down as she woke herself up and succumbed to sleep.

Jay had to be all right. I kept repeating the words over and over as I twisted the bracelet Callie made for me around and around my wrist. It was dirty and starting to fray, but I knew I'd never be able to take it off. Not now she was gone.

Jay had to survive because I'd promised. It appeared I wasn't very good at keeping my promises, but what was I supposed to do? Jay and Ollie had gone in the opposite direction. I couldn't have left Gemma behind. I'd promised Callie I'd keep them all safe, but I couldn't split myself into four and go with each group. I would have if that were possible.

It'd been hard enough keeping myself alive, let alone the three of them as well. And what about Mum? And Savannah? And Ollie?

I rubbed my thumb over the string, back and forth, back and forth.

Come on, Jay. *I'm not giving up on you.*

I awoke with a crick in my neck as Gemma jumped awake. It appeared I'd fallen asleep resting on her shoulder. She went to say something but closed her mouth again as the silence of the room engulfed us. Instead, she let out a deep breath and shut her eyes, burying her face in her hands.

I stretched my legs and went to stand next to Lisa.

"He's coming," she said. "He has to be. I'm not leaving here without him."

I squeezed her shoulders tight for a moment before leaning up against the doorframe and watching the day go by. When my cheeks were so cold I felt as though I'd freeze, I turned back to the group to see Savannah and Mum huddled in the corner, as far away from Tom and Gemma as they could be. Savannah was crying, and Mum was whispering something to her.

"No," Savannah said so we could all hear. "Why should I? We've all got our opinions. Why can't I share?"

Mum whispered something else to her, but Savannah shook her head.

"It's stupid. You're all delusional. They're both dead."

Lisa spun round to look at Savannah. "You don't know that."

"We don't know that," Mum said. "What's the harm in staying here a little longer? We've got food here and real beds and everything. We're in no danger."

"But it's stupid. Look at them. Waiting for them. They're not coming."

"I'm not giving up on Jay," I said. "I'm not going to move on just because I couldn't wait long enough."

Savannah was glaring at me. "How are you still here? How did you find us? How were you on your own and alive? She was—she was with all of us and now…"

Mum rubbed Savannah's arms. "It's not Zane's fault."

"No." Her eyes shot to Tom. "It's his."

Tom crossed his arms over his chest but didn't say anything.

"Savannah, it's not his fault." Mum tried to recapture her attention.

"He killed her."

"No. He didn't. She was already gone. It was the Infected. It wasn't Tom. He wouldn't do something like that."

"How do you know? We don't know him. We just let him come in here and start killing us."

314

"Hey!" Gemma shuffled in front of Tom to block Savannah's death glare. "That is not fair. He's a good man. He saved Zane's life."

Savannah gave a dark laugh. "You would say that. He may have saved the one you love, but he killed the one I love."

"Savannah." Gemma clenched her jaw. "I don't want to argue with you, but you're being ridiculous. He stopped her from getting back up and killing the rest of us."

Savannah was shaking her head, and her hair was whipping back and forth. "We could've saved her."

"No, we couldn't."

"You don't know that! All of you have made a little family here, and then there's me. You didn't care about Aniya. You never even spoke to her. You couldn't care less if I walked out of here right now. You're not even worried about Ollie, just Jay."

"I'm sorry." Gemma jumped up. "I'm sorry Jay is like a brother to me. I've known him since the day Lisa brought him home, so I'm so sorry that I care about him more than Ollie. I admit it. Of course I care about Jay's life more. I've known him for fourteen years."

Savannah narrowed her eyes. "You are so manipulative. We always do what Gemma wants. Why? Why does the world seem to revolve around you?"

"What?" Gemma's eyebrows came together. "What the hell are you talking about? We don't always do what I want. I didn't wanna go in the farmhouse, and I didn't wanna leave here the other day."

"So you're all high and mighty because if we'd gone with your choice, people would still be alive?"

"I'm not saying that. We don't know what would've happened if we hadn't gone to the farmhouse. How could I possibly know that? Do you have a problem with me, Savannah?"

"You were moping around here crying about Zane with no thought whatsoever. How do you think Jen was feeling? That's her son, and you were acting like he was your saint or something."

"What's that got to—"

"And she was even comforting *you*. How wrong is that? It's all about Gemma."

"And it's not all about Savannah? You tried to run the show from the day we met you. We saved your life, and you're not even grateful."

"Yeah, well, maybe we would've been better off if we'd just taken your car like I'd wanted."

Silence was like a sledgehammer on the room. I was afraid to breathe.

Mum was still rubbing Savannah's arms, but her eyes were wide with shock. "You don't mean that, Savannah. I can't speak for anyone else, but I care very much about you. You've made me smile at times I didn't think I could. And you know who else cares about you?"

Tears were creeping down Savannah's face.

"Ollie and Jay. We just want to wait. Just for a little while. There's no harm in it."

Lisa's voice was strong and steady. "I'm not leaving here without Jay."

"You're all mad." Savannah stood up and left the room.

Mum sighed and tried to tuck her hair behind her ears before getting up to follow her. "I don't think she meant what she said. About the car." She was biting her lip. "She's just angry. She doesn't mean what she says."

Gemma was the first to speak. "What is her problem with me? What did I ever do to her? Please, suggestions? I genuinely haven't got a bloody clue."

"At least I know what her problem with me is." Tom was

still gripping his arms tight as though holding himself together.

"I knew we were a clash of personalities but…" Gemma pushed her hair back. "She didn't have to get personal." She sat down next to Tom again. "And, Zane, in case you're getting all weird again, I'm not in love with you. For the record."

I watched her before sitting next to the door with my back up against the wall. "I think Mum's right. I don't think she meant what she said. She wants someone to blame for Aniya, and I guess I was wrong before. She doesn't want to blame herself. I guess she and I are very different people."

"In every bloody way." Gemma pulled her knees up to her chest. "I hope Jay and Ollie can talk some sense into her when they get back."

Tom was rubbing his hand over the back of his neck. "You lot don't blame me, do you?"

"For what?" Gemma looked at him.

"Aniya."

"How could we? Don't let her get under your skin, Tom. We all know you did the right thing. We didn't exactly have time to vote on it, but I know which way that vote would've gone. You were the one who noticed the Infected anyway. I didn't see her thanking you for that."

Tom was looking my way, and the fire igniting in my blood was hard to ignore, but I tried to push it down nonetheless. Gemma was right. Things could have been a lot worse if he hadn't been there.

"We don't blame you," I said. "You did the right thing. Savannah's just blind with grief. You didn't do anything wrong."

His mouth pulled up at the corners. "Thank you."

Lisa stood up, and I spun round to look out the door. There were a crowd of Infected in the distance, and they were coming this way. In front, stumbling towards safety, rucksack on their back and some kind of bat in their hand, was a single figure.

FIFTY-TWO

Lisa was squinting. "Is that Jay?" I could hear the tears in her voice. "Jay?"

"It could be him." Gemma was leaning out the door. "But where's the other one?"

Sickness curled around in my stomach and squashed me tight. I couldn't tell whether that was blonde hair auburn with blood or auburn hair.

Tom tried to pull Gemma out the doorframe.

"Hey!" Gemma shrugged him off.

"Look at them. We have to get inside."

"No. We have to get *him* inside."

"What about us?"

"What about him?"

Tom growled and unsheathed his machete, stepping past the doorframe. "I can't promise anything."

I scrabbled around for my golf club and Gemma her baseball bat. Lisa followed after us, bouncing on the balls of her feet, trying to catch another look at the figure. She raised the golf club like she meant business.

We stood steady, the four of us, waiting for Jay or Ollie or a stranger.

"It's Jay," Gemma said. "I know it is. It's Jay."

The wave of groans felt like a boulder to the chest. I clenched my fists to fight the trembles.

"Come on, Jay." I was staring at the figure as he grew closer and closer. He seemed too short to be Ollie.

"It's Jay." There was joy in Gemma's voice.

That hair was in fact blonde with blood caking it. He was

holding the cricket bat we'd found in Gemma's shed. And he was alive.

Just.

His footsteps were unsteady, and it dawned on me that he might have been travelling for hours. He tripped and only just caught himself, and before I had time to think, I was racing towards him.

"Zane!" Gemma was a few footsteps behind me. I heard the whoosh of Tom's machete as he caught up.

My heart tried to halt me as I came face to face with the line of Infected, but I powered through my fear, Jay's hand reaching for me. I yanked him forward and pushed my legs to run harder than they ever had before, dragging Jay along behind me.

Lisa was halfway between the Infected and the door, and she sprinted back with us as we burst through the first door. But I didn't stop. I let go of Jay in the hotel corridor, not even giving him a glance before going back for Gemma. I crashed into Lisa as I turned, flinging her to one side as I exploded out the door again.

They were everywhere.

"Gem!" I yelped, fright making my heart scream.

"Here!" She was to the right, fighting off three Infected.

Tom was slashing heads here, there, and everywhere, only a few steps away from her.

I put my head down and made myself reach her. I blocked out the moans of the Infected. I blocked out the crushing fear of death. I couldn't live with myself if I left Gemma to die. I'd rather die myself than watch her get bitten.

"Zane, no!"

I grabbed her wrist, her bracelet from Callie rough on my healing palm.

"Run!"

She tripped as Jay had, following me, unable to touch her feet to the ground any faster. I hurled her into the front room and put my arms against the doorframe, head swirling.

Tom was there, right in front of me. Maybe two, three metres away. But he wasn't heading in this direction. He was letting them surround him.

I shook my head. "What are you doing?" I breathed the words. "Get back here."

But how could he see where the door was now? How would he know which direction to run?

"Tom!" I yelled it, Infected turning their heads as though they hadn't seen me until now. "Tom! This way!"

With a flourish, three were dead, and Tom was ducking and weaving his way towards the door. I reached out my hand, Infected growing nearer and nearer.

I had a few seconds. Not even that. We had to the shut the door.

But I wasn't about to shut it on him.

The second his fingertips touched mine, I clenched my hand tight and pulled with all my strength. He came tumbling through the door after me.

Gemma threw her weight on the door, slamming it shut and resting her back against it. She bounced as they crushed against the other side.

Before my brain had any time to catch up with me, I spun round with a chair and jammed it in the push down handle. I grabbed for another one to squeeze in and threw all the rest in that direction, hoping they'd trip up once they made their way in.

Tom was lying on the floor on his back, staring up at the ceiling. Gemma offered her hand as we passed and sped to jam more chairs into the second door as we hurried our way into the hotel corridor.

Jay was still gasping for breath, face pale and green as he rested against the wall. Mum's shoulders relaxed as she saw us, and Lisa looked as though she was about to say something.

"No time." Gemma rushed past. "We have to find a way out. Now. Come on."

Jay pulled himself up and followed us into the food court. We were so close, someone stepped on the back of my trainers more than once. We headed straight for the supermarket, and Gemma paused at the fire escape.

"Everyone ready?" Her eyes darted everywhere. "I have no idea how many of them are going to see us, but we're going to have to run. Okay? Jay?"

"Fine," he wheezed. "I can't feel my legs anyway."

"We all look out for each other. Nobody else dies on my watch. Ready?"

I gave a nod. Gemma threw open the door, and we were running. Gemma was at the front, Tom and I a step behind her, keeping Jay safe between us. Mum and Lisa and Savannah brought up the rear.

A few Infected turned their heads, but we were gone before they could work their way round cars or fences to reach us. The huge horde was still banging on the door of our latest failed haven. Some on the outskirts of the pack noticed us, but they were too far away to cause a threat. They crept this way, but we'd be out of sight by the time they reached the motorway.

We only slowed once we'd been on the motorway for five minutes, but we didn't stop. The heavy breathing and groaning made me want to rest, but I couldn't pause now. My legs wouldn't let me. Fear kept me running and running and running.

When darkness started to fall, we stopped in a clearing of trees to the side of the road. Jay fell to his knees and curled up in a ball on the ground. Lisa hugged him close as though she'd never let go again. Mum occupied Savannah with making a fire, and Gemma and Tom stood with me, watching the road, making sure the Infected weren't about to appear on the horizon.

No one spoke until everyone's breath had been caught, and we were certain the horde wasn't after us. I checked my arms and hands for bites even though I was sure I hadn't been bitten. I watched as Gemma checked herself too, grinning when she came back clean.

Lisa only unravelled herself from Jay when he was asleep in front of the fire. She put one arm around my shoulder and the other around Gemma's.

"Thank you. You saved his life. I can't ever repay you, but thank you so much."

Gemma grinned. "I wasn't about to leave him. And anyway, Zane and Tom saved my life, so I think we're all even now."

"And, Zane." Tom's face was open, and he was fighting down a smile. "You saved my life too."

I pressed my lips together for a moment. "I wasn't going to leave you out there to die."

He nodded and offered his hand. "Thank you."

I looked him up and down for a moment, wondering what was going through his head as I tried to work out what was going through mine. A rush of emotion filled me up, and I acted on impulse, throwing my arms around Tom and squeezing him tight.

"You didn't have to risk your life for Jay," I said.

"And you didn't have to risk your life for me."

"But you saved my life, and you asked me to repay the favour."

He was smiling freely when I pulled back. "But you didn't have to."

Gemma hugged Tom when I let go. "You risked your life for us. You could've died. I think you're part of the family now." She offered her hand to me when they parted. "Zane?"

"What's this?" I raised my eyebrows at her.

"Thank you for saving my life."

I bundled her into a hug. "And thank you for not dying."

"Right back at you."

Her stormy-grey eyes seemed to sparkle as they met mine, and though I couldn't understand the desire, I could resist temptation no longer.

"I'm never going anywhere. Trust me," I whispered, caressing her face and pulling her closer to me. I rested my nose on her soft cheek, listening to her breathe, listening to her live. I shut my eyes and brushed my lips over hers. It lasted no more than a few seconds.

I wouldn't even call it a kiss. I would call it a promise. Between two best friends.

I wasn't going anywhere. And there was no way in hell I was letting her leave me.

FIFTY-THREE

In the morning, we carried on moving. Lisa kept thanking us over and over again for saving Jay, but the more I watched him, the more I came to the conclusion we hadn't saved him at all. He hadn't spoken since we'd left the services, and he looked as though he was only walking because that's what everyone else was doing.

Gemma tried to engage him in conversation, but he was giving nothing at all. No one was brave enough to bring up Ollie. Not even Savannah spoke his name.

"Where are we going?" Lisa asked after a few hours.

"Nowhere," Savannah answered. "We're going absolutely nowhere."

"We're looking for shelter." Gemma's voice had some bite. "Obviously. We're not just walking because it's fun."

"Why are we going this way?" Savannah asked.

"It's just the way we were going before. If you really think about it, I guess we were running away from the coast originally."

"What about London?"

"What *about* London?"

"We're getting closer. It's in this direction."

"We're not going to walk to freaking London."

"Okay, okay." Mum jumped in. "We're just trying to find a place to stay so we can rest for a few days at least. That's all any of us wants."

Savannah started muttering under her breath, but she was ignored. I dropped back to walk beside Jay and gave him a nod of acknowledgement. He gave me nothing.

It must have been at least a quarter of an hour before I caved. "If you want to talk about what happened, you can always talk to me. It backfired last time I told you that, but I'm telling you it again."

He kept looking ahead.

I tried another tactic. "You know, Callie once told me that nothing in the universe can be created or destroyed. Everything here is what's always been here."

"I told her that."

"Oh."

"And I told it better than you did."

"What do I know? Just passing on the information."

"You don't have to walk with me," he said. "I'm more than happy by myself."

"And I'm more than happy walking next to you."

"Maybe I want to be by myself."

"Maybe I won't let you."

"Zane, please."

"Do you remember when Callie—"

"No."

"But I didn't even—"

"No. I don't want to talk about Callie. I don't want to talk about Dad. Or Aniya. Or Ollie. Please, Zane. Just leave me alone."

I didn't say a word while we walked. A dark, crushing force was gripping my heart as I tried not to think of Callie. Tried not to think about what she'd say to me if she were still here.

But if she were still here, everything would be different.

Something had twisted. My grief wasn't as black and gut-wrenching as it had been at Mandeville Farmhouse. I wanted to talk about Callie for the first time since I lost her. Something was making me want to remember her in a way I'd been too afraid of before. I wanted to think about the things we'd done and seen. Try and smile about the fact she'd existed at all. And I'd loved her, and she'd loved me back.

I didn't know whether that meant my heart had decided to start healing, or it meant I was guiltier than I thought I was.

"Hey look." Gemma pointed to one of the huge signs. "What are the chances?"

The sign read *Thrill Island*, and it struck me how many miles we must have walked since meeting Savannah. I hadn't been to Thrill Island since the summer. Another memory of Callie punched me in the stomach. I did nothing to block it out. After passing my driving test the month before, I'd driven Callie, Gemma, and Jay there for the day in Mum's car. We'd laughed all the way there and all the way back.

That felt like it was in another century. Another time. Another universe.

I looked to Jay, wondering if he was thinking the same thing, but his expression was blank and emotionless.

"How about it?" Gemma was grinning.

"Absolutely not," Savannah snapped.

"Well, you would say that. What does everyone else think?"

"I dunno, Gem." I rubbed my hand over the back of my neck. "It'll probably be really dangerous. It'll probably be crammed with Infected."

"Nah. I bet they shut up as normal on the Saturday everything went to hell and never opened again on the Sunday. I bet you."

"You are not serious?" Savannah pulled her nails out of her mouth. It was strange to see her without lipstick on. "Really? This is the most idiotic idea I've ever heard."

"Why? It's got gates and shelter and most likely food."

"I can't believe that you, Gemma, Little Miss I Don't Want to Go, actually wants to go."

"Well, staying in places doesn't seem to have treated us any better than moving on, so what can it hurt?"

"We could all die."

Gemma rolled her eyes. "I just wanna look through the fence and see if it's clear. If there are Infected, we can just walk away again, because they'll all be trapped inside."

Lisa raised her hand. "I trust Gem. If she thinks it'll be safe, I think it will be too."

I nodded. "Me too."

"Well, obviously I'm out." Savannah crossed her arms over her chest. "It's utter suicide."

Mum wet her lips. "I think I'm with Savannah on this one. I just don't know what'll be over there."

"I'm with Jenny," Tom said.

"Stop calling me that." Mum's eyes were dark as she shot a glare at him.

"Well then, Jay?" Gemma turned to him before anyone else could speak. "You have the deciding vote."

"I don't care."

"You've got to cast your vote."

"Why?"

"It's what we do."

"Maybe I don't want to do it any more. Maybe I'm done with all this."

"Well, you have to this time. We'll be stuck here arguing for eternity if you don't." Gemma breezed over the more sinister undertones of his words.

"Fine." He threw his arms out wide. "Whatever. Let's go for it."

"No!" Savannah marched up to him. "What are you doing?"

"Forget it." He walked by her. "We're going. It's done. Keep moving."

Gemma and I exchanged a look as the group trekked

onwards, Savannah complaining to Mum about our unfair system. I hung at the rear, Gemma dropping back to walk beside me.

"That didn't go as I imagined. We're back at square one again. Jay's hurting, and there's nothing I can say to make it go away."

"He won't even share what happened, so we don't even know where to start," I said. "He hasn't mentioned Ollie. I'm not sure what happened to him. I'm just assuming he's dead."

"He's got to be. Jay would want to go after him otherwise." She shook her head. "Is this just gonna carry on getting more and more depressing until there's only one of us left?"

.I shrugged. "I dunno."

"I don't want to be the last one."

"What?" I tried to lighten the mood by chuckling, but it felt wrong in the air. "You'll be queen of the ZA, for sure. The Infected would be afraid of you if they had any sense."

"I don't want to be queen of the ZA. Can you imagine? Wandering lonely through the streets with nothing to live for apart from the fact you haven't fought this hard for this long to give in. No. That's no life."

"I don't think any of us want that. That's worse, isn't it, than being the next to go?"

She nodded. "For certain."

"Not that I want to die."

"Well, no, obviously not. Me neither." She gave a growl. "It's so stupid. Even if it came down to me and a horde of Infected and no way out and a gun, I don't think I'd be able to pull the trigger on myself. Is that cowardly?"

"No. But I think you'd think differently if you were in that situation." A shiver took hold of my body. I tried to push the images of the Infected crowding around me, getting closer and closer, out of my mind.

"How would you kn—" She stopped and bit her lip. "You were really that close, huh?"

I nodded. "Really. I even thought about the gun from Mandeville Farmhouse. If I'd been in charge of it and not Jay, I wouldn't be standing here talking to you now. Tom would never have had the chance to save me. I thought I was going to die the most horrific and painful way I could think of. I would've done anything to get out of it."

She put her arm round my waist and squeezed. "Not on my watch, Carlisle."

FIFTY-FOUR

We reached the entrance of Thrill Island as the sky started to grey. The place felt like a scene from a horror film. Cars were dotted around, but there was no sense to the pattern. There were receipts and pieces of paper floating around the car park. The whole place was silent. The epic adventure music they used to play as you entered the park came to mind, and I didn't know which was creepier, it not playing, or the idea of it playing to no one.

Ducking under the barriers and sneaking past the booths, we reached the metal gates, and as Gemma predicted, they seemed to be locked as normal. We all stood staring for a few minutes before Gemma pulled back.

"It's perfect. I don't see any Infected. The whole place has been shut off, and it's pretty much an island on its own. They won't be able to reach us."

"Says you." Savannah's hands were on her hips. She was glaring at Gemma, but no one else took any notice as we continued onwards.

We checked the gate all the way along, and Tom discovered a set of keys hanging from the lock of a hut-like structure.

"Let the adventure begin." He was smirking, his lip curled up in a playfulness I hadn't seen before. Something about his enthusiasm made me want to smile too.

Tom clicked open the door, and we shuffled into a tidy office that hadn't appeared to be hit by the ZA. There was a bowl of wrapped sweets between two computers, and we each grabbed a handful as we passed. We didn't need to exchange words, just the look of euphoria. I'd forgotten what blackcurrant tasted like. I felt like I could have melted as I finished off my first sweet and shoved another into my mouth.

The door on the other side of the office led through to a long bridge with a building at the end. We crossed the bridge and snuck our way into the entrance hall, which was a mesh of arcades and shops and restaurants. Out the other side, the bright colours of Thrill Island had us staring in silence for a full minute.

"Weird." Gemma shook her head. "Last time we were here we had to practically shove people to get to anything."

"And queue for two hours," I added.

"We'd have to queue forever these days. I bet the power's out here too."

"Unless it's got its own power source." Tom dashed back into the entrance hall, and we waited, tapping our feet until he returned. "Never mind. Forget it."

"Damn." Gemma ran her hand through her hair. "Oh well, could be worse."

We wandered towards the high dinghy slide that was dry and bizarre-looking without people on it. Never before had I missed the sound of laugher so much in any one moment. It was so wrong, this place of such joy and noise being quiet and solemn.

Gemma nudged my arm and grinned. "I'd beat you on the slide if it weren't shut."

"My friend, this is the ZA. Nothing's shut."

She raced towards the metal stairs, leaping over the chain stopping the public from queuing for the abandoned slide. I shrugged off the two rucksacks I was carrying and sprinted after her, unable to suppress the laughter building in my chest. I jumped and almost slipped as my feet touched back onto the floor.

"Come on, Carlisle!" Her feet were banging above me. "I thought you wanted to qualify for the Olympics?"

I pushed my legs harder and skidded to a halt as she did at the top. She rested her hands on her knees and couldn't breathe.

"I beat speedy Carlisle."

"It was a tie." I couldn't erase the smirk on my lips. "Anyway, we didn't start at the same time."

"Excuses, excuses." She stood to full height, grin lighting up the whole world around us.

Forget the blueberry muffin. Forget the bubble gum. Forget the blackcurrant sweets.

This was the best moment of the ZA so far. It was the first time I could remember feeling normal. Feeling like me again.

"Right." Gemma crawled under the barrier and pulled up two dinghies from the conveyor belt.

"Are you serious?" I raised my eyebrows. "There's no water on it."

She threw the boats down. "What do you suggest?"

"It's a slide, right?"

She was creeping towards the slide closest to her.

"No, you don't." I flung myself down, using the rail to push myself faster.

Gemma cackled as she flew down at the same time.

The landing wasn't as spectacular as I imagined as my bloody and filthy combat trousers shuffled against the slide. I shot a look to Gemma, who was using the sides to propel herself forward.

"No!" She was panting. "Victory will be mine!"

When we reached halfway, Gemma jumped up and tried to surf on her feet, her boots squeaking against the plastic. I leapt up too, legs scuttling as fast as I could manage without falling on my face.

I reached the end of the slide first with seconds to spare and threw my hands up in celebration. "That'll teach you to challenge me to a race."

She shook her head as she arrived next to me. "I'll get you one day."

I noticed the others for the first time. Mum was hugging herself, my rucksacks at her feet, a small smile on her face. Lisa was watching us, lips pressed together and almost turning up. Tom had his hands in his pockets, eyes also on us. Savannah had her arms crossed and her nose turned up. My heart dropped as I spotted her. Savannah would be giggling and smiling and maybe joining in if Aniya were here. And the same went for Jay. If he hadn't lost Ollie. Jay wasn't even looking this way. He was gazing at the doughnut stand.

I wandered over to him. "Thinking about doughnuts, huh?"

He looked up at me, baby-blue eyes dull and sad. "Aren't you?"

"I am now."

He dragged his feet as we marched towards the stand. Gemma bounced our way and gave Jay a quick squeeze. "Hands off the candyfloss."

The door wasn't locked, and we let ourselves in to scavenge. There were uncooked doughnuts and a fryer, but with no way to run the fryer, we had to look at the batter and lick our lips.

"No candyfloss, Gem."

"Dammit."

A shiny wrapper caught my eye, and I pulled out a box to reveal bags of sweets. My legs felt like they were going to buckle.

Gemma's eyes went wide. "No. Way."

The rest of them tried to cram through the door all at once to reach, their hands snatching packets up. There was a chorus of pleasure-filled moans as everyone stuck their noses over the packets and breathed in like air was a sweet, rare treat.

Gemma put her hand over her mouth. "I'm actually dribbling."

No other words were spoken until we'd each polished off a packet and shoved the rest into our rucksacks.

"Wow." Gemma's grin was infectious. "That felt like one of those amazing moments you remember forever."

"Chocolate." Mum was shaking her head. "You'd think we'd never seen it before."

It was safe to say we were in high spirits as we continued further into the park, and the sun grew lower and lower in the sky. Gemma even hooked her arms through Mum and Lisa's, the three of them skipping along, giggling like they didn't have a care in the world. And in that moment, we didn't. Sometimes there was enough time to forget about what we'd lost and enjoy the moment right in front of us.

The life right in front of us.

We reached the tallest coaster and looked up at it.

"I'm halfway between thinking it looks like the most fun in the world and it being boring these days." Gemma had her hands like scales. "After all, my body's so used to adrenaline I'm not sure my heart rate would even increase."

"I seem to remember a lot of screaming and swearing on that in the summer."

"What did I know then? That was a different time entirely. A different life in fact."

There was a shriek from Lisa, and we all jumped to face the danger as a single Infected appeared from behind a building, dragging its body along. Its flesh was stretched over its bones, and the stink of its rot made me hold my stomach and my breath. Its hair was matted and knotted, solid with blood, and some of it was missing in clumps. Its stomach was vomiting guts, and it was difficult not to stare as they drooled all over the ground.

To my surprise, Savannah jumped forward with the wheel brace rather than the cricket bat. She forced it into the Infected's skull until it dropped to the ground, half of the weapon still sticking out. All sorts of liquids oozed from the hole. I had to abstain from letting the gag reflex engulf me.

"Where did that come from?" Tom asked, machete held out ready.

A quiet so intense I could hear everyone else's breathing took hold of us, and there, in the distance, was the song of the Infected.

"I knew it!" Savannah was growling. "Stupid idea, Gemma."

Gemma didn't even argue, her face growing pale.

"Let's get out of here," Mum said.

We spun round and went to race back towards the entrance, and that's when we saw them. A mob of Infected.

And they were coming this way.

FIFTY-FIVE

We all backed away, making no sound as we eyed one another, like someone else was going to have a brainwave and figure out a way to save us.

"Jay?" I looked to him out of desperation. "What do we do?"

"Come on." Tom found his head first. "This way. We'll go the long way round."

We fell into line and ran towards the back of the park, hoping we could do a full circle and outsmart them. After all, they were just reanimated corpses carrying a deadly infection. How hard could they be to outsmart?

But the further we ran, the more Infected popped out from behind bins and queue lines and stalls. We didn't engage, just dodged past them. We couldn't waste our energy killing any of them when that would bring the rest of the horde closer.

Lisa sounded as though she was hyperventilating by the time we shot past all the arcades and shops and restaurants, bursting back through the front doors of the entrance hall. We sprinted along the bridge, back the way we came, but we all skidded to a halt when we saw them.

We didn't reach the gates. We didn't have to. We could already see that our escape was blocked by too many hungry mouths.

My stomach dropped into my shoes, my lungs clogged up my throat, and I wanted to scream and pass out all at the same time.

We were trapped.

"No!" Savannah cried. "They must've heard. They must've heard and come after us."

"Shut up," Gemma hissed. "We need to move."

"Don't tell me to shut up. You're the one who told us to come here. You're the one who was making all the noise."

"Shut it, Savannah. We need to get back in the park."

"What? There's no way out."

"There's no way out this way either. We've got to climb something. Come on!"

We dashed back towards the entrance hall as the Infected burst through the doors on the other side.

"No." Lisa was chanting the word. "No, no, no, no, no."

"There!" Gemma pointed to a set of stairs on the other half of the room. "We can get to the park that way."

"You sure?" Mum's fingers were white as she gripped her golf club.

"Do we have a better plan?"

Following Gemma without thought—as the more I thought the less my legs wanted to work—we powered our way towards the Infected at the front. Tom peeled off to detach a few heads, and we knocked a few more down as we passed and all tried to barge through the passageway.

My jelly legs almost had me tripping down the stairs as the Infected's moans filled my ears, and their hands grew closer and closer to my back.

"Wait."

Someone stopped dead in front of me. It sounded like Savannah or Lisa. I pushed them down in a panic, hands beginning to shake now.

"It's too dark."

"I don't care!" I snarled the words, the animal of survival fighting to be unleashed and keep me alive above all others.

A terrified squeak sounded in front of me, and I took the hand of whoever it was. Both her hands clasped mine tight, and I felt the cold of a wedding ring. Lisa.

"Don't make a sound," I whispered to her as we descended into a darkness like I'd never seen.

The blackness was like ice in my heart, and I wanted to crawl under the stairwell and rock backwards and forwards until this was all over. I couldn't even swallow my fear down. I had to let it fill me up as we tiptoed forward, listening for the tap of Gemma's boots in front.

My heart was galloping in my chest so hard and loud I was terrified the Infected would hear it. I couldn't breathe through the panic in my heart. Each breath was pointless, like I hadn't breathed at all. My lungs were squeezing tight like I was suffocating, and as the Infected's chorus swelled, I couldn't take a breath at all.

The hums of murmurs and growls bounced off the walls and rang in my ears. I thought it would swallow me up. There was a sensation of the sound vibrating the world in front of me. I was unsteady on my feet. A small part of me wanted to give in. But I couldn't. I hadn't come this far for nothing.

The terror was so engulfing I felt a spin in my head. If I could see anything at all, the world would be tilting. But all I knew was the beating of shoes in front of me and the desperate longing in the tuneless voices behind me. And of course, Lisa's sweaty hand in mine. I couldn't be sure if the trembling was so violent because her fright was encouraging mine or if all the fear belonged to me.

It was all I could do to keep breathing and keep putting one foot in front of the other. Just keep going.

I had to crush my lips shut to stop from crying out when I walked into the back of someone. There was a furious muttering, and the panic grew and grew.

"What's happening?" Lisa squeaked. "Why've we stopped?"

"Wall," was Gemma's response. "I know there's a door here somewhere."

"You've led us to death, you idiot!" Savannah's voice was too loud and too high-pitched, and they were coming right behind us.

"It feels like a door."

"Open it!"

"I'm trying." I could hear the fumble of her hands against the door or wall, and my body was shaking with anticipation, wanting to act. But do what?

The putrid stink of the Infected was growing closer and closer and closer, and we didn't even know when they would strike. How many seconds did we have? Sixty? Twenty? Two?

The hissing was louder now. Louder by the moment.

This couldn't be the end. I didn't want to never see the sky again, the stars. I didn't want to die in the dark.

I bit my lip to stop from screaming and willed Lisa to do the same. Her hand was grasping mine so tight it felt as though my bones were crunching together. She could break it for all I cared. What use was my left hand? I'd rather know she was still next to me. Still breathing.

"Come on, Gem." I forced the words through gritted teeth. "Save us."

There was a banging in front as someone tried to break their way through. A squeak escaped from someone, and we were all clawing our way to the door, and I swear I could feel an Infected's rotting breath over my shoulder and—

I was going to die. No. Please.

Not like this.

I yanked Lisa forward into the mob of the others, all throwing themselves at the door. Tears blurred my eyes like it mattered. Like I could save myself. Save anyone.

My breath was like gunfire. My skin was alight with panic,

every nerve tensed, waiting, wanting to do something. My heart was like a drumroll building up to the execution. I feared the moment it would go silent.

Then I'd be dead.

I couldn't accept it. I couldn't. I could only just stop myself from screaming and diving head first into the Infected to try and bat my way out. At least then I'd be trying. At least I wouldn't be standing here waiting to die.

Something was building in my chest, and I exploded with a growl. What did it matter if I was quiet now? Everyone was making so much noise.

"Gemma! Please! Open the damn door!"

"I can't."

"Gemma!"

"Zane!" It was Mum. She was screaming.

"Mum!" It came out as a sob.

"Break it open!" Tom yelled. "We'll break it down. Pull down the handle."

"It's locked."

"So what? On three. One!"

"Wait! I can't find the handle!"

"Two!"

Lisa shrieked. The Infected howled.

"Three!"

I hurled my weight into the person in front of me. There was a crack, and some of the dying daylight broke through.

"Again!"

Jay was in front of me, his face pale and green and shining with sweat. I gave him a look and a nod, and he nodded back as we lunged towards the door, throwing everything we had into the wood because there was nothing left now.

"Again!"

I yelped as something touched my back, and I launched

myself into the door. The lock gave way, and we tumbled over each other to the ground, scraping our elbows and knees.

As fast as I fell, I was up again, tugging Lisa back to standing and flinging her into the huddle. I wasn't losing her now.

Our feet pounded hard on pavement as the crowd of hungry, frantic monsters chased us. A horde that would never stop. All the Infected were heading this way after the racket we'd made. Tom was slashing heads, and Gemma was shoving them away as we ran.

And ran. And ran.

"What now?" Savannah screeched.

"Just don't stop!" It was the only response I could think to give.

They were everywhere, creeping out from behind everything.

And there was no way out.

We could run and run and run, and they could stumble as slow as they liked, and they'd still reach us. They outnumbered us. Ten to one.

Gemma skidded to a halt in front of a giant pyramid building that had an old ride hidden inside. There were only two ways round. To the right, which had Infected shuffling this way already. Or through the pyramid.

Her chest was billowing up and down as she faced us. "We've got to go in there. It's our only option."

"No." I shook my head. "Not in the dark again. There's got to be another way."

Jay dropped to the ground, searching his rucksack for something. The rest of us created a circle around him, watching as they grew closer. He pulled out the gun, tucked it into his trousers, and produced a torch.

Gemma, Savannah, and Tom had torches too. Tom tugged Mum closer as Jay grabbed Lisa.

"I love you," Gemma said. "All of you. And I'm sorry."

Tom and Mum took off first, and Lisa and Jay were less than a step behind, followed by Savannah. Into the darkness of the pyramid.

To our dooms.

Gemma offered her hand, head whipping around and meeting the eyes of the Infected. "Carlisle? Watch my back?"

I swallowed and took her right hand with my left. She had her baseball bat and torch clenched in her other hand. With one last look into each other's eyes, we headed back into darkness.

I wasn't letting go for anything.

As I was consumed by the blackness of nothing, a shiver ran over my body. The cool air bit at my cheeks though my skin was on fire. The corridors of the pyramid were thinner than I remembered, and I felt squashed and smothered.

But the torchlight Gemma was shining down the corridor made it much easier to breathe and keep going. There was a sharp left and then up some stairs and round a corner. Dread was clenching my throat tight.

What if we couldn't find a way out?

The walls were painted black with slithers of silver and neon paint that jumped out and toyed with my eyes as we rushed by, twisting this way and that.

We halted as we found the others at the start of the coaster. They were looking through the window into the control booth and down onto the tracks. A hungry, guttural cry sounded from somewhere deeper in the tunnels, and everyone's eyes grew wide, torchlight jumping from face to face.

"Where now?" Mum's hand was still in Tom's.

Jay was looking underneath the track. "We've got to jump down there."

"Are you mad?" Savannah pulled him back. "What if there's no way out? We'll be stuck down there."

"There'll be an emergency exit. I'm sure I remember seeing one last year."

"While you were on the roller coaster? No. That's insane."

"There'd have to be an emergency exit somewhere. It's an enclosed space. What if there was a fire?"

"Or a Zombie Armageddon," Gemma cut in.

"The people on the ride would have to get out somehow."

The sound of the Infected was turning to thunder, and my legs felt like they were going to collapse.

I had to do something.

I raced to the edge and sat dangling my legs. Gemma shone her torch down to the floor. Reaching for the track, I swung for a moment before dropping down to the ground, eyes darting everywhere.

"Zane!" Savannah's face was bright-white with terror.

"Come on. They're coming."

Gemma threw me the torch, and it almost dropped out of my hands they were shaking so much. There was a wild rush as everyone passed weapons and torches to me and swung their way down. Lisa was the last one, looking behind her. She was trembling.

"You can do it, Lisa." Gemma had her hands up as though she was going to catch her. "Come on."

"We won't let you fall," Mum said.

My heart was pounding so hard in my chest, begging for me to start moving again, but I couldn't leave without Lisa. And not just for Callie. For Jay. For all of us.

"We'll catch you." I offered a hand for her to take, and Tom stood beside me and did the same. He looked at me for a moment before Lisa took a hand each, and we lowered her to the ground.

Then we were running again. Weaving our way through

the metal holding the track up. The corpse of the coaster stared down at us.

There was a blip of sound, and my breath choked me as someone's torch revealed an Infected only a few centimetres away from my face. I swung my golf club around without time for thought, and the thing was on the ground. Mum drove her club down seconds later, and there was a splat and a crack. She went to smile at me, and I went to smile back when an Infected's head appeared from nowhere.

I tried to scream, but someone's hand was over my mouth. I reached out for her, but I was too far away.

Not Mum.

I didn't have time to feel guilty for the selfish thought. I didn't care. They could take anyone before they took her.

The hands clamped down on her shoulders, and I wrestled with the pairs of arms holding me. Its teeth were moments from her neck, and the thing had no head.

Before my brain could catch up, I flew into Mum's arms as the others let go of me. We both would have gone tumbling to the ground if not for Tom, holding us steady, machete dripping blood. Mum's breath was firing in my ear, and tears were streaming down my face. My legs were shaking, and it was hard to remain standing, but we had to keep moving.

Keep running.

Torchlight zipped across the room as we hurried towards a beam of light. Just as Jay said. A fire exit.

We burst through the door, weapons raised, breath ragged. With a moment to clear our heads, we ran, pushing back the Infected that dared to get close to us. Jay was in the lead now, pumping his arms faster than I'd ever seen. We crossed a train track and entered a Wild West themed area. I paid no attention to the doughnut and waffle stalls now. They meant nothing.

Turning, taking in the area clear of Infected for now, I saw them all stumbling in the distance, some appearing from the pyramid and others making their way round. We had a minute at least. If we were lucky, two or three.

But they would never relent. How long could we keep this up? There was only a limited amount of time we could keep on fighting. Keep on running.

There needed to be a way out.

Jay was hanging over a waist-high fence with water guns mounted to it. On the other side was the log flume, which looked as though it was built onto the lake. We were at the edge of the park again. Nowhere to turn.

"We're going to die." Savannah was crying. "Aren't we? We're all going to die."

Gemma smacked her hand over Savannah's mouth to quiet the shrill noises escaping. Savannah threw Gemma off in a fierce spin, and Gemma huffed as she hit the floor, catching herself before her head smashed against the concrete.

Savannah's face was red, her eyes glowering as she kicked Gemma hard in the ribs. "You're a sick waste of space! You've killed us all. I bet you're happy now."

Gemma cried out and curled into a ball, covering her head as Savannah's foot connected with her again. Hard.

I felt as though the steaming blood inside me was going to explode, and I tore towards Savannah. But Tom was there first, grabbing Savannah's arms and pulling her back.

"No! This is all her fault. We're all going to die. Let go of me!"

Gemma was struggling for breath as I heaved her up to standing. She put her arm around my shoulder to steady herself, and her skin took on a sallow paleness as she eyed Savannah.

No one spoke. The Infected grew closer.

"Get off me!" Savannah shrieked it again. "Don't touch me. You killed Aniya. You deserve to die."

"Stop this!" Mum jumped in front of Savannah. "Stop all this hating. We need to get out of here. Please. Just forget all this for now."

"How can I?" Savannah's face was dark, and for the first time, I was afraid of her. "He killed her."

"Savannah?" Jay's voice was as menacing as Savannah's face. "Are you going to be a danger to us?"

"What?" She was fighting to break out of Tom's arms and trying to scratch and kick him. She looked like an animal.

"Do you want to come with us?"

"I don't want to die."

"Do you want to kill Tom? Or Gemma?" He approached slow, with meaning.

She was clawing and letting out little screams.

Gemma squeezed me tight.

"Do you?"

"What's this about? Leave me alone!"

"Savannah."

"He killed Aniya." Tears choked her and filled her eyes.

Jay shook his head. "You can't believe that."

"Jay?" There was a wobble in my voice as I helped Gemma towards the log flume. "They're coming. We need to go." As I passed him, I noticed his hand was hovering over the gun.

My heart leapt, and I almost gave the game away, but Gemma pulled me forward, shaking her head. He couldn't...

"I don't trust you. Do you trust us?"

She looked to each of us in turn. "Some of you."

"What if the people you trusted weren't here, and it was just Tom and Gemma left? What then?"

She was shaking her head, and her mouth opened as she noticed the gun. "I'm sorry!" She screamed it. "Don't! Please. I won't do anything. I swear."

Jay tipped his head to the side, and the Infected started tripping over the train track.

"We need to go," I said.

Gemma let go of me and scrabbled to climb over the wooden fence. Everyone looked round as she dropped to the other side, splashing into the tube of water.

"Now, Jay!" I flung myself over too. The icy temperature of the water froze my mouth for a moment, and I couldn't move as shivers took over my system. My combats were soaked, the tight running trousers underneath making a second skin. The water was lapping against my mid-thigh from where I'd jumped.

Gemma was wading towards the slide, water grazing the base of her hips. I had to drag my clothes through the water as Tom tumbled over and caught himself before he fell. My combats felt like iron weights. I was glad that, unlike Tom, I wasn't wearing jeans.

We both turned to wait for the others as Mum climbed her way over. I could hear Gemma sloshing in the distance.

"Jay, please," Savannah said from the other side of the fence. "I'm sorry. I would never hurt you. Please don't."

"You're letting your grief control you."

"And you aren't?"

"I'm dealing with it."

"How? How can you possibly be dealing with it? You've barely spoken since..."

"At least I'm not trying to kill my friends."

"I didn't try and kill anyone! Jay, let me come with you. I can protect you. I can."

"I don't trust you. I don't trust you with them. We need Tom and Gemma. And I don't have the energy to sleep with one eye open watching you, making sure they aren't in any danger."

"They aren't! You'll kill me, Jay. Please."

"I don't want to leave you here, Savannah. But I will."

"You can't do this! You can't speak for everyone. We're a democracy."

There was a pause, and I strained to listen, the blood pulsing so hard in my ears I almost couldn't hear Jay's response.

"Are we? Let's do the count, shall we? Me, Gemma, and Tom. That's half already."

"The others would never agree."

"I don't care. It doesn't matter any more."

"Since when were you the one in charge?"

"Since I killed Ollie."

There was no response from Savannah, and I wanted with everything I had to look over the fence and rush to save her, but the other half of me was too afraid to look. I didn't want to see Jay's threatening face or Savannah's petrified one.

I wasn't strong enough for this any more.

"Jay!" The scream was Lisa's, and we all tried to jump to see over the fence, forgetting the danger for a second. "Run! Now!"

The breath pounced out of my lungs as I waited. My hands clenched so tight my old grazes stung. But I couldn't stop. My heart felt as though it was making my legs shake.

I waited for what felt like an eternity, and I could see that Tom was about to turn round and continue on when Lisa and Jay tumbled over the fence together. Tom grabbed Mum's hand again and pulled her towards the slide.

I waited for a count of five seconds. "Where's Savannah?"

Lisa was crying. Jay pushed past me and made his way towards the others. Gemma was about halfway up, gripping tight onto the side as not to fall down and take the others with her.

I watched them walk off for a second before fumbling up the fence again to search for Savannah's sunset-golden hair with the pink ends. My eyes scouted everywhere, but there was just a sea of Infected. What had Jay done? Where was she?

I wanted to call out, but it was useless. She knew where we were. And I couldn't hear her screaming. Did that mean she'd escaped? Or was she dead?

The Infected grew nearer and more excited by my presence. Like my head over the fence was some sort of menu board. I hung on until I couldn't wait a second longer, and then I raced up the slide, everyone else waiting for me at the top, waving like I couldn't see them.

My blood felt hot as I climbed and gritted my teeth. My arms were shuddering with fatigue as I pulled myself up and up the slide. I had to puff out hard breaths as I climbed, feeling as though my arms were going to give way.

There was a crack down below as the Infected tried to break through the fence. I made the mistake of looking round when the crunch sounded again. My hand slipped. I went to catch myself, but there was nothing to hold onto, and my feet skidded from under me.

"Zane!" There were five calls of my name all at once.

I scrabbled for purchase, dropping my golf club, but my arms were too heavy, and my hands were too cold and clammy.

I couldn't hold on.

My stomach jumped out of my mouth as I fell down the slide. I shrieked and kicked with my legs, trying to climb, but it was too steep. I spun so I was on my back. The Infected began falling into the water. I gave a yelp as I crashed to the bottom, trainers and socks and combats and underwear and T-shirt and hoodie and coat sopping wet.

I knew I had to jump up and get out of there, but I couldn't control the violent shudders of my freezing body. My limbs didn't want to work. The Infected were slowed by the water but cheered as they saw me there waiting for them. Like a prize.

"Zane!" The screech sounded like Mum, but I couldn't turn my head and look at them.

More Infected dropped into the water one by one, and the fear they might be swimming this way out of sight made my arms turn into propellers as I tried to get a grip of the slide again. I flung the rucksacks off and grabbed the side. What use were supplies if I wasn't alive to use them?

As I went to move forward, there was a roar, and an Infected with golden-blonde hair with pink ends and a hole torn out of her neck sprinted this way, tripping over the other Infected to reach me first. The water jumped away from her feet as she raced towards me.

She was a hundred times faster than the average Infected. Just like the Infected that had appeared inside Callie.

"Zane!" The shout sounded further away.

"Savannah." I mouthed her name, but it was useless now. That thing wasn't Savannah. It didn't know it'd ever been her.

She was growing nearer. I had to beat her to the top. I had nothing to hit her with. No way to defend myself. My golf club was gone, as was the axe from Mandeville Farmhouse that was sticking out the top of one of the rucksacks. There was no time to find them now.

I flung myself at the slide and took the biggest steps I could, ignoring the screaming of my arm muscles and the water dripping off me. Something grabbed my leg, and I shrieked, crashing back into the water. Jerking my legs this way and that, I met the dead hands and body of the one who had hold of me. I kicked myself free and scurried away, but she was after me. I turned to face her and without thinking, struck out, punching her square in the face.

My knuckles stung, and she swayed back a moment before

coming for me again. I swiped across with my foot, knocking her off balance. Before she could jump back to standing, I slammed my feet into her head over and over again, grunting with the effort, until something cracked.

The fear and freeze and despair had my nerves jittering, and my vision was pulling in, making some colours jump out and others mute. I could hear my name in the distance but so far away.

I looked up at the slide, perhaps ten seconds away from the next attack. It was so high. So steep. And I was so tired.

Pulling everything I had left into my system, I put one foot in front of the other, not afraid of crying out as the pain shot through my body. Tired, cold, and exhausted muscles screamed, and I powered on, thinking of Lisa and Jay and Mum and Tom and Gemma. And Aniya and Ollie and Savannah. And Michael. And Callie.

There was no time for giving up.

The hands of the Infected reached up, waiting for me to fall. The hands of the people I loved dangled down, waiting for me to be safe. The question was, which hands would reach me first?

I'd never felt such weight in my arms and legs. Never felt a fierceness in my heart like it.

But I was—against all odds—still alive. And I wasn't going to let anything change that.

There was no giving up.

Time seemed to slow down as I put one foot in front of the other, gripping the side of the slide with both hands and hauling myself up. It felt as though I'd been climbing for miles. But I would climb for miles more.

The hands above reached for my arms as soon as I was near the top, and they all pulled me up together, groaning with the effort. Arms were around me and squeezing me and hugging

351

me close, but I was concentrating on breathing and staying conscious as I knelt on the hard metal of the safety deck to the side of the flume.

When I opened my eyes and everything stopped spinning and blurring, Gemma was in front of me. Her arms were the strongest as she pulled me close.

"Never scare me like that again."

My mouth was dry, and my tongue felt too big, so I couldn't form a reply. Couldn't make a sound at all.

She refused to let go of me as the six of us sat there and watched the Infected struggle and flurry at the bottom of the slide, never getting more than one foot up before sliding back down, knocking the other Infected over until they started it up again.

"They're not clever enough to get up here," Tom said.

"But we're not safe." Lisa's eyes were huge. "How long can we stay up here? How long until we freeze to death?"

"We won't." Gemma shook her head. "We're fine."

"Look at Zane. We are not fine."

The shuddering was so violent I couldn't stop my teeth from chattering. I had no control over my body whatsoever. It was bouncing this way and that, trying to create any sort of heat at all.

"Take your coat off, Zane." Mum appeared in front of me.

"Wh-wh-wh-what?"

"Now."

I couldn't make my hands work any more, let alone my fingers. I watched, numb, as Mum pulled my coat, hoodie, and T-shirt off and pushed them to one side. I was no warmer than before. But no colder either. She took off her own coat and jumper and forced the jumper over my head. Gemma gave me her hoodie as well, and Tom wrapped his coat round me. The shivering didn't stop.

Jay pulled off my hat and shoved his own onto my head. Gemma bundled me up in a blanket and wouldn't let go of me. I fought to keep all of my attention on the sound and swell of their voices.

"Okay then. Now what?"

"We need to get out of here."

"How?"

"Where? We can't get out the way we came. And we can't even find somewhere in here that's safe. There are too many of them."

"We can't just stay up here, we'll die."

"If we go back down there, we'll die."

The light of the day was almost gone, and the Infected were getting harder and harder to see. I didn't know whether it was because my body was calming down or because I couldn't see them, but the Infected were louder than ever.

I blinked to see better in the fading light, and their voices grew crisper as the shuddering at last became a gentle shiver. Squinting at the world around us, I couldn't drag my eyes from the mountain-like structure jutting out in the distance. It was one of the few things I could still pinpoint in the night.

"What about that?" My arm juddered as I pointed.

They all shut up to look.

"How are we going to get to it?" Lisa asked.

"There." Jay pointed to the side of the flume. There was an area of grass hidden behind the fence. It didn't appear to go anywhere, but it was the safest passage we had.

"I don't know." Lisa was biting her lip. "It's getting dark."

"We can't stay up here all night." Gemma pulled me to standing.

"We can't survive the night like this," Tom said. "Let's go for it."

There were nods all around, and Tom was the first one to

skid and surf his way down the conveyor belt on the other side. It wasn't as steep, and the Infected weren't waiting for us at the bottom, so the others hurried on after him.

It might not have been salvation, but we would go for anything we could get. Anything that meant we didn't have to sit around and watch each other starve or freeze to death.

My legs were heavy as Gemma and I made our way down together, her arm always there to catch me, ready, in case I needed it. We jumped off the side before we reached the water, and Tom's hand was outstretched to steady us as we landed.

We all stood there in a huddle for a moment, watching and listening to the Infected.

"If we're really quiet, they might not know we've moved. There's no way they can see us now." Jay was whispering.

"Yeah, but, Jay?" Gemma pulled off her rainbow hat and forced it on Jay's honey-blonde hair. "We can't see them either."

"We've just got to be quiet." He nodded. "We can do that, can't we?"

Before we could argue any more, Jay jogged along the fence line, stopping to pick up a stick. He launched it in the direction of the lake, and as it landed with a splash, the Infected shrieked and whooped.

Jay had a sick, twisted grin on his lips. "That'll distract them."

We scampered round towards the mountain, almost tripping over each other's footsteps, but not making a sound other than the necessary breathing. I didn't know how well the Infected could hear, but it couldn't be that well, not with all the noise surrounding the log flume.

The mountain loomed in front of us, and a mesh fence encircled the metal struts holding the coaster up. It was only about a metre away. Tom knelt down and used his hands knotted together as a step, and Mum was the first one over. She looked around for a minute before jumping and tumbling over the fence. Jay and Lisa followed, and Gemma was looking at me.

"Go on." I ushered her forwards. "Me and Tom know what it is to climb a fence." I smirked his way, and he smiled back.

By the time I dropped over to the other side, they were helping each other over the mesh fence, Gemma shoving Mum up. Tom and I jogged our way over, and I went to help Gemma when she held up one finger and shot into the park.

Tom clapped his hand over my mouth as I reached out for her and used his other arm to pull me back. My heart was trying to escape my chest, and my eyes filled with tears as she wiggled a door handle of a shop and disappeared inside.

"Over the fence," Tom hissed in my ear.

I squirmed and tried to go after Gemma, but his grip was stronger than mine, and he was lifting me and trying to throw me over the fence. Clinging to the mesh with both hands, I refused to move, staring at the place Gemma had been as I heard the first of the straying Infected somewhere in her direction. I had to bite my tongue hard to stop myself calling out for her.

My breaths felt like they were going to kill me, lungs sucking in so much air that did nothing I might as well have held my breath. Tom pushed me up, but I wouldn't budge. I wasn't going to leave Gemma out there.

I almost fell off the fence with relief when she sprinted back this way, holding an armful of what appeared to be clothes. She flew up the fence and to safety, and it was all I could do to scrabble after her.

"Now what?" Lisa was turning around and around, watching the few Infected who were tripping over themselves to get this way.

I was confident they wouldn't be able to scale the fence. Not before we pushed them off anyhow. But for how long? How long until they started climbing on top of each other? We were enclosed in this mesh fence with no way out other than back over to where the Infected were. Were we safe?

I was sure safety was something that no longer existed.

Gemma threw something soft my way, and it turned out to be a huge Thrill Island hoodie, which I managed to fit over my other layers and under Tom's coat. She threw one to Mum and Tom before yanking another over her head and straightening a Thrill Island hat.

"Right." She looked out towards the park. "This is it, I reckon."

Mum handed me the spare baseball bat that'd been sticking out the top of her rucksack. It felt heavy in my hands and awkward. I hadn't realised how at home I'd been with a golf club in my hands and how wrong it felt to be holding something different after all this time.

I turned back to Gemma. "Why did you run off like that?"

"I don't want you dying of hypothermia, Carlisle. What a stupid way to go. Speaking of which, where are those spare socks you made such a fuss about?"

I ignored her. "It's not as stupid as getting ambushed while hunting for a stupid hoodie."

A few more Infected were creeping out, but my heart was so tired of racing that nothing happened. I watched them draw nearer, unsure whether I was the safest I'd been since entering the park or the total opposite.

"What now?" Mum put her arm around me. "Where else is there to run?"

Gemma shook her head. "Nowhere."

It wasn't that word but a lack of arguing that made my muscles tense.

"What are you saying?" Lisa was twisting her hands around each other. "We're going to die here?"

"Or die trying." Tom tucked a hammer from inside his rucksack into his belt and unsheathed his machete once again.

Jay had sat himself on the floor in the middle of the enclosure. I made my way over to him and stood there, looking down at him.

He noticed me at last. "What?"

"Why did you leave Savannah?" There was a rumble in my voice, and I fought the tears back.

"She was a danger to everyone."

"Really?"

"Zane, did you not see what she did to Gemma?"

At the sound of her name, Gemma hurried over, lifting her layers and shining her torch to reveal the angry, red marks Savannah's feet had made.

"Damn right. It freaking hurts to breathe." She looked at me, dropping her clothes back down. "Jay was right. She was losing it, Zane."

"Since when is it okay for us to decide who lives and who dies?"

"Since she started attacking Gemma." Jay was rubbing his hand over his head, not moving Gemma's hat out of his way. "I didn't want to do it, but I didn't want to wake up one morning and find anyone dead. It was a small price to pay."

"Small price? What's the matter with you?"

"Shush." Mum hissed it towards us. "They're coming. Be quiet. We don't want them all here at once. If they come in waves, we might be safe."

"Might be?" Lisa was shaking her head. "Might be?"

"I can't promise anything."

"And Ollie?" I looked back at Jay again. "Why did you tell Savannah you killed him?"

"What?" Gemma's eyes widened.

"Because I did kill him."

I took a step back. "Why?"

"He asked me to."

My shoulders dropped.

"He got bitten. He was all right. He would've made it back to the services, but he didn't want Savannah to see him like that. He didn't want to turn. He just wanted to die. He asked me, so I..."

Gemma put her arms around Jay and squeezed. "Well, I'm with you on this." She met my eye again. "Zane, do you not think on some level that Savannah would've lost the plot and come after me? What would've happened then?"

"I'm not gonna tell him it's all right to leave somebody like that. It's not."

"Get over it, Zane. There's no right and wrong any more. Just living and dying."

I turned my back on them, sick to my stomach. I couldn't look at either of them if they truly believed that. Jay let Savannah die without a hint of remorse. Maybe it wasn't her we should've been afraid of. Maybe it was him.

The first Infected hit the fence, and Mum and Tom got to work. I rooted around in one of the rucksacks and found a screwdriver. Without much thought to the position we were in or how we were going to escape, I started plunging the metal into decaying skulls and yanking it back out again.

My breath was gasping in and out as the anger surged up inside me. My heart was pumping hard, drumming a steady rhythm. I wasn't afraid of the Infected any longer.

But what about Jay?

The Infected swarmed the fence, and Gemma jumped to action beside me with Jay's hedge clippers. Their faces were everywhere, growling, flinging saliva in our direction. Blood splattered all over my hands and Tom's coat, but I didn't even flinch.

When had killing become so easy? How hard was it to change target?

I pushed the thoughts out of my mind and kept going. The Infected were creating a second layer and a third. They dropped to the ground, but the others walked on top of them like they weren't there at all.

"How long can we do this?" Gemma was panting. "How long do we keep fighting?"

"Until we can't fight any more," was Tom's answer.

I didn't look at her.

On and on and on. Darkness fell. We kept killing. The groans didn't grow any quieter. The amount of Infected never dropped. My arm was shaking again, and my legs were ready to give way.

Mum wiped sweat off her forehead, and Tom's face spoke of nothing but agony as the torchlight hit him. Lisa was standing behind us with the torch, making sure we could see what we were doing. Jay was taking care of any that tried to go round the back.

I couldn't look at him either. What little thing did I have to do for him to turn on me next? In this world of dead people, how was one more going to make any difference?

More time passed. An hour, two? It was impossible to tell. Since the chocolate of the afternoon, my stomach had grown hungry again. It felt as though it was caving in on itself as it tried to eat its way out of my body.

Tears filled my eyes out of starvation and desperation and exhaustion.

"This is stupid." Gemma took a step back. "We can't beat them."

"We can!" Tom looked as though he wouldn't stop until he

dropped dead. "We can get out of this."

"No." Gemma dropped the hedge clippers and collapsed to her knees. "We can't."

"Don't give up, Gem!" Mum was wheezing with the effort.

"What's the point?"

There was an awkward kind of quiet, a click, and a scream from Gemma.

I spun round, the reserve of my energy force firing to life inside me. She'd dived on top of Jay and was wrestling him to the ground. Jay was shaking from side to side, trying to fling her off, but she was holding on too tight.

"Drop it!" She growled the words, and I dashed over to them as Lisa shone the torch to reveal the gun in Jay's hand.

I stepped on his wrist until he let go of the weapon, and I snatched it up, holding it away from my body. It felt awkward in my hands. Wrong.

"Don't you dare, Jay Ashford. Don't you dare." She moved off him but looked ready to pounce at a moment's notice as they both sat there.

"What?" Tears were streaming down his face. "We're all gonna die here. Why not speed up the process?"

A slither of cold dripped down my spine as the true seriousness of the situation fell on me.

"Jay," I breathed.

"Shut up, Zane. You don't care."

"What? Of course I care. We all care."

"It's just good sense. How long can we keep going like this? We're only human. Why not take the easy option?"

"Because we've come this far on the hard road. I'm not ready to give in yet."

"Maybe not now, but what about in five hours? Ten? How long, Zane? How long can you keep fighting?"

"As long as it takes."

There was quiet, the huff of Mum and Tom still sounding in the background.

"We need help!" Mum cried.

No one went to the rescue.

Jay's eyes were dead as he looked at us. "Callie. Dad. Aniya. Ollie. Savannah. Who next?"

"Nobody."

"I can't." He shook his head. "I can't lose any more."

Lisa dropped down beside him. "And I can? We'll get through this together, Jay."

"How?"

"With each other. You can't leave us here. You can't leave me here."

He was sobbing. "Why are we still trying?"

"Because that's what we do." I took a step closer. "We survive. And we help each other." I shook my head. "I'm sorry about what I said before. You were right with what you did. If Savannah was here right now, things might be different. They might be worse." I didn't believe my own words, but I didn't need to believe them. Jay did.

"What's the point of all this? They're all dead. They're not coming back."

"But look at what you've still got left."

Lisa pulled him into a hug. "I can't lose you too, Jay. I can't."

"Me neither." Gemma stood up.

"Nor me," I said.

We were all staring at him.

"Help!" Tom yelped. "We need all of you!"

"We can still win this, Jay." I forced out a smile. "But not without you."

"Come on, Jay." Gemma took my hand. "You're the ZA ready one. Tell it to us straight." She took the gun away from me and threw it in his direction.

There we waited, Mum and Tom still fighting for our lives, and by the sounds of the swearing and squeaking, they were losing. Lisa held Jay as though that was enough to save us all. And Gemma and I stood hand in hand. Our lives were in the hands of Jay Ashford now, and all we could do was stand there and hope.

Emotions raged across his face as he looked to each of us.

I held my breath. If the ZA had defeated Jay Ashford, it had defeated us all.

Gemma took a deep breath. "Do we live, or do we die?"

FIFTY-SIX

"Live."

FIFTY-SEVEN

With Jay fighting at our sides once again, a new lease of life filled me up as we stabbed and slashed our way through the night. I felt invincible. How many times had I almost lost my life? Yet I was still breathing. Still fighting.

I would never stop fighting. We would survive this. All of us. For all of them. For Callie and Michael and the Mandevilles and the Penningtons and Gemma's mum and Joel and Aniya and Ollie and Savannah. Every last one of them.

"I can see the ground again." Gemma let out a sound that was all happiness, almost like a cheer. "We've nearly killed them all!"

A smile lit up my face, and she winked at me. I was beaming and so alive I could burst with it. What did it matter what had happened before? There was no before. Only now. Only right now in the moment we were living in. There was no other way to live this life.

Although I knew that was stupid, and life and grief were bound to catch up to me, right then it didn't matter.

It didn't matter because we were alive.

Mum and Tom dropped down to the floor and shut their eyes, breathing in and out, chests heaving. I stumbled back too, wondering how many minutes I could remain awake.

Lisa went to lay next to them, and Gemma pulled back.

There was one Infected left. Its jaw was hanging loose, its skin grey and decaying.

"Jay?" Gemma wheezed. "Do the honours?" She was holding out the hedge clippers.

He took them, marching towards it. He looked it right in the face and drove the end straight through its eyeball. It was then he slumped down to the ground and curled up next to Lisa. I fell next to Gemma, and although we were in the middle of the most dangerous place we'd ever found and we didn't know whether we were safe, I shut my eyes. And it took only seconds until I was asleep.

When I awoke, sunlight was beaming down on us, not warm but bright and demanding. I squinted and covered my eyes, sitting up and observing the fence. The fact I was still alive meant the fence was still standing. To my surprise, there were only two Infected trying to push their hands through the metal to greet us. I jumped up, pulling off the blanket Gemma must have laid there in the night. I eyed the thing for a second before forcing the screwdriver into its mouldy head and that of its friend.

The stink of bodies was unbelievable, but I looked past the corpses to the colours of the park around me. The top of the pyramid was peeking out in the distance, and I could see most of the big roller coasters from my position. It may not have been conventional, but this place was now my idea of heaven. Against all odds, it'd kept us safe.

I continued staring out into the distance, breathing through my mouth until the others awoke, and one by one, we climbed out of the cage and back into the park. The squelch of the bodies underfoot made me gag, and they laughed at me.

Gemma nudged my arm. "Really? Really? After all that violence?"

I pushed her back, holding her spare golf club, the baseball bat back with Mum. There was something about the golf club that made me feel safer. It felt right in my hands.

My eyes were alight, darting from place to place, waiting for the stray Infected. We crept around the whole park, checking in all the buildings and queue lines and stalls, killing them off one by one. We filled our stomachs with more chocolate and sweets as we passed, and I felt unbalanced and sick as we made our way towards the entrance building.

With the torches ready, we snuck down the stairs and into the dark pit of abyss we'd found ourselves in yesterday, the place I thought would be my tomb. In reality it was filled with lockers and things, and I breathed a sigh of relief. Gemma's mouth quirked up as she saw me, and I looked away, pretending not to have noticed. We killed the loitering Infected and made our way over the bridge.

"You know when I said Thrill Island was probably safe?"

We all looked to her. "Yeah."

"That was stupid. Let's not do that."

I laughed, and she stuck her tongue out at me, pulling a face. Everyone was smiling. Even Jay wasn't frowning. It dawned on me that right in front of me was my new forever. With Lisa and Jay Ashford, Gemma Stuart, Mum, and though I never would have thought so in a thousand years, Thomas Reyes. The old world was well and truly gone, but I knew I'd always have them. They were my reason to keep on smiling.

A group of three or four Infected were stumbling across the bridge towards us. Without anyone flinching or panicking, Tom beheaded them all one after another. He sprinted to the office we'd entered through, slashing another head from the look of it, and slammed the door shut.

The Infected sung us a tune as we approached them.

"I've locked the door for now." Tom appeared, shoving the keys into his pocket. "One of them must've fallen on the door handle."

"No wonder there were so many last night." Gemma pulled off her Thrill Island beanie to scratch her head. "They were coming through there. I don't think there are nearly as many here as yesterday."

There were mumbles of approval, and we began slaying the Infected on the other side of the gate. Unlike last night, the sun was shining down on us, and my heart felt lighter in my chest.

When the last Infected dropped to the ground, the groaning quiet for once, we all looked at one another, deflating.

"What now?" Mum shrugged. "Stay? Go?"

I smirked. "You know what? I'll bet Thrill Island is safe."

Gemma chuckled and put her hand in the middle. "I second that. Let's stay."

Mum and Tom and Lisa put their hands in the middle. Jay watched us for a minute.

"Wanna stay?" Gemma was chewing on her lip.

Jay let out a breath and looked to the sky, contemplating something. When he looked back at us, his eyes were a little brighter, and he even forced a smile onto his lips.

"Yeah. Why not? I'm in."

Gemma flung her arms around him and danced about for a moment before pulling back and kissing his cheek. "Love you, Jay."

I bundled him up in a hug next, and he squeezed me back.

"Me too," I said. "Love you, Jay."

He tried to bat us off as Lisa and Mum kissed his cheeks. They hooked arms with him and Tom, and Gemma joined on the end.

I shook my head before taking Gemma's outstretched arm and joining my bizarre and mismatched family.

Thrill Island was safe for now but wouldn't be forever. This apocalypse was unforgiving, and something told me we'd be on the move again before we were ready. But for now we were safe, something I would never take for granted again.

Safe and free and alive.

And really, ZA or no ZA, what more could I ask for?

ACKNOWLEDGEMENTS

First I need to thank Kimberly Ito for her editing genius. Without her, the ZA would be a tame inconvenience instead of the chaos inspired by her suggestions.

Huge thanks to Chris Kemp for creating a cover more incredible than I could've imagined.

Thanks to my beta readers: Anna Grove, who's scared of zombies; and Jerry Beckett, who made sure the Zombie Armageddon sounded real. I'll miss your wisdom and words more than I can express.

Next, I need to send lots of Viking hats and coffee beans to the entire NaNoWriMo community for existing. I need to thank everyone who works for NaNoWriMo, who's connected with me as a buddy, and anyone who's ever listened to me ramble about it. They are to thank for ZA and many other extraordinary stories. (www.nanowrimo.org)

My writing home, Movellas, deserves a colossal hug for always being there to support me, offer advice, and make me laugh. I owe so much to you guys. (www.movellas.com)

Love and kisses to my amazing James Terry for being there always. For showing me that Zane's capacity for love does exist.

More thanks than I can ever express to Dad for being there each and every single step of the way.

And thanks to James Looby for simply being yourself (and of course for being cooler than me).

Hybrid Publishing—
Free the Publishing Industry,
Unleash Your Voice!

Disrupt the old world of traditional publishing, and say yes to the wonderful world of hybrid publishing. If we support our creative people, they can and will take over the world. The 'traditional' publishers are terrified. They should be. They are the zombies and we are the survivors.

Whatever your dream is, you can do it. Rise up with us. Say no to the way things have always been done, and say yes to the new way of doing everything. Join the publishing revolution.

Don't let them discourage you. You are good enough. We believe in your magic and your outstanding talent.

Phenomenal books don't just come out of the 'traditional' world. They come from everywhere. Let's rally together and make our voices heard.

#HybridPublishing @MoltenPublish

Lightning Source UK Ltd.
Milton Keynes UK
UKOW02f1223061216
289306UK00004B/166/P